The Rood and the Torc:

The Song of Kristinge, Son of Finn

Some other works by Matthew Dickerson:

Nonfiction

Following Gandalf:
Epic Battles and Moral Victory in The Lord of the Rings

From Homer to Harry Potter:
A Handbook on Myth and Fantasy

Narnia and the Fields of Arbol:
The Environmental Vision of C.S. Lewis

Ents, Elves, and Eriador:
The Environmental Vision of J.R.R. Tolkien

A Hobbit Journey:
Discovering the Enchantment of J.R.R. Tolkien's Middle Earth

Novels

The Finnsburg Encounter

The Rood and the Torc:

The Song of Kristinge, Son of Finn

Matthew Dickerson

WingsPress

San Antonio, Texas
2014

The Rood and Torc: The Song of Kristinge, Son of Finn
© 2014 by Wings Press for Matthew T. Dickerson

First Edition:
Print Edition ISBN: 978-1-60940-298-3
ePub ISBN: 978-1-60940-299-0
Kindle ISBN: 978-1-60940-300-3
Library PDF ISBN: 978-1-60940-301-0

Wings Press
627 E. Guenther
San Antonio, Texas 78210
Phone/fax: (210) 271-7805
On-line catalogue and ordering:
www.wingspress.com
All Wings Press titles are distributed to the trade by
Independent Publishers Group
www.ipgbook.com

Library of Congress Cataloging-in-Publication Data:

Dickerson, Matthew T., 1963-
 The Rood and the Torc : the song of Kristinge, son of Finn /
Matthew Dickerson. -- First edition.
      pages cm
 ISBN 978-1-60940-298-3 (trade pbk. : alk. paper) -- ISBN 978-1-
60940-299-0 -- ISBN 978-1-60940-300-3 -- ISBN 978-1-60940-
301-0
 1. Finn, King of the Frisians (Legendary character)--Fiction. 2.
Fight at Finnesburg (Anglo-Saxon poem)--Adaptations. 3. Epic
poetry, English (Old)--Adaptations. 4. Middle Ages--Fiction. 5.
Beowulf--Adaptations. 6. Historical fiction. I. Title.
 PS3554.I316R66 2013
 813'.54--dc23
                                    2013007838

THE TALE

For my parents, Willard W. and Clara May Dickerson,
who instilled in me early in life a love of books and of story.
And for my parents-in-law, Robert and Judy Forrest,
who prepared and shared with me an even greater love of my life.

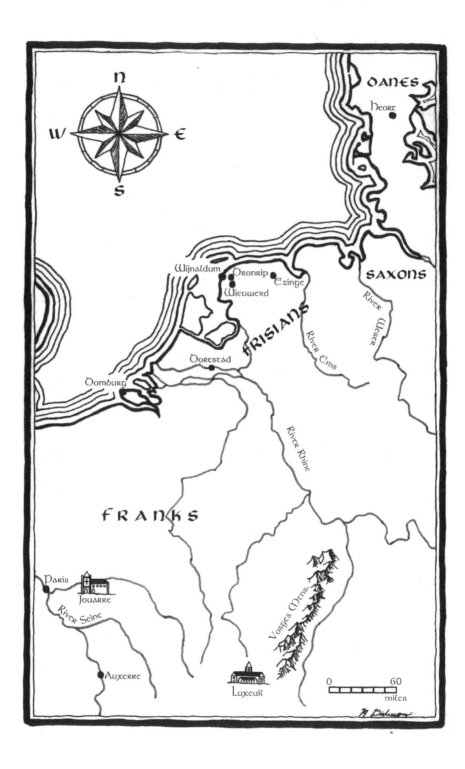

The Rood and the Torc:

The Song of Kristinge, Son of Finn

From Hwitstan he went, the wise thane Ulestan,
from hearth, from home, from hall and from king.
No foe drove him forth. No fear made him leave.
He did not seek that sorrowful way.
One command he received, one care from his ruler.
To him was trusted the highest of tasks:
this boy to keep, the king's own blood.

CHAPTER 1:
ULESTAN'S FINAL DUTY

Kristinge rose from his seat in the corner of the mead hall. He approached the fire, making his way past the haughty stares of battle-scarred warriors seated on heavy wooden benches. His eyes darted around the crowded room. It was smaller than the great walled burgs of the Franks where, not many days earlier, he had played his harp and sung before their ruler. Smaller and warmer. More comfortable. More like Finnsburg, the hall of the Frisian king Finn in the days of his glory—at least as far as that hall remained in Kristinge's fading memory from his days as a child in the village of Hwitstan. Nonetheless, despite the familiarity of this scene, he felt ill at ease. The hall was full. Fifty men at least were gathered there that evening. The chieftain Frotha and his kin, along with a few of his loyal retainers, sat on the benches in the center of the hall, closest to the fire. The rest of his war band filled the benches further from the hearthstone. Most were still seated. Some had already slipped to the ground, succumbed to the food and strong drink. The traveling merchants and their retinues occupied the far wall, but in the smoky firelight Kristinge could not make out their faces.

"Sing," commanded Frotha in his hearty bellowing voice. As he motioned toward an open space by the hearth, his bare arms, thicker than the traveler's thighs, gleamed with the gold of a half-dozen armbands. Around his neck was an even heavier wound-gold torc of a chieftain. "We are ready."

Kristinge approached. It had been many years since he had been in such a place, a true Frisian mead hall. How long since he had last been in Friesland? Six years, was it? Nearly a third of his life. He fidgeted with the pegs of his harp, making sure it was in tune while he dredged his small repertoire for some song or tale appropriate to the setting. Why was he afraid? This should have been far more comfortable than the cold palace on the Isle of the Parisii. It was no time for his memory to fail him.

"Do you have a song, or must we wait all night?" the chieftain bellowed.

Kristinge took a deep breath and nodded. Though Frotha was not a mighty chieftain, not even by the reckoning of the small clans of Friesland, he was nonetheless the lord of the hall and the giver of treasure. It would not do well to displease him. And so, still hoping desperately for some sudden inspiration, the young man lifted his harp. But then his eyes strayed once more to the graceful figure who sat on the far side of the hearth.

Aewin. It was probable that she didn't even recognize him. But he could make no mistake about her. He almost said her name aloud. Glowing in the enchanted light of an evening fire, her face was even more beautiful than when he had seen her among the Franks. Her dark hair—hair that had been hidden beneath a bronze helmet when last he saw her—hung free, braided and bound with golden pins as befitted one of her station. Emerald eyes, which in her distress a few days earlier had flashed with a dangerous vigor, now sparkled with light-hearted mischief as she spoke with one the young retainers seated at her side. Nor did Kristinge miss the smooth curves of her shoulders and hips, which by the warmth of the fire were no longer hidden beneath several layers of fur. He tried to turn away, to discipline his thoughts to the task at hand. After all, he knew what her station was. And he knew his own. For a lowly bard to think of a woman so close in kinship with a chieftain was brash and foolhardy. Just to look at her might well put his life in danger from her family. And for a monk there was an even greater danger—a danger to the soul as well as the body.

For a bard or monk, yes. Yet what about for a king? Would he be judged so were he the wearer of a torc?

A king? Absently he began plucking the strings of his harp as if to sing, but his thoughts were drifting backward to a spring day, several months earlier...

It was the first warm day of the year, and the fragrant breeze had that particular distracting quality that comes with the season. Feeling its effects, the young monk struggled to prevent his thoughts from drifting too far from the task at hand. It was a struggle he was near to losing. The sun had long since burned off the early morning fog, and signs of new life were exploding from the barrenness of winter. The maples scattered among the pines on the far side of the pond were dotted with tiny red blossoms. Buds on the beeches were such a light green they appeared almost gold against the silvery bark. And on the distant hillsides the tall thick firs were darker and greener and more full of life than they had looked in the winter. Involuntarily, his eyes wandered from the scroll held in front of him upwards toward the treetops, then higher still to the Vosges mountains rising beyond. Even in the higher altitudes, the remnants of the winter's snow were disappearing under the bright blue skies, while in the foothills and valleys around him it was already gone. In its place the first flowers of spring were already in full blossom, and buds were exploding from the trees with the promise of bursting into leaf any day. Even the birds were participating in the event; the woods and fields were filled with their sounds as they celebrated in song the onset of the season. Peas had long since been planted in the gardens at Luxeuil, the fields near Annegray were sown with wheat and barley, and beans would follow in a few weeks. Before long, the yellow gentian—the bitter root that was both food and medicine for the monks—would begin to blossom in the mountains, and the younger monks would be sent into the higher slopes to gather wild roots and seeds.

All of which was making it more difficult for the monk to concentrate.

There was, however, work to be done. Brother Kristinge dropped his eyes from the hills and trees back to the immediate scene where his gaze traced a path around the gathered company. There were seven of them standing there beside the abbey pond on the edge of the monastic land. Father Petrica, garbed in his plain hooded robe, was the central figure in the Luxeuil retinue. He was shorter than Kristinge and slight of build, but his work-hardened hands, stern Roman jaw, and wiry muscles gave him a tough look that belied his small stature and gentle green eyes. In the identifying manner of Luxeuil monks, the front half of his head was shaven ear to ear and forward, leaving the back untouched. However his natural baldness—Petrica was now approaching his fortieth year—was creeping backward making the line of his tonsure indistinct. Kristinge on the other hand, only two years past his twentieth year, still retained a thick head of dark hair where it was unshaven in the back. Perhaps, he thought, that was why the younger monks were required to wear their hoods in the presence of their elders: to hide the blessings of their youth.

Kristinge's gaze continued around the circle. Facing Father Petrica and in sharp contrast to him was a Frankish nobleman richly garbed in a heavy sleeveless bear-skin cloak, a purple tunic, woolen trousers, and fur boots. His attire looked uncomfortably warm for the day, but left no question about his wealth or station. His tunic was fastened at the collar with a large silver brooch which must have cost him more than a few coins, as had his bear skin. Nor did Kristinge miss the elaborate jeweled and ornamented scabbard draped over the nobleman's back. Though empty at present, it was made to hold a hefty blade.

Standing at the nobleman's sides were his two sons. The older of them, about fourteen years of age, bore a striking resemblance to the father, particularly in his heavy round face. He was even garbed in like manner, including a small empty scabbard. The younger son, however, wore only a heavy woolen robe that was cut for a man half again taller than him, and there was no indication that he had a weapon. He looked no more than nine years old, and his face was pale with either fear or illness. He was glancing back toward his mother and the rest of their large retinue who stood a short way off. There were about a dozen of them, family and servants both, taking care of the horses and guarding their master's sword that had been removed in the presence of the monks.

The nobleman, meanwhile, scratched his heavy beard and tugged on the sleeve of his tunic before continuing. "The land, alls of it from the muddy river to the hill by the old sheep brook," he said, in his heavy Frankish tongue. "I gives it all to Father Petrica and I doesn't never going to ask for it back."

Kristinge dipped his pen in the ink and prepared to write. On the ground in front of him, holding the scroll and the ink, knelt two untonsured novices. A few years younger than himself and new to

Luxeuil, they were the final members of the monastic retinue. Though Kristinge had not yet learned their names, he could see they were from the mountains. They were nervous, as peasants were in the presence of nobles, and stared wide-eyed at the strangers. Kristinge hoped Father Petrica would not be too hard on them when the nobleman had left. Only a few years had passed since Kristinge had been in their place. Fortunately, Petrica was too busy to scold them now. "The land along the Doubs river from Annegray stream to the northwest ridge and its tributary stream," Father Petrica repeated slowly. Kristinge wrote quickly and neatly on the sheepskin scroll held before him by the two novices. He would later translate the document into Latin back at the abbey. For now, the barbarian tongue would have to do. When the monk had finished scrawling, Petrica went on, "I hereby bequeath, free of cost to the monastery at Luxeuil, with no further hindrances of any kind."

"Further... hindrances... of any... kind," Kristinge repeated under his breath. Then he looked up.

Petrica nodded for the nobleman to continue. At that moment, however, the ceremony came to a temporary halt. The nobleman had stopped speaking and was staring over the monks' shoulders in the direction of the monastery. Petrica, noticing that their newest benefactor had been distracted, turned to see what it was. Instinctively, Kristinge turned as well.

Another monk had appeared at the top of the hill, and was now approaching with a determined gait. His features were visible. He was about the same height as Petrica but a little plumper, and though his hair was gray it was still full in the places it was left unshaven. He wore a robe similar to that of the other monks, but his hood was down as he walked, revealing a different tonsure than the monks of St. Peter's at Luxeuil—a curious detail that might have been lost on the guests yet was obvious to the other monks. Thus Kristinge recognized him quickly. He came to a stop next to Petrica, and put his hood up in respect as he sought to catch his breath.

Petrica looked upon the newcomer with a sharp, penetrating glance that indicated some annoyance. It would not do to lose this gift of land because of a poorly timed interruption. With a slight nod of his head, he addressed him in a level voice. "Willimond?"

"Father," Willimond replied, addressing his monastic superior with a tone of reverence, despite the fact that Petrica was a few years younger.

"Is your business so urgent?" Petrica asked, motioning with his hand in such as way as to indicate that he was busy. "Where is patience?"

"I am sorry," Willimond said. He gave a sidelong glance at Kristinge, then leaned forward and whispered into Petrica's ear.

Petrica's eyes registered his surprise and concern, and he also glanced at Kristinge. The young monk's curiosity was fully aroused now. Whatever had brought Willimond out there must have been important or he would not have risked interrupting such an occasion. What could it be? He looked at Petrica. For a moment Petrica said nothing as he pondered whatever news had been brought to him. Finally he turned around again to face the curious eyes of the nobleman and his two sons. "We will continue," he said.

Kristinge saw Willimond's face and shoulders drop slightly, but the older monk stepped back out of the way in obedience and he said no more.

The nobleman cleared his throat and continued. "Me, Lord Charlethax of Billenford, gives these lands that is my own to give." Kristinge returned to his work, trying not to think about whatever urgent message had brought Willimond out there. He listened as Petrica interpreted the speech of Charlethax, still in the Frankish tongue but with words more fitting the more formal language of such documents. Kristinge had helped with this task before, when other uneducated Frankish nobles had made gifts of land to the monks of Luxeuil. He knew what to expect.

"This I do on the third day of May," Petrica said. There was a pause as Kristinge finished transcribing. "And now," Petrica said to the nobleman, "is there some way by which we shall remember this day before God and before men?"

"There is," Charlethax replied. "We can remember it as the day when my son John was thrown into the abbey pond by his brother Charleson."

"But father," the younger son protested. "The ice has barely—" His sentence was cut short by a solid cuff to his head by his father.

"Witnessed and hereafter remembered," Petrica dictated, "as the day in which John son of Charlethax, Lord of Billenford, was thrown into the abbey pond."

"Sons," the Lord of Billenford said. "It is time."

Charleson grinned wickedly at his younger brother as he grabbed him by the collar of his robe. John squirmed momentarily, trying to elude the grip, but once again a cuff to his head convinced him to stop resisting. He was dragged ten feet to the edge of the pond, where Charleson waited only long enough for him to disrobe before heaving him into the chilly water. The younger son sank beneath the surface and came up a moment later gasping and sputtering from the cold, his only consolation being that a moment later his older brother slipped on the spring mud, lost his balance, and with his arms and legs flailing plunged in to join him. When the two boys came dripping from the water, their mother was already running down to the shore to help dry them off.

"Can you make a mark on the scroll?" Petrica asked of Charlethax, ignoring the scene at the water's edge.

"I can," Charlethax answered, grinning in pride at his ability to hold a pen to make a mark for his name. The monk dipped the pen in ink and handed it to the nobleman, who scratched something illegible on the scroll held for him by the novices.

"It is finished," Petrica said. "May God grant you rich blessings for your generosity."

"The Lord be kind to you also, Father," Charlethax replied. He was still grinning. "Now come and share the mead cup with my family. We has brought enough for all!"

"My thanks," Petrica said. "I will gladly join you."

"Father," Willimond interrupted hesitantly.

"Ah," Petrica said. Kristinge thought he saw a shadow pass over Petrica's face as he turned toward him. "Kristinge."

"Yes, Father?"

"You have done well. You are released from your duties this day. Return now with Willimond."

"Thank you," Kristinge answered. After checking that the ink was dry, he carefully rolled up the scroll and handed it to Petrica, along with the pen. Then he turned to join Willimond who at once set off with good speed in the direction of the Monastery. When they were far enough away from the gathering, Kristinge could contain himself no longer. "What is it?" he asked, ignoring the rule of silence.

"Ulestan," Willimond answered. "He is dying."

In its first incarnation, the monastery of St. Peter had been built by Columbanus among the ruins of *Annegray*, an old stone fort remaining from Roman times before Gaul had fallen to Clovis and the invading Frankish hordes and become the Merovingian-ruled Francia. Perhaps at one time Annegray had been an important outpost on the frontier of the great Roman empire. But when the empire had expanded far to the north, it had lost its usefulness; in later years it served as a way post from which a small battalion might guard against the numerous outlaws in the mountains. Eventually the fort was abandoned altogether, and it had long since fallen into disrepair; the once strong walls crumbled inward, and only a few of the stone buildings remained standing through the decades turning into centuries before Columbanus received the land from King Childebert for the founding of a new monastery. Yet despite the condition of the buildings, the site of the old fort was ideal for Columbanus' vision. It was the folk of these rough mountains to whom he had come: the Suevian tribes who, after their defeat by Caesar five centuries earlier, had settled here in this out-of-the-way place where they could continue to resist Romanization. Nestled in a green hollow in the foothills of the Vosges mountains, with fresh springs, clear rivers, deep forests, inaccessible defiles, and stern mountainous surroundings, Annegray was thus at once austere and idyllic.

For a time, Columbanus and his followers lived on wild seeds, nuts, and even bark. But within a handful of years, the land surrounding the fort began to show the results of the discipline, toughness and organization of that small band of monks. The ground was cleared and planted, cultivated grain and vegetables sprung from the soil, apple and pear trees were planted, and the old walls and buildings took a new form: that of a monastic village rather than a hostile fort. Then the local peasant populace began to stream into the monastery, not to rob its unarmed occupants as they had done during that first winter, but for food, healing, and the preaching of the monks. As its reputation spread throughout Frankish Gaul, the monastery built by Columbanus and dedicated to St. Peter grew. Soon even the sons of nobles, lured by the Irish monks who were both practical and devout, were coming to join the peasant farmers. Only a few years passed before Columbanus' monastery had outgrown Annegray. So the king gave him another abandoned castle, eight miles away in a more spacious vale lower in the foothills. Luxovium, the Romans had called it. Luxeuil it was to the Gauls who did not speak Latin. It had long ago been overrun by pine trees, but Columbanus and his hard-working followers had cleared the land and rebuilt the forest, and his monastery expanded.

And still more followers came, seeking something both physical and spiritual in the teachings and lives of the monks. Columbanus needed more space. Three miles away they built Fontaines, a third site in the growing monastic community. Yet the original site at Annegray had not been abandoned. Quieter and more secluded than the larger new settlements, Annegray was a place of deep contemplation, of intense study, and of difficult work. It was there that the most serious of the monks went, Willimond and Kristinge among them. There, too, Ulestan had come.

Through those gates built centuries ago by Roman architects and soldiers, and later raised again by Columbanus himself, Kristinge entered at Willimond's side. Now, however, as he strode briskly across the grounds of Annegray, his gaze fixed upon a small building set against the base of the wall on the other side of the monastery. He could feel his heart pounding, not from the exertion of the walk, but from fear of what awaited him: fear that Willimond had spoken the truth, and their friend was dying.

He followed Willimond past the chapel to the guest house where Ulestan had been a permanent "guest" since the day of their arrival. Only Kristinge's discipline, implanted in him through those six years of monastic life, kept him from sprinting across the grounds ahead of Willimond. He took a deep breath as he ducked through the low door and tried to steel himself against what he would find inside.

Ulestan's room was a small stone chamber, with a single shelf for a candle plus two hooks on which to hang his belongings. In the winter, a vent in the wall provided heat from a central fireplace. It did not have the warmth of the great wooden hall of Finnsburg. No poet ever sang in this room. Yet Ulestan had been content. Kristinge stepped into the room ahead of Willimond to find the old warrior half-sitting, half-lying on the straw mattress in the corner. A young novice sat with him trying to offer him some wine, but Ulestan was coughing too much to drink. At the sight of Willimond and Kristinge, he motioned for the novice to leave.

The novice looked to the monks for confirmation. Kristinge could not find his voice, but Willimond responded with a nod and said in Latin. "We will take care of him now." The novice placed the wine cup into the older monk's hand and disappeared from the room.

Willimond sat down at the foot of the bed, while Kristinge rushed over to Ulestan's side and knelt beside him. "What is wrong?" he asked, speaking in Frisian. Though it was his native tongue, after years of speaking Latin the Frisian dialect sounded harsh in his ears and on his lips. It had been so long since he had spoken it regularly.

"My time has come," Ulestan replied.

"No!" Kristinge protested.

"Ah, my friends," Ulestan smiled deeply. His smile was interrupted by a long coughing fit. "My young friend," he continued a minute later. "Do not grieve, nor seek to prolong my departure. I have made my peace with the Father, thanks to Willimond."

"Thanks be to God, not me, my friend," Willimond gently corrected him.

"Yes," Ulestan agreed. "Thanks be to God." His voice was soft now with fatigue—not the fatigue of an afternoon's exertion, or even of a long battle, but the fatigue of a life filled with its share of suffering. "Soon I will be home," the old warrior said.

"No," Kristinge started to protest again, but Willimond put his hand on him and silenced him so that Ulestan could continue.

"My young friend." Ulestan was now looking Kristinge in the eye. "There is but one final duty I must carry out, though I confess I have no joy in it."

"Can it not wait?" Kristinge asked, not caring what the duty was.

"It cannot," Ulestan answered.

Beside him, Willimond winced as if struck by some unseen rod, but he said nothing.

"May I not then perform this duty in your place?" Kristinge suggested in all sincerity.

"Perhaps. Perhaps it is indeed a duty I am passing to you."

Confused, Kristinge turned to Willimond, but Willimond's eyes never left Ulestan. He turned back to look at the old warrior. "Speak to me, then. I will do whatever I can."

"Yes, I must," Ulestan said, as if to himself. He took a slow breath, but it did little to clear his old lungs. "I was charged by Finn himself, and I agreed. I gave my word." He coughed again and paused.

Kristinge was confused. Finn? Old memories began to well up, brought back by the sound of the Frisian tongue and by the mention of Finn, a name Kristinge had not heard in many years. "What is it?"

Ulestan did not answer directly. "Kristinge, do you know who your father is?"

"Willimond has always been a father to me." Kristinge replied at once. It was true. Though he knew Willimond was not his blood father, he was the only father Kristinge had ever known. He was as true of a father as Kristinge could have had.

With a feeble gesture of his right hand, Ulestan brushed Kristinge's answer aside. He stared at the ceiling for a moment as if staring into heaven, gathering strength. Then the thane who had served two kings and one God began the fulfillment of his final duty.

"There was once a great king," he began. "His name was Finn."

Tears in his eyes, Kristinge sat still and listened. In Ulestan's tired voice, he heard an echo of the old poet Daelga, and a hundred memories of his youth in Friesland—memories he had not relived in a long time—began to rush up within him.

"The king had a son who was strong and handsome and very much like the king himself. His name was Finnlaf." Somehow, the speaking of this tale strengthened Ulestan. He went on. "But upon a time, the son became sick—sick unto death. And all the kingdom grieved for him, but none more than Finn his father and Hildeburh his mother."

Images of the chieftain-king Finn, and of his Danish queen Hildeburh, flashed briefly across Kristinge's mind. Years ago Ulestan had been Finn's friend and his champion. But Ulestan had been sent away. And rumor had eventually come even as far south as Luxeuil that Finn had been killed in battle by the Danes, his own wife's people. What had that story to do with them now?

Ulestan paused briefly, as though giving Kristinge's memories a chance to wrap around these old names. Then he continued. "It also happened about that time that a great Man of God had come to Friesland to dwell in the village of the king. His name was Willimond."

Kristinge's heart began to beat faster, though he was not sure why. He turned again and looked over at the older monk, but Willimond's face was set in stone. Ulestan continued now without pause, his eyes staring at the ceiling above him as if he saw the story unfolding there even as he spoke. And perhaps he did. "This Man of God was called before the king to pray for the king's son, that he might be healed. And when the Man of God prayed all night, God heard the prayer and answered it, showing His mercy both to the king and to His servant Willimond. Finnlaf was healed and his life was spared."

"I remember Finnlaf," Kristinge said softly. He remembered the young prince's proud but kind face, as he walked around the village at his father's side. And often at Ulestan's side. On rare occasions Finnlaf shared with Kristinge a lesson from the bard Daelga.

Kristinge remembered also Finnlaf's pale face, laying in the boat upon the funeral pyre after he had been slain in the horrible fight that precipitated the later battle at which Finn himself fell.

"Thus it was," Ulestan continued, "that Finn in his gratitude—or perhaps in his own crafty wisdom—gave as payment to the Man of God an unasked-for gift."

A third time Kristinge looked at Willimond, trying to guess the outcome of this story that had taken place in a time before his memory. But the older monk still said nothing. And alone Kristinge could not so quickly solve the riddle. He could think only that Ulestan was dying.

"The present was a baby child," Ulestan continued. He turned his gaze back upon Kristinge, and studied him as he continued. "Given to Willimond was a child, the offspring of Finn and Hildeburh, the newborn brother of the one whose life had just been spared. The king gave to Willimond *his own son*, and told him to raise the child well, but with one additional charge: none should know the child's identity. Thus the child would be safe not only from the king's enemies but also from a rivalry with his brother for the torc of his father."

"I do not understand—" Kristinge started to say.

Ulestan finished. "Willimond took the child from Finn, and he named him Kristinge, and from that day forth he raised him as his own, Kristinge, the son of Finn."

For a brief second Kristinge's thoughts hung poised, like an hawk hovering, preparing to dive for a field mouse. Then the implications of what Ulestan had told him struck, and he felt himself plunging downward. "It cannot be!" He turned to Willimond half expecting the older monk to contradict Ulestan's story.

Willimond looked back in Kristinge's eyes, and after a brief pause gave a single silent nod.

"But," Kristinge objected. "Finn? My *father*? Why—?"

He didn't have time to ask any of the innumerable questions that rushed into his head like the incoming tide. Ulestan still had more to say. "There is more," he went on. "Much of Finn's story you have heard, but not all. All who knew your identity were sworn to secrecy, and though there must have been many more who guessed, it was never spoken of. When Finn saw his own end coming, he sent us away from Friesland to protect you. It was Finn who sent us here to Luxeuil."

"Luxeuil? To protect *me*? Sent us away? *Why*? I do not understand."

But Ulestan was beginning to reach the final point of his own exhaustion. That story had cost him. His head drooped back upon his bed-mat and his eyes fell shut. "Because you were his only remaining son, the heir of his torc," he whispered.

"The heir—?"

"Finnlaf had been killed. In the fight."

"In the fight with the Danes," Kristinge mumbled, closing his eyes as he dredged the history from his memories. Yes. He knew. *But the heir —?*

"It was a lie," Ulestan went on. The passing years had done little to lessen the pain for him. It was legible upon his brow.

"A lie? What lie? Why?" Kristinge had not been at the battle, but he knew the stories. The Danish king Hnaef had come to Finnsburg to see his sister Hildeburh before the onset of winter. With him were three warships, loaded with booty from successful raids along the Frankish and Saxon coasts. He had even brought gifts to Finn and Hildeburh. But something had happened. Something had caused a fight between their peoples. A tragic fight. Both Finnlaf and Hnaef had been killed that day. Some of the Danes had claimed it was Finnlaf who had killed their king, and Finnlaf, lying dead, could not dispute his accusers. Seeking the *weregild*, the powerful Danes had come back the following spring and killed Finn. Finnlaf and Hnaef? *His brother and uncle?* And Finn his *father?* Those past events suddenly became more important to him. More real.

"Lies," Ulestan said again. "Finnlaf did not strike Hnaef. He never did. It was Hunlaf the Jute who killed Hnaef. And it was Hunlaf's brother who struck down Finnlaf. He struck down Finnlaf while I..." his lips trembled.

Willimond placed a comforting hand on the old warrior's leg. "There was nothing you could do."

"Nothing," Ulestan repeated, eyes still closed.

But now Kristinge's mind was racing. "How do you know?" he asked. He had barely even known his brother. "Who saw?"

It took a moment before Ulestan could answer. "Though I did not see, I knew. I knew Finnlaf. He was like a son to me, even as you were to Willimond. I knew Finnlaf, and I saw his love for his uncle. And I knew also that he would not have struck any man from behind—not an enemy, and certainly not his kin. Even though I did not see, I knew."

Kristinge was still shaking his head in disbelief. "My *brother?*"

"But there was one who did see," Ulestan went on. "One who saw it all."

"Who?" Kristinge demanded, his eyes snapping back on Ulestan. "Why did the lies persist?"

"Daelga saw," Ulestan answered, as he found the strength to open his eyes once again and look upon Kristinge's face.

"The poet?" The question came from Willimond. Until that point, the older monk had been silently listening to a tale that he knew too well, but at this news his voice registered his surprise. "Daelga *saw*? Why did he not tell?"

"Daelga saw. From the back of the hall, he watched everything. But he was afraid. Afraid of the Jutes. Afraid of the Danes. Perhaps afraid even of Finn. And he was a poet, not a warrior. He fled the battle. Fled and was ashamed."

"But how—?" Willimond started.

"He told me... later. Weeks later, perhaps. I do not remember."

"And why did *you* not tell?" For a moment, Willimond's voice sounded accusatory, almost harsh. Then he asked again in a more gentle voice. "Why did you not tell?"

"Why?" Ulestan answered, his eyes closing once again. "Because it would not have mattered. Because Finn knew already without being told—knew as well as I did that Finnlaf would never have killed his uncle. Because his anger and hatred were hot enough already and he almost destroyed himself. Because I wished for peace."

"Why did I not tell?" Ulestan said, repeating the question. "I have asked myself that question many times. I do not know. Perhaps I, too, was afraid. And then I was gone."

"Does anybody else—?"

"No. Nobody. Or perhaps Hildeburh. Daelga may have told—" Ulestan coughed loudly. This time, he could not stop. A flu had settled too deeply in his old lungs. The spasm sent Kristinge to his feet, and he started out the room to get help, but Willimond called him back sharply.

A moment later, the coughing stopped.

Willimond reached over and put his hand over Ulestan's mouth. His breathing had stopped too. Gently, Willimond pushed the old warrior's jaw shut. Then he put his head down and wept.

CHAPTER 2:
A King's Son

An important stirring brought the young traveler's thoughts back to the present. The audience was growing restless waiting for him to sing. How long had he been daydreaming? Frotha, the chieftain, was glaring at him as though ready to toss him out of the mead hall. Kristinge looked down at his feet. He was still without a song. Why had his memory failed him on this night of all nights? He thought once more of the young woman seated across the hearth, though he dared not look at her now. *Perhaps for a king...*

But no. He was not a king. He was no more a king than he was a true bard. *And yet...*

An old song that Daelga used to sing sprang to Kristinge's mind. Absently, instinctively, he fingers plucked a few strings of his harp. No, he thought, even as his fingers found the next few notes. This was not the right song for a mead hall full of warriors. It was something the seasoned bard had written for queen Hildeburh long ago, and sung to her at times when the gathering at Finnsburg was small and quiet. It was no war-song. No celebration of battle. It was a song of praise for the beauty of a queen.

Kristinge could hear Daelga's voice. Could remember the day the old bard had first begun to teach him the song. A fall day, but sunny. They'd been seated on a high hill overlooking the seas.

I know not why I teach you this, Daelga had told Kristinge. *It will not inspire warriors to battle nor will it win you gold rings from a chieftain. Yet of all the songs I have sung, not one has Hildeburh praised more. If it was she who was the treasure-giver, I would sing it more often!*

As if it had been six hours ago when last he had heard it, and not six or more years that had passed, the words came back to the young monk. And with the words came something of a chanted melody, and a distant memory of his days in Hwitstan. It would be brash to sing it now, he thought. Impudent and foolish. Yet when he lifted his eyes and saw her sitting there, he threw away his caution. His fingers dampened the harp. He plucked the first few notes again, more clearly now. Then he began.

> A pearl of great price   a prince to delight:
> Graced in wound gold   she glitters so clear.
> I vow, though I voyage   to vast empires grand,
> in price her peer   no other will prove.
> So round and fine   this radiant gem,
> so smooth and soft   her sides did appear,
> that ever in judging   gems that are fair
> I deemed as dear   her only alone.

His nerves calmed as he continued. Instinctively, his eyes were drawn to her. She sat a few feet away, watching him. A strange expression, as of some old memory, flitted across her face. Was this not the very song he had once sung to her so long ago, when both had been but children in Hwitstan? A brash thing even then. Yet now, as then, her eyes had captured him.

> But once did I see her.   One time was I granted
> that marvelous sight;   yet the memory stays
> forever with me   when waking or sleeping.
>
> In a garden she stood,   arrayed in bright glory
> by flowers with blossoms   more bright than silver.
> Her hair like water   fell from her head,
> her laughter the sound   of the sweet cascade.
> While I from afar   that vision did watch.
>
> And while I watched   her, wondrous fair,
> she sang a song   like sweet perfume
> that filled the air   with fragrant scent,
> and bid the birds   themselves to silence.
> The whistling wind,   its wandering ceased
> and sat still to listen,   light breath on her hair.
> The mountains behind,   beneath their white manes
> of snow-capped stillness   so great, stood poised.

Then even the sun   though high in the sky
looked shining downward   deeming her equal
in beauty and grace;   and no less bright.
Enthralled, I at once   then did to her
my own heart bestow.   Or was it stolen?
For seeing her then   in such splendor adorned
by sun, wind, blossom,   and mountain's snow
and voice like crystal,   I had little choice.

Desire then found me,   flowed in my veins
as longer she sang   spinning enchantment
that wrapped my soul   in sweetest caress.
I would from all cares   to her company fly.
Yet on that spot,   though yearning to speak,
still longer I remained   unable to move.
So strong was her spell   like a statue of marble,
my legs were bound   in fetters of bronze.

She danced then too,   thus sealing my doom,
in glistening white gown,   that gentle maid,
her bare feet floating   free from the earth.
Sailing, she rose in   rhythm to her song,
crossed glade of grass   still glistening with dew.
As light as the breath   that filled her bosom,
round the flowered glade   she glided and spun.
No trace of her touch   tarried on the earth.

What marvels there   my mind did amaze.
Such wealth I watched   in wonderment glad.
The great trees bowed,   trembling at the sight,
but dared not touch her   with twig or branch.
But I, great fool,   then forward strode,
moved from my trance.   The trees' restraint
I no longer heeded,   but longing to reach
that unbounded beauty   I broke the spell.

My advance she saw   yet did not cease
her song or dance,   but smile she gave,
while with her hand   she told me wait
'til dance was done   and then to come.
And still she sang   with sweetest voice
that beckoned flowers   bloom at the sound,
and fruit to fall   ripe at her feet.
What mortal man   that call could resist?

I did not then know   of the more powerful spell
which in that meadow   that fair maiden bound.
Earnestly she warned   that I must wait
at edge of wood,   not wander in,
but too swiftly I strode.   I could not hold still.
My heart did not heed   her solemn warning.
Compelled by her beauty,   the boundary I crossed,
and she then vanished   from my vision.

O great delight!   For the dear radiance
cast 'pon my brow   by her blessed smile
I would willingly wait   one thousand winters
beneath the bows   of silvered birch.
But in my mortal mind   a madness had reigned
my headlong haste   me heedless bore
one step too far   on that fair grass;
and I thus drove away   the delight I sought.

And with her parting   all other beauty passed:
the wind its heavy   howling then resumed;
the grass once green   grew old and withered;
and flower pedals bright   fell stale and brown.
The distant mountains   rumbled their dreary moans
while in the sky saddened   the face of sun.
A swoon of longing   then smote me there
where that great beauty   I once had seen.

And piteously I cried   'O pearl, beyond compare,
to see thee once again   I would all dangers face.'

When the song ended, there was a low murmur of approval through the hall. Kristinge looked nervously at Frotha. When he saw the chieftain nodding his satisfaction, he breathed a sigh of relief. The singer bowed to the treasure-giver, then to the others in the hall, risking as he did the briefest glance in the direction of the woman for whom he had sung. Her face was glowing more than ever, and there was also a strange tilt to her eyebrows as if she, too, had been lost in a memory. She was watching Kristinge closely, almost admiringly—if it were possible for one so full of pride to admire—but also shyly. Kristinge turned away and smiled.

"Sing another," Frotha ordered, then added with a good-natured laugh, "this time, one for the warriors."

Kristinge nodded and bowed again. Suddenly his nervousness was gone. Like a slight breeze blowing away a morning haze, the singing of that first song had loosened his tongue. The barding mood was upon him now, and a host of old songs came flooding back across his memory. He latched onto the first one that came to mind—a song he knew well enough; one he would not have to think twice about; and one also that would please a chieftain and his warriors.

A song I will share,   will sing of a tale
of a mighty thane   who a thousand men slew.
That man of old   though mortal in body
was tall and stout   with the strength of ten.
The fame of Friesland,   his name was Friesc,
no better retainer   has a chieftain beheld.

Kristinge strummed the harp and lifted his voice louder, filling the hall with the sound of his singing. And even as he sang the familiar song, his mind drifted back once more to Luxeuil and to the days that followed the death of Ulestan. He thought again of the events that had propelled him along the path to where he now stood, singing as a bard in the hall of a Frisian chieftain.

Ulestan was buried the afternoon after his death. He was a scarred old warrior from a pagan land—one who had never learned Latin, and had never taken the vows of a monk. Yet the burial he received at Annegray was a Christian burial. He was a baptized man. And in those last six years of his life he had somehow captured the affection of many at Luxeuil. Perhaps in his sufferings he had come to understand Grace better than most ever do. *For he who has been forgiven much, loves much,* Petrica had once said of him. Even Abbot Walbert, from his prayer retreat deep in the woods, heard of his death and returned to pay him honor. At the command of the abbot, Ulestan was given a plot in Luxeuil's small cemetery down in the vale, and Kristinge was allowed to dig the grave. Willimond dug beside him and later spoke a short eulogy. The abbot said the prayers. Then, as the community gathered around the grave to sing *Compline* at the end of the day, Ulestan's two friends filled the deep hole into which the old warrior had been laid, marking the warrior's final resting spot with a small Irish cross.

However the work of Luxeuil did not stop after Ulestan's death. The labor of translation and copying needed to continue. There was cultivated grain to be planted and wild seeds and roots to be harvested. Peasants came to be taught. And *Compline* was only one prayer in the continual singing: the *Laus Perennis,* that was one of the blessings made possible by the many voices at a such a large community. On the morning after the burial, the young monk was aroused as usual two hours before sunrise for *Matins* and the morning mass. At the peal of the bells, he rolled off his mat on which he had passed a second sleepless night, wearily donned his robe, and stumbled from his room. Though the ache in his arms reminded him as clearly as the ache in his heart that he had spent the previous day shoveling dirt onto a grave, there was nonetheless work to be done from which he was not excused. His body mechanically led him through the day: singing the chants, morning prayers, the communal reading of scripture, followed by private meditation and study. Then, shortly after sunrise, work in the fields. And to all of this Kristinge submitted. Luxeuil's routine was so ingrained in him that to do otherwise would have required more work than to comply. But his mind was far from his chores, and even the discipline of the monastic life was unable to shake his thoughts free of the final words spoken by the old warrior.

Willimond took the child... He named him Kristinge...Kristinge, the son of Finn. The Heir of Finn's torc.

Finn? Kristinge could scarcely believe what he had heard. *His father?* Images of the warrior king whom a much younger Kristinge had known only from a distance crowded their way into his already confused mind. He could still hear the authoritative sound of Finn's voice. He could see his dark eyes and long black hair; the huge broad-sword draped over his back; the group of thanes and hearth companions surrounding him in his hall. He could see him, staff in hand, standing atop his tower at sunset looking out over Hwitstanwic toward the great North Sea. When Hildeburh the queen was at his side their presence there was a sign that all was well in Friesland.

And Kristinge was his *son?* *The heir of his torc?* What did that mean? Why, six years later and hundreds of leagues distant from Hwitstan, did the knowledge bring him such turmoil? How had it invaded the peace of Luxeuil? Finn was dead. Finnlaf was dead. And what of Hildeburh? *His mother!* Images of her were more haunting still. A twelve year old Kristinge had more than once thought that her piercing gaze was focused on him alone. Perhaps it *had* been. Would not any mother have eagerly watched her child grow whether she could hold him or not? Or perhaps all the youth of the village had fancied the eyes of the queen upon them. It did not matter. It was a gaze that Kristinge still remembered. And as Luxeuil's spring rolled into summer he thought of that gaze more and more often.

Nor were these the only memories that returned to disturb Kristinge. Memories of the small chapel which Willimond had built. Memories of his training from the monk as well as from the bard Daelga. And memories of a young girl who had come to Hwitstan during his last summer there. It was just a face. He had forgotten even her name. Only the dark hair, and the sharp green eyes. She was three years younger than he; at the time, just a girl of a dozen summers. Too young for marriage, though old enough for her chieftain father to be making plans for her. And old enough already to be pretty. Old enough to catch the eye of a young Kristinge. She had been brought to Finnsburg to be offered in marriage to Finnlaf. Or so she had boasted. While her father was conversing with Finn in the mead hall, she had slipped out and come down to the river where Kristinge was working. They had talked. He had shown her the weirs, and brought her to the chapel. He even played for her on the harp. Then three days later she was gone. Kristinge had not seen her again. Why, six years later, had the memory come back to him?

The Danes he defeated,   he alone that day
when fallen in fight   were all his fellows.
That man of old   though mortal in body
was tall and stout   with the strength of ten.
The fame of Friesland,   his name was Friesc,
no better retainer   has a chieftain beheld.

The song came to an end. The audience responded with a loud din of cheers. Several beer-laden warriors beat on their shields and benches. Frotha picked up his sword and hit his bench with the flat of it. The hall was warming to the performance. Distracted as Kristinge was by his memories of Luxeuil—even as at Luxeuil he had been distracted from his work by memories of his childhood in Friesland—he had still succeeded with the song. The chieftain ordered the bard's mug filled with ale. Kristinge took a swig and sat down for a short rest while the board and mead were passed around the hall. A few of the nearby warriors shouted out words of praise to the him as their cups were filled. He barely heard. He was still lost in memories of his departure from Luxeuil.

Many weeks had passed after the death of Ulestan. And difficult weeks they were. Kristinge had been given no chance to speak with anybody about what Ulestan had told him. Except for times of prayer and communal recitation of scripture, the Benedectine rule of silence governed life at Luxeuil. Still, even had he been free to speak, he might not have known what to say or even whom to tell. Other than Willimond, who else would have understood? To whom could he have spoken? Some novice whom he barely knew? Petrica? Abbot Walbert? What would they have said? What would they have advised? Would they have had any sympathy? Perhaps, had he been able to talk to somebody, Ulestan's death and his parting words might not have so overwhelmed young Kristinge. Or perhaps it would not have mattered. But those were what-ifs. He had not spoken to anybody. And he had made his decision before the end of summer.

"I hereby bequeath with no further hindrances..." the voice of Petrica recited while Kristinge scribbled. The occasion was similar to that on the day when Ulestan had died; another aristocrat was granting a small piece of land to the monastery. On this day Abbot Walbert himself was there with Petrica, while Kristinge with his steady hand transcribed the occasion. Under the rule of Walbert, Luxeuil had expanded considerably. Her reputation among both Franks and Gauls even as far as Rome had been established. It was a good time for the monastery. The passion of Columbanus and the Irishmen who had founded Luxeuil still infused the monastery with life, but the founding abbot's hot temper and his propensity for making political enemies were now gone, replaced by the calm patience of its newest abbot. The day of this particular grant would be remembered by the cutting off of a lock of hair from the head of the nobleman's daughter. The deed was transacted, only this time it was the mother and not the child who cried. *"Your beautiful hair! Your beautiful hair!"*

A few days later Kristinge stood in the chamber of Abbot Walbert, asking to leave Luxeuil and seeking the abbot's blessing on his departure. He did not expect it to be easy. But when he found Willimond standing at the Abbot's side, his heart sank. He feared his old mentor was there dissuade the abbot from granting him leave.

"I still remember the excitement you first had when we arrived here," Willimond said, after Kristinge had explained his request. "The thrill of learning the scriptures. Of studying here. Of the chance to leave the small village in the middle of a pagan land. What would lead you back there? What would make you give up this—this life of the Lord's work?"

Kristinge wasn't sure how to answer. He wasn't sure he knew. "I watched a servant eat a lock of his master's daughter's hair. He did it just so we could remember the day his master gave land to us."

"And?"

"It's not what I came here for."

Willimond shrugged. "No. Nor is weeding the garden, but it is work that must be done. And it has its place. You know as well as I that the Franks—even the rulers—cannot read or write. If cutting off a lock of hair or throwing a young boy into a pond will help them remember the covenant they have made with us and with God, then so be it. Did not God *Himself* instruct even Israel to make monuments that they might remember the days when he rescued them?"

"It was a lock of hair, not a monument."

"A lock of hair or a pile of rocks. What is the difference? We are still in this world. Even on a monastery."

"But it is not—"

"It is not what you came here for?" Willimond finished. He was growing agitated and the tension showed in his tightening voice. "And what *did* you come for?"

"To learn. To study. To understand the Word of God."

"To do God's work?" Willimond asked.

Kristinge paused. "Yes," he finally said.

"And is this not what you are doing?"

"I am," Kristinge conceded.

"And have you learned?"

"I have learned more than I had ever hoped. I did not know that in all the world so many books existed to be read."

"And you have read it all?"

The question embarrassed Kristinge. "No," he replied.

"Then what?" Willimond asked, holding Kristinge's gaze in his own.

Kristinge lowered his eyes. "I don't belong here."

"Because you are the son of a king?"

Kristinge blinked and looked around. Though that was indeed the issue at heart, still he cringed to hear Willimond say it so openly. Yet Abbot Walbert did not even lift his eyebrow. Was it possible that he already knew?

Willimond's voice took on a new passion as he continued. "Kristinge look around you. Who did you see in the field this morning working together? Do you see Chlotair? He is the son of Charibert II, who ruled Aquitaine. A Frankish king!"

"An illegitimate son," Kristinge replied without thinking.

He wished he hadn't. Willimond's voice was stern when he answered. "Do you pass judgment? He was knit together in his mother's womb by the same God who knit you together. And he has given his life to the Lord."

"But he had no claim on the throne—the king's torc."

"The throne and torc? Is that what this is all about? Kristinge do you really desire your father's torc? Have you learned *nothing* about the Frankish kings? Nothing from their treachery? Their short-lived reigns? And what of your own people? Do you desire such tragedy—"

"No," Kristinge answered. "I have no desire for the torc. I desire only to know who I am. Who my father and brother and mother were."

"What is it that you do not know?" Willimond asked.

Kristinge never had the opportunity to answer. Abruptly, Abbot Walbert brought the conversation to an end. In a voice much gentler than Kristinge expected, he asked, "When will you leave?"

The question was blunt and unexpected. "I... I... I don't know, Father," Kristinge answered. "I had hoped... I had hoped to depart as soon as possible."

"Sit down." There was another small wooden stool. Kristinge took it. Petrica, who had also entered the room, stood behind him. There were four of them in the small office now—not the private council with the abbot Kristinge had sought. "Autumn has already begun," Walbert continued. "In the north, it will not be long before snows come. Do you know how far you will travel this year, and by what route?"

Kristinge looked at Walbert, then back at Willimond, then at the abbot again. "Then you do not object to my leaving?"

"We hold none here against their will," Walbert answered.

"But you *knew* I wanted to leave even before I asked?"

It was Petrica who, at a nod from Walbert, answered the question. "We have watched all summer the trouble in your eyes. Could anybody have failed to see your distraction? It was evident in your every thought and deed. As for the reason, it was not difficult to guess."

"Then you know what Ulestan told me?"

"Willimond told us many weeks ago of Ulestan's dying words," Petrica acknowledged.

"But..." Kristinge wanted to object. Oddly enough, he wanted *them* to object. He needed them to argue against his departure. He needed to defend himself. He preferred Willimond's questions to Walbert's placid acceptance. Suddenly the young monk was not sure he wanted to depart.

"We do not counsel you against leaving," Walbert said, as if he read Kristinge's mind. "God leads us on many different paths. Few have ever left here in bitterness, but many *have* gone on. Columbanus himself did not die at Luxeuil. If he had, then the monastery at *Bobbio* would never have been founded."

"But how do I know God *wants* me to go?" Kristinge finally asked.

Petrica and Walbert both laughed. Even Willimond chuckled. "A well-phrased question, brother Kristinge," Walbert answered. "And if I guess rightly, one that you had expected *us* to ask *you*." Kristinge nodded, and the abbot continued. "The answers are many. His Word is our final guide, but there is much that it does not say. With some it is visions. With others it is their hearts." He raised his hand as if to forestall any objection, though Kristinge had not formulated any. "Truly, the heart of man is wicked, and yet God will use it if you let him; he will incline even the human heart to his will." Walbert paused. "What does your heart tell you, my son?"

"It urges me on," Kristinge answered. "But it is not because I do not love this—"

Again Walbert put up his hand to stop him. "You need say no more. We know your love. Yet if God called you on and you could not leave this behind, you would be greatly diminished. I will tell you this, for I am not one who believes in secrets. We have known for some time that you would one day leave. The Spirit has been making this clear in our hearts even from the day you came. Nor was your heritage unknown to us. Willimond is a wise one. He is too wise to keep such knowledge hidden. I think perhaps he hoped you would find a home here—the home that he never had." Kristinge closed his eyes to hold in a tear as Walbert looked over at the older monk and continued. "But a deeper hope that we all share is that your true home will be in the Lord, wherever he leads you."

"You have a gift, son," Petrica added. "We have seen it in your Spirit, though perhaps this place gave you little chance to us it."

"A gift?" Kristinge asked. His pulse was racing faster now. They could not be speaking of his work as a scribe—his labors copying the old manuscripts. His hand was steady and clear, but it was not beautiful. He had once gone back to one of his copies, and seen in the margins notes written by other monks ridiculing the plainness of his script. Not that he didn't enjoy the work. He especially loved copying the ancient Greek works. He loved myths and stories about gods of Olympus. Pagan gods, they were, yet they were also wonderful stories which so often had glimmers of truth about the one real God and his ways of mercy and justice. Pointers to the truth such as the Apostle Paul himself might have used when he preached by the temple of Athena. If Kristinge could tell such stories, he would be glad. But no, they could not be speaking of his work as a scribe. What, then? What was this gift of which they spoke?

"You will be a prophet," Walbert said. "A poet. Or are the two one and the same?"

"Had you lived among the pagans," Petrica explained, "you would be a great bard—a scop in the tongue of your people. It is written in you, somewhere, and it will come out."

"But how do you know these things?" Kristinge questioned them. He felt dumbfounded. *Why did everybody else know more about him than he himself did?* Another question that would continue to plague him.

"Willimond saw it in you," Petrica answered. "And he has known you longer than any."

Kristinge turned toward Willimond in surprise.

"Thank Daelga, not me," the older monk said. His voice was no longer challenging. "He told me when you were still young that you could be a great bard. This he told me even before he heard you sing! I think he read it in your eyes, your fingers. His opinion only grew stronger as you became older. If I had watched you less closely, I think he might have stolen you away as his own disciple. When Daelga was later baptized, he prophesied about you again. All that he said then, I have forgotten. Perhaps I did not listen as carefully as I ought to have."

Kristinge wanted to question Willimond more, but he did not have a chance. Everything was happening too quickly now. Walbert was already querying him again. "How far will you go this winter?"

Kristinge was embarrassed that he had given the question so little thought. Up until then, the decision to leave had occupied him, rather than the particulars of how. "To Friesland, at least," he said, giving the first answer that came to his head. "Perhaps to Danemark. If my mother is still alive—"

"Then you should leave tomorrow. Travel will soon grow difficult. And Danemark is far. Snow comes early there."

"We can be ready tomorrow," Willimond said.

It took a moment for the import of Willimond's comment to reach Kristinge. "*We?*" he asked, almost falling off of his stool. All of Willimond's laments of his many uprootings rushed into his mind. "You are going too?"

"I am."

"But Willimond," he objected. It was more than he could ask for. "Your home? You don't need to—"

"I have already packed my belongings. I have known this day was coming for some time."

"Then you've already decided—"

Willimond cut him off before he could finish. "And Walbert, in his great kindness, has even said I could bring my scrolls that have been with me since Lindisfarne."

Kristinge could barely believe what he was hearing. "And our horses too?" he asked, spinning back to the Abbot. He had given little thought to his *mode* of transport. Now he considered how great a distance he was planning on going, and how long it would take on foot. "The ones we—"

Walbert shook his head no. "They are no longer *your* horses. They were given to Luxeuil when you arrived. You gave up your personal possessions."

Kristinge's heart sank, but only a little. He was still feeling overwhelmed and overjoyed by Willimond's news. "Tomorrow?"

Walbert nodded. "Now if I could speak with you alone," he said, motioning for Willimond and Petrica to depart.

The following morning, as their last act of participation in the community that had been their home, Kristinge and Willimond took part in Luxeuil's prayers. Then they departed. Kristinge carried with him his few belongings: an extra robe, a warm woolen cloak and blanket, a walking staff, and a wallet of food containing provisions for three days if they were careful. Willimond had only a few more possessions than Kristinge; the older monk's carefully rolled sheepskin parchments were bound together and tucked under one arm, and a larger odd-shaped bag was slung over his other shoulder. When they came to the edge of the cloister, they stopped. Kristinge and Willimond knelt before Walbert who prayed over them and blessed them. Then they rose to depart.

"You remember your instructions?" The abbot asked Kristinge, handing him a package resembling a small scroll.

"I do," Kristinge replied, placing the package into his satchel. He saw the curious look on Willimond's face and was about to explain when Father Petrica appeared from behind a hut at the northern edge of the cloister, slowly making his way in their direction. Kristinge was glad to see him. Despite the discipline he had received at his superior's hand—especially during his final distracted summer at Annegray—he nonetheless felt a certain fondness for the older monk. He fell silent as he watched him approach, wondering what to say in farewell. But as was fitting for a Benedictine monastery, words did not matter. When Father Petrica arrived, he proved less formal than Walbert. In contrast to the sober and at times almost stern demeanor he had so often exhibited, there was both a smile and a tear upon his face as he wrapped his wiry arms around Kristinge and squeezed him in a tight hug. His strength surprised the young monk. "God be with you, brother," he said.

"And with you, Father," Kristinge replied, returning the affectionate embrace.

Then with a sly grin—another uncharacteristic expression on his normally austere face—Petrica handed Kristinge a palm-sized purse. "May this speed your voyage."

Surprised by the gift, Kristinge inspected the contents. The purse contained a dozen Roman coins, with a few Frankish and Danish coins also. It was enough, perhaps, for a few nights lodging along the way, or even for passage on a trading ship. Kristinge eyes lit up with gratitude. He didn't know what to say. "Father! Thank you!" He turned to Abbot Walbert. "And you as well. Thank you."

"It is not much by the world's standards," Walbert explained. "It is what we can spare to send with you. And perhaps you will find that with God's blessings it will last longer than you think." Tears came to Kristinge's eyes and a lump to his throat, but he could say nothing more. The abbot then turned to Willimond. "And you, brother? You came here with little, and you depart with little. If I know your heart, then I know that the greatest treasure you have is the Word, and that is hidden in your heart more clearly than it is written on your prized scrolls. Yet I would still give you something for your voyage. And so, as you go to be a shepherd, perhaps the most fitting gift I can give you is this." He extended his left arm and presented Willimond with the ash walking staff he was carrying. "May this lighten the burden on your feet."

Willimond received the staff with gratitude. "You honor me. Truly I came here with little, and have left with much. I dwelt longer here than I did at Iona or Lindisfarne, and richly have I felt the blessing. It is not easily that I depart."

"It is not lightly that we let you depart," Walbert smiled. "Go now with our blessings, and do not forget where you came from. Be as shrewd as serpents and as innocent as doves. Remember that you are ambassadors of the Gospel. If you are welcomed into a home, let your blessings rest on that place. If you are turned away, shake the dust from your sandals and move on."

His blessing given, Abbot Walbert embraced Willimond and Kristinge. Then he turned and strode back toward the barley fields with Petrica at his side.

CHAPTER 3:
OAELGA'S HARP

It was the booming voice of the chieftain that brought Kristinge back to the present. "Another song, bard. Or you will make me regret filling your cup with drink."

Kristinge glanced over at Willimond. The older monk was still seated on a bench against the wall, watching the performance from the shadows away from the fire. Not for the last time, the young monk-turned-bard wondered what he would have done without his friend and former mentor. When the older monk gave him a nod of confirmation, he smiled at him then stood. He took a final swig of the ale followed by a deep breath. Then he lifted his harp and stepped back toward the hearth. Everyone in the hall was watching him expectantly now. The chieftain Frotha. His thanes and hearth companions. The traders who were present. Willimond. And *Aewin*. She was no longer talking with the warrior at her side. Her gaze was upon the bard now. Kristinge's neck tingled with the excitement of her glance. He plucked a few strings on the harp. He could still feel the barding spirit upon him. He knew what he must sing. It would not be long. An ode to many heroes of the north who had passed through hardships and on to joy. It was another song to please the warriors, but one that might also please a chieftain's daughter.

> Weland by hindrances,   by hardship was tested,
> endured the exile,   that strong-minded earl.
> He found often woe,   his friend was his sorrow,
> his companion was longing,   the cold winter loneliness.
> His supple sinews,   by Niphad were severed,
> his legs thus were bound,   though he a better man.
>   That passed over.   This will as well.

Was Beaduhilde's doom—   the deaths of her brothers
were not as sorrowful   as her own troubled state.
She knew without doubt,   and now was her dread,
a child she carried;   she could never now
demand any answer,   how it was destined.
        That passed over.   This will as well.

The moans of Maethild   many have learned
came without count,   the Geat's lady's cries;
A languishing love   deprived her of sleep.
The joys of life,   laughter and song,
strength and passion,   she could not possess.
        That passed over.   This will as well.

Theoderic was exiled   thirty long winters
in the Maering's city;   many knew of his sorrow.
        That passed over.   This will as well.

Lo! We have heard   tales of great horror:
how Attila ruled,   rode from the East
with fell horsemen,   the foul hunters.
Their yoke was heavy.   Hard were those years.
        That passed over.   This will as well.

We have learned as well   of the wolfish thoughts
of Eormanic the king;   how he cruelly ruled
the wide Gothic country;   that was a grim king.
Brave warriors sat   bound in their sorrow,
expecting only misery,   many times wishing
that this cruel kingdom   would be overcome.
        That passed over.   This will as well.

He who sits sorrow-bound,   stripped of his pleasures,
gloom in his heart,   himself ever thinking
that his heavy hardships   will have no end,
bethink on these words!   In this world you are living,
where God in his wisdom,   that we do not have,
sends among men   both joy and sorrow.

About myself I will   say only this much:
I was the Heodening's scop,   before them I sang.
I was dear to my lord.   Deor was my name.
High was the honor   I held for long years
in my master's heart,   until Heorrenda,
that song-crafty man,   stole all my honors
which the leader of men   had long lent to me.
     That passed over.   This will as well.

The song was done. It was too pensive, too full of longing and emotion to be applauded, but Kristinge could see in the eyes of his audience that they had not gone unmoved. Quickly, before the mood of the hall was lost, he launched into another song—a longer tale of a young warrior who fell under the enchantment of the Fairy folk and with the help of a battered old war-blade became a mighty hero before losing all his strength when his chieftain unknowingly broke the enchantment by giving him a new sword. All the men-of-arms who knew the value of a battle-tested weapon cheered loudly when this song was over. Now Kristinge was warmed. Not even the eyes of the maiden could wholly distract him. Three more songs he sang, each as well-received as their predecessors, until Frotha tossed him a small gold ring and told him to sit. "Well done, bard," the chieftain acknowledged. "You have earned your keep."

Kristinge collapsed back to his bench, exhilarated but exhausted. *You have earned your keep.* How odd it was to hear a chieftain say that to him. The title *bard* still sounded strange to his ears. That he had even come to take up the harp again was still something of a surprise to him. Despite all that Petrica and Walbert had said of his gifts—despite even what Willimond had told him about Daelga's prophecy—Kristinge had not left Luxeuil with any intention of being a bard or scop. He had remembered little if *any* of what the old bard Daelga had taught him long ago; neither the songs, nor the plucking of the harp, nor even the rules by which the true bards composed. The little training he had received as a young boy in Hwitstan was too far in the past. The road and its dangers gave him enough to think about without trying to dredge from his memory a long list of old Frisian lays. Until the morning he had departed from

Luxeuil, he hadn't been sure how he would be traveling. His travels as a young novice and monk had been limited to a few short trips into nearby villages, either to aid Walbert in the preaching of the Gospel or to help the poor.

"Which direction?" Willimond asked, after they turned their backs on the monastery.

"Northwest. Toward Paris," Kristinge replied. The direction surprised Willimond, who had thought to travel north and east, around the mountains and on to the Rhine in hopes of hiring passage to Dorestad or Utrecht on a sea-bound ship. But Kristinge had opted for the longer route. Though no road could be said to be safe for two unarmed monks traveling alone, the better traveled route might be the lesser of the two dangers. Poor though they were, they were easy prey for robbers. And many of the wild mountain folk did not take kindly to monks. Kristinge did not want to become a sacrifice to some pagan idol before he even reached Danemark. Instead, the plan was to walk by road as far as the Seine river, and from Paris or Auxerre to find a trade ship to the sea. Two week's journey by foot should bring them from Luxeuil to the city of Auxerre, Walbert had told them. Ten if they pressed hard. Another week from Auxerre to Paris would bring the total to three weeks. It was said that Columbanus once made the entire trip in ten days, but that required him to walk longer each day than Pheidippides walked from Athens to Marathon. And Pheidippides died when he arrived. Yet such a feat would have been no more miraculous for Columbanus than other things he accomplished by God's power. And if Kristinge and Willimond could make it in twice that number of days, it would be good enough; at that time of year, they were still likely to find Frisian traders in Francia, and maybe even a ship bound for the north.

The only possible delay was that Abbot Walbert had requested that Kristinge carry a message for him to the monastery at Jouarre, a days journey by wagon to the north and east of Paris. It would take a three day round trip by foot if they had to detour from Paris.

"Jouarre?" Willimond had asked in surprise when he heard of Kristinge's plan.

"A monastery near Paris. It was founded by Adon, a disciple of Columbanus—"

"I know some of Jouarre's history," Willimond interrupted impatiently. "I am only surprised that we are traveling there. You have some purpose at Jouarre?"

"Walbert asked me if I might deliver some parchments to the abbess. That is what is in the package he gave me," he added, lifting his satchel slightly, "and part of the reason he requested we follow this route, though he also believes it will be safer for us. He suggested we could find lodging in the guest house at Jouarre before we look for passage on a trading ship." Then he laughed. "The Lord's mercy upon us both. I have messages from Walbert for half a dozen daughter monasteries of Luxeuil. I could spend all year delivering them. Fortunately, all Walbert asked was that I bring them as far as Jouarre."

They talked more as they walked, at times speaking idly of the terrain, or of their memories of Friesland, or of Finn and Hildeburh. Kristinge said nothing about the young girl he remembered from his final summer in Hwitstan, though her piercing gaze still haunted his memory. He did speak of the poet Daelga and others they had both known. At the mention of Daelga and his minstrelsy, a sly smile slipped onto Willimond's face, but he said nothing for the time. Late in the afternoon, they shared a loaf of bread together and also found some wild seeds by the roadside. Willimond was still looking for more seeds when Kristinge urged him on.

"There is an estate ahead," Kristinge explained as Willimond came trotting out of the woods to join him. "So I am told by Father Petrica. It belongs to a Gallo-Roman by the name of Benetus. He is Latin-speaking. In the past, he has made gifts to Luxeuil, and he might be hospitable to traveling monks. Father Petrica said we could make it there in one day if we walked briskly. It cannot be much farther."

"Then let us proceed," Willimond agreed. "I would gladly forfeit the chance to gather few wild seeds for a roof under which to lay my head this night."

Together they marched on. Shortly before sunset, they arrived at a large fortified stone house surrounded by cultivated fields. As Petrica had guessed, the nobleman was more than happy to feed and house two monks for the night. As soon as he learned whom his visitors were and where they had come from, Benetus gathered his whole household to meet them. By the time he had finished introducing four children and thirteen grandchildren, it was dark. Then, though his family had already eaten their evening meal, he brought out another board of bread, cheese, and roasted grains for his guests. "Modest fare", he called it, but by monastic standards it was a feast. Benetus ushered his family into a large adjoining hall, and then rejoined Kristinge and Willimond in the smaller room to make sure they ate enough.

When the monks had finished eating, Benetus led them into the large lantern-lit hall where the family was waiting. He then insisted they sit and join in conversation, though it soon become clear that what he meant by conversation was the monks answering his questions. And the questions he asked were as endless as they were varied: questions about Luxeuil, where the nobleman was considering sending his oldest grandson the next year; about God; about the "savage peasants" of the Vosges mountains; about wild fruits and seeds, and about crops and farming—the monks at Luxeuil had a reputation for their ability to conjure a healthy crop from notoriously poor soil—and even about Columbanus, whose famous miracles and exploits the host knew as much about as Kristinge. The questions lasted long into the evening, but Kristinge did not mind. It was more conversation than he had had in the past six months put together. There was a warm blaze in the fireplace that cut the chill of the autumn air, and plenty of mead to share. Both were a welcome treat for the travelers. And as they soon discovered, Benetus was well educated. Though for daily trade he spoke the Frankish tongue of his country's rulers, in the home his family spoke Latin. He could both read and write, and had even received some years of education at a Roman monastery in southern Burgundy near Arles. However he had been disillusioned by what he thought was hypocrisy and greed there, and had given up religious life—or at least the Gaul-influenced monastic life—and returned to his estate. He was well enough versed not only in holy scriptures but also in secular writings ranging from Tacitus to Sidonius, so that the questions he posed for the two monks were often quite challenging and led to some interesting dialogue and provocative debate about various philosophies. His wife was also educated, though not formally, and could read Latin. At times, she participated with questions as thoughtful as those of her husband. Late into the night and long after all of his children and grandchildren had departed for sleep, Benetus and his wife kept the two monks occupied.

Such was the monks' reintroduction to the world. In the end it was Kristinge's exhaustion that brought their conversation to an end at an hour much later than he was accustomed to. Benetus reluctantly led his guests to a small room where two mats had already been rolled out on the floor. Kristinge was asleep within moments.

The next morning, the two monks joined Benetus' family for a rich meal of baked bread and fresh goat's milk along with some scraps of grilled ham—a even rarer delicacy to the pair of monks for whom any morning meal was a luxury. After breaking their fast, the host and his wife both encouraged Kristinge and Willimond to remain for the day and continue their conversations. It was a strange feeling not to have any duties—no *enforced* discipline, or *regimen* of spiritual activity. Kristinge, having enjoyed the previous evening's dialogue, was tempted by the offer. It was Willimond, despite Benetus' kind and persuasive manner, who politely declined and insisted they must continue on. They thanked their host for his hospitality, and after he had given them some guidance for their next few days, they departed.

For the first hour or so, they marched along in silence. The air was cold—there had been a frost up in the hills—and it took time for their bones to warm. Once the sun was high, however, the day turned mild. The landscape was also changing as they made their way farther from the mountains and closer to the center of Francia. The steeper slopes of the Vosges gave way to wide, rolling hills, while the old deep forests were replaced by younger, more civilized woodlands, and cultivated farms.

"It looks as though we will be sleeping in the open tonight," Kristinge commented, repeating information they had heard up from Benetus. He was tired of the silence and ready to talk.

"It is well we each brought a blanket," Willimond answered in a quiet voice.

Kristinge wondered at Willimond's strangely solemn mood, but he wasn't yet ready to pursue it. "Tomorrow night we should be able to find lodging." He was referring to a village near the estate of another wealthy Frankish nobleman whom Benetus had told them of. "There will likely be a guest house or inn for traders there."

"Yes," Willimond said. "And an inn will cost money, too. Do not forget that we have many nights ahead of us."

"We have coins," Kristinge replied. "Enough for a few nights." He was not excited about sleeping outside throughout the months of September and October.

"Or, if we can earn our night's keep in some other way and save those coins, we might keep enough to buy passage to Danemark."

"You mean we can do like Columbanus?" Kristinge joked. "We can kick some bear out of its den?"

Willimond shrugged enigmatically. They strode on. At noon, a small caravan of traders passed by in the opposite direction. They were Goths from Spain, returning with a load of Saxon wool and Frisian cloth, gained from the trade of wine and glass. The traders spoke little Latin, but they had a trade knowledge of Frankish. They confirmed what Benetus had told the monks of the road ahead. Then, after asking for guidance to the estate of Benetus, they passed on.

"Will Benetus be safe?" Kristinge wondered aloud. "With the barbarians, I mean? They were all armed."

"They did us no harm," Willimond answered.

"We have no treasure worth anything to them."

"We have greater treasure than you know," Willimond said, referring obliquely to his scrolls which he held up in his hand. Then, more to the point of Kristinge's question he added, "Benetus' home is protected. His hired band numbers at least as many as the trader's band, and it would take a small army to throw down his walls."

"Still, I had heard they were not safe. The Goths are Arians, aren't they?"

"More likely just pagans."

"Barbarians?"

"You Frisians, too, are considered barbarians here," Willimond reminded Kristinge.

Kristinge took the jibe with a smile. "I wonder," he said, replying to Willimond's earlier comment, "why in the end Walbert let you take your scrolls, but did not offer to me any of those I labored on." He paused for a minute, then added a little wistfully, "Or the horses."

"He was generous."

"Generous? But we brought those horses with us from Friesland when we came six years ago."

"We did. And when we arrived, we gave them to Luxeuil as we did all our possessions. And we lived there for many years, eating their food, sleeping in their beds—"

"And working," Kristinge added. "Cultivating their fields, copying scrolls."

"Do you feel cheated for your labor?"

Kristinge sighed. "No. Walbert *was* very generous. He needed give us nothing. He sent us with honor as if we were apostles."

"We are," Willimond answered. This time it was Kristinge who raised his eyebrows. "They gave us what they could afford, and perhaps more" Willimond went on. "What they thought we would need. It was indeed a sacrifice. We had no claim even on these things, and certainly none on horses."

"And your scrolls?"

Willimond looked down. The scrolls he carried were old, the work of his own youth when he was a monk at Lindisfarne the same age Kristinge was now. "No," he said. "Only the Word of God is the treasure. I fear that they gave me these because they perceived that *my* work was of no great value." He laughed. "The same reason the Abbot of Lindisfarne sent me with these scrolls so long ago when I left there for Friesland." Then his voice became distant. "Oh, the beauty of the work done at Lindisfarne! The magnificence of Aidan's work, and the Gospels there. I wish I could one day see the final work." He paused. Then he startled to chuckle again inwardly. "Did I ever tell you about when Finn—your father—burned one of my scrolls? How foolish I was. I felt as if he had burned the world's greatest treasure. Ha. Now your work, on the other hand, I have seen. And it *is* a treasure. That is probably why Walbert sent us with my scrolls. Yours were too highly valued."

"You tease me," Kristinge said, catching some of Willimond's humor. "I am no artist."

"Perhaps not with pictures. That is true. Your script is clear enough, but it lacks the beautiful lines that even some of the poor peasants sometimes discover. Yet you are an artist with words. I have read your translations. You have a gift."

"So Walbert was not quite as generous as we thought."

"He was. Walbert *has* sent us out in honor. You may be assured he will pray for our safety, and that is a gift beyond measure."

The night was cool, but not as cold as Kristinge had feared. They were further from the mountains now and autumn had not progressed as far in the lower lands. The cloudy skies held off the frost, and the traveling monks remained comfortably warm under their heavy wool blankets. The next morning, as they rolled the blankets and prepared to depart, Kristinge spoke.

"I have wanted to ask you a question ever since our meeting with Abbot Walbert." At Willimond's prompting, he went on. "I was terrified when I went to speak to the Abbot and found you there too—when once more you sought to dissuade me from the journey. Yet later Abbot Walbert told me that you yourself who persuaded him to send me with his blessing, and that *he* had initially been against my departure."

"He said that, did he?"

"He did."

"I suppose, then, that there is truth in it. Though I do not think he needed much persuading. He is a man who is keenly aware of God's will. But come, what was your question?"

"What changed your mind?"

Willimond was silent for a moment before answering. "My mind was never changed."

The answer took Kristinge by surprise. "I do not understand. You still think I should not have left Luxeuil?"

"No. It was never my belief that you should remain there forever. It is rather to the contrary. I spoke the truth when I said that Hwitstan was my home; that I loved Friesland. I have always longed to return. Oh, I was content at Luxeuil," he quickly added, "and I am glad for my years there; I learned much. But I feel that my work on the *outside* is not yet finished. Though I am not sure how or where I will continue. I have heard that my church was left in ashes when the Danes attacked. No," he concluded, "my desire has been to return to Friesland. To see again my *flock* that I labored with for so long. Even to see Hildeburh, your mother."

"But that does not explain—" Kristinge began.

Willimond cut him off with a wave of his new staff. "Does it not? Do you not now see why I *had* to question you? Why I had to be sure? I am all too aware of my own weakness. I knew where my own selfish desire lay. I could not, in my selfishness, let you leave too quickly and easily. It would have been too convenient for me. I had to make sure that it was God who was leading you away, and not me. I had to test. Perhaps I tested too hard. I do not know. But there was also this, as Walbert said when he read my heart: I truly wanted you to have a real home such as I never had."

When Willimond was done, they both fell silent. The day progressed much as the previous day had, except that they saw no other travelers until late in the afternoon when they approached a small village. After unsuccessfully searching and inquiring for lodging, they walked on and spent another night in the open a mile past the village. This night was colder than the last. Kristinge was up well before sunrise, pacing around trying to warm his legs. Willimond soon joined him, and they set off on their fourth day of travel. When the sun was high enough in the sky to have melted the frost and dried the ground, they stopped for a rest. They finished the last loaf of bread, shared a small block of cheese, and then set off again. Their legs were now growing more used to walking, and with the stiffness of a second night's sleep on hard ground wearing off, they set a quicker pace.

By evening they had come to a much larger estate set in a wide shallow valley by a large stream. They had a good view as they came down the hill. A big hall, as big as the largest building at Luxeuil, was surrounded by a number of smaller structures: stables, pens, granaries, and a smithy. The whole cluster of buildings was enclosed by a high stone wall a few hundred yards in circumference. It was not a true burg, or fortress as Annegray had once been, but the wall was wide and well built; in places it rose as high as ten feet. It was enough to offer at least some protection against a small band of robbers. A number of sheep and pigs roamed inside the enclosure, watched casually by a swineherd-shepherd. A larger flock of sheep grazed on a hillside to the south. On the other side of the wall, about a quarter mile away from the main enclosure, was a separate cluster of small huts, likely for the peasant workers. Most were above-ground timber structures, but Kristinge also saw a few sunken mud houses that reminded him of the Frisian terpen. Seeing them gave him a sudden sense of urgency about his return, and also a desire for company. "Let us pay for lodging if we must," he suggested as they approached. "There is a large hall here. For a gold Roman coin, they must be able to accommodate guests."

"Perhaps," Willimond said softly as they came to a stop a few hundred yards from the outskirts of the village. He stood for a moment scanning the area. The late afternoon had grown warm and the peasants in the field—men and women dressed in plain skin trousers with no shirts or shoes—looked up and saw the strangers, but they returned quickly to their work and paid little heed. "Perhaps," Willimond said again. "However I am not so eager to lose even one coin. We have many days ahead of us, and we are far from Friesland and farther still from the Danemark. I do not fancy walking all the way if there is a chance of hiring passage on a Frisian trading ship."

"And I do not fancy sleeping in the cold for the rest of the journey," Kristinge rejoined, more sarcastically than he intended.

"Perhaps we will not need to," Willimond went on calmly, ignoring Kristinge's tone. "This must be the home of a wealthy nobleman. He might be of kindred spirit to Benetus."

"You think he will offer free lodging?"

"No. I speak of *earning* our keep."

Kristinge sighed. He was feeling too tired to work more and too tired to argue. "What labor could we perform?"

"In the days past a wandering bard or minstrel, if he was talented, could earn his keep at the hall of a king or wealthy noble." Willimond turned toward Kristinge. "There is one more treasure Walbert gave to us. Or rather returned to us, for it was once yours. It may prove of greatest value yet."

Kristinge was curious as Willimond pulled his large satchel off his back. He had noticed the bag's odd shape—odd, though strangely familiar—and had wondered more than once at its contents. Still, he was not prepared when Willimond reached in and removed a small harp. It was not *any* harp. It was Kristinge's own harp—the harp that had once been Daelga's, and that Daelga had given to him the year before his departure from Hwitstan. It was the harp on which he had played and sung so many Psalms in his days at Hwitstan. The harp on which he had once sat by the river and played a song for a young daughter of a Frisian chieftain, pledged in marriage to Finnlaf. He trembled with joy at the touch of the wood and strings. But the joy was overshadowed with a dread of what Willimond was asking of him. He had not played in six years. He was afraid even to touch the strings. "You can not be speaking of *me?*" he protested.

"If we are given the chance," Willimond went on, ignoring the protest, "then tell a story—a pagan lay, such as Daelga used to tell. This is not the time for your psalms, but for a heroic poem."

"A pagan lay?" Kristinge was surprised by Willimond's advice and for the moment forgot his fears. "Should we not be working *against* the ancient pagan ways?"

"We are no longer at Luxeuil. Story is more pleasing to the ears. And we *do* want lodging."

"But—"

"It is no compromise. Story is powerful. It will touch ears that would never hear the preaching of a monk."

"But why me?"

"Ah, my friend. You have a gift." Without waiting for an answer, he started forward leaving Kristinge still holding the harp. Kristinge paused for just a moment to caress his old instrument. Then he caught up with his companion. They passed around the edge of the village and headed straight for the gate to the main estate. When they arrived, they were met by two young girls of about seven and nine years. Though covered in dirt and dust from an afternoon of playing outside with the animals, Kristinge could see that they were well-dressed in expensive cloth. He guessed they were the daughters or perhaps granddaughters of the manor lord. With a lightly armed gatekeeper watching them carefully and protectively from atop the wall, the girls ran over to the open gate to see who the strangers were. Before Kristinge could say a word, Willimond introduced him as a traveling bard. At the word bard, Kristinge cringed with dread that not even robbers on the road would have elicited. But it was too late. The girls had already turned, and ran giggling back to the house to fetch their father, leaving the guests standing at the gate.

There was no time for Kristinge to protest. The lord of the house emerged a moment later, with his lady beside him. He was a heavy man, and tall, dressed even more richly than his daughters—though only slightly less dirty—in dark wool trousers, with a heavy blue tunic pinned at the shoulder by a large horse-shaped gold brooch. He wore real leather shoes. His wife, considerably shorter but no less plump, wore a simple ankle-length dress bunched at the shoulders and at her ample waist. She stood at the door holding her two daughters while her husband walked over to the gate. In his right hand, he carried a stout staff taller than he was. He bore a large Frankish broadsword as well, but it stayed in its sheath. The man appeared strong enough that just his staff, which he gripped more like a weapon than a walking stick, would suffice against most enemies. Next to it, the beautiful staff given to Willimond by Abbot Walbert looked like a mere twig. Kristinge, already in dread, wanted to turn and run. Onward the manor lord came until he stood just a few inches from the monks. There he stopped and just stood looking them over with squinty, suspicious eyes. Finally, in a heavy gruff slurred Frankish dialect, he spoke. "What you want? You don't look like bards to me."

He took his staff in both hands now, holding it in a threatening manner that made Kristinge—who was himself taller than most—take a step back. But Willimond, though he was gripping his own staff rather nervously, held his ground and, to Kristinge's surprise, replied in Frankish almost as heavy as the nobleman's, "We are as we appear, monks from Luxeuil." He spread his arms in an wide open gesture. "I am named Willimond, and this is Kristinge."

"Monks?" the man grunted. "My daughter said you were bards."

"So they claimed," shouted down the gatekeeper, speaking for the first time. "I heard them myself."

"And so we are. Or rather my companion is," he said, pointing toward Kristinge whose stomach had just slid a few more inches up his throat. "For a meal and lodging, we will gladly entertain you. Or," he added, pointing to the young girls, "we will entertain your daughters if you wish."

"We got a nursemaid already," the man grunted again.

The gatekeeper laughed.

"I don't need nothing from you," the man yelled up at his servant. "If you was doing your job, they'd have been a mile gone by now." He reached up suddenly with his staff and knocked the gatekeeper backward off the wall. Kristinge heard him land on the far side with a thud and groan.

Kristinge, eager to avoid the same treatment, took another step backward and prepared to leave. Another night in the cold might not be so bad after all.

"Monks, you say?" the man went on. "Well I suppose you can't do us much harm." He looked at their arms. "Don't look like you could hurt much. If it's lodging you want, you can sleep in the stable. But if it's a meal you want, you'll have to earn it first. We're eating now. Entertain us." Without a further word, he turned and strode toward the house.

CHAPTER 4:
MONK AND BARD

Willimond and Kristinge glanced at each other, then turned and followed him into the house. It was a far cruder building than the home of Benetus, and a little smaller, though together with all the out-buildings it formed a larger overall estate. Through the main door they found a large central hall with a high angled roof running the entire length of the house. A door on one side led off into a side corridor where the occupants bedded, but most of the activity took place in this main hall. In the middle was a large table, big enough to seat twelve or more men. Around it were four long benches, and at the far end was a hearth and some cooking utensils. Shelves on the walls were covered with pottery, bronze bowls and utensils, glass drinking horns, a few silver bowls, and some wooden bowls. Further from the hearth were stacks of clothing and blankets, along with a few weapons hanging from hooks: bows, battle-axes, an assortment of spears, and a pair of swords. Where the walls weren't lined with useful commodities, they were decorated with woven hanging carpets—a luxury uncommon in Friesland save in halls of the richest chieftains, and not to be found at all in Luxeuil.

Without a further word to the traveling monks, the lord of the house seated himself at the table. His wife crossed the room and began to serve him dinner. Only when he was well into the meal, did she and her daughters sit to join him, and even then—in contrast to the wife of Benetus who spoke freely and intelligently during the evening—she said nothing while her husband ate. All of this took several minutes during which time Kristinge stood nervously, wondering whether he should just turn and flee. He had no idea what to sing, and didn't even know if the harp was in tune. Over the previous six years he had sung nothing other than the chants, and he didn't think they would be well-received at the moment. How had Willimond gotten him into this? He was a monk, not a bard.

"Now," Willimond whispered in his ear.

Now? Kristinge asked wordlessly.

Now, Willimond responded with a nod.

Kristinge took the leather cover off of his harp. He plucked a few strings. It was as out of tune as he expected, and it took him many minutes to adjust the pegs to his satisfaction. The delay seemed terribly long. The Frankish lord grunted as he savagely ate his meal of wild game, occasionally taking a break to swig ale from his huge glass drinking horn. "Well?" he said once, turning and fixing a stare at Kristinge. "Will you make me wait all night, and regret my offer of lodging, too?"

Kristinge cleared his throat. Only one song had come to mind. It was an old Saxon poem that Daelga had brought to Friesland from the isle of the Britons. Fortunately, the characters were wholly Germanic, and—as long as he didn't forget it in the middle—would suit a Frankish as well as Frisian audience. Daelga had sung it many times at Folcwalda's court, and he had patiently taught it to Kristinge. Somehow the intervening years had left the words in his memory. He cleared his throat and began.

> Weland by hindrances,   by hardship was tested,
> endured his exile,   that strong-minded earl.
> He found often woe,   his friend was his sorrow,
> his companion was longing,   the cold winter loneliness.
> Though a better person,   by pain he was bound
> when his supple sinews   by Niphad were severed.
>   That passed over.   This will as well.

Contrary to his fears, he did not forget the words as he went. Each new stanza rose to his mind as the time came, and somehow the act of singing took his mind off his own fears, freeing him of his awareness of the audience that sat in judgment. He closed his eyes and sank into the mood of the song. As his apprehension faded, he became less self-conscious and less tentative. His fingers, rusty as they were from lack of practice, still remembered some of their old skill. His voice grew in strength.

> Was Beaduhilde's doom—   the deaths of her brothers
> were not as sorrowful   as her own troubled state.

It was his voice that was his real gift. As Willimond had told him, he had the true voice of a bard—clean, clear and spellbinding; at one moment loud and ringing off the walls, and the next so soft his listeners had to hush and lean forward. It was a voice that could cover many imperfections in his playing of the harp. Remembering something of what Daelga had taught him, or perhaps singing from sheer instinct alone, he used that now. Before the song was half-over, the lord of the manor had stopped eating. He had even stopped chewing, his mouth half full of food. When Kristinge opened his eyes, he could almost see the gruffness sliding from the man's face. When the older daughter climbed into his lap and he absently put his arm around her, the bard knew he had succeeded.

High was the honor   I held for long years,
the maker of music,   in my master's heart,
'til a song-crafty man   stole all my favor
which the leader of men   had long lent to me.
     That passed over.   This will as well.

The song was over. Their host, realizing there was still food in his mouth, quickly finished chewing as he rose. "I am Gundomer," he said. "Welcome to my house." He extended his right arm and gave a firm greeting to Kristinge then to Willimond.

Kristinge set the harp down and bowed. "May your hospitality return to bless you," he said.

"Please, sit," Gundomer said, motioning to the monks. "Wife. Bring more food." He looked at his wife, but she just stood there expectantly, holding a slight curtsy. "Ah," he said, realizing what she wanted. "Excuse me. My hospitality indeed! If it returns upon my head I will be a poor man. This is my wife Berta. And my daughters Elfhild and Hildegund. Please, accept our welcome. Would you join us in a meal? Elfhild, tell Celestine to bring in more poultry."

Before either monk could say a word, Berta had scurried off to the cooking end of the hall. She returned with two bowls of hot barley soup, and some bread, cheese, and nuts along with a drinking horn of beer for each of them. A short time later, one of the servants came in with some poultry ready for cooking. Willimond and Kristinge then spent the next two hours sitting at the table with Gundomer and Berta, the two of whom proceeded to consume a second dinner at least as large as the monks' first. When all was done, the host insisted first that Willimond and Kristinge share the hospitality of their house rather than the stable, and second that Kristinge sing again that evening. Kristinge readily consented to the first demand and reluctantly to the second. He dredged from his memory a longer story about Merovech's famous defeat of Attila the Hun at the battle of Orleans—a place near Gundomer's home—and the conquering of Francia. He forget several lines, and fumbled somewhat with the harp, but the host did not mind nor even notice; Kristinge's stature as a bard had already been established.

Thus began Kristinge's trifling as a bard. Not by any decision of his own. It was not a path he would have sought. A mere two songs in Gundomer's house had left him drenched in nervous sweat and silently thinking he would never again play the harp no matter how desperately he needed lodging. And yet he couldn't help feeling a little satisfaction at having conquered in such a short time the inhospitable Frankish manor lord. For his songs had possessed a certain power, in which Kristinge himself had been swept up. When a short time later the elder daughter Elfhild came shyly back into the main hall and asked him if he might tell her a story before she went to sleep, he obliged her and her sister with a story about Luxeuil's founder Columbanus, which he half chanted to the plucking of his harp. On a whim of the moment, he even made up a short song and wouldn't let the girls go to sleep until they had learned to sing it with him, which pleased their mother to no end. The rest of the evening the monks spent talking with Gundomer. They said little about the purpose of their own quest other than that their first destination was Paris. Instead they indulged their host's curiosity with several stories about Luxeuil.

The following morning, when the monks came to say farewell, Gundomer scratched his face in a sly way. "I have a wagon of goods to be brought to Auxerre and Paris for trade. My driver might enjoy your company along the road. He likes to talk, and my soldiers are tired of his chatter. If you're willing for your ears to be taxed instead of your legs, the ox-drawn wagon is sure to cut your voyage short a few days." He paused and his eyes narrowed. "Of course the wagon won't be ready to go until tomorrow, but if you'd stay the night with us again I could send you along the road with a good word or two for when you next need lodging. By foot, it will be many nights to Paris."

Lured by the promise of speeding their voyage to Paris as much as by the possibility of lodging on route, Kristinge and Willimond accepted the offer, consenting to spend another day with Gundomer waiting for the wagon-master to have everything ready. Only later did Kristinge discover the manor lord's motivation for keeping them at his estate. During the day, without the knowledge or consent of either monk, he sent messages to several nearby nobleman, landowners, and traders inviting them to hear his new bard. When Kristinge saw the crowd gathered in the hall that evening, and discovered that he was expected to sing before them all, the rich barley and wild nut stew became unappetizing. Whatever Willimond thought of his voice, Kristinge did not have a true bard's repertoire. To survive the previous night, he had already performed the only two songs he could dredge from his memory. What would he sing? Had he been given the day to work at it, he might have come up with something. But Gundomer, assuming Kristinge was a real bard, gave no thought to such matters.

Miraculously, however, the second evening proved as successful as the first. Gundomer, with a house full of guests who had not heard Kristinge's earlier performance, insisted that he sing the same two songs again. It was such a relief to Kristinge that he almost hugged the great bear of a man and he went on to sing with more energy and confidence than he had the night before.

Sitting in the hall of Frotha several weeks later, having just sung the *Lament of Deor* yet again, Kristinge cringed. How many times had he performed that song since the first night at Gundomer's estate? He could not even count. He supposed it was one advantage of being a traveling scop rather than a bard in the permanent service of a chieftain; performing for a different audience every night he could get away with such limited repertoire. The poet Daelga on the other hand would never have prospered under Finn had he sung the same songs evening after evening, month after month, winter after winter. Not that there were no songs worth repeating. There were lays even a true bard like Daelga would come back to time and again—proven poems tried and battle-tested like a good sword, sharpened from time to time or given a new sheath but keeping always the same shape, retaining its original metal. Yet even the greatest of songs grew wearisome if overused, like an arm holding a blade through a long battle.

Fortunately Kristinge's repertoire had expanded a little since his nerve-wracking beginning at Gundomer's small burg. Though he had continued to rely on just a few songs, memories from years past had slowly returned to him. As the leagues had gone by between Luxeuil and Paris, as evening after evening his fingers had stroked his old harp in order to earn his keep, he had recalled more of the old songs from the days when he would sit at the feet of Daelga listening to the old bard sing. He had even composed a few new poems during the long days in the wagon, and from time to time had ventured beyond the safe confines to perform them.

Nonetheless, until he had sung for Aewin in the hall of Frotha, not once had he enjoyed his task. For a *task* it was. Though the previous six years had made his voice and harp-fingers rusty from lack of use, only a few days into the voyage they had become sore from *overuse*. The wagon-master, a short fat talkative fellow named Ulfgar, had kept the young monk busy singing nearly every night. When Kristinge hadn't spent the evening sweating in the walled estate of a rich kin of Gundomer, trying to entertain the household and all its guests, he had spent it singing to a rowdy crowd of merchants and artisans in some little tavern or wayfarers' inn such as could be found in the larger settlements.

Neither setting had pleased the neophyte bard, but if he had felt a preference for the safer manors of the nobleman, the wagon-master had shown a stronger preference for the bawdier inns—places in which he was usually known by name. In fact, Ulfgar's knowledge of the inns had been equal to his knowledge of the roads themselves; he took considerable pride in his assessment of which served the best beer and mead, and which where most likely to have a strumpet, or a maid whose morals were loose enough that she might be bought for the evening. Kristinge was not sure which had horrified him more, Ulfgar's unashamed patronage of such services, or his use of his master's wealth to pay for it. But during the day, the wagon-master was friendly enough to the monks, keeping them well-entertained with his endless stories and his wealth of knowledge about the land through which they traveled. And he had known his business. He had steered the wagons well, protected the merchandise, and proven himself a stingy bargainer. Thus even if Gundomer knew about his servant's occasional pilfering, he was probably happy with him.

And Kristinge also, tiring as the journey was and little though he looked forward to his work each night, had no real cause for complaint. At least not against Gundomer. Though more than once he grumbled against Willimond for having forced him into an unwanted vocation, he had eaten well and slept beneath a roof every night but one after leaving Gundomer's estate. And he had grown in both his skill and confidence as a bard. By the time he reached Friesland and performed for the first time on his home soil in the Frisian mead hall of Frotha— singing for the young Aewin whose sparkling eyes he still remembered from years earlier, though he doubted she remembered him—he had a large enough repertoire to occupy an audience through a least a few mugs of mead. Thus the evening, despite his renewed anxiety, had been a success. Once he had gotten over his initial nervousness, the excitement of being back among his own people and the flutter of seeing Aewin again, he had done well. Even Aewin had been pleased.

The journey had been a blessing in another way also. As Gundomer had promised, it had proven much faster than a journey on foot. And safer also. With Ulfgar's savvy dealing, two wagons nearly full of good quality tanned skins—wolf and sheep acquired from peasants in the mountains and also bear taken in hunt in the woods surrounding Gundomer's estate—had garnered a fair price in Auxerre and at a few estates along the way. While hidden beneath the skins was an even more valuable load: iron weapons fashioned by Gundomer's smith. As the miserly nobleman had not been one to risk a loss of his valuable merchandise to robbers, a small escort of mercenary guards had been sent with Ulfgar and the monks. Two rode on horse and another three drove the second wagon. Altogether there were eight of them. Not a war band by any means, but a larger party than some. And though the monks would have proved useless with a sword had they been called upon, each soldier was a match for three or four poorly armed robbers. As a result, they had been left alone. Had it not been for the anxiety that awaited him every evening, Kristinge would have traveled in relative peace for many days.

But poor Willimond. Along with Ulfgar and the mercenaries, he *had* been forced to listen to the same songs night after night. Kristinge looked across the hall toward the older monk, thinking how tired he must have become of hearing *Deor's Lament* repeated so often. It took a minute to spot Willimond's form, supine on one of the benches. The old monk had already fallen asleep. Kristinge smiled. So *that* was the reason was why his traveling companion hadn't complained. He slept through the songs each night.

Kristinge then turned back toward Frotha. It was now a late hour. The singing was done. The feasting was over. Others around the hall were growing quiet. The traders with whom Kristinge had been traveling since Paris—others who had now heard his songs more than once—had also laid their heads down for the night. The chieftain was talking privately with two of his thanes. For a brief moment, as he looked at Frotha, Kristinge imagined Finn seated in his hall in Hwitstan talking with his thane Ulestan. A sudden twinge of regret came simmering to the surface of the young monk's emotions—a hint of sorrow that he had never know his own father. Or his brother Finnlaf. Only Hildeburh had he known, and she only as one of Willimond's flock, not as his *mother*. He turned away before any tears could well in his eyes.

He looked next for Aewin, still afraid to meet her eyes but unable to resist any longer. To his disappointment, however, she was nowhere to be seen. Some time after the final song, she had slipped from the hall with some of her retinue. Where she had gone to spend the night, Kristinge didn't know, but her absence added to his sense of sadness. He was almost sure now that this was the same young girl he remembered from Hwitstan. Though she had grown in the intervening years, as had he, her eyes had not changed. And no two women could have those same eyes. Did she still remember him? Did she remember those few days she had spent at Finnsburg? Did she still wish she had married Finnlaf?

Suddenly Kristinge's heart was pounding. He knew that Aewin had long since reached the age when she might be given in marriage. Was she now promised to another? Or perhaps already married? It was a question he shouldn't be concerned with. He knew that well enough. He could not allow himself even to imagine. He was not Finnlaf. He was not Finn. He was a monk, not a chieftain. Still, he wondered how she saw him. As a bard? As a stranger? Or perhaps she didn't think of him at all. It was foolish to think she would. It was foolish to wonder if he would see her again.

Foolish. He repeated the word. He should have long since given up trying to foresee where his path would take him. He cleaned off his harp and replaced it in its skin case. Several of the hall's guests had now left for other lodging. Only Frotha's thanes along with a few others such as Willimond and Kristinge remained. There was room on the bench beside the monk-bard. He laid his head down beside him and lifted his feet. It was time to sleep. Earlier the next morning, he would be departing for Danemark. He closed his eyes.

But sleep did not come. His heart was still beating too fast. *Foolish... He should not even imagine...*

He opened his eyes. The red light of a fading fire still flickered on the ceiling. Where indeed would his path take him, and whose paths would his cross? What of the prophecies that had been spoken of him? Was he really destined to lay aside the monk's calling and take up the harp's bard forever? What he had found in Paris had shaken every perception he had of his vocation.

"You wish to go to the monastery?" Ulfgar asked as the wagons rattled through the Marne valley approaching Paris.

"To Jouarre, yes," Willimond answered slowly, as if he had been disturbed out of a trance or waking dream.

"That is too bad. Then you will not see the king."

"The king?" Kristinge asked eagerly.

"I heard rumor in Auxerre," the wagon-master explained, "that Clovis has come from Burgundy to meet with the Austrasian seigniors to discuss the kingship of Austrasia. With him are the queen and palace mayor."

"But I thought Childebert, the son of the mayor, had been named king of Austrasia," Kristinge said, repeating the rumor he had heard at Luxeuil.

The wagon-master looked at him oddly. Then he laughed. "That's true enough. He was *named* king."

Kristinge wanted him to explain, but Willimond was uninterested. "You know where Jouarre is?"

"I do."

"Is it far from Paris?"

Ulfgar shrugged. "A long day's walk. Forty miles. Maybe more."

Kristinge felt a twinge of disappointment at the wagonmaster's words, as he was reminded again that he could spend an extra three days of travel delivering Walbert's message. Yet the journey by wagon all the way to Auxerre and beyond had already saved him several days. And as they learned the next day, Ulfgar had managed to save them another by detouring further north and coming into the city from the other side, closer to the monastery. In the morning when Ulfgar let the monks off he surprised them, "Jouarre is not far from here. With a steady stride, three hours of walking will suffice."

Kristinge breathed a sigh of relief. They thanked the wagonmaster and gave him their blessings, then turned and strode in the direction he had sent them. By early afternoon they were approaching the monastery. As Walbert had told them, Jouarre was a masterpiece of stonework. Its patrons, the aristocracy of Paris and the Marne valley, had desired through this architecture and artwork to establish prestige for the young monastery, and thus fame for themselves as well. Not monks but professional Gallic artisans, likely trained by Greeks, or perhaps by Byzantine and Coptic masters, had carved and dressed the stone. The main walls and door frames were engraved with traditional religious scenes: Christ and the Apostles, the Symbols of the Evangelists, and other depictions of the life of the Lord. While the cornerstones, foundations, and even the crypt walls were decorated with elaborate geometric patterns: squares, diamonds, octagons, and an assortment of intricate shapes. It was an impressive work. The effect was made even more striking by the contrasting pink clay used as cement. Kristinge, who had never been to any monastery other than Luxeuil, stood in awe at the architecture as he waited by the gate. The structures of Luxeuil and Annegray, constructed from timbers and rough-hewn rocks of the surrounding lands by the unskilled hands of monks and local peasants, were crude by contrast.

Yet Jouarre's *order* was similar to that of the monastery Kristinge had just left. Both had adopted the rule of *Benedictus*. And though the implementation of the rule depended as much on the personality of the current abbot or abbess as on any written codification, at present both still had a strong Irish influence. Jouarre's founder, Adon, had been a disciple of Columbanus and a Luxeuil monk. Like Columbanus, he believed his monks should lead a simple life of vigorous work, meager food, as little sleep as possible, and immediate unquestioned obedience to their superiors. The result was that both monasteries were small and austere compared the much older Gallic monasteries under the rule of the Roman bishops. And yet their severity was neither self-centered nor proud, but rather holy and humble. It was, perhaps, this humility that the Franks found so refreshing and which was leading so many to join the Irish monastic ranks while the Gallic monasteries dwindled.

But now Kristinge's thoughts were on something else. Jouarre did differ from Luxeuil in one significant way. It was a double monastery with separate cloisters for women and men. This was a fact that Kristinge found somewhat curious. Columbanus had never despised nor been afraid of women, nor had he preached as some monks did that women were the root of evil; the Irish monk had been a well-educated scholar as well as poet, and was equally comfortable with women as men; even his first patroness had been the Dowager Queen Brunhild with whom he had spent considerable time before the infamous feud between them had erupted. Still there were no women at Luxeuil except for rare occasions when female guests were welcomed. And so Kristinge wondered if the presence of women monks in close proximity to the men made some difference to the nature of life there, despite the fact that there was very little interaction between them. He was staring at a stone on the front gate with a scene of Christ at the Judgment day, and wondering about the nature of the double monastery, when a young monk approached.

Speaking in the Frankish tongue used for visitors, he asked them who they were seeking.

"We are looking for the Abbot," Willimond answered him in Latin.

Kristinge wrestled his eyes back down from the beautiful art work. The young Jouarre monk was now looking them over carefully, taking note of their monastic robes. His eyes stopped when he saw Willimond's unusual tonsure. "Brother Agilbert is at prayer," he replied in Latin. "He may be gone for several hours."

"Willimond," Kristinge whispered. "Jouarre is ruled by an abbess. Her name is Telchild. Walbert's message is to be delivered to *her*."

Willimond corrected himself. "Pardon me, brother," he said to the monk at the gate. "We seek the abbess. We have a message from Abbot Walbert of Luxeuil."

At the mention of Luxeuil and Walbert, the monk grew more attentive. He looked at Kristinge and then back at Willimond. "I will inform brother Agilbert of your presence. The abbess is his sister, and he may wish to meet you or to hear your message." Before Kristinge or Willimond could stop him, he turned and disappeared. He did not reutrn for several minutes. While he was gone, Kristinge apologized to Willimond for not having told him earlier who the message was for, but Willimond only shrugged. Then they both fell quiet, inspired perhaps by the architecture or the spirit of the place to return to their monastic practice of silence. Eventually the young monk returned. He appeared embarrassed. "Brother Agilbert is busy with other duties and cannot be disturbed, but he has asked me to lead you to the Abbess Telchild." He paused, then bowed in greeting. "I am sorry. Forgive my lack of hospitality. I am brother Wilfrid." He led the two visitors through the outer gate, past a small cluster of buildings toward another large chapel surrounded by a low wall with a gate. Within was the cloister of the women's monastery. He rang a bell at the gate, and then waited. "We will meet outside," he said. "Men do not enter here."

A few minutes later a young woman appeared dressed in a simple hooded robe similar to that of Wilfrid. She bowed in greeting to the three men, then turned toward Wilfrid. They exchanged a few words, and then she turned and left. A minute later she returned with another woman whom Kristinge had no difficulty guessing was the abbess. She was tall and stately, forty years old or older, and wore her hood down revealing long auburn hair streaked with gray and bound in the back with a single strand of wool the same color as her robe. In her face was a look that Kristinge found at first hard to identify, but later came to name as *holiness*. She greeted Wilfrid with a kiss on each cheek, and then turned to the guests.

"Abbess Telchild, these are Brother Willimond and Brother Kristinge, guests from Luxeuil," Wilfrid explained. "They bring you a message from Abbot Walbert."

"Greetings in the name of Christ," Telchild said, in a rich voice that sounded more feminine than Kristinge expected.

"Greetings," Willimond and Kristinge answered simultaneously. Hands folded at the waist, they bowed. Kristinge noticed then that Willimond had put his hood back up, and he did the same.

Wilfrid, having done his task, turned to leave. "You will stay with us this evening," he said. "I will see that guest rooms are prepared." He departed before they had a chance to accept or decline.

"Come then," Telchild said. "Let us walk. We will talk in the garden." She turned to the young female monk beside her. "Dear Begga, please bring us a loaf of bread. And some wine."

"Yes, Mother," the younger woman replied.

Kristinge was surprised by the abbess's offer of hospitality. He had expected simply to deliver the message, and then to depart—though he wasn't sure why he had that expectation since Walbert and Petrica had also always greeted visitors at Luxeuil hospitably. But Telchild did not yet take any interest in Kristinge's message. Instead, as they walked around the perimeter of the monastery wall, she spoke casually to Willimond. "You are from Britain?"

"I am from Iona, and then Lindisfarne in Northumbria."

Telchild looked him over carefully. "*Lindisfarena*? I know that name well enough. I should have known from your tonsure. Were you there during the rule of Aidan?"

Willimond smiled in appreciation to hear the abbess refer to his old monastery using its Saxon name rather than the Latin version. "For a time I dwelt there," he said. "Too short a time. Aidan was like a father to me. I was a young child when he took me into Iona, and I went with him to Lindisfarena at the call of the English king Oswald. But I spent only one year there before I was sent to Friesland. I did not even see it finished. That was so many years ago."

"To the Frisii?" Telchild said. Now she looked even more surprised. "Time passes quickly, does it not? Friesland. I did not know there was a mission there. Put your hoods down, my brothers," she said. Whether it was command from a ruling abbess or a gesture of friendship and equality, Kristinge did not know. But she was studying Willimond through deep green eyes that Kristinge only now noticed. As he and Willimond rolled back their hoods, she continued. "My brother Agilbert has been to Lindisfarne. He may be able to tell you something about it since you left. He will be returning to Britain soon. He has been called there by the *Roman* church, though I confess he has a difficult time with the Anglo-Saxon tongue. I, too, once met Aidan before his death. He was a holy man—fierce in his love of peace, and fiercer still in his zeal for the Gospel."

"He was a father to me," Willimond repeated.

Telchild nodded. There was both knowledge and understanding hidden behind her sea-green eyes; both gentleness and authority in her manner. Though she was twice Kristinge's age, he was surprised to find himself suddenly attracted to this abbess. He flushed with a mixture of guilt and embarrassment at feelings that were foreign.

"And you, brother Kristinge," she said, turning her eyes on the younger monk, making his flush deepen. "Not Irish, nor a Celt, I should think. There is something Norse in your blood. Swedish, perhaps? Or a Dane?"

At that moment, they found themselves at the edge of a small garden where the monks were experimenting with a cultivated variety of pea. Most of the plants had been harvested, but some pods remained on the vines to dry and seed for the next year's crop. "Frisian, mother Telchild," Kristinge answered.

"Another from the Frisii? Yet I am not wholly wrong that you have more Northern blood."

"My mother was a Dane," Kristinge replied. Her questions had caught him off guard. They were at once both casual and probing, comforting and intimidating. He kept his answers brief.

"A strange marriage even in this day," Telchild said. Again her gentle manner and soft voice belied the shrewdness of her guesses.

"You must, then, be of the blood of a clan-chief?"

"My father was King Finn," Kristinge answered. "And my mother the queen Hildeburh, a Danish princess." Again he found himself blushing. He had already revealed far more than he had intended. Not only Willimond but Walbert himself had warned him against making his heritage widely known. Yet something about this abbess disarmed him. Did he have to fear her? Even if he did, he could not imagine telling her anything less than she asked. He ignored Willimond's warning glances and went on. "My brother was Finnlaf, who was killed in battle with the Danes." How odd those words sounded on his tongue. *My father... my mother... my brother...* He wondered as he spoke how much Telchild knew of them.

"A tragic tale," the abbess said, answering his unspoken question. Their eyes met and she guessed his thoughts. "Yes. It is a tale that is known among us. A wandering poet came to Paris not long after the fall of Finnsburg and told us a long lay of the death of Finn and Finnlaf. Daelga was his name."

Kristinge took a sharp breath and found his heart racing at the mention of the old bard. Beside him, Willimond was also listening intently.

"He told the tale only once," Telchild went on, "as though he needed to tell it more than we needed to hear it. And then he entered the monastery and gave up the life of a bard. He died a monk just a few months later."

There was a long, somber silence. "Is his grave nearby?" Willimond finally asked. Kristinge noticed tears in the older monk's eyes, and then realized that he himself was crying.

"Yes," Telchild answered. "You knew him then? I will see that you are taken to the grave later."

"Thank you," Willimond said. Then they fell silent. A short time later, Begga returned with a hot loaf of bread and a flask of wine.

"We will break bread together," Telchild said. She administered the sacred elements of communion in silence, and the three of them together entered into the Mystery. Only after the sacrament was over did they continue the conversation.

"You have a message for me from Walbert?" the abbess finally asked.

Kristinge had already forgotten about the messages he carried, but he nodded in response to her questions. He removed from his pack a small scroll and handed it to Telchild. She unrolled it and read it through silently. Kristinge avoided the temptation of trying to lean over and read it. He was glad when Telchild explained. "A great surprise."

"What is it?" Kristinge asked.

"Walbert asks if we might send some sisters to Luxeuil to found a monastery for women." The contents of the message left Kristinge somewhat disappointed. After the recent death of Sigibert III, and all of his own questions about his heritage as the son of Finn, he expected the letter to have political implications. Still, he listened as Telchild went on. The letter was obviously interesting to her. "He says the need there is great among the mountain peasants as well as the nearby aristocracy." Her eyes glanced heavenward as she pondered the situation. "I shall have to pray about this. There are some sisters here who are capable of the task. And yet..." she paused. "Well there are some wealthy patrons who would like abbeys in other regions. Queen Balthild herself would have us found a monastery at Chelles. I wonder if we would find the necessary patronage in a place so removed as Luxeuil. So far from anything." Then she shook her head and shrugged, causing a light rippling of her long hair. In the bright afternoon sun, Kristinge could now see the remnants of Irish red in her tresses. "But come. This is not a concern of yours. And it is time we returned." She rose, and Kristinge and Willimond stood with her.

"Unless I have forgotten," she said as they walked, "the poet Daelga said nothing about Finn having a second son." She didn't wait for a response. "Friesland is a small kingdom. It is too small for two kings. I wonder if even Francia might be better off had Clovis not divided the kingdom among so many sons. So your story comes as no wonder. Perhaps Daelga himself did not even know of you. I should think it wise, then," she said, turning now directly toward Kristinge, "if you take care to keep the same secret. At least until you know more where you stand in that realm. I understand you are going there now; that you will not be returning to Luxeuil."

"You are very astute," Willimond said, answering for Kristinge.

"Ah," she laughed. "Not so. Walbert mentioned in his letter what your destination was, and asked if you might be housed here and given some provision for your journey. Two requests I would hope Brother Agilbert will already have seen to without any request from Walbert. Though with Agilbert, one cannot always be sure."

They were nearly around the wall now, and as they approached the front entrance Kristinge saw a young woman sitting on the hard ground beside the gate. She was dressed in a tattered and filthy robe, and her wild bright red hair hung limply all around, half covering her face. Her forehead and hands were smudged in dirt, and her arms were wrapped tightly around her breasts as she rocked from side to side. It was an odd scene at a monastery, and Kristinge found himself staring at her, unable to take his eyes off. *A local peasant looking for charity?* he wondered.

"Sister Osanne," Telchild explained in a low voice.

"Sister?" Kristinge mumbled in surprise. *A monk?*

"Yes," Telchild affirmed. In a soft whisper, she explained Osanne's story as they approached. "She was an Irish princess, the youngest of three. When she decided to dedicate herself to the Lord at an early age, her pagan parents were greatly angered. They refused. Against her objections, they betrothed her to a wicked Frankish prince named Ebroin—a scoundrel in the service of King Clovis. Osanne had no choice. But when he violated her weeks before their wedding, she escaped from him and fled here."

"Is she—?" Kristinge paused, unsure how to ask.

"Ill of mind? Is that the phrase you seek?" Telchild responded. "Yes. She has not yet recovered from what she was put through. At times she is very lucid, though still somber. At other times, she gets like this. All we can do is love her and be patient. I believe, though, that God will one day heal her mind and she will be a great saint. Certainly she will know compassion."

As they approached the gate, Kristinge watched Osanne closely, though he tried hard not to stare. He heard her mumbling to herself.

"And Kristinge," Telchild added, stopping him with a touch on his shoulder. She looked directly into his eyes now. "We believe that she is also a prophetess."

As if on cue, Osanne lifted her head. Her candle eyes flickered at the sight of the approaching group, then turned to Kristinge and grew brighter. He returned her look, mesmerized now by the mystery that surrounded her. Her hair, matted as it was and filled with leaves, still looked soft. For the first time, he realized how young she was. Despite her haunted expression, she couldn't have been older than he was. From her eyes, he guessed she was even younger, only sixteen. He remembered his own mother, and the young children of Lopystre whom he had grown up playing with—the girl Blostma who had told him bedtime stories as a child. He remembered the young chieftain's daughter to whom he had innocently sung many years ago. Kristinge had a sudden longing to lift Osanne in his arms. When she called him, he obeyed.

"You," she said, her eyes glittering at Kristinge as her right hand flashed out in a pointing gesture that was slightly off target. "Sit." Kristinge looked over at the abbess for council. Her nod told him to obey. He turned back to the former princess. "Sit," she said again. He dropped hesitantly to his knees. What was he to think of this? *A prophetess?* Yet he consented. Osanne was looking in his eyes now, her orbs flashing with some hidden gift. "Closer," she whispered. He inched forward on his knees. His muscles tensed as she put her hands on his forehead, but he did not pull away. She held him for a moment, then stroked his eyes shut with her fingers. He began to relax in her touch, but almost at once she cried out in pain. Kristinge winced and tried to pull away, but her grip on his face was firm. For a brief second, he was afraid she was going to poke out his eyes. "The pain. The pain," she moaned. "Fire everywhere. Flames and destruction. Oh the women. And the church. The church, too, is in flames."

Kristinge recoiled, but she did not let go. "It is passed. Ashes, now. All ashes. The village lies in ruins. Black. Nothing remains. The angel has departed," she shuttered, then sighed as if in great anguish of sorrow. An instant later, however, she began again. "But no. I see another has returned. A bright beacon in the darkness. Kings and princes. A wound ring of shining gold. A new church. It rises from the ashes. It grows and grows. Oh the light! It shines before kings. Throughout the nation." She sighed again. "Ah. But it is not you. A new church. But no. Not you. You will build no church. One who comes after you will build it. You will build no church. No church. You are just a voice crying in the wilderness. 'Prepare the way.' Yes. You are the one who will go ahead. You will prepare the way for ones who come after you. I see you laying the stones around the Cornerstone. Setting the foundation. But the one who comes after will build. He will build. And you... you..." she shivered and fell silent, rocking back and forth. As quickly as she had called him, she removed her hands from Kristinge's head and wrapped her arms once more about her body. Her eyes were closed.

Wait, Kristinge wanted to shout. She had touched a nerve. *What do you mean?* How *was* he returning to Friesland? As a monk or king? What did she mean he was not the one who would build a church? Was he to wear the torc instead? Was that the shining gold? *You can't do this*, he protested. He looked to Telchild for help, but she offered none. A new question arose in his mind now. Was this really a prophecy? Or just the ravings of an unwell mind? Kristinge already had too many questions to wrestle with, without more being piled on. He turned to Willimond, but his old mentor had nothing to offer either. He looked back at Osanne. She was rocking back and forth, staring ahead, eyes on some unknown distance, leaving Kristinge to wonder. Not for the last time, he began to envy the simplicity to be found in weeding a garden.

CHAPTER 5:
THE LONG-HAIRED KING

Several days later many hundreds of leagues away, as Kristinge lay on the mead bench of Frotha's hall trying unsuccessfully to sleep, the memory of that incident still brought unease. He could not ignore it. The encounter with the princess-turned-prophetess Osanne had shaken him more than anything that had happened since his departure from Luxeuil. It terrified him. Fire and ashes? Was that what she had seen? What had it meant? Had she been looking into Kristinge's *past*? Or into his *future*? And what had she seen at the end that had so frightened her? Why did he feel the same fear? He had tried to forget what she said, to convince himself that there was no truth to her vision. After all, not even the abbess had known the meaning of what Osanne foresaw. But still the memory of her touch on his face was painful.

Nor had the unexpected meeting with Osanne been his only encounter near Paris. It was the first of many. After so many years cloistered at Luxeuil, the world had suddenly come crashing in on him. Not that Luxeuil had made any attempt at complete seclusion. It was not a hermitage, nor a monastery like those of the ancients where one might go thirty years without seeing any face save those of his fellow monks. Columbanus had not been one to flee the world. He had chosen the site of Annegray in the Vosges mountains *because* of the inhabitants there, not to escape them. When he and his fellow Irish monks had met robbers coming to steal their last bite of food, they had greeted them with echoes of the same charity that Christ had shown on the cross.

Kristinge, however, had experienced little of that turmoil himself. His time at Luxeuil had been one of work and study. Raids had become infrequent, and with the departure of its founder the kings of Francia had ceased to care about the dealings of that such a small monastery. If even half the tales of Columbanus were true then life at Luxeuil had grown considerably calmer during Walbert's tenure. Thus Kristinge been ill prepared for his own encounter with the new

Frankish king—an encounter only too similar to those that had filled the life of Columbanus. Nor had he expected that Frankish city to be the first place he would see a face he knew, one of the few people from his Frisian past he still remembered.

After his meeting with Osanne, the young monk had retained enough of his wits to deliver to Telchild Walbert's messages for the other monasteries near Paris. The abbess had promised to see to their delivery, then had given Kristinge and Willimond to the keeping of Brother Agilbert who let them spend a few moments at Daelga's grave before leading them to the men's cloister. There, because of their robes, the guests had been treated as brothers of Jouarre and put to work. Kristinge had earned his meal not by singing but by laboring with the other monks. Yet it was work for which he had been glad, and he had fallen easily into its routine. He had almost forgotten the cathartic effect that labor had on the soul.

Only at the end of the day did Jouarre present Kristinge with something unfamiliar. As a younger monastery, it had been founded with the Benedictine rule in mind. Monks were housed in large dormitories rather than small private cells such as those at Annegray. Between the unfamiliar environment of crowded bodies, the loud breathing, and the echoes in his ears of the strange prophetesses pronouncing his fate, Kristinge slept poorly. Had he not been once more within monastic walls, he might have risen much later. Alas, he was awaked well before dawn and by the time the sun was near to rising he had already joined Jouarre in Matins, and was ready to depart. After prayer, Agilbert led them to the gate where he provided them with a small satchel of light fare to keep them from starving over the next few days as they sought passage from Paris to Danemark. There they had found waiting for them the Abbess Telchild. Accompanying the abbess was another female monk named Beatrice. Older than Telchild by several years, she had gray wispy hair and a wrinkled face to match the wide, leathery hands that gripped several scrolls and a large satchel of goods.

"We will walk with you," Telchild explained. "I must speak with Queen Balthild while she is in Paris. I had hoped to start on the journey tomorrow, but we will take your presence here as God's provision and begin the journey today instead. That is, if you will consent to allowing us to accompany you. I can give you no command."

"Command or no, you are more than welcome," Willimond replied.

Kristinge, however, had caught something else in Telchild's comment. "The queen?"

Now Telchild turned her smile upon Kristinge. "You are surprised?"

"No," Kristinge lied, not wanted to offend the abbess with any unintended insinuations. An instant later, with a blush of guilt and embarrassment, he confessed, "Yes. A little."

"Surprised that an abbess would be *interested* in speaking with the queen, or that she would be *allowed* to speak with the queen?"

Both, Kristinge thought, but he did not voice his opinion aloud.

"Balthild is a holy woman," Telchild explained. "Come with me in Paris and you will meet her."

Before Kristinge could answer, Telchild had begun to walk. It could be nearly a two-day journey by foot to Paris, yet here was the abbess setting out as though for a morning stroll. The others took a few quick steps and joined her. When they had set a good pace, the abbess began to tell them more. "The queen was slave girl. A Saxon. Whether taken in a raid or sold by her parents, she has never told me and I do not ask. I know only that Clovis bought her for his own pleasures, and by the time he had tired of her he found that she was too wise to be easily gotten rid of. So he took her as a wife and made her his queen. Now he gets his pleasure elsewhere."

Kristinge looked at Telchild in surprise as she spoke. The abbess's voice was as close to contempt as Kristinge could imagine from one so gentle and holy. Here was an unabashedly critical appraisal of a powerful king: a king who wielded enough might and influence that if he ordered the destruction of Jouarre there were none who could stand in his way. And yet Kristinge's impression was that Telchild would have said the same thing even were Clovis present with them. Here was picture of what Columbanus must have been like—and perhaps an explanation of why the old Irish Abbot had also eventually lost the sympathies of the ruling powers of Francia.

"Her generosity is great," Telchild went on, oblivious of Kristinge's thoughts. "She has used her authority and wealth to purchase the freedom of many of her fellow slaves, and she is one of Jouarre's greatest benefactors. She has even spoken of starting a new monastery at Chelles, and I believe she will succeed, though she will get no help from the king." Again the abbess shook her head. "Clovis thinks nothing of our work. There have been Frankish kings in the past who aided the monasteries, though most have given in the names of their queens. Even Childebert aided Columbanus for many years. But not Clovis. He would just as soon tear Jouarre down as give us a single coin. I fear little stands in his way except God himself—and Queen Balthild. I would warn you about Clovis. What they say is true; he is insane."

At this, Kristinge couldn't help but think about Osanne sitting by the gate of Jouarre, but Telchild guessed his thoughts. "Not like Osanne. She is a holy woman. Her insanity was brought on by harm done *to* her, not *by* her. The insanity of Clovis is of an altogether different sort. He has done evil that it is best not even to mention. Why God permits him to live, I do not know. Perhaps he has been spared for the sake of his holy wife. Beware of Clovis. His ways have an ungodly appeal for some. He is a man of many lusts, and he has a way of getting them satisfied. But do not fall for the seduction of that life."

Kristinge nodded. Another warning to heed. He wondered if he would remember them all. As they walked down out of the village and onto the main highway, Telchild told them more about Clovis and Balthild, and about recent events in Paris and in the various remaining Merovingian courts. She was at once knowledgeable of the events of the world around her and distant from them, as if the governing of nations was not the *real* stuff of life. Kristinge, mesmerized by her voice and manner, was content to listen.

They walked until after dusk the first day of the journey, spent the night in the trees near the road, and rose before dawn the next morning. But the time went by quickly. Kristinge learned much from Telchild and also from Beatrice as they walked. Through the abbess's subtle questions, she also learned much from him, some of which

Kristinge hadn't been aware he even knew until he had had to answer her questions.

On their second morning Balthild began to prepare Kristinge for the city itself. "Paris is an old city," she explained. "Older than the Romans. Long ago it was the home of the *Parisii*, a Celtic tribe, ancestors of the Gauls. They were a strong people then, ruling most of what is now Francia. Lutetia, the little island settlement, was their seat of power. Some traces of them remain, though most have vanished." There was a sad look upon Telchild's face now, as if something beautiful had been lost in the Roman conquest. She was Irish after all, Kristinge thought, closer in kinship to the Celts than the Romans. Her sympathies were clear. "It was the Romans who renamed the city Paris after the tribe they had conquered. In the earlier days of the Roman empire, Julian ruled all of Gaul from there. That was when it became a great trade city. It is told that Attila almost captured Paris when he invaded nearly a century after Julian. The city was saved only through the prayers of Saint Geneviéve." She shook her head. "Would that Geneviéve were here today, for the city is again in need of prayer."

Telchild paused again, but she continued a moment later. "Another century passed after Attila. Rome fell, and the Franks came. Paris remained, though more of her splendor was lost. After the death of Clovis the Conqueror, the first of the Merovingian kings, Francia was divided among Clovis's four sons. Ruthless tyrants they were, inheriting all of their father's cruel determination and none of his savvy. Officially Paris was given to Childebert as part of his realm, but it became a meeting ground—a neutral city where the four oft-warring siblings would meet to settle matters. Or at least *attempt* to settle them. If but a fifth of the stories about the sons of Clovis are true, they rarely settled *anything* with words. But that is the way of the Merovingians. I do not doubt it was that spirit that had made the kingdom of Francia possible. I know as well that it is now ripping it apart."

At that she fell silent. Kristinge sensed a finality to what she had said. She would speak no more on the subject. Listening to Telchild, he had barely noticed the slow brightening of the sky from black to gray to blue. The sun was well above the horizon now, and it was not long before they began to encounter other travelers along the road. Several wagons passed them, most moving toward Paris.

"So you will return to Friesland now?" Telchild asked, some time later.

"That is my hope," Kristinge replied. He told her a little of his departure from Hwitstan six years earlier, and of what he had learned at Ulestan's death. "I feel drawn back to Friesland now, as if there is some work for me to finish—something left undone by my family. That is why I left Luxeuil. But at the same time I fear returning." It was the first time he had admitted this even to himself. He paused a moment to reflect on his own words before continuing. "There is so much I do not know or understand. I will not return to Friesland yet, except in passing. First I must travel to Danemark, this winter if I can. I must at least seek my mother. I know that both Finn and Finnlaf are dead, but I know not if she still lives—or whether she even survived the battle. No word ever came to Luxeuil, save that Finn had been killed and Finnsburg burned and all of Hwitstan with it. In my heart, I think Hildeburh must be alive—that the Danes would not have killed one of their own, but would have brought her back to Danemark. Yet I do not know."

Telchild appeared surprised at Kristinge's last comment. "You have not heard? Then perhaps I do know more than you. Whether your mother is alive today I cannot say, but I know for sure that she survived the battle. It was she who pleaded for Daelga's life after the battle was over. The two of them stood on the tower and watched the battle together, for he was unwilling to forsake her. By the time it was over, it was too late for the poet to escape. This, Daelga himself told me. The Danes spared his life at Hildeburh's request, but her they took back with them. Thus your heart has spoken the truth."

Though Kristinge's spirit had told him this all along, there was nonetheless a sudden upwelling of relief. Despite the years that had passed, he now was more hopeful than ever that his mother still lived. There was silence for a time as tears rolled from his eyes.

"I will not ask how you will return to Friesland," Telchild eventually said. "Whether you go as a monk from Luxeuil or as the son of Finn is for you to decide. I sense you do not know yourself.

But I will ask in what cloak you will travel to Danemark. Do you go as Hildeburh's son? Or do you go as a Christian monk? There will be danger on either path. With either identity you choose, you will not lack enemies in Danemark."

Kristinge thought for a time. This was another question he had not yet pondered, but he knew that Telchild spoke truth about the danger. "I go to seek my mother," he finally answered.

On they walked as the sun crept into the sky. About the second hour of daylight, many miles away from Jouarre, an ox-drawn cart stopped beside them. The driver, a burly gray-haired man with a long scar on his left arm, had noticed the monastic robes and offered them a ride in exchange for a blessing. Fortunately his wagon was nearly empty. It was too late in the season to be selling produce. More likely he was a wagon-driver going to Paris to purchase goods for his lord. Whatever the case, he was acquainted with the abbess and had a high view of her blessings, though from what little he said it appeared he thought of them more as powerful magic than the work of God. Still, he offered the ride and Telchild accepted on behalf of the four monks. For the rest of the journey, Telchild spoke mostly with Beatrice while Willimond sat in his own thoughts and Kristinge reflected on the news that his mother's life had been spared. It was still before the noon hour when they approached the outskirts of the town. Before long, they were making their way down the dusty dirt streets toward the bridges across the Seine river.

From what Kristinge had heard along the route and learned from Telchild, Paris had less political importance than it had once had in the days of Julian or even Childebert. Still, the city had continued to grow and had long since expanded beyond the confines of the little island. Like Auxerre, it was dirty, busy, and full of markets. Only it was bigger than Auxerre, and more permanent. Here and there were signs of wealth and power: palaces, large estates, Roman monasteries, numerous stone buildings. It was larger than any settlement Kristinge had ever been in.

So mesmerized was he by the city—stunned as much by its size and wealth as by the dirt, noise, and crowds—that when the wagon came to a stop near Clovis' palace, Willimond had to nudge him. Kristinge blinked and turned his head. The abbess was rewarding the wagon-driver with her blessing, and had already been recognized by the palace guards. Before Kristinge could take in the exterior of the impressive stone architecture, he was being ushered into the place through the thick wooden doors. Only then, when he stood within the high, stone, torch-lit corridor, did it dawn on him what was happening. And all the stories of Columbanus's tumultuous relationships with the Frankish rules flashed in an instant across his mind. Yet before the tales had time to terrify him, he was overwhelmed by the palace itself. He had not imagined anything so big. Any one of a dozen rooms he passed were large enough to engulf half of Luxeuil. Even the hallways were grand. The walls were lined with colored mosaics and woolen tapestries of exceptional workmanship and value. Where the stonework was visible, it was masterful—even more ornate than that of Jouarre. To one who had never traveled south to see the great architecture of Rome or east to the famed palaces of Byzantium, the proportions and grandeur of the Frankish palace were breathtaking. Kristinge could only gape in awe as they walked from one hall to the next. Nothing he had seen—not Luxeuil, nor the estates of Benetus or Gundomer, nor the mead hall of Finnsburg—could equal Clovis' palace. Finn's mead-hall was petty and barbaric compared with this. The wealth of Gundomer was not even a grain of sand.

As Kristinge gazed about, they were led down a palace hallway that would have stretched end-to-end across the main cloister at Luxeuil, and into a large throne room. There a group of richly dressed noblemen were seated around a table in front of an empty throne. Their boisterous conversation came to an abrupt end at the sight of monastic robes.

"Be seated," the courtier instructed Telchild. "The king will return momentarily."

"I have no wish to see the king," Telchild objected quickly. "I desire an audience with Queen Balthild." But the courtier, either not hearing her or choosing to ignore her, had disappeared before she was done. An instant later, the huge doors of the throne room were swung shut, and the four monks found themselves standing in Clovis' council hall. Kristinge turned toward the abbess wondering what she would do. From all he had heard of the king, he had no desire to meet him. Telchild, however, was unperturbed by the turn of events. "God's plans were different from mine," she said in a quiet voice and with a slight smile at Kristinge. "And if God's plan is that I speak to the king, we will stay and find out why." Without another word, she and Beatrice sat themselves in two chairs on the opposite side of the door.

Kristinge stood where he was for a moment longer. He was feeling considerably less confident than the abbess. Only when he realized that his legs were shaking did he follow the abbess's example and take a seat. His eyes darted around the room, and what he saw did nothing did ease his anxiety. His glance fell first on the pagan statues and idols that adorned the tables and walls alongside the occasional Christian symbols remaining from previous kings. Then he looked to the throne itself, adorned with jewels and surrounded on the four corners by the weapons of the king. A double-edged broad sword leaned against one corner of the throne in an enameled ornamented sheath. A Roman short saber, or *scramasax* leaned against another. A long spear stood against the third, and a shorter Frankish lance against the forth. And sitting on the right arm of the throne was a *francisc*—a heavy one-piece Frankish throwing ax. The sight of these weapons along with the pagan statues and wooden idols of Frankish fertility gods made Kristinge even more anxious. He glanced at the table in front of the throne. The group of nobleman had resumed their conversation in lower tones.

"Have I told you of my first meeting with Finn?" Willimond asked in whisper. "I was a young monk, with little experience outside monastic walls, coming before a great warrior-king whose sword I was barely even strong enough to lift. And the first thing I did was to trip and fall face first in the mud right in the center of the village—"

His story was interrupted by the sound of loud voices mingled with uneven footsteps and laughter. Immediately the nobles sitting by the throne fell silent and looked around expectantly. Then a door in the far corner of the hall swung open and slammed against the back wall. What Kristinge saw next was an image he never forgot. Into the throne room stumbled a young man with long locks of golden hair reaching down to his waist, and a youthful smooth face that was at once both beautiful and wild. Along with tight-fitting red trousers and high soft leather boots, he wore a woven purple tunic left unfastened and open down to his belly. He was bedecked in silver and gold jewelry from his neck to his wrists, and in his right hand he carried, almost casually, a beautiful gold cloisonné necklace. This, as Kristinge guessed from Telchild's description, was Clovis the king, descendant of the more famous conqueror of the same name. He was surprised at how young the king looked. And how wild. But what he saw next almost made him fall off his seat. Hanging on to Clovis' back like a white leech was a young girl of fifteen or sixteen winters, dressed only in linen underwear that reached to her knees, and a flimsy neck scarf that didn't even cover her breasts. Before Clovis could escape her, she reached a hand into his tunic, and though he was twice her weight she pulled him back toward her and gave him a long sensuous kiss while her hands moved up and down his back and thighs. *Was this the holy queen Balthild of whom the abbess had spoken?*

Kristinge stared for just a moment before turning away, embarrassed by the display. When he looked back up, the woman was slipping out the door wearing the cloisonné necklace, but the king was still holding her scarf. With a lewd grin on his face, he walked over to the throne and sat down. The noblemen all rose and gave half-hearted bows before returning to their seats. Only then, when Telchild loudly cleared her throat, did Clovis turn toward the door and notice the four robed monks seated there. Fumbling clumsily, he fastened his shirt at the neck with a gold brooch, and then rudely called the guests forward.

"What in the name of Woden do you want here?" he asked of the abbess. It was obvious that he had made her acquaintance in the past. "I hope you haven't come to tell me how wicked I am. I've got plenty of my own bishops and monks to tell me that." Then, for no reason, he burst into a strange fit of laughter. He jumped onto his throne and started dancing around, until one of the nobleman rose and helped him back to his seat. Kristinge just stood there, watching the scene half in horror and half in fascination.

"The sensible Ebroin," Clovis said. "Always spoiling my fun."

Ebroin? Kristinge wondered. Where had he heard that name before?

"And speaking of spoiling fun," the king went on, "back to you." He released one more squeal of high-pitched laughter then turned his eyes on the abbess. "What do you want from me?"

"Nothing," Telchild said coldly.

"Then what do you have to give me?" he asked.

"Everything," Telchild answered. "But nothing that you would accept."

"Nothing to give and nothing to take? Then why are you here?" Only now did Kristinge notice that Clovis was flinching away from the abbess, as if he was afraid of her, or as if her presence made him feel guilty.

"I wish to speak with Queen Balthild," the abbess replied.

"Sapping more money from our treasury?" Ebroin asked.

Telchild refused even to look at Ebroin, and Kristinge remembered where he had heard the name before. *Osanne! Ebroin was the one who had raped her.*

"Some day you may find a palace mayor who is not so pliable," Ebroin said. "I suggest that you return to me soon what you have unrightfully taken."

Still Telchild refused to look at Ebroin, but Kristinge could see her face growing red with anger. He wondered if she had the same Irish temper as Columbanus. "I wish to speak with Queen Balthild," she repeated.

"Send her away," Ebroin said.

"What?" Clovis replied angrily, suddenly turning on his servant Ebroin. "Are *you* giving me orders now? Would you have her pestering *me* instead of Balthild? Give her what she wants and let her go."

Turning from Ebroin, the king gave orders for one of his servants to fetch the queen. After a few long minutes of waiting, filled with icy stares and unspoken accusations, another woman entered the hall through the main doors. She wore long, heavy, loose-fitting trousers which, unlike the king's, had been made more for rugged wear than for luxury. Above the trousers she wore a tunic and cape which in color and fabric were not unlike the robes of the women monks. Upon seeing the abbess, she broke into a warm smile and ran over at once to welcome her with an embrace. This, then, and not the other woman, was Queen Balthild.

"Why did you not tell me you were here?" she asked. Before

Telchild could reply, the queen was ushering her and Beatrice out of the room. And all of a sudden, Kristinge and Willimond found themselves alone with the king and his court.

"And you," Clovis said, turning his eyes upon the monks. "Your requests can wait. Be seated."

Kristinge, who had been foundering at a loss for something to say, breathed a sigh of relief and followed Willimond back to the door. "What are we going to say?" he whispered after they once again took their seats.

"I do not know," Willimond answered. "But it appears that God brought us here, so I trust He will give us the words when it is time."

At the present moment, that did not come as a great comfort to Kristinge, but he held his tongue and waited. As nervous as he was, something about the scene intrigued him. He listened to the conversation with fascination, hoping to glean as much as possible from what he heard. With the exception of Ebroin, it turned out that the noblemen in the room were not from the Neustrian court of Clovis, but were Austrasian seigniors and aristocrats come to discuss the future state of their realm. The conversation centered on who would run the realm after the recent deaths of King Sigibert and his son Dagobert.

"You have taken care of Grimoald," they queried. "And his son Childebert?"

"Of course," Clovis answered, grinning with evil delight.

"How?" they pressed.

"The way one ought to deal with usurpers and pretenders to the throne," Clovis said. He lifted a sword from beside his throne and made a slitting motion along his neck.

"So the reign of Childebert was short-lived, eh?" one of them joked.

"I'll bet old Grimoald would have been satisfied to keep the position of Mayor had he known what would happen when he named his own son king," another said.

The conversation continued, centering on the remaining heirs of the Merovingian dynasty. Clovis continued to put forth his own oldest son, Chlotar, as the only rightful heir of the entire Frankish kingdom. Though none gainsaid him, they kept asking who would rule in *practice*. But the king was oblivious to the implication that anybody but the rightful Merovingian king himself would have authority. As the conversation progressed, it became clear that Ebroin was the real spokesperson for the throne. Eventually, the Austrasian nobles ceased even to address Clovis.

In the end, Clovis' young son Chlotar was named as the King of all Francia, much to the glee of Clovis. Kristinge could hardly believe he had just witnessed the naming of a king. He wasn't sure whether to be thrilled or appalled. When the deed was done, Clovis announced that it was time for a celebration. He started to jump on his chair when he noticed that the monks were still waiting by the door. "Hasn't anybody taken care of them yet?" he asked. The nobles appeared surprised to see the monks still there. They shook their heads. "Well, bring them over here. I feel like granting a boon to celebrate the crowning of my son. Where is my son? We must crown him this very day." He began to look around the room as if Chlotar might be hiding under his throne. Ebroin tried to get his attention again.

"Yes. I was saying. Come forward."

Willimond and Kristinge looked nervously at each other, then approached the throne. "Ask of me anything," Clovis said. At that, Ebroin looked very nervous.

"We seek only passage to Danemark," Kristinge replied in a shaky voice.

"To Danemark? Who wants to visit that barbaric country? Ask me instead for passage to... to South Burgundy, yes. To Genoa, or Agde. To the Mediterranean. Yes, much warmer there. Ebroin, buy them passage on a trading ship to Italy."

"Oh gracious king," Willimond said, with a severe tone that did not match the courtesy of the words themselves. "We seek passage to Danemark. If you have changed your mind about the boon, then we will buy our own passage."

"Changed my mind? Do you insult me?" He picked up the *francisc* off the arm of his throne and held it menacingly in his right hand as if he meant to hurl it at the monks. At that moment, however, he caught sight of Kristinge's sack near the door, and the harp which was half-visible out the top. He let the ax drop with a thud on his seat. "Danemark, yes. Tomorrow morning we will buy you passage on the next trading ship bound for Danemark. Of course you will entertain us this evening, for I see *you* are a bard." He was pointing at Willimond, mistaking him for the owner of the harp. "Yes. After this evening's feast we will expect a song from the bard. But now, it is I who will entertain."

Now he did jump up on his throne. The nearest of the Austrasian nobles jumped back, tipping over his chair in the process. "Send in the entertainment," Clovis shouted at the top of his lungs. Somebody was awaiting his order. The moment he shouted, the front door of the hall burst open. In came five young slave-girls, barely clad. "Entertain!" Clovis shouted, and he began to rip open his tunic.

On the heels of Willimond, Kristinge fled from the hall as if he were fleeing for his life.

Fortunately it took only a short time to find abbess Telchild. The same servant who had ushered the slave-girls into the throne room led Kristinge and Willimond to the queen's chambers where they found Queen Balthild in quiet conversation with Telchild and Beatrice. The queen greeted the monks warmly, and spent a long time querying them about Luxeuil and about Walbert, though she already revealed more knowledge about both than Kristinge expected. Then she asked about their meeting with King Clovis. Leaving out any reference to Clovis' entry into the hall, or to the conditions surrounding their departure, Willimond explained what they had heard of the conversation. Telchild was far less enthused than Clovis about the naming of her son as the new king of Francia. "My son will be more a slave than I ever was," she said sadly. Willimond then went on to tell of Clovis' granting of their request for passage to Danemark, as well as of his command that Kristinge play the harp for him that evening.

"Do not worry about entertaining the king," Balthild said at once. "I will see that your passage to Danemark is purchased. As for the king, he has enough entertainment already." At this, Kristinge blushed. The queen saw him and laughed a low, almost self-deprecating laugh. "I guessed there was something that Willimond graciously left out of his story for my sake. But alas, I know all too well of the king's exploits."

"And it does not bother you?" Kristinge asked. Willimond shot him quick warning glance, but the question had already been spoken.

"Bother me?" Balthild said. "It grieves me deeply, but there is little I can do. Little I can do for *him*, anyway, other than run his kingdom as best I am able, and give what help I can to his sons. For you, however, I can do more. I will tell you again that you have no obligation to entertain the king or his wicked court. There are some privileges to being queen. If my position does not suffice to rescue you from this, then what benefit has it?" Then she laughed again. "He has likely already forgotten you anyway. I will take care of paying for your passage. And now, I request that you please join us in our own feast."

Balthild signaled to one of her maids who went to the door. A moment later, a small group of servants appeared at the entrance to the queens' chambers. She called them in at once, and they entered carrying many trays laden with food—food the likes of which Kristinge had not before partaken. There were a half dozen varieties of fresh fowl and game, wine imported from Italy, fall fruits and nuts, and a large block of cheese to go with the loaves of bread. The young monk sat staring wide-eyed at all the fare, unable to believe his eyes. It was more than ten monks at Luxeuil would eat in a week.

"As I told you," Balthild said, guessing Kristinge's thoughts, "for all I have been through at the hands of Clovis, there are still some advantages to being a queen. Eat. It may be many months before you dine this well again."

Telchild gave thanks to the Lord for His provision, and they shared a meal together. The meal lasted for some time, in part because they were enjoying the conversation and in no hurry to finish, and in part because more food kept coming in. Eventually, however, the flow of victuals came to an end. There was more wine, and then a rest. It was late when another servant entered with a message from Clovis.

"The king commands the presence of his honored bard," the servant told the queen. He appeared nervous to be the bearer of tidings, as if he guessed how the queen might respond. Kristinge started to rise and reach for his harp.

"No," Balthild said, speaking to both Kristinge and the servant, and motioning for Kristinge to sit back down. "It is not necessary. He promised a boon before he made any demands. He will honor his promise."

But Kristinge didn't sit down again. Some time earlier in the evening, a seed had been planted in his mind. It had been growing through dinner, and now it was beginning to flower. He wasn't sure he could explain. He wasn't even sure *he* knew what he was doing himself, but something compelled him—something that he would only later relate to words spoken to him by Abbot Walbert before his departure from Luxeuil. "I will honor *his* request," Kristinge said. "I will tell sing a story for the court if the king so desires."

Willimond did not show any surprise, but he gave a warning. "Be careful. This is not a gruff land-owner who would punish a distasteful song by sentencing you to a night in the stable. If the king decides to make a martyr of you, I fear there are none who will be able to stop him."

"There is One," Kristinge answered.

"I will not be there," Balthild objected. "I will not sit at his side when his concubines are dancing."

It was Telchild who gently answered the queen, rightly guessing what Kristinge had meant. "It is not you of whom he spoke, but One far greater." Then she turned to Kristinge. "There is a prophet's spirit upon you tonight. That much I see. Prophets must speak the word— though they are sometimes killed for it. May God bless your tongue."

"Thank you, Abbess," Kristinge replied. A strange mood had fallen on him now. *Was this the prophet's spirit of which she spoke?* Yet at the mention of concubines, and the realization that neither the queen nor the abbess would be with him, he began to feel fear. He was glad when Willimond arose to join him.

"You will be in our prayers," the abbess said, as Kristinge and Willimond followed the servant out of the room.

CHAPTER 6:
THE PROPHET

*T*here was once a great and mighty king, one who wore the golden torc, a chieftain of chieftains who ruled many nations. The realm of this king extended to the farthest corners of the earth, and he held dominion over many kings and princes. Countless were the other tribes who paid tribute to him. No other had ever been more powerful than he, nor would there ever be another ruling tribe like his.

One night this king had a dream. He had a powerful vision, a night-seeing. He saw a mighty tree, a great ash of numerous branches that reached to the heavens. Its leaves were fair to look upon, and it bore much fruit, and in its branches nested many birds, and beneath its boughs the beasts of the field came to find shelter. But an ax was laid to the tree, a metal blade was put to the wood, and its glory was chopped down. All that remained of the once proud tree was the stump, and its only food was the dew of Heaven.

This was the king's dream, the vision that came to the ruler, and he did not understand it. So he called his wise men. He sent for his priests, and summoned his bards and skalds. He told the dream to his councilors, made the mystery known so that they would answer him. But the skalds could not speak. No bard knew the dream. His councilors fell mute. Only one in all the kingdom could help—one councilor wiser than all the rest whose wisdom came from God, and was given to him from the Heavens. This wise man, the one of surpassing knowledge, replied to the king and explained the dream. He spoke with prudent words.

'Your dream,' he explained, 'was given you by the God that you might have wisdom and know what is to happen in days to come.' Then the knowing bard explained to the king the meaning of his dream. He told him its interpretation. 'Your dream was about you, O king. You are the great tree. You are the glorious ash. And in your splendor you reach to the heavens, and all of the nations of the earth are under your care, like birds that nest in your leaves. Yet you have grown too proud, O king, too haughty and full of conceit so that you call yourself a god and have forsaken justice and righteousness. Therefore, unless you repent of your *pride and show mercy to the poor, unless you humble yourself before the One God, your kingdom will be taken from you and given to another, and you will become like a wild animal driven from the dwellings of men and made to live like a beast of the field until you repent and acknowledge the true Lord of Heaven, the Maker of men, and King over all the middle-earth.'*

So the dream came to pass. The vision was fulfilled. One day the king stood upon the roof of his great hall, looking out over his royal city, casting his eyes to the horizon and knowing that as far as he could see in every direction was under his dominion. He felt great and overbearing pride such as he should not have had. And in his pride he proclaimed, 'Indeed I am like a god, for all that I see I have built by my own power and for my great glory and majesty.' And in the moment that he spoke these words a voice came from Heaven saying, 'Today the kingdom is taken from you.'

And so the mightiest king of all the earth, the chieftain of chieftains and bearer of the golden torc, was cast from the dwellings of men, thrown from his castle and banished from the mead hall. For seven periods of time he lived like a beast of the field, drinking dew and eating grass, and his face was not shaven and his hair became like feathers and his nails like the claws of birds. Until seven periods had passed, and after that time the king lifted his eyes to Heaven and his sanity was restored to him and he humbled himself before the God of Heaven and praised His Name and acknowledged His Lordship. And then was His kingdom returned to him.

The hall was stone silent. The revelry that filled the air when Kristinge first began to sing had ceased. The Frankish nobility with their wives and concubines stared in silence at the brash monk-bard as if they expected him to be struck dead. Yet Clovis just sat there, slumped in his throne. On his lap sat another young concubine, but his roving hands had fallen off her. She had pulled a fur shawl back over her exposed breasts. For that, Kristinge was thankful; he needed no distractions.

There was yet another king, he went on chanting, after only a momentary pause. The Frankish tongue was coming easier to him that night than ever before. It was too late to stop. The prophets' spirit was indeed upon him. Plucking a few rare notes on his harp, he continued.

He was the son of the first king, the offspring of the mighty chieftain. And like his father, his pride too became very great. His arrogance exceeded even his glory and wealth. And he threw a great feast, a splendid banquet in the grandest of mead halls; he celebrated with men, and invited his wealthiest nobles and thanes, and princes from many lands. And when it came time to drink the wine, the hour to share the mead, he called for his golden vessels—vessels he had stolen from the house of God, mead cups that did not belong to him but to the Ruler of the Heavens and Maker of men. He called for the holy cups so that his princes and nobles and wives and concubines might drink and praise his pagan gods made of wood.

And as he sat drinking wine and worshipping his idols and giving his body to his concubines, in that very hour a great hand came out of the walls of his banquet hall in the royal palace, an arm emerged from the stone, and the hand took a candlestick and began to write upon the plaster walls, made letters that all might see. All who were there could see the hand, yet none knew the meaning of the writing; none understood the mystery. And the countenance of the king was changed, and his thoughts troubled, and fear came upon him, and his knees began to shake like those of a young man going to battle. He called to himself all his pagan priests, his skalds and his diviners and astrologers, his wise men and councilors. But none of them could read the writing. They did not know its meaning.

But the queen came into the banquet hall. The wife of the king entered. And she was more righteous than the king, and wiser. And she knew of a man of God who had great wisdom and understanding, and could understand all manner of hard sayings and dreams, 'for the Spirit of God is upon him,' she said, 'and his wisdom is from Heaven.' So the king called this wise man before him, the very same wise man who had once explained the dreams of the king's father, and the king asked him what was the meaning of these words.

The wise man appeared before the king as he was commanded, came to the throne as he was ordered. Without delay, he told the young king the tale of his father, how the former king and once great chieftain had been cast from his throne like a wild beast and restored only when he humbled himself before God. Then this is what the wise man told the king. 'You, too, O king have not humbled yourself, but have lifted yourself against the

Lord of Heaven. You have stolen the drinking vessels from His house and have drunk wine in them, and you have praised your gods of wood. This then is the message which has been given for you, the words which were sent. "Mene, Mene, Tekel, Upharsin." And the meaning of the message is this. "God has numbered the days of your kingdom and finished it. You have been weighed on the scales and found deficient. Your kingdom will be divided."

Then the king ordered the wise man to be clothed in a cloak of rich fabric, adorned with gold, and richly rewarded, though indeed the wise man wanted none of these things; he had no desire for riches or reward. Then the king sent the wise man from the hall in great honor, paid him tribute and made him depart. But the king did not heed the message, and he did not humble himself. And that very night, he was slain and his kingdom was given to his enemies.

Kristinge lowered his harp which he had been plucking throughout the telling of his story. With just a glance at Willimond, he turned and strode hurriedly toward the door of the hall, anxious to be gone as soon as possible. He knew not how the king would interpret the story, but if it was unfavorably he did not want to wait for the consequences. Willimond followed him toward the door.

"Wait!" Clovis commanded. His voice was surprisingly stern and powerful. Kristinge froze, a knot of fear rising in his throat. He turned around and walked slowly back to the throne, with Willimond still beside him.

"Is it cloaks and reward you want, then?" the king asked loudly, sounding more lucid than he had all afternoon. He rose suddenly from his throne, causing his concubine slave to fall to the floor at his feet. His hands were trembling. "Take it, then." He ripped the fur shawl from the shoulders of the girl. She was left exposed once again as Clovis threw the fur on the ground at the monk's feet. Kristinge could see the shame in the young girl's face as she clutched her arms around her breasts and tried to hide. Feeling no longer condemnation but pity for her, he picked up the fur shawl—appreciating for just a moment the beautiful extravagance—and then gently set it around her shoulders. Though she said not a word, he could see the gratitude in her eyes.

"Is it gold you desire? My offer of passage to Danemark was not enough? Take it then, also." He unbent a gold ring from his left wrist, and threw that at Kristinge. Kristinge instinctively caught it in his free hand. Clovis was already stripping another one off. He threw this one also, followed by a heavy neck-band. "How much do you want?"

"King," Ebroin objected, eyeing the wealth accumulating in Kristinge's hand. "The monk has gone too far. He deserves death for his insolence, not reward."

"Silence!" Clovis screamed at his advisor. He picked up his francisc and brandished it until Ebroin slunk back to his chair. Then the king turned and raised the ax toward Kristinge. "Take what I have given you, and leave."

Kristinge bowed his head slightly, then turned and strode from the hall, only barely resisting the urge to run. It was not until he was out the door and the full terror of the situation struck him that he realized how fortunate he was to be alive. His knees grew weak beneath him.

Willimond reached out a hand and steadied him as he stumbled. In a soft voice he said, "I know not whether to berate you for your foolishness, or praise you for your faith. Had I known you would tell a tale from the Word—"

"You would have recommended against the tales of Daniel?"

"You could not have chosen a more risky tale. Nor one more appropriate. If God led you, so be it. We must obey and trust Him." Then the older monk smiled slightly. "But next time, give me warning."

Kristinge didn't answer, but he returned the smile. How much of the song had been God's leading, he did not know. Nor was he ready to think about it. Not having made other plans, they now found their way back to the where they had left the queen and the abbess. When they arrived at the outer door to her suite of chambers, one of her own servants was waiting for them. "The queen will see you in the morning," he told them. "She has instructed me to bring you to the guest chambers."

Whether it was God's grace, the fact that his exhaustion outweighed the lingering terror, or the comfort of the softest bed he had ever slept on, Kristinge was asleep within moments. It was not until late the next morning, after they had been well fed, that he and Willimond were led back the queen.

"My servants arose early and have found two Frisian trading ships," Balthild explained at once. Kristinge's heart leapt with anticipation as the queen continued. "They are northward bound on a last voyage to Danemark before the winter sets in, and have agreed to take two passengers, one in each ship. I have paid already for your passage. They will leave at midday."

Kristinge and Willimond thanked the queen many times. "It is little," she finally replied. "I would do more if I knew how. Telchild tells me that God will do mighty things in your lives."

"The abbess said this?" Kristinge asked in amazement.

"She did. Though not, perhaps, what you expect. And not without..." she cut herself short before she finished.

Perplexed, Kristinge waited expectantly for her to finish. When she said no more, he asked, "What did she mean? Not without what? What is it I expect?"

At this, however, the queen only shook her head. "It is best that I say no more. Perhaps I have already told you more than I should have. You must ask Telchild herself. She is visiting a small chapel on the island and desires to see you again before you depart. Come. I will go with you."

Followed by four guards and a pair of servants, the queen proceeded out of the palace and began walking northward through the busy streets of Paris. As they passed the shops of various artisans and tradesmen, she spoke to Kristinge. "I heard of your tale last night. It was boldly done. Though had I known what you proposed, I might have counseled you against it. What they say is true. Clovis is no longer sane. But that only makes him more deadly. And he is still strong. I have seen him kill men with his francisc, hurling it with enough force and vengeance to split skulls." She shivered now, as if at a gruesome memory.

"I was afraid," Kristinge admitted for the first time. He didn't want to think about split skulls and throwing axes.

"But the Lord was with him," Willimond added.

"That I know beyond doubt," Balthild replied with an enigmatic smile. A moment later they arrived at a small stone chapel where they found Abbess Telchild and Beatrice. They joined them in silent prayer until it was time for Willimond and Kristinge to depart. Then all of them walked the remaining distance down the river to where the two trading ships were waiting. Once there, Kristinge and Willimond knelt again before Telchild and received her blessing. When they rose, Balthild also came forward. She had taken a large bundle from one of her servants. "I have many questions for you, and I wish you had the time to stay with us longer," she said. She smiled at Kristinge, who looked again at her dark brown hair and green eyes; at her soft, bare arms and her flesh that looked so warm even on a cool October day. He could see why Clovis had desired her. He wondered whether given the freedom to choose her own path, she would have followed the one she had been sent upon. And what path was he himself being given? Had he chosen it for himself?

"Were it not for your safety," the queen went on, "I wish you could sing for the king's court every night. I would that you could return with us to Burgundy to our court there. It would be good for us to hear you. But alas, I think there are not many who would gladly listen." She sighed, as one who has accepted the fate of living under constant sorrow. "I would know what drives you to Danemark, to that cold and hostile land. Or what sends you to Friesland. But I sense you carry within you, in addition to the future of which Telchild has spoken, a history best left unquestioned for a time." She laughed. "Why is it that I can see that past so much more clearly than the future?"

And I can see neither, Kristinge thought.

"You are gracious, dear queen," Willimond answered, when Kristinge could not. "We will remember your gentleness even as we remember the hospitality of your house."

With nothing else to say, she stepped forward with her bundle and handed half of it to Willimond and the other half to Kristinge. Standing on her toes, she pulled them forward and gave each a kiss on the forehead. Kristinge blushed, and to avoid her eyes he looked down at what she had given him. It was a pile of clothing, new and costly by the looks: a heavy fur cloak such as a wealthy nobleman might wear, along with a pair each of woolen trousers and tunics, and some soft leather shoes like those of the king. Knowing something of the value of such things, Kristinge realized that his whole bag of coins would not have sufficed to have purchased half of what he held. His eyes opened wide with surprise and gratitude, and he looked over at Willimond and saw that he, too, was holding up similar items.

"We cannot accept this," Willimond said at once, starting to hand the bundle back to the queen.

Kristinge's jaw dropped at Willimond's words. *Cannot accept? Why not?* The garments were beautiful. He was glad that Balthild refused to take the bundles back. "It is a gift," she replied. "Show me your love by accepting it

"But—" Willimond started to object.

"It would be better," the queen said before Willimond could finish his objection, "if you did not arrive in Danemark in the cloak of a monk. It is still a pagan land, more so even than Friesland. Few missionaries have gone there, and those who have gone have not returned. The Danes are jealous for their gods, and quick to make martyrs of any who threaten them. This is for your own protection. If they are going to put you to death, at least let them hear what you have to say first."

"But—" Willimond tried again.

"Do not turn down what God provides," Abbess Telchild interrupted, taking the part of the queen. "You might well regret it later if you do. Would you find yourself cold and wet in the weeks to come, wondering why God has not provided for you, when it was you yourself who refused his provision when he did?"

Kristinge watched Willimond ponder these words. Then the older monk bowed to Queen Balthild. "Your generosity is as abundant as your hospitality. I will not refuse what you have graciously given." But then he turned back to Telchild. "Yet as for our robes, do you truly council that we hide them and show shame for our Lord?"

"I council only that you heed the queen's advice," Telchild replied. "She is wise and her advice sound. Consider again your purpose in going to Danemark. When I asked that question of Kristinge yesterday, I did not ask it lightly. If your purpose is as Kristinge said, to find the one you seek, you will be better able to accomplish it without the attire of a monk."

Kristinge's thoughts flashed back to their conversation of the day before—the conversation of which the abbess was reminding them as clearly as she could without giving away Kristinge's identity in the presence of others. *Do you go as Hildeburh's son? Or do you go as a Christian monk?* She had asked.

I go to seek my mother, was Kristinge's response.

"There is no cowardice in putting aside the robe for a time," Telchild went on. "One may hide a robe without showing shame for the Lord. Even Paul the Apostle wore the cloak of a tentmaker when it suited him." Then her voice lightened. "Of course unless your hair grows in quickly, you will ill be able to hide what you are."

Willimond bowed. "Again I am humbled."

The abbess shrugged. "'As iron sharpens iron, so one man sharpens another.' It is I who am humbled by your fearless zeal for the Lord's glory. Nonetheless, in this you might better accomplish your work—the Lord's work, it may be—without your robes." She turned then to Kristinge. "And I will say a final time that it may also be well for you if *all* of your identities are hidden for the time. Among the Danes, there may be crimes even greater than following Jesus."

Kristinge nodded. Though her allusion was veiled, he knew of what the abbess spoke. He was not only the heir of Finn's torc, but in Germanic eyes he was the heir of Finn's blood feuds. If the Danes still sought the weregild for the death of their nobles, then six years would not be a long wait for them. For the time, he would heed her advice to keep his secret. Yet he wondered if the secrecy were necessary in front of the Frankish queen. Balthild could certainly be trusted, he thought. He risked another glance in her direction, but she was staring down the river as if trying not to listen. He wondered whether she had not already guessed who he was, and he wondered how much longer he would be wondering what others did and did not know about him.

Soon it was time for the ships to depart. Kristinge could see the merchants standing beside their ships a few paces away, waiting impatiently for the monks. Though too wise to risk rushing a ruling queen, their frequent looks showed their displeasure at the delay. Finally, Telchild and Beatrice turned to leave and the queen's servant notified the traders that their passengers were now ready to depart. Willimond was ushered to the center of the front ship where, with rowers fore and aft of him, he was given a small space surrounded by the cargo. The traders had not been generous with room. Kristinge looked nervously at the other ship, and the small space he would be allotted for the duration of the voyage. For how many days? Yet his hope of what lay at the end of the voyage was enough to endure anything.

"God's blessings," Queen Balthild said again.

"His blessings upon you as well," Kristinge replied. Then, under orders from the merchant, he prepared to step down upon the keel board.

Yet there was to be one last delay. Not far behind them, rising over the steady din of haggling merchants, came an angry voice shouting in the distinctive Frisian dialect. The sound of his native tongue caught Kristinge's attention, and he turned to look. What he saw took him by surprise. A few dozen yards upriver, a single Frisian trading ship had come ashore to unload its goods. The ship's sailors, however, were being accosted by a pair of Frankish soldiers. One had seized some of the merchandise, a bundle of woolen cloth, as if to confiscate it. Such a scuffle over customs fees between guards and merchants was not uncommon. What was surprising was that the merchant facing the soldiers was a *woman*—a fiery young Frisian woman, clad in a rich but well-worn sleeveless woolen cloak and dark trousers. At least Kristinge *guessed* she was the owner of the goods. But he knew that women merchants were as rare among the Frisians as were monks. And she didn't look like a merchant, but more like a princess or the proud daughter of some great warrior. Her hair, bound below a bronze war helmet, was long and black, contrasting sharply with the smooth white skin of her bare forearms. And though she was not large, her arms looked strong and finely tuned.

And her face. Her eyes! Kristinge's own eyes opened wide. Could it be? He took an involuntary step forward. He had seen that face before. Those emerald eyes. They had haunted his memory for many years.

Not intimidated, the young Frisian woman stood toe-to-toe with the soldiers, demanding that they return her goods. But the soldiers, over a head taller than her and well armed, only grinned at her fiercely. Suddenly the one holding her merchandise dropped the goods and grabbed her shoulder. Before she could pull away, he reached toward her breasts with his other hand.

What happened next caught everyone off guard, especially the soldier. Rather than trying to escape his grip, the woman's knee came up hard into the soldier's groin faster than he could pull away. With his eyes wide open in surprise and pain, he fell doubled over into a heap on the ground, while the woman quickly reached over and picked up her goods. And the mischievous expression that flashed across her face erased many of the doubts remaining in Kristinge's mind about her identity. Could this be anyone by her? *Aewin?* The young girl he had met so long before in Hwitstan—the one who had been promised in betrothal to his brother before...

But she was no longer a young girl. Her beauty was astonishing. What was she doing here? Where was her chieftain father? Kristinge took another step forward. His concern was no longer merely for a fellow Frisian in trouble. Yet what was he to do? He could only watch.

With one guard still bent over clutching his groin, the woman stepped back toward her boat. Unfortunately, there were two soldiers. The other one drew his sword. He was no longer smiling as he stepped toward her. Seeing him approach with blood in his eyes, the woman's look of triumph vanished. The seriousness of the situation struck her. She took another step backwards, looking around for help. But most of the sailors in her ship were unarmed and not eager to come to her aid. A few had drawn swords but they had yet to disembark. They saw as clearly as she did: a few dozen paces away, a much larger group of Frankish soldiers was watching the scene closely, ready to enter the fray if any of the Frisians attempted to interfere. A battle would not go well for the woman's company, and her people knew it.

The remaining Frankish soldier came toward the woman. She stepped back again, and found herself ankle-deep in the river. "Come here," the soldier said in his own Frankish dialect, beckoning with his hand. The woman looked around once more for help. There was no aid. She reached into her belt and pulled a short knife. It was no match for the soldier's sword. Even had she a weapon equal to his, he was twice her weight.

No! Kristinge thought. In his mind it was a shout, but afterward he did not know if any words had even come forth from his mouth.

He was terrified. Still, he took another step. The woman had now turned in his direction. For an instant their eyes met, and he could read in her glance the silent plea for help. A vision flashed across his mind of her as a younger girl sitting beside him on the banks of the Hwitstan, listening as he played the harp. He had to do something. He started forward. Then a hand came firmly upon his shoulders. It was the merchant in whose ship he was to sail—a fellow Frisian. Kristinge tried vainly to pull away, but the grip was firm. "Unwise to involve yourself," the merchant said. "Nothing you can do here."

"She's one of our people," Kristinge argued, but the merchant only shook his head. Kristinge looked back upon the scene. The soldier was advancing now. He stood at the edge of the water. The woman, still holding her knife, took another step back. Two of her people near the front of the ship had leapt into the water, but then stopped when ten or more Frankish guards took several threatening steps forward. The young woman looked at her people with scorn, then turned back toward the advancing soldier. She was up to her knees now. Behind her, the river dropped off steeply. She could retreat no farther. The soldier lowered his blade until its point was just below her neck. Kristinge's heart was pounding.

"Stop!" another voice rang out.

Kristinge looked to his side. Queen Balthild had stepped forward. "Stop!" she shouted again, in a voice not as loud as the Frisian woman's but full of authority. The soldier stopped and looked. His comrade had now regained his feet and turned toward the queen also. His anger and hatred were written clearly on his face, but he recognized who it was who spoke and bowed. Moved perhaps by sympathy for her kindred sex, Balthild spoke. "Leave the Frisian woman alone. Let her unload her merchandise."

"She has not paid—"

"Leave her," The queen commanded sternly. "I know what custom fees you loot, and I know how little of it makes it to the throne. This one you will not accost." As she spoke, her personal guards from the palace took a step toward the two soldiers who still stood menacingly over the Frisian woman. It was, however, unnecessary. Balthild was queen. The soldiers reluctantly obeyed, and backed away from the young woman.

The Frisian woman did not leave the water until the soldiers had disappeared. When they were gone, she stepped up on the bank and resheathed her knife. Then she turned and looked at Balthild, bowing her head slightly in acknowledgment of the favor done her. No words were exchanged between them. None were necessary. When she had silently thanked the queen, her eyes scanned again the company of her rescuer. Kristinge could only watch. She had grown beautiful since he had last seen her, from a sparkling young girl to a woman full grown. Her face—forehead high and proud, eyes black and flashing, and full lips tightly pursed—was stunning. Enamored by her beauty, he could not look away. When her gaze finally met his, they stopped as if in a glimmer of recognition. Yet she held him captive for only an instant. Then she dismissed him and turned upon her own servants. With words even more fiery than her gaze, she proceeded to scold them for their cowardly faithlessness.

But Kristinge still stood staring at her, unable to forget her face or beauty. Queen Balthild looked back at Kristinge, then at the woman, then at Kristinge again. The monk saw the queen's smile but did not comprehend it. Only the heavy hand still resting upon his shoulder turned his eyes away. The scene had played itself out and the merchant was ready to depart. With a final farewell to the queen and another look back at the Frisian woman, Kristinge stepped into the boat. Within a few moments, he had started down the Seine toward the North Sea doubting he would ever see Luxeuil or Jouarre again. But he was not thinking about Jouarre. He was thinking about his old acquaintance. Would he see *her* again? Was she now betrothed to another? Would she think differently of him if she knew that he, too, was a son of Finn?

CHAPTER 7:
THE WICS OF FRIESLAND

Though many days of travel had passed between Kristinge's encounters in Paris and his arrival at Frotha's hall, the memories of the events as well as images of Telchild, Balthild, Clovis and Aewin were still fresh in his mind as he lay on the bench trying to sleep. Long after the fire had burned down to a soft glow and the last of Frotha's warriors had fallen asleep, Kristinge lay awake pondering what Telchild had told him. And thinking too, against his will, of Aewin. Not until the young monk's restless mind had recounted almost his entire journey from Luxeuil to Paris and along the wics of Friesland to where he now lay did he finally fall asleep to the heavy breathing of the mead-laden warriors who lined the benches around him. But he did not sleep well. His rest was troubled by dreams of the sea.

It was the chieftain who woke Kristinge the next morning, prodding him in the ribs with his foot. Startled awake, Kristinge fell off his bench and landed on the floor with a painful jolt. He sat up quickly, rubbing his elbow and·looking around. Most of the inhabitants of the hall were still sleeping off the effects of the previous night's drink. But it was not warriors he was looking for. The one he hoped to see was gone. Of course he shouldn't have expected to see her, he reminded himself. This was not her village, and the chieftain Frotha was not her father—though at times the evening before she had seemed so much at home in the hall he almost thought she belonged there. Even if she were the daughter of the chieftain of this hall, she would not have stayed here with the warriors. She had left while they were still drinking, and was probably asleep in one of the nearby dwellings with some of the women of the village. Someone close in kinship to the chieftain, who could offer a more luxurious bed. Or perhaps her ship had already slid off the beach and was even now rowing eastward up the coast. He cast his thoughts forward. Perhaps he would see her again in another hall the next night.

Then the voice belonging to the foot brought him back to the present, with only slightly less of a jolt than when the foot had brought him back from sleep a few seconds earlier. "I won't ask for whom you look," Frotha said. He was standing over Kristinge, looking down with a bemused smile. He had certainly seen the young monk looking around the hall. Could he have guessed for whom Kristinge was searching? For just a moment, Kristinge considered asking him about Aewin. But what pretense could he give for such a question? "Your merchants are awaiting you by the beach," the chieftain continued. "They are eager to depart. If you hope to depart with them, I would suggest you make more haste than you are making."

Kristinge jumped to his feet. He donned his warm cloak which he had used as a sleep covering, picked up his harp and belongings, and then took one last look around, this time hoping to spot a different face. When he saw no sign of Willimond, he felt the beginnings of panic.

The chieftain must have read it in his eye. "You need not fear. The ship has not departed."

"Thank you," Kristinge said as he hurried toward the door.

"Wait," Frotha called. Kristinge stopped and turned. The chieftain watched him for a moment, then spoke. "I am in need of a bard, and you remind me of someone I knew long ago. You may stay and serve in my hall."

Kristinge's jaw dropped in surprise. This was an offer he had neither sought nor expected. Yet he was not unpleased. The chieftain would not have made such an offer had he not been impressed with the young bard's performance the night before. Still, Kristinge knew he could not accept. Regardless of what Petrica and Walbert had told him about his *gift*, he was not sure he wanted to return to Friesland as a bard. And however he was to return, he had first another task to perform—a voyage to Danemark. Besides, he knew he had not yet acquired enough of a true bard's repertoire to risk more than a night or two in one hall. He wondered how much of his previous night's success had come from the inspiration of Aewin's presence in the audience. He could not count on such again. "Your offer is gracious," he replied after a moment. "Yet I cannot accept. Perhaps I may return in the spring, and if you are still willing I will sing again."

"So be it," Frotha said. "The traders tell me you are bound for Danemark. I cannot guess what brings you there, though a good bard can no doubt find service wherever he goes. I warn you, though. Be cautious to whom you sing. Had a certain young woman's rash brother been present in the hall last night, he could not have missed the look in your eyes when you sang. If a young bard wishes to dream, I will not stop him. Perhaps it is necessary to the trade. But some chieftains are more jealous of their sisters and daughters." He laughed. "Had I still a wife or daughter in *my* hall perhaps *I* would have been less pleased."

Kristinge blushed and bowed quickly, then almost fled from the hall. Had he been so obvious? Yet regardless of Frotha's words, he could not help but glance around the village one time hoping for a final glimpse of her. Perhaps... A thought crossed his mind. He had little expected to see Aewin again so soon after their distant encounter in Paris, but he had found her again at Frotha's hall. Or rather she had found him. Was it too much to hope, he wondered again? That her ship might follow a similar course as his own along the coast? That he might yet see her again before his voyage took him beyond Friesland?

Whatever hopes he had, she was not to be seen that morning. And Kristinge could not afford to stand too long looking for her. A frosty wind was blowing from the north. Already his ears were cold. Above, the sky was dark with low gray clouds. It would be a rough day on the water—cold and damp. He was not looking forward to the voyage. Frotha's proposition now sounded more appealing. Nevertheless, down he walked toward the beach and the waiting sailors. Most of the crew were already aboard the two trading ships when he arrived. Willimond was nestled in the center of the smaller ship, wrapped in his warm cloak, with eyes closed in prayer or meditation. Only the chief trader, a red-bearded Frisian named Wyndlaf, along with a fellow merchant and one of the steersmen, were still standing on the beach conversing with one of Frotha's seafaring thanes about the water conditions. Wordlessly, Kristinge gripped the gunnels and climbed down the center plank to his own spot. Over the past fortnight he had grown quite familiar with the small ship. His life, he realized, rested as much on the strength of the thin oak planks beneath his feet as upon the skill of those who guided them. Motivated by that knowledge, and not lacking the time to do so, he had studied the craft's construction on the first few days of his voyage. It had taken the young monk's untrained eyes some time to see how it was all fitted together, but as he eventually realized the design was both ingenious and simple—a work of art of a master shipbuilder. On each side of a heavy keel board were five overlapping oak *strakes* fastened with long narrow shards of iron driven in rows through each overlapping pair. The rowlocks—sixteen of them—were similarly fastened with these iron *nails*. The ship's ribbing, on the other hand, was not attached directly inside the strakes, but was lashed to wooden clamps fixed to the timbers. Kristinge himself could never have designed such a sturdy or complex vessel. Nor even having seen the design could he have replicated its construction. But several days of travel had proven its seaworthiness.

Still, his stomach was uneasy when a minute later they slid off the beach and started rowing out into deeper water. Though Kristinge had been born in Friesland a stone's thrown from the sea, he had never been on a sea-going vessel until his departure from Paris. Travel by ship, after all, was for kings, warriors and merchants—and perhaps for the brave exploring Irish monks—but not for peasants and priests. He had heard enough stories of warships lost to storms, and had times without count in his childhood stood upon the hill above Hwitstanwic watching wild waves crash upon the shore. He knew the sea was a thing to be feared: a wild and unpredictable creature against which a few pieces of wood might account for naught. And yet he had also come to realize how much he missed the salt air of Friesland and the sandy wic of Hwitstan. It had thus been with a sense of fearful excitement that he had stepped aboard this same vessel in Paris, and had set off with an unknown band of Frisian merchants bound for Danemark. He had felt then for the first time, as he said farewell to the queen and abbess and started down the Seine river toward the great North sea, that his journey had really begun.

A far cry from the slow jarring rattle of Gundomer's wagons, he had at first found their smooth speed exhilarating as they sliced through the water behind the strokes of eight pairs of oarsmen. But his excitement had not lasted, and he had soon grown weary of the ship. As large as it was, nearly fifty feet in length and wider than the young monk was tall, there was little space left for the passenger.

Between the rowers, the traders, and the goods, Kristinge found himself hunched in a small ball. Well before the end of the first day, a short afternoon of rowing, he had been ready to escape. But after a brief night in a small village, they had continued at first light—with the second day being twice as long as the first. On the middle of the third day, rounding a bend in the river, Kristinge had caught sight of the long-awaited North Sea. As it came into view, sparkling in the distance under the afternoon sun, he had momentarily forgotten the discomfort of his position. But even that thrill had faded a short time later when they moved down through the mouth of the river, past the tidal water, and out into the surf—when the first swell hit the boat and he felt the dismal sensation of having his stomach drop into his bowels one moment and rise into his throat the next. Any romantic ideals he had ever had of the seafaring life had disappeared almost at once, vanishing in the mist of the first icy spray that caught him in the face, and the first feeling of nausea that crept over him. Suddenly, Kristinge had not only had to deal with the cramped quarters, but with the wind, waves, and swell of the North Sea in October. When the chop and swell were at odds, which grew more usual as the month progressed, it was next to impossible to stay dry in the boat. Even dressed in his new woolen garments, which on the council of both the queen and abbess he and Willimond had donned in replacement of their monastic robes, he could not stay warm. He soon gave up trying, and resigned himself to shivering away the days.

Night had brought only a little relief when they pulled ashore to sleep on a lonely bank or to find shelter in a trading village. Evenings were barely long enough for Kristinge to stretch his legs, and never long enough for him to get completely dry. Willimond, who had long ago taken a sea voyage from Lindisfarne to Friesland, had tried to encourage him, reminding him how richly God had blessed them already. Kristinge had been forced to admit that his purse, if nothing else, had grown rather than shrunk. Indeed, at Clovis' expense, it had bulged like a pregnant sow. Two heavy gold armbands and a rich necklace—any one of the three worth more than the sum of all the coins he had been given Luxeuil—now weighed him down. Not to mention that to his meager wardrobe had been added the beautiful wool trousers, tunics, and fur cloak given him by Queen Balthild, while in addition he had been provided with passage on a trading ship and had not had to purchase a single meal or night's lodging in all his many days of travel. But he had been little in the mood for cheering.

It not been until the evening after the fourth day of travel that he had pulled out his harp to take his mind off his concerns. The sound of music and the feel of strings beneath his fingers had a soothing effect, especially when he was most distraught. Though his fingers had been cold and cramped from a long day in the boat, he had found solace and distraction in his playing. So, apparently had the traders and sailors who heard him. He had not been playing and singing more than a few minutes before they had gathered around him to listen. Soon they had built up his little fire with their own wood and were cheering him on. And though he had not performed since his appearance before Clovis four nights earlier, Kristinge was infected by their enthusiasm. He was in the right mood to entertain. Dredging from his memory the few seafaring songs he knew, from the most somber and lonely to the most adventurous, he stumbled from one song after another until late into the evening when the fires had burned low and his fingers were nearly frozen to his strings—and still Wyndlaf had to rescue him by sending his crew to sleep.

It was that night that had planted the seed necessary for Wyndlaf to present him to Frotha as a bard—the seed that resulted in his singing once again, after many years, for Aewin. And though Kristinge had not planned on returning to Friesland as a bard, he had not been altogether unhappy with the proposal. His singing had also provided one additional benefit. The following morning, to his pleasant surprise, both he and Willimond had found a little more room in the boat and a greater willingness on the part of the merchants to talk. Thus they had made their way along the Frankish coast and started up the western shore of Friesland. And so, not far beyond the Rhine, they had eventually come to the clan village where Frotha ruled. And Kristinge had once again sung for his acquaintance of long ago. And now he departed, wondering if he would ever see her again. Perhaps her ships would also be traveling up the coast, following him from mead hall to another. Until he sailed past her home and onward to Danemark.

It was not long, however, before he had other thoughts to occupy his mind. The merchants were working their way along the Frisian coast, from village to village, bay to bay, hoping to reach Danemark before it was too stormy. But winter was fast approaching. There had already been days between Paris and the shores of Friesland when they had been unable to travel due to rough weather. As they sailed onward from Frotha's hall, these days became more frequent. The islands and wics of Friesland protected them from the worst of the North Sea, but the waters were still rough. To the inexperienced Kristinge, it felt as if they were traveling through constant storm. One evening after the weather had been particularly rough and cold, and they had been forced to stop early when the boat had nearly swamped, he overheard the merchants wondering whether they would make it to Danemark at all that year. If winter came too soon, they would go no further than their homes in Friesland. At these words, Kristinge's heart froze as cold as his fingers. Having learned from Telchild that his mother had survived the battle, he was now more eager than ever to reach Danemark. And he was not ready to return to Friesland. Not yet.

That night he felt in no mood to play his harp for the sailors. He spent the rest of his waking time praying fervently that they would make it to Danemark before the winter set in. He did not feel close to God, and wondered if his prayer would be answered—or even heard.

The following morning, for the first time in many days, the sun was shining. Despite the lingering discomfort in his legs and back, Kristinge was eager to board and press on. So were the sailors. Before the sun had risen full above the eastern horizon, they had set off, and with favorable winds they were soon able to pull in the oars and raise sail. An hour later, they had rounded a long peninsula and turned eastward across the great bay. The seas were nearly flat. There was no chop and the swells rose no more than two feet. With the unseasonably calm waters, they made good headway. They had crossed the great bay by the end of the morning, and were approaching Wijnaldum early in the afternoon, half a day ahead of Wyndlaf's prediction. For the first time in many days, Kristinge grew confident again that they might make Danemark. They would cover many more leagues on the famed swan road before resting for the night. To his dismay, however, he looked up to see Wyndlaf signaling the two steersmen to shore. A minute later, they were sliding ashore at Wijnaldumwic while several warriors stood watching from the beach.

"Welcome, Wyndlaf," came the booming voice of a burly red-haired war-leader. "If had you passed us by this trip, my welcome next time might not have been as heart-felt. Come ashore. Show us your wares." Kristinge saw from the man's torc that he was a chieftain. Accepting the invitation, the trader ordered his men ashore and followed them out of the ship.

"We have made good time today," Kristinge heard him saying in a quiet voice to his steersman. "Let us rest for the night. We may fetch a good price for our few Frankish-forged weapons here. This clan has no smith of its own." When the other nodded his agreement, Kristinge's heart sunk. *No*, he wanted to protest. They would be losing precious hours of travel. *We can not afford such a delay*. But his words would be futile. His legs felt unduly heavy as he stepped out of the ship.

"I hear your thoughts, friend," came Willimond's voice from behind. "I am no happier about this delay than you, but perhaps it is God's will."

"That we fail to reach Danemark?" Kristinge replied in frustration.

"I was thinking of something else. That there are some believers here. Or there *were*; I know not if they still remain. There were only three: a peasant farmer and his wife whom Ulestan once helped, and a metal smith. I came here on more than one occasion to preach to them. We are not far from Hwitstan, or from where Finnsburg once stood."

"I was with you the last time," Kristinge answered. The memory was coming back to him and for a moment he forgot his impatience.

"You remember this village?"

"Yes. It was the *only* time you ever allowed me to join you on your travels."

"I did not travel much beyond Hwitstan and Ezinge," Willimond replied defensively. "There was enough to do there. But I had a vision to one day bring the Gospel throughout all of Friesland—to see many churches grow here. Alas, it was a vision I was not to see fulfilled."

"Not *yet* ," Kristinge corrected.

"Come," Willimond said soberly. "Let us see if there are still any here of the Faith."

Putting his own concerns aside for the moment, Kristinge followed Willimond into the village in hopes of finding their fellow followers of Christ. That hope, however, was not to be fulfilled. Seven years was a long time. After two hours of searching for the metal smith, Willimond even began to doubt his memory. "There is no smith here," they were told by three different people. Finally they met an old peasant who remembered the smith, and told Willimond he had died of illness during the winter four or five years past. The monks lowered their heads in sadness.

They searched next for the peasant farmer. Though Willimond had forgotten his name, they eventually found him. He and his wife lived in a sunken hut on the far side of the main terp, near the village lands where they worked. Willimond found the two of them in the nearby woods collecting wild nuts and seeds to supplement the grain harvest which was now past. The reunion brought no joy. Neither the man nor women at first recognized the monks who were not wearing their robes. When Willimond reminded them who he was, they looked sheepish and acted eager to be rid of him. When Kristinge later walked past their hut he saw the reason why. Near their door were a pair of wooden stick idols of the fertility gods Njord and Nerthus, along with sacred wooden cow's horns. Perhaps under pressure from the other villagers they had given up their Christian faith and returned to the idol worship. Kristinge had never seen Willimond so dejected as when he walked away from that house.

Disheartened and with no other purpose in the village, they returned to the beach. "What fate have the other believers come to?" Willimond wondered aloud. "Have all my years here come to naught?"

Kristinge did not know how to answer. He sat silently beside his old companion a few yards upriver from the pair of guards who stood watch over the ships. They were still sitting there some time later when Wyndlaf returned to the ship with the chieftain and a pair of his thanes. He watched absently as the trader ordered one of his men to unload a few items from the ship. The chieftain desired to look over some of the goods. As expected, there was some dickering. Kristinge had seen it several times before. In the end Wyndlaf traded three new Frankish-forged iron weapons for a large load of native Frisian cloth:

the *pallia Fresonica* they would later sell in Danemark—if they made it that far—or the following spring at the fairs of St. Denis. When the barter was complete, the merchant fell into easy conversation with the chieftain. Kristinge, seated downwind, heard all but a few words which got lost here and there to the squawk of a gull or sudden gust of wind.

Most of the conversation held little interest to the young monk. However, when the chieftain began updating the merchants on the present struggle for the Frisian torc, Kristinge began to pay closer attention. It was the first news of Friesland he had heard since word had reached Luxeuil of the battle of Finnsburg and the death of Finn.

"Aldgisl is strong and well-liked," the chieftain was saying. "And he has a good war band—a strong hearthwerod. He will be king soon, I think. I will follow him. But old Réadban, he is a real question. He is crafty and unpredictable, and just as ambitious as he was in his youth when he challenged Finn."

At the name of Finn, Kristinge's heart started to beat faster and he sat upright. *Finn? Somebody had challenged him? Who? Why?* His dilemma came rushing back at him. Was he truly returning to Friesland as the son of Finn? The heir of the torc? Was this his *own* history he was hearing—the history of Finn?

"You know Réadban is the chieftain at Dorestad now," the chieftain continued. His voice was calm, giving little hint of emotion, as if the events were distant and impersonal. It was Kristinge whose emotions were beginning to rise. "It was his son, Radbod the Young, who overthrew Frotha's kin in Dorestad many years ago. But Radbod is dead, and he was childless. Réadban has claimed Dorestad until Ultar's son Rathbod is old enough to rule."

"Do the people follow him *willingly?*" Wyndlaf asked.

"The peasants?" He shrugged. "They do not care. As long as they get something to eat. What matters is that Réadban has a loyal hearthwerod—a large war band and many thanes. Mercenaries, half of them, but it doesn't matter much. It is a large enough band to back his ambitions. He claims Utrecht as well now. No one is strong enough to oppose him. I imagine old Frotha would try to claim Dorestad back were he a few years younger. And if he still ruled a large enough clan to have a real war band. He always hated Réadban even before he lost to him the rule over the southern villages. Frotha was loyal to Finn."

Kristinge's head was spinning now. Loyalty to Finn? Why had he not known this when he had sung in Frotha's hall a few nights ago? Is that what Frotha had recognized in Kristinge? And who was this Réadban?

"What of Aldgisl?" the trader pursued, his eyes narrowing hungrily at this rare morsel of information being doled out so freely. "Friesland is not as large as Francia. There can be no more than one king or one torc around a king's neck. Réadban's ambitions cannot be hidden from Aldgisl. Does Réadban seek the torc for himself? Does he oppose Aldgisl?"

"Not now. Not openly. They are kin, after all—Aldgisl and Réadban. Distant kin, perhaps, but kin. No. Since the deaths of Radbod and Ultar—"

"Ultar is dead?" Wyndlaf asked, surprised.

"He was killed in a summer raid upon the Swedes," the chieftain confirmed. "You had not heard? Ultar had gone to join his brother Radbod, and Réadban has been made childless. Thus he has pledged his sword to Aldgisl. Or so Aldgisl claims, and I do not doubt him. But Ultar left behind a son; Rathbod, he is called. An ill name, I think. Still, though he is just an infant, he is kin of Réadban. I wonder what will happen when Rathbod is old enough to rule. Will Réadban still support Aldgisl when one of his own is old enough for the torc? I wonder. If Aldgisl really covets the torc, he would do well to watch them both."

There was a pause as the chieftain gazed contemplatively out toward sea. "Réadban is raising a war band to drive the Franks out of Domburg," he finally continued. "He is ambitious. He wants to raise eight hundred or more—a war band such as has not been seen in Friesland in a long time. If enough follow him, he promises even to cross the Rhine to regain territory to the south. Or so he claims is his purpose. Some think otherwise. If he really raises so many thanes, no chieftain in Friesland could equal him. And he is doing it all in the name of Rathbod, who is still suckling at his mother's breast."

Kristinge heard breathing at his side and realized that Willimond was listening too.

"What do *you* think?" Wyndlaf asked. Merchants were notorious for staying uninvolved and neutral in matters of Frisian political affairs, but equally notorious for knowing more of what was happening than anybody else, perhaps because their livelihood depended on being well-informed. "Will he succeed? Will he drive out the Franks? Can he raise such a large war band?"

The chieftain thought for a moment. He was not likely to speak openly against Réadban. Nor against Aldgisl. That much Kristinge knew. Likely, this young chieftain had already pledged his sword to one or both of them. So Kristinge was not surprised when he deflected the question. "It was Réadban's son Radbod who usurped Frotha's torc and drove his family from Dorestad. There could be no love there, so don't expect Frotha to follow him. Indeed, knowing Réadban, I am surprised Frotha still lives. Still, it is a popular campaign against the Franks, and Réadban is gaining support. The Frisians have feared the Franks for too long. We have been threatened too often, especially those of us close to the great river. The Franks have taken Domburg back since the time of Finn, and have crossed the Rhine in many places. But now their kings appear weak. Many among the Frisian clans think it is the time to attack them. I do not disagree. A number of chieftains have already pledged themselves to this battle—though not necessarily to Réadban himself. I think if Aldgisl takes up the cause, there will be a war with the Franks."

He paused and looked out to sea for several moments before continuing. "If he does not, then I do not know. It could happen anyway. Réadban has somewhere acquired treasure, and with it he has attracted a large war band of his own. I hear it now numbers three hundred. If he wins a victory against the Franks without Aldgisl, then Aldgisl's claim on the Frisian torc will be greatly weakened. With such victories, kings are made! If pressed, I think Réadban could already put up a good fight against Aldgisl. Though as I said, I do not think he will—at least not until Rathbod is older. And by that time, Réadban will be long in his grave, I think. He's already lived longer than a warrior ought. Valhalla is not far away from that one. Valhalla or Hel, but for now he remains on this *middan-gearth*."

"And you?" the other younger merchant asked slyly, pressing the question yet a step further than Wyndlaf had taken it. "Who will you support for king if it comes to a contest between them?"

The chieftain laughed and put his hand on the hilt of his blade. "I will protect my people. Keep them alive and well-fed. Any Frisian chieftain or king who can help me with that will have my support." But then he looked around, and in a lower voice which Kristinge could only barely hear added, "And yet I tell you that I have no more love for Réadban than Frotha does. There are some who will never forget that it was Réadban who betrayed Finn at the end."

What? Kristinge's heart lurched, and he almost shouted aloud. He would have leapt to his feet had it not been for Willimond's hand on his shoulder restraining him. *Betrayed Finn?!* He felt his anger rising. It did not matter that he had barely known Finn—or that it had happened many years ago. *Who was this chieftain Réadban?*

"Betrayed Finn?" Wyndlaf asked, in a surprised voice. "This is a new tale to me. News may travel slowly, but we have ears in my trade. What do you mean?"

"Finn knew the Danes were coming to attack. It was not only Finn's son who died in the first battle. The Danish king perished also, so there was a weregild to be paid. Finn knew that in the spring he would see battle, and he sent to his chieftains for aid, calling his war band to gather at Finnsburg. It was then he was betrayed—betrayed by those he had trusted."

"How—" the trader started to ask.

"Some of the blame lay in Finn himself. At the death of his son Finnlaf—slain in his own hall upon his own hearthstone—many of Finn's thanes lost confidence in their king. And in his self-pity, Finn did nothing to regain their trust. Yet even so, many remained loyal and would have come to his aid had it not been for Réadban. Réadban and his sons spoke evil words of the king, inciting others to abandon Finn as well. And where words did not suffice, they issued threats. For Réadban was already powerful enough that other chieftains were afraid of him. Or if not afraid, his words conveniently gave them excuses to follow their own petty ambitions."

Is this what I have inherited? Kristinge wondered. *Do I claim this inheritance?*

The chieftain was not yet finished. "Despite Réadban's threats, Frotha's brother Froda answered Finn's call. He took his band of twenty loyal warriors and fought to the death at Finn's side. He was a brave warrior, Froda was, and loyal until the end. I have often heard Frotha wish he had been in his brother's place. But alas, the line of Finn is now gone, and it is the likes of Réadban that lives on in his grandson Rathbod."

After that, his voice grew so hushed that Kristinge could no longer hear without stepping closer. Yet he had heard enough. In a sullen mood that matched Willimond's, he walked with the older monk back down to the ship with the chieftain's words ringing in his ears. *Alas, the line of Finn is now gone...*

The next day, they encountered more hard northern winds mixed with a cold rain. Though it did not halt their voyage, they were not able to venture far out into the offing. Travel was slow and miserable. Not for the first time on the voyage, Kristinge was on the verge of seasickness in the long rolling swells inside the Frisian islands. The rain trailed off by noon, but the winds only grew colder. It was already approaching dusk when the boats turned into a large, sheltered bay. Further back in the ship, Kristinge overheard the steersman talking with Wyndlaf.

"The Beowic terp is old and high. I could use a dry night. Besides, three of the sailors have families there."

"We will stop at Beowic on the return voyage," Wyndlaf answered him, "but in the morning I would send a message to Ezinge. Let us stay at Hwitstanwic instead—near the old ruins of Finnsburg."

Finnsburg? The word hung frozen in the wind, and Kristinge's heart began to pound with dread. Finnsburg. This was his home. It *had been* his home long ago. But now...? Now...?

"Only if we must," the younger trader was saying. "The place still stinks of death."

"You never saw it during its prime, in the days of Finn," Wyndlaf replied, almost wistfully. "Though not like the Frankish palaces of Paris and St. Denis for grandness, it was a warm hall with a hearty fire and good beer. Finn was a generous lord."

"Well he's dead now," the other grumbled.

Kristinge could not see Wyndlaf's expression, but he could feel his own body tensing with emotions he could not even identify. He was caught between an urge to curse the young steersman who had spoken so callously, and a desire to turn the ship around and head back to Paris.

"Think what you may," Wyndlaf finally said. "The beaches there are good, and there is a high hill. You'll be plenty dry. There are even a few abandoned huts that survived the fire. We'll be able to sleep under a roof."

The other's grumbling reply, Kristinge did not hear. He was overwhelmed with trepidation, and for a long time was unaware even of the lash of wind on his neck or the icy spray against his face. Some time later, the two ships slid onto the sandy beaches of Hwitstanwic. Kristinge sat huddled, unmoving, for many long moments while the sailors around him stepped ashore. When he finally rose, he was trembling. Whether from the cold or from fear of what he might find, he did not know. He found Willimond waiting for him a few yards up the beach. Under the light of the rising moon, the older monk's face looked pale. Neither spoke a word. They had not seen the village since its destruction, and Kristinge was afraid to face what he knew awaited him. In silence they climbed the hill past the ruins of what had once been the tower Finnweard, and descended down the back side into the rubble of Hwitstan.

Tears were streaming down Kristinge's face before he even reached the bottom. Despite all his foreknowledge of the loss that awaited him, the sight was still shocking. Most of the buildings had been torn apart or burned to the ground. Scarred human skeletons in grotesque death poses, their flesh long ago picked apart by birds, dotted the ground, some still clutching their makeshift weapons. Only a few of the sunken houses with turf walls had survived the flames. Miraculously, two or three of the huts still possessed remnants of their roofs, but even these turf skeletons only made the scene more depressing. Without the great mead hall, the village was forlorn. Yet where Finnsburg had once stood, proudly guarding its town, there now lay just a scattering of ash. Only the huge hearthstone and a few charred beams remained in the center of the village, buried in ash beneath the burnt ruins of the roof.

Willimond did not stay long. After a passing glance at the remains of Finnsburg, he passed through the village and around the pond, walking slowly but steadily to the spot where his church had stood. Kristinge paused only a moment longer to look upon the ruins of the great hall of Finnsburg, and then ran to catch up with Willimond. As they expected, the church too had been burned. The Danes had spared little. Kristinge came up behind Willimond who stood over what had once been the door of his chapel. In the moonlight, Kristinge could see the tears on the older monk's face. Putting his own confused thoughts aside for the moment, he placed his hand on Willimond's shoulder, offering what comfort he could. He could see Willimond gaining strength before he stepped through the now imaginary doors. Somehow, though his pulpit had been destroyed, a few of the benches had survived the fire. The monks sat for a long time just staring at the emptiness in front of them. Finally, Kristinge pulled his heavy blanket from his pack and stretched out on a bench. He fell asleep with Willimond still sitting up beside him.

When Kristinge awoke in the morning, Willimond was gone. He arose, splashed water on his face, and then went in search of his friend. He found Willimond sitting down by the river looking out over the tidal water. "Our weirs," Willimond said, pointing out into the river at a couple timbers that marked where they had once been. Since returning to Friesland, they had taken to speaking to one another in the Frisian tongue, in part for the practice but more than anything so that they would not be perceived as strangers. Now Kristinge's native tongue was beginning to feel native again, and he was glad that Willimond continued the practice even when they were alone. Somehow, the speaking of Frisian felt more natural on that soil than did Latin. It was an honoring of their former home.

"The tides have taken them now," Willimond continued, "but once they supplied much of the village with fish."

Kristinge sat down beside his former mentor. As much as he grieved to see for the first time the ruins of his former home, he knew that Willimond was grieving the more.

"Did I ever tell you of when I first came to Hwitstan?" Willimond asked. Kristinge shook his head and waited for the story. "My first friend here was a fisherman named Lopystre. The weir-tender. Do you remember him?" He didn't wait for an answer. "I arrived here late in the evening on a trading ship, just as we did last night, only then it was a Saxon ship that had come from the Isles. And once they let me off here, I was on my own. I was about the same age you are now.

"Anyway, when I arose in the morning I had nothing to put on but my cold, wet cloak. Nonetheless, I went out in search of the king. And the first thing I did was trip and fall flat on my face in the mud and dung, covering myself with filthy stink that almost made me vomit. What do I see when I lift my head from the ground? Who was there looking at me but Ulestan and young Finnlaf. What a sight I was. Covered in filth, wet to the bone—not to mention my tonsure which was a new sight to these Germanic folk who honor the long hair. A fool I made of myself. I think God was teaching me some of the humility I would need for His work. It was a hard thing for me just to rise and face them then. But somehow I managed."

He paused for a moment, and gazed out over the water. Without looking at Kristinge, he continued. "Well after a short dialogue with Ulestan, I decided I ought to clean myself off. Wanting to avoid further blunders, I thought better of bathing in the pond in the middle of the village, so I came down the hill to the river. And there were Lopystre, Lindlaf and Lawyrke out in the cold water working the weirs. Just as I arrived, Lopystre was struggling to drag onto shore a net laden with fish. Well I had worked weirs as a child in Iona, and I immediately jumped into the water—I was going to wash anyway," he laughed, "—and I started to help. That was the beginning of a long friendship."

"I remember Lopystre," Kristinge said, when the story was finished. "And Lindlaf also. Lawyrke I do not remember."

"He drowned in the weirs one day. His foot got caught when nobody was around to help."

"I remember now," Kristinge said. "He had a son my age."

"Yes," Willimond answered. "Did you know that I lived with Lopystre's family until the church was built?"

"It was a beautiful church," Kristinge said, watching Willimond's face closely.

Willimond's eyes had now begun to well with tears, though he was struggling to control them. "In its way, it was. I have seen many grander in the days since I departed, but I have not seen any I have loved more. For it was the people here who made it grand. A small congregation it was, to be sure. As long as Finn clung stubbornly to his pagan ways, his folk were slow to follow the Cross. But there were some who believed, and they were beautiful. Lopystre and his family served the Lord with such joy—his wife Berigyldan with her quiet hospitality, and tall Lindlaf. I can still see the face of his young daughter Blostma when I baptized her. 'Momma, I'm a heathen now!' she sputtered happily as she stepped from the pond."

Kristinge raised his eyebrows in surprise, but Willimond smiled despite the tears that were now flowing freely down his face. "That was the word Finn used to describe those who did not believe in the Frisian gods: *heathens*. From his point of view, unbelievers. Though I suppose the word is not accurate. If anything, those *from the heath* were even less willing to give up their beliefs in the Frisian gods and follow Christ. But for Finn, 'heathen' was a term of contempt—a name for a fool who doesn't know better. *Paganus* we would say in Latin. Blostma must have known it was a name of derision, but she accepted it."

Willimond stopped suddenly, and shook with two heavy sobs. He began speaking against almost at once, in a disciplined effort to maintain his composure. "And Lawyrklaf," he said. "Even after his father died he did not lose his joy in life. The Lord bless and keep his whole family. It was a small flock, but God loved them. I wonder to this day if any of them survive. Does a spark of faith dwell anywhere in this land? Was all my work in vain?"

Kristinge knew that Willimond was referring to the pagan idols he had seen in the homes of former believers—not just in Wijnaldum, but in every village they had stopped at throughout all of Friesland. He knew the sorrow in his former teacher's heart. But he could not let the statement go without a response. He confronted Willimond, as the other had so often confronted him. "Vain?" he asked. "Do you call what you did for Lopystre vain?"

"It is all gone now."

"And not Lopystre only," Kristinge went on, ignoring the comment. "His whole family. And Ulestan, whom you brought up from the pit. Where would he have been without you? And Daelga the poet. And the queen herself, Hildeburh, my mother. All of them.

And me. Where would we all be without you?"

"Had God sent somebody stronger—"

"But He sent *you*. He knew your weaknesses as well as your strength, and He chose you. And for that choice He had a purpose. 'For the sake of those who are chosen, I also endure these things—'"

"'That they may obtain the Salvation that comes with Christ,'" Willimond finished. "'And with it, eternal glory.'" He paused and inhaled a long deep breath. "Come, my young friend. You have lifted my heart. Let us depart from here." They rose and together walked down the river and along the beach to where the sailors were already preparing the ships for departure.

"I wondered if you had been taken by the ghosts that haunt this place," one of the merchants said. "We were getting ready to leave without you."

"I thought you were sending a message to Ezinge," Kristinge said.

"We are, but Ezinge is far to go on foot, and winter is fast approaching. We have not the time to wait for an reply. My brother will stay there until we return. The rest of us will depart."

A short time later, they were sailing out of Hwitstanwic into the reflection of the rising sun. Though he wasn't sure why, Kristinge was glad to be sailing out of Friesland. With the exception of one night in Frotha's hall and his brief encounter with Aewin, all he had seen so far of his former homeland had served only to depress and discourage him. And also to raise more fears about what he would find when he returned for good. What would he say to Réadban and Aldgisl if he met them? And what would he learn of Aewin? Had she indeed become more unreachable than ever? And more beautiful?

The merchants were in a hurry now. They did not stop long at any villages, and though the amount of sunlight grew less with each passing day, the hours of travel were long. The first day out of Hwitstan took them as far as the mouth of the Ems river, and to another important trading community built on the terps. On the third day from Hwitstan, they reached the Weser river. Now, Kristinge knew, they were approaching an end of the Frisian territories and the beginning of the Danish and Jutish lands. Many Saxon clans still dwelt here also. On the forth day out from Hwitstan, they finally reached the Elbe river, which was nearly as long as the Rhine. It also marked the farthest boundary of Friesland, and even there the Saxon and Danish influences were dominant. Though the village was large, the surrounding territory was wild.

After the Elbe, the coast turned sharply to the north. They were sailing along Danemark now. A large remnant of the Angles still dwelt there on the shores, along with Jutish tribes, but all under submission to the ruling Danes. Here Willimond fared well, for he remembered much of the Saxon dialect from his days at Lindisfarne. They worked their way up the coast fighting against the prevailing winds and weather that worsened daily. On the sixth day out of Hwitstan, it snowed all day. The merchants were looking nervous now, and Kristinge could tell they were eager to turn back to the south. At the end of the fourth day after the Elbe river and the eighth since Hwitstan, they reached a sheltered harbor with a large Jutish village. When morning arrived to reveal an inch of fresh snow on the ground, they made their decision.

CHAPTER 8:
ᴛʜᴇ ʜᴏᴄʟɪɴɢᴇѕ

As he stood next to the ship, shivering, looking down at the layer of fresh snow atop the cargo, Kristinge heard Wyndlaf speak the words he had been fearing. "We go no further. We will trade with the Jutish merchants here. Our profit might be greater further north among the Danes, but..." He didn't finish the sentence but merely looked toward the sky and shrugged as if he didn't need to explain. He spoke with resolve. "Tomorrow we sail southward and homeward."

No, Kristinge wanted to object. They were only on the southern edge of the Danish rule, among the Jutes and mixed clans. As he had learned from the traders, the Hoclinges dwelt further north by many days. A journey on foot in this wild and unknown territory would be difficult and dangerous. They were too far from their destination to be abandoned now. But the trader read the look in Kristinge's eyes and forestalled objection. "Winter is upon us. We will go no farther. Already we have risked our boats and lives traveling this far north so late in the autumn. If you wish to continue, you will have to journey on foot. Or you can find a Danish ship more familiar with these waters."

Kristinge's felt his heart sink. Not for the first time since his departure from Luxeuil, doubt began to creep over him—doubt that he might never find his mother, and that the voyage was too great for him. But he staved off his despair. Perhaps the trader was right. A Danish ship could be the answer. He turned his gaze back toward the beach, forgetting already how much he loathed travel by sea. Wyndlaf, however, was not finished. He leaned closer as the young monk stood scanning the shoreline and began speaking with Willimond. "You have paid your fare. Go among this folk as you please. You have not sought my council."

Kristinge understood at once that Wyndlaf was offering advice. Since having attained the stature of a bard, he had found the sailors friendlier and more willing to bestow their wisdom—whether it was sought or not. And at the moment, the monks were not in a position to refuse any aid. Kristinge spun around at once, even as Willimond nodded for Wyndlaf to continue.

"If you ask me, I wouldn't ride with these *Vikings*."

"You don't trust their ships?" Kristinge asked, plying for any scrap of information he might use.

"Their ships? There are none better. The Danes are masters of their craft without questions. Their *ships* are as sound and solid as a tree itself—and they know how to sail them."

"Then what?" Kristinge wondered aloud.

Wyndlaf leaned even closer. "They're *warriors*, not traders, these Danes are. I wouldn't feel safe with them. No. If you *really* want my advice, turn around and return to Friesland. Forsake this barren land. Come back with us to Ezinge. We have visited more than one chieftain who would take a good bard like you. Indeed, you could find no more generous treasure-giver than Frotha himself. Come. We have room in our ships and would charge no more fare. You've got Frisian blood in you, I can tell."

Kristinge stared mutely, his thoughts paralyzed. *Turn back?* This was not the advice he needed. What could he do? He was not yet ready for his return to Friesland. Yet to be left in Danemark...

It was Willimond who answered the trader. "For the safe passages as well as for the generosity and wisdom of your warnings, we thank you. But we will continue if we can find a way."

Wyndlaf shrugged again and stepped back. "Do you know where you go?" He asked in a more distant tone. "How far? Where you will winter?" Then once again his voice lowered. Though the monks had not worn their robes in many days, the traders knew what they were. "Christian monks have not fared well here."

This time Willimond looked at Kristinge for an answer. "We do not know how far," Kristinge replied, finding his thoughts and tongue again. Cautiously he added, "We are looking for somebody. A Dane."

Now the trader's curiosity and nose for information were aroused. "Searching? For whom? A chieftain? Another monk? In this I might be able to help. I have traveled among the Danes before. We have traded in many Danish villages. I know most of the clans and their chieftains."

Kristinge hesitated. The name of Hildeburh would arouse suspicion. He looked around. There were no Danes or Jutes within hearing distance. Though Kristinge placed little faith in the ability of a merchant, even a fellow Frisian, to hold his tongue, he wondered if he had any choice. *Was it worth the risk? What if the trader really did have information? What else could Kristinge do?* "We are looking for Hildeburh, your former queen," he finally said. "We have heard rumor that she still lives."

At the mention of that name, the merchant's eyes narrowed and he looked Kristinge over more carefully. "If I didn't know better..." he started, but didn't finish. "Monks from Luxeuil, you say? And yet you speak the Frisian dialect like natives."

Under the trader's penetrating stare, Kristinge began to grow nervous. Had he made a mistake and compromised his identity? How much would the trader guess? He was glad when Willimond broke the silence. "We have been to Friesland before. In Hwitstan, I served the queen for many years as her priest. We have heard she still lives. As her former priest, I would see her again. We departed from Hwitstan only a few months before the Battle of Finnsburg—"

"Not a good event to speak of here," the trader interrupted with a cautioning word.

"We understand well," Willimond went on more softly. "That is why we are asking *you* where we might find her. As a Frisian, we hoped you might help—"

Again Wyndlaf interrupted. "I also heard this rumor, the same as you. It is said to have come from some who survived the pillage. But nobody I spoke to had themselves met any survivors, and so I did not at first believe. You have seen Hwitstan yourselves. There was little left after the second battle. Finnsburg is in ashes. It is hard to believe any endured the fury of the Danes on that day." Kristinge's heart sank. His hope faltered further and he wondered if Abbess Telchild had been mistaken. But the trader was not finished. "No. I was slow to believe such a thing, until I saw the queen myself."

Now the young monk took a sharp breath. Excitement rose in his chest. "Hildeburh? In Friesland?"

The merchant shook his head. "Not in Friesland. After the battle of Finnsburg she was taken back to Danemark by her people. I saw her two summers ago when I was trading farther north. She had seen I was Frisian and came to speak with me. She asked me about Friesland. Bought some cloth from me. That was all. I only know that she is still alive. Or at least that she was alive two years ago. I have not seen her since."

"Is she well?" Kristinge asked, unable to hide his interest.

"She looked well," the trader answered, once again watching Kristinge closely. "Though I don't know how free she is. After the death of their chieftains, her clan was somewhat inhospitable toward Frisians. Even toward traders. It was three years after the battle before I even ventured north again."

"Do you know *where* she is?" Willimond asked.

"The Hoclinges are her clan. They dwell in two coastal villages in the summer, one north of here a day's journey by boat, and another on the Baltic sea south of Geatland and Swedeland. In the winter they move inland. Best inquire of the villagers here. Do you speak the Danish dialect?"

"Some," Kristinge answered. He was thinking more of Willimond's capacity than his own. The Saxon spoken at Lindisfarne by the elder monk in his youth was close to the Jutish and Danish dialects. Even Kristinge had discovered that Jutish was not so different from Frisian, and he guessed he could get used to the Danish dialect.

"Ask for the Hoclinges," the trader said softly. "That is the queen's clan. The people here should know where they winter."

For the third time, Kristinge and Willimond thanked Wyndlaf for his help. Then, ever more eager to find his mother, Kristinge led the way into the village. It didn't take long to find Danish traders who knew the land. They were a rough looking lot. Dressed in poorly-tanned fur hides, with bare arms, long braided hair, and shaggy beards, they appeared more like mercenaries than merchants. Nor did the Danish battle-axes, visible at their belts, bolster Kristinge's confidence. But he and Willimond knew they had little choice but to seek help. Praying silently, they approached.

Despite Kristinge's reservations, the band proved amiable enough to the strangers. When they heard that Kristinge was looking for the Hoclinges, they grew more friendly still. "We serve Fjorgest, a Hoclinges chieftain," their leader said.

"Is Hengest still king?" Willimond asked.

The trader looked him over. "Irish?" he asked.

"Half," Willimond answered.

Kristinge winced. He knew as well as Willimond that purity of blood was highly valued among the northern tribes, and that mixed-breeds were disdained. Nonetheless, the answer was true, and safer than telling a Hocling that they were from Hwitstan. Or that they were monks.

"And you," he said to Kristinge. "You have Danish blood in your veins." It was a comment, not a question.

"Half," Kristinge echoed, following Willimond's lead in accepting disdain rather than giving up too much information.

"Two halflings, eh? Traders?"

"We've come from southern Francia," Willimond replied, neither lying nor answering the question.

The Danish trader laughed. "Men of few words. I like that. It'll make you easier to travel with."

"Then you will guide us?"

"You are looking for the Hoclinges? We leave for their villages today. Four days of hard travel, but if you can keep up we'll guide you—for a price, of course."

"How much?" Kristinge asked, too eagerly for one hoping to strike a good bargain.

The trader looked them over, as if guessing how much they could pay. "Ten Danish silvers. For that, we'll guide you, guard you, and feed you." He laughed and put his hands on his own healthy girth. "You look as though you could use some more food than you've been getting."

"I have only four," Kristinge answered. "But I can add two Romans." He was trying to bargain the traders down. The Roman coins weighed more than the Danish, but not three times as much.

"It is settled. We leave after our meal."

An hour later, Kristinge and Willimond found the traders packing up their belongings near the edge of the village. There were twelve of them in the band, and it was difficult to tell who was the leader. All of them looked equally rough. Kristinge decided that if he was safe from *them*, he was probably safe from anything. They looked the match for any bandits they might encounter. With a reassuring nod from Willimond, Kristinge swallowed his anxiety and the two of them fell in with their newest guides. Before the sun had reached its peak, they were hiking northeastward into the interior of Danemark.

As Kristinge had been promised, the going was not easy. Though there were signs that other traders had traveled that overland route, there was little that could have been called a road. They were not far out of the village before Kristinge was fighting his way over rough terrain. Bushes and small scraggly trees cluttered the landscape, tearing at the legs of any who wandered too close. Numerous streams and brooks crossed their way. And where the ground was open, it was strewn with small boulders and loose stones that were difficult on the footing. To make matters worse, snow fell on and off all afternoon, accumulating little but making for cold travel and slippery ground. Having been confined to a wagon or boat since leaving Gundomer's house weeks earlier, Kristinge was out of condition for such work. He struggled to keep up the brisk pace set by the leaders of the Danish party—who to his dismay were not the least hampered by either weather or rough ground—and was winded before they had gone more than a few miles.

"Keep it up. This will be good for us," Willimond said softly in Kristinge's ear. Despite his age, the older monk showed no sign of fatigue. Ashamed of his own weakness, Kristinge renewed his determination and kept going. Fortunately, though the way was tough, the guides were as skilled and knowledgeable as promised. On several occasions they found trails through thickets, or discovered shallow fords over rivers where Kristinge would have found nothing. In that alone, they earned the fee they had charged. They were also loose with their tongues, speaking freely and loudly of various happenings in Danemark. The monks soon learned which chieftains were gaining or losing power, which trade-routes had been profitable, and where they thought strife was due to break out. One of the first things they heard was that the Hoclinges no longer held much power. The battle of Finnsburg had cost them dearly, and though Hengest had won the day he had lost many warriors. He was unable to stand up to a challenge the following year, and fell in battle to a rival chieftain. His brother Fjorgest was now the chieftain of the Hoclinges, but he paid tribute to another more powerful Spear-Dane. What to make of this news, Kristinge did not know, but like all that he heard he locked it in his mind.

The second day was a little easier than the first. The sky was overcast but it did not snow. The traders awoke at first light and started at once with a pace almost as swift as that of the previous day. By day's end, Kristinge was exhausted. Nonetheless, on the second night he took up his harp and sang, hoping for a response like he had received among the Frisian traders. Whether due to his own impatient mood, or the disposition of the company to whom he sang, or the less familiar dialect, or simply the effect of cold dry air on his voice and harp, however, the Danish company was not as enthusiastic as Kristinge's earlier audiences. Thus he did not sing for very long. On the third night there were no requests for his harp, nor did any of the traders ask if he was a bard. And after a hard day of hiking, he felt little like singing to an unappreciative audience.

At noon of the fourth day, the company finally came to the first of the Hoclinges villages. It was small settlement. No more than a dozen huts dotted the side of a low hill, with nothing resembling a mead hall or chieftain's home. Nonetheless, Kristinge's excitement was mounting. He had been waiting for too long. He could barely contain himself as they passed the first huts. His eyes darted around from house to house searching for Hildeburh, however unlikely that might be. But the village was quiet and nearly empty, and the traders did not stop. They greeted a few villagers they saw and continued through, and Kristinge's heart sank. A short time later they reached another small settlement, and again Kristinge's hopes rose. And again, to his disappointment, they passed through without stopping. Doubts began to rise. He had given no thought to how he would find his mother once he arrived in Danemark. Would he even recognize her after so many years? Would she recognize him? He hadn't even considered that there would be many Hoclinges villages. In which did she dwell? Perhaps he had passed her already. Even now, each step might be carrying him farther from her rather than closer. He felt like Orpheus of Virgil's tale, not knowing whether each step brought him closer or farther from his beloved Eurydice. This was almost more than Kristinge could bear. Yet he kept moving, glad that the monks of Luxeuil had valued not only the Gospels but also the Greek myths.

Still, even with Virgil's hero in his mind, with each step his mixed sense of dread and anticipation grew. The late afternoon light faded quickly, but the company marched onward. The sky above was clear and the air sharp. The traders talked enthusiastically among themselves as they went. Kristinge could sense in their voices that they were almost home. But what would that mean for him?

Evening was upon them and the sun barely above the horizon before they reached the next settlement. At first it did not look large, and Kristinge feared it was another small outlying village. His patience was nearly exhausted. As he walked past the first few houses and around a small knoll, he was relieved to see that it was larger than the previous two villages. Unlike the villages of Francia and Friesland where the dwellings radiating outward in circles around a central mead hall—with perhaps a small wall around the outermost dwellings—he found instead a long narrow strip of buildings scattered haphazardly for some distance along a central ox-road and so it wasn't apparent just how big the village was. He also had to look more closely before he realized that the houses, too, were bigger than they had first appeared. With good timber rarer in Danemark and more likely to be used in ships than houses, most of the dwellings were of stone and turf, and had been built narrow and long to allow for shorter roof beams. After Kristinge had passed some fifteen such houses, and several more still stretched before him including a larger mead hall, he realized it was a sizable settlement, with near as many inhabitants as Hwitstan in its prime—perhaps sixty or more houses and half as many livestock pens and other small structures. This must be the main village of the Hoclinges clan, he thought. He would find his mother here, or not at all.

By the time Kristinge had realized this, the first of the members of the small band to break away from his fellows turned in to one of the homes. A second later, another said a word of farewell to his companions and turned to another house. As if that were the spark setting a pile of dry wood a blaze, the whole band suddenly began dispersing. This was the end of the voyage. This time he was sure of it. His heart began to pound.

"Be careful," Willimond warned him. At the sound of the voice, Kristinge jumped. He was as tense as a bowstring. Willimond's hand was on his shoulder. Speaking in a low tone and in Latin to be doubly safe, the older monk went on. "It would be an odd sight were a stranger with Frisian blood and Frankish accent to come out of nowhere and embrace Hildeburh. Remember that she is of a chieftain's blood. And though your resemblance to Finn is not as great as was Finnlaf's, if there are any here who knew your father you could well be recognized." He paused and looked more closely at Kristinge as if seeing him for the first time. "For that matter, you look startling like your mother. I know not if any blood-feud yet remains, or if they consider the weregild paid with the death of Finn and Finnlaf, but do not forget that the Danes believe *your* brother killed their former chieftain, Hnaef."

Kristinge nodded, trying to take to heart Willimond's warning and to conceal his excitement. But how was he *not* to show affection for a long-lost mother? A mother whom he had never known—never known and always known. Many months of tension and longing were compressed into this moment. Kristinge was a wave that had rolled in from far out to sea, and was now on the verge of cresting.

Yet the wave only kept building, towering ever higher. It did not break. There was no shore. For there was no sight of Hildeburh. Why would there be? Had he expected to see her standing out in the village waiting for him? On they marched through the village, with the band of traders disappearing around them, making their way to various houses where they were greeted by family, until by the time they reached the far end of the settlement only the two of them remained. Then, for the first time, Kristinge really understood the possibility that his mother no longer lived—a possibility that until that moment had been but meaningless words in the mouths of strangers, but was now threatening to be a reality. He had given no thought to how he would actually *find* her once they arrived in Danemark.

"What do we do now?" Willimond asked, when they had come to a stop at the far end of the settlement.

Kristinge almost burst at the question. *I die.* But he held his tongue, blinked the tears back in his eyes, and forced himself to think. There was no sign of Hildeburh. Yet that meant nothing, he told himself. There were a thousand places she *might* be, and still be *alive.* He looked around. The village looked nearly empty now. It was almost dark. Only a few peasants were still working around the fringes of the settlement. Back in the center of the village, a handful of warriors gathered in the twilight around the door of a large hall. Kristinge's eyes were drawn there. The only large building in the village, it had to be the hall of the chieftain—the mead hall. *Could there be a better place to find his mother?*

"I do not know what to do," Kristinge admitted with a sigh, finally answering Willimond's question. "I confess I had given little thought to how we would find her once we made it this far. My thoughts had only been to find this village. I suppose it would not be wise to ask for her." He knew before it was spoken what Willimond's response would be, but he had run out of ideas.

"No," Willimond answered abruptly, putting the suggestion out of the question. "Not wise at all. And yet, we can hardly remain inconspicuous for long. They cannot help but to have noticed two strangers walking through the village." He too was staring back toward the village in the direction of the hall as he continued his thought. "Even now the chieftain is questioning the traders about who we are, and they are telling him first what they know, and then what they have guessed." He did not pause long before he made the suggestion Kristinge knew would be coming. "Perhaps you would be well-advised to take up again the role of bard."

"Ha," Kristinge said, though there was little laughter in his mood. "After my performance among that band I doubt such a claim would be taken seriously." But in his mind he was pondering the more serious problem: despite several weeks of travel with his harp, he had not yet acquired the true bard's repertoire. How long until he ran out of songs? Would he be able to compose new ones fast enough?

Willimond smiled. "Even the best bards fall short at times. Be glad it happened when it did. There are heathen kings and chieftains who would kill a bard for displeasing them."

Kristinge did not return the smile. He was still thinking about how poorly received his songs were among the Danish traders. "I do not know what it is best to sing among the pagans," he admitted. "Am I truly a bard, as you have begun to call me? Or an apostle—an evangelist?"

Willimond was silent for a time. When he spoke, his voice was low and tentative. "Maybe we have been speaking the church's Latin for too long."

Kristinge raised a curious brow. Was the older monk speaking metaphorically? Or literally? Or both?

"At Luxeuil we spoke of the *evangelium*: the good *message*," Willimond explained. "But in the native tongues of our Saxon and Frisian kin—and your Danish kin, too, I would guess—we would speak instead of the *gód spel*."

Kristinge did not need an explanation. "The good *story*," he said. He had never before considered the difference between the two words, for in his mind they both refered to the same thing. But there was a difference, and he knew his native tongue well enough to know it.

"Yes, the good story. It is a message, that is true. And a good one. Both true and joyful. Death has been conquered. What greater message could there be? And what a delight to be the messengers. But the heart of that message is more than an idea. It is a story. So the translation from Latin to these Germanic tongues—for the 'good message' to the 'good story'—is appropriate. We tell the good *story*."

Kristinge nodded. "Yes, it is a story." He paused. "But what makes a story good?"

At this Willimond smiled. "That is a question. A story, I think, like a message, can be good because it is true. Indeed, there are ancient poets who say that truth can only be found in story. Does not God himself speaks to us in story? And a story can be good because— well, because it has a joyful ending; because it gives reason to turn our weeping into dancing. But I think a story can be good in other ways too. It can be good because it is beautiful." He paused, and Kristinge could see his eyes staring off into the distance as though seeing something far away or remembering something long past. "The monks at Lindisfarne had a vision. They wanted to make copies of the ancient texts—even God's own word; especially God's word—that were beautiful just to look at. So that there would be beauty in the colors and the shapes and the images, as well as in the words. For all beauty, at its deepest, is goodness. It is truth. And I think God is pleased in that beauty and goodness."

Though the idea was not new to him, something about the moment, about the past few days and weeks, or simply about the way Willimond was speaking reached Kristinge perhaps for the first time. "So a beautiful story is a good story." He didn't wait for Willimond to answer. "There is, I think, a certain beauty in the old pagan lays. It is a cold harsh northern beauty, full of the lies and false myths of their gods, but it is a beauty nonetheless and one that reflects truth. That much, if nothing else, I learned from Daelga. Could not the evangelium itself—the *gód spel*—be captured in these tales, and brought to life in a new way?"

He began to turn the idea over in his mind. He did not know yet the fruit it might later bear, but if nothing else, it was good to put his mind on concerns other than finding his mother. "You know, when I told the tale of Daniel before Clovis' throne, I felt as though I was almost there. However angry he was, something about that tale moved him. Had it not, he would have killed me. Could the tale have been made more..." he paused. "More Germanic? More Frankish? Or, for the Danes, more Norse? And yet still be the same tale?"

"That is a difficult question," Willimond replied after a moment's thought. "It is thought to be one of the greatest sins to change the Word of God—to add or remove even the smallest word. And yet did not Jesus himself bring his preaching to the people with a language and stories they could understand? Can the stories change and yet remain the same? I do not know. Saint Paul found truth even in the myths and poems and prophecies of the Greeks. He used those tales to speak the truth in Athens. If you succeeded at such a task here among the Danes, you would have a lifetime of songs. I wish Walbert were with us."

Now Kristinge did laugh. "What a scene we are, standing in the desolate wastes of Danemark discussing difficult questions of

Christian teaching that nobody within a five days journey could care about. Could any doubt that we are monks? Come. Let us return to the hall. Let us meet this chieftain Fjorgest. I will take up the harp and see what the Lord will provide for us."

Now it was Willimond who stood staring at Kristinge. "My friend and son, you speak in a voice and with a tone I have never before heard from you. Could it be you have grown so much in just a few days?"

"Grown? Certainly not. The only thing I have grown is cold and hungry, standing at the edge of the village. My thoughts have turned to fire and food. If I can earn us these things with my harp and voice, praise God. If not, better to find out soon while we still have a few coins left."

Together, they turned back toward the village and began walking in the direction of the chieftain's hall. But there was something else on Kristinge's mind—something he hadn't told Willimond. Truly he desired more than anything else to find his mother. Yet if Willimond was right, it would not be safe for him to seek her. What else could he do, then, except make himself as visible as possible as soon as possible? And how better to do this than as a bard? If he couldn't find Hildeburh, let her find him.

If she was still alive.

It didn't take long for Kristinge and Willimond to find the Hoclinges' chieftain Fjorgest, though at first they did not know they had found him. He was standing near the entrance of his hall, talking and laughing with a dozen other men, all warriors. They were dressed in heavy wool tunics and trousers. A few had fur cloaks thrown over their shoulders. Save for the gold necklace and gold armbands, Fjorgest did not stand out. He was about the same height as the others, and median in age. And when Kristinge asked for him, he did not at first identify himself.

"Who are you?" he said gruffly and in a thick Danish accent that Kristinge had to work to understand.

"A traveling bard," Kristinge answered. "We have journeyed from Francia."

Fjorgest's eyes narrowed and Kristinge guessed from his expression what he was thinking. A Frankish bard showing up in a northern

Danish village made for a strange and implausible story. "And you?" the chieftain asked Willimond.

"I was his tutor once."

Fjorgest snorted contemptuously. "You are far from your home. That much I hear in your voices."

"I have spent my life traveling," Willimond replied. "Danemark is no further from the western coast of Britain than southern Francia is."

"A Saxon?"

"Irish and Celt," Willimond replied, repeating the answer he had given to the traders four days earlier.

The chieftain, Kristinge guessed, had already learned as much from the chief trader. Still, he turned to Kristinge. "And you, bard?"

"I am told I have some Danish blood."

"That may be," the chieftain replied, looking him over. He still had not identified himself. "If you are a good enough bard, I will not care what kind of blood you have. But if you are not, we will examine your blood by spilling it. I am not a patient chieftain."

At that, several of his thanes laughed. Kristinge, however, was concentrating on understanding the heavy dialect, and he missed the veiled threat. He had noticed the gold necklaces and armbands around the chieftain's neck. "You are Fjorgest?"

"I am."

"And you are seeking the service of a bard?"

"Sceaptung, my *skald*, has a voice like a sore goat. And I have just *lost* the service of my former bard."

As Kristinge had earlier learned, it was not uncommon for a Danish village to have both a bard and skald. Their functions, though similar, were not the same. A bard was a singer of songs. He was a musician, a tale-teller, a writer of poems, and most importantly an entertainer. A skald on the other hand was an *historian*. He was the historian of the *gods*, remembering their tales that they could be passed from generation to generation. Consequently, a skald was an historian of his people as well. The fate of the folk, after all, was never far from the fate of their gods—Midgard and Asgard, the land of the people and the land of the gods. So the Danes believed. Of course the best skalds were often gifted bards as well, but it was not necessary for the vocation. As often as not, skalds were chosen for political or religious reasons rather than for any skill or talent. The priests had as much influences as the chieftain in appointing the skald. Thus it was that Kristinge was not bothered by the mention of a skald. "So you are without a bard?" he asked again, his hope rising.

"My former bard did not serve me well," Fjorgest replied, fingering his battle-ax. "He has gone where he will trouble no more chieftains."

This time, Kristinge did not miss the gesture. He swallowed hard, but thinking still of his mother he pressed his offer. "Then allow me to enter your service."

"That I will do," Fjorgest replied. Now the chieftain smiled for the first time. "The gods have been good to me today. No sooner do I lose one bard to the misfortunes of the trade than another arrives to take his place. And on the very day I return to Heort from my coastal hall. We will feast tonight. And you will be our bard. Let the skald croak with the chickens."

Kristinge bowed low. "I am honored," he said, but Fjorgest had disappeared into the hall.

The short days and long nights of the northern winter were fast approaching. By the time they finished the conversation with Fjorgest, stars were shining in the sky and the warriors were already gathering in the hall. It would not be long before the celebration began. The monks walked to the edge of the village to spend a few moments in prayer together, then returned to the door. For all his boldness before Fjorgest, Kristinge had once again grown afraid and was beginning to doubt the wisdom of his offer. Perhaps there was another way he might find his mother. But Willimond did not allow a delay. "Let us see what the Lord brings us now," he said quietly. "Perhaps we will find Hildeburh tonight. Only do not forget your caution. Be patient and allow the Lord to work." Then, seeing Kristinge's fear, Willimond put a hand on his younger companions shoulder. "God is with you. Do not be afraid."

Kristinge nodded. There was more at stake on this night than any other since their departure from Luxeuil. Yet at Willimond's words, Kristinge sensed a strange peace settling over him. The nervousness that had been threatening him suddenly dwindled, or was at least held at bay for a time. With renewed resolve, he followed Willimond inside.

At once, Kristinge was assailed with warm smoky air, the smell of hearty drink, and the sound of many voices. He turned to Willimond, but his friend was already weaving his way along one wall toward an empty bench on the far side of the fire. Kristinge followed him more slowly, looking around as he went. It took many minutes to sort through all he saw. Unlike the elder monk who at times past had been close to the counsels of Finn, Kristinge had not often been inside Finnsburg, and never to share mead with the warriors. The manors of Frankish nobles where he had performed along the journey to Paris were sterile by contrast. Heort was a true mead hall in the northern tradition—the center of life in the clan village. Only Frotha's hall where he had sung for Aewin could compare. The chieftain Fjorgest was seated beside his hearth near the back center of the hall, still dressed as he had been a short time earlier. Filling the benches around him were forty or fifty of his warriors and thanes, talking with one another and laughing over loud stories and jokes. Though with the noise and the abundance of food and drink, Kristinge would not at first have thought of Luxeuil, in some ways the hall was more akin to his former monastery than to the palace and hall of Clovis. There was a warmth of fellowship and loyalty that was nearly palpable. These were men who had fought at each other's sides. Men who more than once had saved each other's lives. For a moment Kristinge almost forgot about Hildeburh as he wondered about their stories.

But he did not for long forsake his purpose. His eyes continued around the hall looking for some sign of her. There were women present there, though only a few. Some were the age of Telchild or Beatrice. A few were younger than himself, and for a moment Kristinge's thoughts again turned to Aewin. Had she dwelt in the village, she too would have been present at the hall. Here were the wives and daughters of the chieftains and influential thanes. Fjorgest's own wife was likely among them, and during the evening would speak to her husband's hearthwerod on behalf of the treasure-giver. But Kristinge didn't care about her now. He wondered only whether Hildeburh were among them. And whether he would recognize her if she were. His pulse was racing as he studied the faces of the women present. How much would she have changed in those six years?

Across the hall Willimond had found an empty seat. Before Kristinge could reach him, a pair of young thanes filled the bench beside the older monk. Disappointed that he had not seen his mother, Kristinge sighed silently, then looked for a bench for himself. The only empty seat he saw was closer to the hearth than he cared to be. Yet even as he thought this, Fjorgest caught sight of him and motioned for him to sit. Kristinge acquiesced and took a seat not far from the fire, near to the chieftain's right hand. He kept a tight grip on the harp in his lap, and thought about Aewin. He had not seen her since his departure from Frotha's hall. Even if her ship had continued behind his along the Frisian coast, he had now left it far behind. He would have to put the thought of her from his mind. He looked again toward Fjorgest's bench. Seated closest to the chieftain were two warriors, taller than the rest. Kristinge now saw that they also bore gold torcs about their necks and numerous rings on their arms. They must be chieftains of neighboring clans, though from the deference they showed to Fjorgest ie was clear they owed their allegiance to the Hoclinges' overlord. The two of them were speaking quietly with Fjorgest as Kristinge watched. A moment later, the treasure-giver rose to speak. Those who saw him rise, fell silent in anticipation.

"It is time for our hearts to be glad," Fjorgest began in a booming voice that brought instant silence to the rest of the hall. "It is time for the spirits of the Spear-Danes to rejoice, for our voices to be glad. To us has been given the joy of earth, a stronghold to protect us, and folk from afar who pay us tribute. Our enemies are silenced. Victory has been given in battle. And now comes winter and the warrior is home again, the shield hangs above the door, the sword-bearer sleeps with his wife." As the speech continued, Kristinge watched the chieftain closely, mesmerized by the authority in his voice. If Fjorgest was as mighty in battle as he was in voice, it was clear how he had become the ruler of the people.

The speech lasted several more minutes, though to Kristinge it did not seem long. As was the custom of chieftains, Fjorgest spoke words of welcome to the gathered company, and promised with astounding verbosity a great celebration including treasure-giving and praise for worthy thanes. Several of his thanes who had won particular glory in battle through the raiding season were mentioned right then—though afterwards Kristinge could not remember any of their names. Then Fjorgest ended with words of welcome to the chieftains who sat beside him, praising their strength and skill and promising friendship between their tribes. Kristinge later learned that younger one, Aesher, was Fjorgest's cousin and ruled over a coastal clan related to the Hoclinges. The other, Healfas, was a Jutish chieftain whose sister was married to Aesher and who paid tribute to the Hoclinges. Several of the warriors in the hall were thanes and retainers in the service of these other chieftains. When Fjorgest's welcoming speech was over, Aesher and Healfas spoke similar words to the gathered company though with greater brevity. They promised gifts to their own thanes, and also—as their treaty with Fjorgest demanded—gifts to the Hoclinges.

Then, when all three chieftains had spoken, the feasting began in earnest. At a word from Fjorgest, servants appeared from the back of the hall carrying great jugs of mead and beer. An enthusiastic cheer resounded as mugs and mead-cups were filled with the strong drink. "Fjorgest," the men shouted. And "Aesher", "Healfas", and "Love live the Gods." Then, while the beverage was still being poured, more servants entered bearing more hearty fare: boards of bread, cheese, and roasted grains along with dried fruits and salted meats and fish. The men cheered again, and attacked the plates of food as if they were looting a Saxon village. The women, too, took part in the feasting equally ravenously.

Kristinge, fearing his fingers would be hacked off if they got too close to the meat board, managed to stab a slab of cheese and some bread and sat silently chewing on them while the celebration raged around him. One thing about Fjorgest: he did not lack in generosity for his thanes. Though the food was not as tasty or extravagant as that served to the monks by Queen Balthild, at least Kristinge could see that there would be no shortage of it, nor of strong beverage nor treasure-giving. If he could earn the chieftain's favor with his barding, he would not lack food during the winter. Nonetheless, as the evening progressed he began slipping into a strangely solemn and heavy mood—a mood darker than he remembered in many months. It was not fear. After Willimond's assurance, he had entered the hall confident that night with a peace he was sure had come from God. Nor was it his failure to find his mother. Though he could not deny the initial disappointment, he was far from giving up hope. There was something more—more than his fatigue and the physical and emotional exhaustion of many days of travel. It was almost as if the celebration itself weighed upon him. It was a strange mix of fellowship, loyalty, and familiarity that Kristinge found seductively appealing, yet also appalling. It was a fellowship rooted in a warrior society where glory and status came from prowess in battle. From the ability to kill and not be killed. Here Kristinge was an outsider, excluded from the real celebration, desiring at once both to be accepted into it and to flee from it. More than once he thought to rise and find a seat at Willimond's side, but something kept him from moving. Food was again passed in his direction, but he no longer felt hungry. He ate nothing but the cheese and bread, and sat instead listening for fragments of conversation in the midst of the loud din of their collective voices.

Only when the feasting began to slow did Fjorgest's skald Sceaptung finally stand to speak. He was an unimpressive man—pale of skin, thin-haired, half a head shorter than Kristinge and many pounds lighter. As the chieftain had said, he was not among those skalds who were also gifted as bards. He had a droning voice like bleating goat. He was easy to ignore as he rambled on about the history of the Hoclinges and their gods in a fashion that gave more of a sense of duty and obligation than of joy in the telling. As for the stories themselves, they were dark and distressing and did nothing to lift Kristinge's mood. The young bard was left wondering how Sceaptung had avoided the same fate as Fjorgest's previous bard. When he could tolerate no more of the droning voice and disturbing tales, he tried to block out the sound from his ears and think ahead to the songs he himself would soon sing. But he could not concentrate. He was glad when the skald finished and sat down on his bench. Now Kristinge readied himself. Perhaps singing would break the gloom and lift his spirits.

when Fjorgest rose again, however, it was not to call upon his new bard but to give a speech of his own. "Bravest of warriors and mightiest of men," he began. All fell silent. "Hoclinges and War-Scyldings, glory is yours—glory in battle, and glory in peace. Table-companions, mead-fellows, and shoulder-comrades, strength belongs to you. The pride of the Spear-Danes, and the honor of those blessed by Thunar. Over the great Swan Road we have traveled in our ring-prowed ships, and we have returned laden with wealth. Far-away tribes have paid us tribute, and nearby clans have trembled with fear at the rumor of our coming. The wind that drives our sails is the wind of Woden himself, and the star Aurvandil shines brightly to lead us home."

As Kristinge sat and listened, he was again surprised by the loftiness and eloquence of Fjorgest's speech. This chieftain, whose *physical* stature was no more impressive than any of a dozen of the mightier warriors who surrounded him, spoke with the authority of a king and the voice of true bard. He put even his own skald to shame as he recounted, in a history fresh, potent, and poetic, the tales of their recent summer battles. He spoke in great detail of their plunder and warfare, of the strength and swiftness of his warriors as they slew their enemies, of the villages they had burned and raided, the treasure they had gained, and of his stout-hearted warriors who had been lost to Valhalla. And already he spoke of the glory that awaited them in the spring when the winter's snow melted—of the Frankish coast ripe for plundering. And ever the Danish eyes looked northward as well, to the great isle where the Angles and Saxons, having driven out the Britons and thrown back the Scots and Picts, were already growing soft in their new land. Listening to him tell of the successful season of raids, Kristinge almost could believe he was listening to Caesar himself, returned from the conquest of Gaul to claim the entire empire as his own. It was clear from his speech how Fjorgest had become a chieftain. And for a time, Kristinge listened transfixed. Yet the high tone of the oratory only belied its dark violence, at once captivating him with the energy of the tales and repelling him with its savagery. As Fjorgest continued, Kristinge could feel his own mood darken even further. Unwanted images began to form in his mind. He saw himself once again in the ship sailing along the Frisian coast, icy spray splashing on his face and dripping down his back. Only now it was not a trade ship; it was a war ship. Women and children ran from him screaming. Halls went up in flames. Halls like Finnsburg.

The realization struck Kristinge full-force. It was raids such as the ones of which Fjorgest now spoke that had killed Finn and burned

Finnsburg to the ground. Only a few days earlier, Kristinge had visited the ashes of Hwitstan and seen the work of these Vikings. It was *this* that repelled him, not the fellowship of the hall. This was what Fjorgest was glorifying: the honor of his warriors, and the blessings of their gods in giving them so many victories. Their *gods?* Gods of violence and destruction. Songs fled from Kristinge's mind. He could sense it now, like a palpable presence. A dark spirit of oppression that hovered over the place. Even in the midst of the celebration, it was gnawing on him, stealing his courage. He could not resist it. The image of Finnsburg's ashes would not go away. *And now Kristinge was to sing to these folk?* He was to entertain them—the slayers of his kin? How could he?

As Fjorgest concluded, he turned toward Sceaptung who now sat near the hearth. "Let not the skalds forget our deeds, the victories won by our hands and given us by the gods, the conquests of our spears. Nor let the skalds forget the mighty warriors fallen in battle, and sent to Valhalla in the funeral pyre. Let the skalds take note of these things, that our deeds may be remembered to the children of our children when they carry their own spears to victory or lift again the battle-tested blades of their grandfathers. When fate sweeps us away, chieftain and thane alike at the end of the days given, let the histories speak of *our* deeds."

"O noble lord and giver of treasure," the skald replied in a voice that by comparison with Fjorgest's sounded even drier than before, "your deeds shall not be forgotten."

With that assurance, Fjorgest sat down. He had finished. It was time for the bard. "Let us have song," the chieftain called out. "Let us hear the new bard who comes to us from far away." He was looking at Kristinge, motioning for him to rise. But Kristinge could not move. A winter night had fallen upon the young monk. Thoughts of Hildeburh fled from his mind. He could no longer remember even his first song. His harp turned cold in his hands. How could he sing here? To the murderers of his own father and brother. In a flash, he saw himself as a betrayer of his own people. The betrayer of his own God. He wanted to grab Willimond. To rush from the hall. But he couldn't. He was a prisoner. He had already failed once before the Danes. If he failed again, Fjorgest would cut him to pieces as he had done to his last bard.

He could not even rise.

This time, it was not the sight of Aewin that saved him. It was something else.

Love.

It was a single thought, flashing across his mind like lightning, erasing for a moment the ashes of his old home. Driving away the oppressing darkness.

Love? Even my enemies? Even those who persecute me? Those who killed?

He struggled against the fear and darkness. I cannot. *Love even them?*

Perfect love casts out fear.

Not now. Not here. Kristinge was losing the battle, moving toward panic. *Love.*

Something caught his attention, made his head turn and his heart jump. Somebody had entered. Somebody he had not before noticed. In the far corner of the hall, across the glowing flames of the hearth-fire—a pair of eyes beneath a high smooth forehead. Even in the red firelight, he could see their emerald sparkle, just beginning to fade with age to a green-gray. And they were looking at him.

More than half a decade had not erased his memory. *Fifty* years could not have erased this memory. Kristinge recognized them in an instant. It was Hildeburh. She had come. She was *alive*. Not only alive, but *alive and here*. He had seen those eyes a thousand times before, yet only now did he look upon them as a child looks upon his mother. And she was looking at him too. *Did she recognize him? Did she see her son? Or only a strange bard?*

Kristinge could hardly contain his emotions. He wanted to jump from his seat and leap into her arms. But before he could move a strong hand clamped on his leg, startling him. He turned to see Willimond beside him. The older monk had somehow found his way across the hall and taken an empty seat vacated earlier by one of Fjorgest's thanes.

"Wait," Willimond whispered in his ears.

At the sudden sight of Willimond appearing beside Kristinge, Hildeburh's eyes had lit up even brighter. Seeing them together, she surely recognized her son. Yet a brief smile was all she allowed herself. "So she, too, must know the danger," Willimond whispered.

"What do I do?"

"It is time. You must sing."

Kristinge nodded. *For my mother.* For a moment longer he stared at her, gathering strength. She was still beautiful, he thought. Her hair, bound in two braids and tossed over her shoulders, was still light and long and fair to look upon. From where he was sitting, Kristinge could see little of her features other than her face, but he guessed she was still slim and strong. When he saw the small circlet of gold on her neck—a gift from Finn made by Deomaer many years earlier—his heart leapt with joy. They still treated her like a queen! *There was so much to ask her. So much to hear. And so much to tell her.* But now was not the time. Fjorgest had called him. For the moment at least, Kristinge put aside his qualms. He rose to his feet with a strength and excitement that he had felt only once before, when he had sung for Aewin. He almost leapt to the stool by the hearth where the chieftain of the Hoclinges had made a place for him.

And when he began to sing, harp in hand, he was once again a bard—a bard whom the Danish traders would not have recognized. Tales and poems—Danish songs that he had not heard since childhood when the poet Daelga sang them in Hwitstan—came rushing back to his mind. He nearly burst with them. Tales of Scyld Scefing, and Beow; of Niphad and Beaduhild; of Hrothgar and Beowulf. He sang them all. And he did not stop. Did not grow tired. For the emerald eyes of Hildeburh the Fair, his mother, were ever before him. At the end of each song, when the voices of the Danish warriors rose in loud applause, he only gained strength and continued on.

It was the audience who lost strength before the bard. Some dropped to the floors beside their benches from too many cups of mead. Others, weary from their travels, lay to rest upon the benches. Finally, only a few remained awake. After a long version of *Deor's Lament*, Kristinge fell silent. He sat down on his bench. When he turned to Fjorgest and saw the chieftain looking at him, he knew he had succeeded. He could read it in Fjorgest's glance. Yet even without that glance, he would have known. He had felt the bard's spirit upon him, and he had submitted to it. Tired from his exertion but exhilarated, he breathed deeply. He felt Hildeburh's eyes upon him, but for the moment he could not return her glance. *Was she proud of her son?* he wondered.

"You will stay here," the chieftain said. As if to reinforce his point, he tossed a small gold finger ring on Kristinge's lap.

"For the winter," Kristinge replied, opening his eyes and looking at Fjorgest.

"We will see for how long," Fjorgest said enigmatically. "There is a hut not far from here. It belonged to a warrior who passed on to Valhalla. You may sleep there. You will eat with me."

Kristinge nodded. "You are most generous," he said. But his thoughts had taken a new twist. What did Fjorgest mean that he would 'see for how long.' Did he mean that Kristinge was not likely to last very long? Or that he might be *required* to stay even longer against his will? Had his skill made him a prisoner like Weland the Smith?

"And you," Fjorgest said, looking at Willimond and pointing.

Willimond rose to his feet and bowed. "I am under your mercy."

"You may share the bard's hut, but you will *earn* your keep. One bard is enough."

Willimond nodded. "That is good, for I am no bard. Do you have weirs?"

"At the sea, but none here" the chieftain replied. "The rivers here do not lend themselves to weirs, or so I am told." He narrowed his eyes and looked at Willimond more closely. "Do you fish, then?"

"I do," Willimond replied, and Kristinge could see his eyes water with memories of his days in Hwitstan. *And for men, too,* the younger monk thought.

"The river flows swift and is clear of ice much of the winter," Fjorgest said. "There are fish to be found there." Kristinge saw Willimond's face rise at the prospect. But it fell again a moment later when the chieftain continued. "There is already one working the river with nets. Jiorlic, he is named. A chieftain's son, he sits in this hall as my fosterling."

Instinctively, Kristinge glanced around, though he knew not whose face he sought.

"He sleeps, already. Drunk," Fjorgest replied, motioning indistinctly toward a bench across the hall. "The youngest of five sons and the smallest in stature, he is unlikely ever to wear a torc about his neck. Nonetheless, he is a chieftain's son and in my care. He must be given first preference."

"I understand," Willimond acknowledged with disappointment. "I will seek other labor."

"Perhaps that is not necessary. The river is long. The hall will rejoice to see more fish in the winter—something other than the salted herring that does little for the stomach but give one an appetite for mead. If you are good enough at your trade, by which I mean *if* the gods are with you, then you will find fish elsewhere in the river where Jiorlic is not. And if not in the river, there is a nearby lake as well. It is an hour's journey by foot. Longer in the snow. Yet there is a hut there, with a hearth. And if you have a line, you can bring in fish through the ice. If you bring fish to my hall, I will see that you are well provided for. Only yield to Jiorlic the spot he wants. If there is a dispute, know that I will side with him."

"You are gracious, Fjorgest," Willimond replied. "I will see that Jiorlic has no cause for complaint. And we will see as well if the God is with me." After thanking Fjorgest again, he returned to his seat.

Kristinge smiled to see Willimond once more in the mead hall of a chieftain, and to see the manner with which he humbly replied to the proud warrior as he had done in the days when he served Finn so long ago. Yet he wondered where Willimond would get nets or a line, and whether he could survive as a fisherman. It had been six years since he had worked weirs, and those had been in tidal waters, not in a river. At the very least, a net could take many days to make and many more to master. As for a fishing *line*, Kristinge had only heard of such things. Rumor had reached Luxeuil of fishing families in the mountain lakes who had used lines for generations, but he had never seen one himself and he knew not how they were made. Yet despite the apparent obstacles—difficulties he was sure were already in Willimond's mind—his old mentor did not refuse the opportunity. Even now, he was probably thanking God

Kristinge himself was about to thank Fjorgest again and then depart to find his hut when a voice stopped him. He turned. While he had been talking with Fjorgest, Hildeburh had left her seat and walked over to his bench. She was so close he could have reached out to touch her.

"My lord," she said, bowing to Fjorgest. "Your hall, as always, is full of joy."

"Welcome, Hildeburh," the chieftain replied in a softer voice than he had used all evening. "The joy is greater with your presence."

Hildeburh bowed again. Without taking her eyes off Fjorgest, she asked, "May I speak with this new bard?"

Fjorgest smiled. "You honor me with the pretense of service, daughter of Hoc and Hnaef-sister. I do not doubt you would find a way to speak with *this* bard whether I permit it or not. Speak then, and may your beauty be enough to persuade him to stay with us."

Hildeburh bowed again, and turned toward Kristinge. Toward her son. Willimond made room for her on the bench, and she sat down now between the two newcomers. Kristinge's hands trembled with longing to reach out and touch her. But what was she doing? Surely she knew who he was and the danger he would face were his name to be known—though almost he did not care. "Bard," she said in a soft voice. A small tear had appeared in her eyes.

"Bard?" Fjorgest interrupted with a loud laugh. Kristinge had to struggle to turn his eyes away from his mother and look back at the chieftain. "A good title indeed, but not a name. If you are to remain with the Hoclinges, I must know your name."

"I am called Kristinge."

"Kristinge" Fjorgest repeated. "It is a strange name. As strange as the cut of your hair." But he said no more.

Kristinge turned back to Hildeburh. Now she could safely call him by his name. "Bard Kristinge."

"Yes, queen?"

"Would you sing one more song for me?"

"It would give me great pleasure to obey the queen."

"I understand you come from Francia?"

"I do."

"I once lived among the Frisians." A strange silence followed this announcement, and Kristinge was afraid to look around. "Could you sing for me a song from the Frisii—if my lord Fjorgest will permit it?"

There was a long silence. At the mention of Friesland, more than one of Fjorgest's warriors lifted their heads. Could it be that hatred still lingered? Were there any among them who had fought at the battle of Finnsburg? Kristinge caught the warning glance that Willimond shot him, but at the moment that fear was far from his mind. His hands trembled as he put them to the harp. He closed his eyes. Had he satisfied Fjorgest's desire for things Danish? Could he sing now as a Christian? Or would his identity as a monk place him in as great a danger as his identity as the son of Finn?

Alas, the questions proved irrelevant. For better or worse, the song rose within, unbidden. It was the bard's spirit. It was still upon him, and it left little choice but to give voice to what was within.

> Lo, I shall sing   of the sweetest of dreams,
> a vision for me   in the middle of night
> when bearers of speech   in their beds do stay.
> It seemed that I saw,   soaring on high
> a wonderful wood cross   all wound with light.
> A blazing beacon,   the brightest of trees,
> it glittered with gold.   Gems too, it had.
> Where wood met soil   were four gems set.
> Upon the cross span,   there stood five more.
>
> A great host of heaven   this hallowed tree saw.
> Fair in their form,   the Father-God's angels,
> the band of spirits,   beheld this same scene.
> While I with sin wounded,   stained with wrongs,
> saw also this sight,   the shining tree.
> And as I watched   this wondrous cross,
> the Lord's own tree,   trouble overcame me.
> It began to bleed,   that beacon of wood,
> in ancient agony   adorned in pain.
> Dark blood flowed down   drenched its right side.
> I lay a long while   in silence looking
> at the Savior's tree,   troubled in soul,
> until I heard speak   the Savior's cross,
> heard it give voice,   the holy wood:

"Has long since past   yet still I remember
how I was hewn   hacked from my stump.
Fiercest of foes   felled me that day,
and seized me then   to shape as they wished:
a gallows, a cross,   criminals to hang.
Then I was born   on the backs of men,
fastened by foes   firm on a hill.

I saw then the King,   the Lord of mankind,
the Creator of man   coming toward me.
Willing he came;   he desired to climb me.
There I then stood,   still and unmoving.
I did not bend   nor did I break
against God's own word,   the will of the King.
The ground did tremble   while I, the great tree,
could have felled all foes   yet I firmly stood.

The young holy Hero,   who was God Himself,
stout-hearted and strong,   stripped for the fight.
Girded for battle, He   climbed the high gallows
in sight of many,   man's race to redeem.
When the Hero held me   with hands, I trembled,
yet dared not to fall;   I had to stand fast.
A rood I was reared: I raised up the King,
Heaven's mighty Lord.   I dared not bow low.
They pierced us with nails   pounded through our flesh,
made vicious wounds   and visible scars.
They mocked us both.   I was drenched with blood
that poured from His side   when His spirit departed.

I on that hill   have thus experienced
a cruel hostile fate;   the God of hosts
was dreadfully stretched.   The strange darkness
had covered with clouds   the corpse of the Ruler,
and his shining splendor.   A thick black shadow
covered the sky.   All creation wept
at Christ on the cross,   bewailed the king's death.

Yet some then appeared;   servants of the Prince,
thanes from far off,   fearful but willing
to take back his body   now cold without breath.

All this I saw.   Sore I was troubled.
Yet with humble heart   to their hands I bent.
They took from my trunk   that tormented body:
the Almighty God   who had given his life.
Valiant men let me stand   stained with his blood,
and wounded with arrows.   They, weary of limb,
laid down their Lord   and looked at his head,
stood by his body   and saw Heaven's King.
They sang their ballads.   His body grew cold,
His spirit's fair dwelling,   while I was felled down.
An earth-cave they built,   in bright stone carved
the tomb for their leader   the Lord of triumphs.
Now I bid you   beloved listener
that you of this sight   shall say to men,
with words make plain   that on this wondrous tree
Almighty God suffered   for the sins of men.
For deeds done by Adam   He tasted of death.
Yet by his great might   to give to mankind
the Lord again rose   from death back to life,
and climbed to Heaven   the Healer of man.
But again He will come   Hither to Man's kind
on the day of doom,   to seek or destroy,
The Lord Himself,   Ruler of Heaven.
Thus sang the rood,   the wood in men's words,
this good tale he told   of trouble and great joy.

"Stranger still," Fjorgest said, when Kristinge had finished the song. The chieftain's voice was softer now, less abrasive, but his glance was penetrating. This was a different man than the gruff battle-hard warrior who had stood outside the hall earlier in the evening, or the proud clan-chieftain who had recently spoken to his people. "What manner of bard you are, I do not know. I believe there is more to you than meets the eye. I will look forward to the sound of your voice and harp to keep me sane during the long dark winter. But now it is sleep that will keep me sane. The last of my warriors has fallen into the darkness of rest and will not awake for some time. We have now only the light of Aurvandil, but the hope of dawn is still far off."

Kristinge looked around. Fjorgest had spoken truly. The hall had begun to empty of guests, and the thanes and warriors who remained within had set down their ale-mugs and were sprawled out on benches to sleep—lulled there, the new bard hoped, not by his singing but by the strong mead and their own fatigue. Yet though the night was well advanced, Kristinge's excitement had not yet given way to his exhaustion. He looked around a final time, avoiding for the moment the temptation to gaze at Hildeburh. As his glance brushed past a dark corner of the hall, two red glints of reflected firelight caught his notice. The eyes of Sceaptung glared back at him from the darkness. The occasional flickers of light illuminated a chilling scowl upon the skald's face. And for just an instant, Kristinge thought he saw something else there: a spirit far darker than Sceaptung's brooding visage. Kristinge drew back like one caught too near a fire when it flares up or spits a shower of sparks. This was more than a scowl. More than a jealous response to a potential new rival. There was a tangible presence of animosity in the skald's glare: an evil as palpable as that in Clovis throne-room, only more focused and alert. Kristinge could almost see a darker presence behind or within Sceaptung. This was what he had been sensing all evening. Yet he resisted his impulse to turn away. Buoyed by a strange strength, he probed Sceaptung's eyes deeper, locking gazes with the skald as if in battle. What he saw there—or *felt*, rather, with some extra sense—nearly took his breath away. There could be no mistaking the hostility. The last song had caught Sceaptung's attention, and Kristinge realized with startling clarity that in singing that song he had made himself an adversary. And with the eyes of prophecy he foresaw also that the conflict between them would not end peacefully.

Then the flames dimmed. The skald's face vanished into the darkness of shadow. As quickly as it had come, Kristinge's feeling of strength passed, and the strange foreboding started to return. He shivered and turned away. Perhaps it *was* time to depart. He looked back toward Fjorgest. "Then I will leave and find my hut."

"Your hut will be cold. There is room on my benches, and this fire will burn for some time still. Take your rest, bard. You have earned it."

Kristinge received the offer with gratitude. He turned around hoping to risk a few more words with Hildeburh, but found that she was even then slipping silently from the hall. Swallowing his disappointment, he resisted the urge to run after her. For the time it was safer to wait. He and Willimond gathered their belongings, then made themselves as comfortable as they could on low benches near the wall. Despite the fire on the hearth, the hall had grown cool and the monks were glad of the gifts of queen Balthild. It wasn't many days before Kristinge realized just how long and cold winter in Danemark was going to be. At the moment, however, winter was far from his thoughts. The memory of Hildeburh's gray-green eyes staring at him from across the hall was still with him as he drifted into sleep.

CHAPTER 9:

WINTER

They were pleasant dreams that filled Kristinge's sleep that night, though like most dreams, strange and fleeting. He was playing the harp for Hildeburh, but as he sang he realized that he did not know the meaning of the words coming from his mouth. Only Hildeburh knew their meaning, but she was unable to speak or explain them. This part of the dream lasted the longest. Then slowly Hildeburh grew larger until Kristinge was again a small infant in her arms. The harp faded. His fingers reached to retrieve it but found only handfuls of his mother's hair. Then Hildeburh changed again, becoming once more a young queen sitting in Finnsburg as Daelga played harp. Then it was no longer Daelga, but Hildeburh herself playing the harp and singing songs to Kristinge—a mother not so much Hildeburh as it was *all* of the women Kristinge had met over the long voyage from Luxeuil to the Danemark, yet always with Hildeburh's eyes. Telchild and Balthild were there among them, blending into one image as they laid their hands upon Kristinge and placed him in a great ship, covering him with warm furs and setting him to drift into the quiet center of Luxeuil's pond. The mysterious Aewin, proud eyes flaring, became the wild-haired prophetess Osanne. Even Gundomer's wife appeared, in the dream nearly as wide as she was tall. She stood beside her two daughters bending over to wake Kristinge who found himself in a wide meadow surrounded by bleating sheep—the women themselves having become the sheep, their woolen coats nearly smothering Kristinge with warm embraces...

Kristinge awoke slowly, the sounds of bleating sheep gradually becoming the heavy snores of mead-sodden warriors. He squeezed his eyes shut, preferring the sheep, but the dream would not return. Then he remembered where he was, and sat up quickly. Morning had already come. Light was seeping into the hall through the smoke vent in the roof and a thin gap of a slightly open door. He looked around. Willimond was gone. There was no sign of Hildeburh either.

He sat still for a time collecting his thoughts. His mother also must have known the danger to Kristinge were it to become known that he was the son of Finn. For now he would have to content himself with the knowledge that she was still alive, and bide his time until an opportunity arose. He took a deep breath, trying to prepare for the patience he would need, and wondering what he would say to her when he finally got the chance. Then he rolled his blanket and gathered his belongings.

Around Kristinge, sprawled out on the benches and cold dirt floor, paying the price for their excesses the evening before, were Fjorgest's thanes and warriors. A few were just beginning to stir. Ulestan had once compared the scene in the mead hall the morning after a celebration to the scene on a battle-field after a battle. Kristinge now understood the comparison. As he picked his way across the hall, over the benches and still supine forms of warriors, he began to form a plan. The first thing was to find Willimond. Together they would look for the hut Fjorgest had offered them. After they found it and settled their belongings, then they would think about Hildeburh. Kristinge passed the last sleeping warrior and stepped through the doorway. It was a bright day, though cold. The young monk shivered with the excitement as he emerged into daylight and took a look around at a strange and unknown place.

The first person Kristinge saw was Fjorgest. The chieftain stood just outside the door of his hall. It was, as Kristinge soon discovered, the place where he could most often be found, his arms crossed and a stone expression on his face as he watched the goings and comings of his clan-village. He greeted his new bard by name. His voice and demeanor had once again taken on their gruff exterior. Kristinge returned the greeting, while casting about for some sign of Willimond.

"I will show you to your dwelling," Fjorgest said. Without waiting for a reply, he turned and began walking northward through the village. Kristinge followed. As they walked, the chieftain informed his new bard that he would be gone for three or four days. He had not visited the other clan-villages since the beginning of the summer, and wanted to do so now before winter set in and traveling grew more difficult. He would depart as soon as his warriors were awake and recovered, and would return three nights hence. Then he would hear his new bard sing again.

"On my future winter journeys," Fjorgest added, "I will expect my bard to travel with me. But not today." He halted beside a rectangular turf building, whose roof was only about the level of Kristinge's chin. "This shall be your abode as long as you remain in my service." Without waiting for a response, he turned and walked back to the center of the village where he retook his place at the door of his hall.

Kristinge watched Fjorgest leave. As the same time, Willimond emerged from a small grotto near the far end of the village and began making his way back toward the hut where Kristinge stood waiting. After exchanging greetings in Latin, they turned and stepped inside to survey their new dwelling. The hut in which they found themselves was a one room stone and turf shelter, about fifteen feet long and ten feet wide. It was located in the northern half of the village just a few hundred steps from the mead hall where Kristinge would be earning his keep. Its hard dirt floor, dug two feet below the level of the ground, had been packed down firmly and worn smooth over a few years of use. A stone and turf wall, rising another four and a half foot above the ground, supported the few precious roof timbers which in turn supported a turf ceiling just high enough that both of their heads were safe. The hut had no furniture save a single wooden bench, nor was there anything in the door to prevent a draft. Whatever door covering it once possessed had been torn free in the months since its last occupation. All that was left from the previous tenant was an old skin sleeping mat, rotting and stinky. The only real hope of warmth was a small hearthstone near the back of the room, with a smoke hole in the corner above it. The debris of the last fire were scattered about the floor, but the hut did not look to have housed an occupant or seen a fire in many months.

Fortunately, the monks were not shy of work. The first thing they did was dispose of the sleeping mat, whose smell nonetheless lingered some days after its departure. Then they set to work cleaning debris from the floor and hearth. By midday they had acquired a new skin to cover the entrance and additional skins for sleeping mats, and the dwelling was soon habitable. Willimond was in good spirits to be working again instead of traveling. He hummed to himself and labored energetically. Kristinge, on the other hand, was far from content. He soon grew tired of the silence and irritated by Willimond's good mood. As they worked, he couldn't help but walk to the door now and then and look out into the streets, hoping for a sight of his mother. "Don't you wonder where she is?" he finally asked, speaking in the Latin tongue.

Willimond's answer took the younger monk by surprise. "I have not ceased to wonder about her since she disappeared last night."

"Then why do you just stand there?" Kristinge replied, his exasperation evident in his voice.

Willimond smiled and shrugged. "What else can I do?" He sat down on the dirt floor and sighed. "Ah. I will admit my unease. I long to see her perhaps as much as you. Do not forget, she may be your mother—"

"Sh!" Kristinge warned, fearing that somebody might be listening and forgetting for a moment that their Latin was unlikely to be understood by anybody in Danemark.

Willimond waited until Kristinge was looking at him again. "She was a treasure to me. You know that she was among the first to be baptized in Hwitstan, despite the objections of her husband who also happened to be king. She was fortunate he allowed her the freedom to follow Christ. Most Frisian chieftains would not have been so tolerant. To the day I left she was among the most faithful of the Frisian believers. How has she fared for these six long years in this pagan place with no fellowship? Does she still serve our Lord? I do not know."

But she is my mother, Kristinge wanted to add, but he nodded his understanding and kept his silence. He had pondered that final question himself. *How had she fared?* At Willimond's suggestion, the two monks spent the afternoon in quiet meditation and prayer so that they would not utterly forget nor forsake their monastic discipline, despite having given up their tonsures when they departed Paris. Before long, the sun was sinking low in the late autumn sky.

Fjorgest and most of his warriors had left at midday. The village was quiet. Evening came quickly, and the sun burned red at the horizon. The air was cold and a few light flakes of snow fell from a single large cloud that wandered low overhead and then disappeared into the south. Kristinge huddled under his blankets on the mats they had made for their beds. He could feel pangs of hunger in his stomach. He pulled the hood of his cloak up over his ears and tried not to look at Willimond, who sat in a posture of prayer. He looked at the door instead.

"A fast will be good for us," Willimond spoke into the silence. "We have not fasted since leaving Luxeuil."

"This fast may last three days," Kristinge replied, his voice on the verge of grumbling. But though he was hungry, Hildeburh was foremost on his mind and not food.

"If God calls us to fast three days, it is because we need it. You know Columbanus—"

"I know," Kristinge interrupted sharply. "And Walbert too. And Jesus fasted forty days. I'm not a novice any more."

Willimond smiled. "I'm sorry, my friend. Old habits die hard. You *were* once my pupil."

Kristinge closed his eyes and sighed. He had not meant to snap at Willimond like that. If his discipline had so deteriorated, then a longer fast *would* be good for him. He whispered an apology to his old instructor and friend—the one whom he had once called *father*. Then his thoughts began drifting once more back to his mother. He knew he needed to get his mind off her. There was nothing he could do to find her until she chose to appear. He cast his glance around the hut looking for something to distract him. His eyes fell on the hearth, and he shivered at the thought of a night in that hut without a fire. He considered trying to build one, but he did not know where wood was to be found, and he didn't feel like leaving the warmth of his blanket to go searching.

The sudden sound of a voice at their door startled them both. Kristinge, recognizing the voice, jumped to his feet. Throwing off his blanket he raced Willimond to the door, winning by a step. Heart in his mouth, he pulled back the covering.

She was standing there wrapped in a heavy cloak, her face glowing in the light of the sunset. Kristinge tried to speak but couldn't. Willimond took her hand and helped her step down into the hut. When the door covering was pulled shut behind her, she tilted her head back and let her hood fall off, revealing her full face and head. Kristinge stared at her now, from close. Her face was still smooth. No wrinkles had yet touched her brow, nor had many gray hairs invaded her locks. She looked first at Willimond—slowly and steadily as if to convince herself of his real identity—and then she turned toward Kristinge. For a moment she said nothing, as if she too suffered from the same paralysis that had struck Kristinge. Then she pulled her right hand from her cloak to reveal a bag with two loaves of bread and some other provisions. "You never used to keep a fire in your home in Hwitstan either," she said to Willimond in the Danish dialect. "If it wasn't for Lopystre and Berigyldan, I think you would have frozen to death long ago." She pulled her left hand from her cloak and held out as a second gift a small fagot of firewood. "It won't last long but..."

The sound of her voice shook Kristinge free from his trance. In a single stride, he was at her side. Hesitating only a second—unsure if he really had the right—he wrapped his arms around her. Hildeburh dropped the bread and bundle of sticks to the floor and returned her son's embrace with a strength that surprised him. She was sobbing. "How I longed to do this for so many years, my son," she wept. "My son. My son. My son."

They held each other, mother and son, for a long time, until both were able to slow their tears. Kristinge did not know what to say. Hildeburh turned to Willimond, who was looking upon the scene, his own eyes full of the tears of joy. "Is it proper, father?" she asked.

"Proper?" Willimond echoed, confused by the question.

Kristinge understood a moment later when Hildeburh threw her arms around the older monk. If Willimond was embarrassed, he didn't show it. He returned the embrace with vigor. "We have so much to talk about," Hildeburh finally said to both of them. "But come, let us have a fire. And some light. And food."

"Is it safe, your being here?" Willimond asked.

Hildeburh lowered her eyes and sighed. "Oh, I am safe. I have not been treated poorly. To Hengest, I was a prisoner, though he still held me in honor. Fjorgest has been more generous—almost like a brother to me. He is embarrassed by my treatment. The daughter of Hoc a captive among her own people. And so many years have passed since the battle—"

"I meant is Kristinge safe," Willimond explained. "Will *he* be safe with you here? Will they guess—"

"I do not know," Hildeburh answered before Willimond could finish. "There are few left who fought at Finnsburg, but there are some." She sighed. "There is so much we have to talk about. So much."

That, at least, nobody questioned. Willimond built a small fire and lit it with tinder brought from Fjorgest's hearth. Then, as Kristinge broke the bread and shared the provisions amongst the three of them, Hildeburh told them much of what had happened to her over the past six years. When the battle of Hwitstanwic ended, she had been taken captive by Hengest and made to watch as the great hall Finnsburg was plundered and burned. Some of the villagers managed to escape. Others tried to fight back, though few had weapons. Most were killed. Miraculously, Daelga's life had been spared at Hildeburh's request. She knew not what had become of him since. It was a horrible experience, watching the flames engulf Finnsburg and seeing the slaughter of many of her folk—a moment engraved still in her memory though it had lasted but a few hours.

When all was over, she had been brought back to Danemark. But after the heat of battle had receded, Hengest realized that he didn't know what to do with her. She was, after all, the daughter of Hoc and the sister of Hnaef. She was a Dane, not a Frisian. She had royal Danish blood within her. But she had also been the wife of Finn and the mother of Finnlaf. Hengest might have been tempted to set her free—though where she would have gone, Hildeburh did not know—but matters were complicated by the fact that she had turned her heart to the Christian God. She had forsaken the gods of the Danes. That was no small crime in the eyes of many, and there were some—including the skald, the priests, and a few of her family's long-time enemies—who advocated putting her to death. For a few days she had been prepared to be a martyr for her faith. Indeed, at that time she had felt little desire to live. Her husband, brother, and oldest son had all been taken away from her in the course of but a few months. And her other son, the son who didn't even know her, had been driven south by his father. What reason was left to live?

But God had given her strength, and sent to her an unlikely aid. Fjorgest, the brother of Hengest, spoke on her behalf. It was he who pointed out who the real victim of the battle was—that *she* was the one who had suffered most. Both a Dane and a Frisian, she had watched as all whom she loved most dearly were destroyed. The words of Fjorgest eventually swayed the people. Yet life was not easy. As Hoc's daughter, Hildeburh was shown some honor in the days that followed, but it was a distant honor. People feared and mistrusted her as much because of her new religion as because of her kinship by marriage and blood with the killers of their lord. It was a lonely time. "Fjorgest' wife, Brytta, alone was willing to befriend me," Hildeburh concluded. "What joy I have known has come from the Lord and from the times I have spent with her. She was so young, and so beautiful. I think she believed in Christ, though she was afraid to tell anyone."

"Fjorgest has a wife?" Kristinge asked. "I looked around the hall last night, but could not guess whom it might be."

"He *had* a wife," Hildeburh answered. "But no longer. She died in childbirth last winter. She was always weak. 'Not a real Dane,' some said about her, laughing behind her back at her frailty. But Fjorgest loved her." She paused long enough to wipe another tear from her eyes. Then her thoughts returned to the present. "But never have I known such joy as when I looked across the hall last night and saw the face of my own son looking back at me. Right here, in the middle of Danemark! I could not believe my eyes. I thought I was imagining it, that I was dreaming. Or that after so many years I no longer knew what you looked like. For you have changed, my son. Only when Willimond appeared at your side did I know for certain that I was not deceived. But tell me what has brought you here? Can I believe it was an accident? That the fates brought you here? Or have you come looking for me?"

"It was no accident," Kristinge replied. "I came to find you. We were hoping—" he choked back a tear. "Hoping that you still lived."

"But how did you know? How long have you known you were—" she paused. "Were my son?"

"Only a few months," Kristinge answered. Beginning from his first days at Luxeuil, he then told his own tale: of his life at the monastery, and of Ulestan's death, and of the discontentment that the old warrior's final words had brought on him.

"Perhaps it would have been better had he not told you who you were," Hildeburh said solemnly. "Then you would not have had to seek for me."

Kristinge shook his head and forced a grin. "And had I not sought, I would not have found." Hildeburh blushed, and he continued his tale up until the previous evening and their meeting. Willimond adding only an occasional detail to fill in the gaps. By the time they were finished, the fire had nearly died out.

"There is so much more to talk about," Hildeburh finally said. "But Willimond is right. It would be dangerous for men to know you were my son—"

"I *want* them to know," Kristinge said, feeling a sudden defensiveness for the father and brother he had never known, as well as a desire to be associated with the mother who had always been kept from him. "I want them to know who Finn was. Who my brother was. To vindicate them both from—"

"I know well enough your desire," Hildeburh interrupted, shaking her head. There was clear conviction in her voice. "I too have known the urge to convince them of the truth—that my son did not kill my brother. Do you think I have not told them a thousand times?"

"Why do they not listen?"

"In this land, vindication comes by the sword, not by words. Truth is whatever is spoken by the mightiest warrior. No. I was already known to them as the mother of Finnlaf, and so I risked nothing in speaking for the dead. But you must be silent, unless you desire to join your brother and father in the grave."

Kristinge was about to object, but Willimond spoke first. "She is right. The event is many years past and there are no witnesses whom the Danes will accept. They will believe only what they want to believe. History will remain veiled to all but a few. I tell you also that you bear a striking resemblance to Hildeburh. When you sit side by side with heads unveiled, it is difficult to miss. Even if you hold your tongue on this matter, they may still guess soon enough whose child you are if you are not careful."

"And I do not want to lose another son," Hildeburh added, with tears in her eyes. "Not so soon after finding you. We must show great care. Your secret must remain hidden." She paused and then turned to

Willimond. "So also should your identity as monks."

Now it was Willimond who objected. "Hide our faith in the Lord?"

Hildeburh looked in his eyes. "Have you come here as monks to preach our Lord's gospel? Then do so in obedience and accept your martyrdom. But if you have come to find me, then take care." Kristinge was surprised to hear from his mother echoes of the wisdom of the Abbess Telchild. "I tell you the truth that it is more dangerous for you to be monks here than to be blood-kin of Finn." She glanced at the tops of their heads. Though they had ceased shaving, and some hair had returned to their pates, their tonsures were still evident. "I fear some may have guessed already what you are. Our boats have seen the monasteries on the Frankish, Anglish, and Saxon coasts. And the skald could not have missed your final song." She looked at Kristinge as she said this, but whether it was pride or fear in her eyes he could not tell. "He is a shrewd one, and wicked. He was responsible for the death of our last bard, and for less reason than you have already given him. You were wise to come as a bard and not a monk. But what will you do?"

"Continue as a bard," Kristinge replied with no small amount of pride. "At Fjorgest' own invitation!"

"And I as a fisherman," Willimond added. "But we will not hide our faith. For I am first and foremost a fisher of men. The monk's garb we can lay aside. Our faith we cannot."

"We do have much to speak about," Hildeburh said. "How I have missed your teaching, but I have not forsaken the Faith."

Though he had guessed already that his mother was still a follower of Christ, Kristinge's heart leapt at Hildeburh's proclamation. The older monk—with so many of his past flock having died or abandoned the Christian faith—also beamed with joy at the news. They might have talked much longer despite the late hour, but as Hildeburh pointed out it was not so large a village that by sunset the next day half the clan would not know of her visit and how long it had lasted. "There is little privacy here," she sighed. "Not for me." And so she departed from the hut a short time later, promising to return as soon as it was wise. The monks let her depart with God's blessings, and praised their Lord for his goodness in bringing about their reunion. It was with a deep sense of peace and contentment that Kristinge fell asleep a short time later, and he slept more soundly than he had in many days.

When Kristinge awoke the next morning, the air was cold, still and damp with a thick fog. And with the chieftain and most of his warriors gone, the village seemed deathly quiet. The young monk, however, was not the least troubled by the weather, and the quiet was welcome. With Psalms already on his lips, he arose early—as he had not done more than a handful of times in the many weeks since his departure from Luxeuil—and spent the hour before dawn wrapped in his warm cloak sitting at the edge of the village in meditation. The hour after dawn he spent reciting the Gospels so that he would not forget what he had struggled for so long to learn. Then he returned to the hut to find Willimond also in meditation. Together they chanted the prayers of *Matins*.

No sooner had they lifted their eyes after finishing their prayers, than Hildeburh stood at the entrance of their abode. "I come with another meal for our new bard," she said. Kristinge stared at her, still finding it difficult to believe he had found her. "Must I stand outside forever?" she asked.

Willimond motioned for her to enter, which she had already begun to do without invitation. Kristinge saw that she was bearing a large wallet. She proceeded to empty its contents: a supply of dried fruit and meats, sufficient for two people for a day. "I am, after all, still a daughter of Hoc and close kin of Fjorgest," she explained when she saw the Willimond looking nervously out the door. "I need no excuse to visit a bard."

"It is not *your* safety I worry about," Willimond replied, with a sidelong glance at Kristinge. "Whether you are free or not, if one guesses—"

"I understand," Hildeburh interrupted. "But perhaps there is less cause for fear then we imagined."

Kristinge's hopes rose. "Why?" he asked.

"Consider it providential that Fjorgest is gone these few days. In his absence I can provide for his new bard without arousing suspicion. Indeed, since Kristinge has been taken into his service, it is my *responsibility* as Fjorgest's closest kin to do so. Is it not the duty of the chieftain's wife to present the mead cup to the honored guest? Well Fjorgest has no wife."

Willimond shook his head in doubt. "I do not mean to lessen your son's accomplishments, but he is a bard, not an honored guest. And I am under the impression that bards are given little honor in Fjorgest's hall."

Hildeburh paled for an instant, and Kristinge guessed that she was remembering the fate of the previous bard. But she smiled again. "Perhaps a bard is not held in the same high honor as a visiting chieftain, but neither am I held in the same honor as were I a chieftain's wife." Then she sighed more deeply, half in relief and half in lament. "If truth be known, I do not believe any among the Hoclinges any longer notice what I do or do not do."

Willimond still looked doubtful, but he said nothing. Kristinge, more willing to accept any excuse to be with his mother, welcomed her reasoning without question. "Come and share the meal with us," he said. He sat on floor beside the small table where the food was laid out, offering his mother the one seat in their hut. But she also chose the floor, apologizing as she sat down that there was so little to eat.

"It is a feast," Willimond replied cheerfully. "At Luxeuil we ate but a single meal a day, smaller than this." He spoke a prayer of thanksgiving for the food. Then they broke the night's fast together. When Kristinge, feeling a suddenly awkwardness in Hildeburh's presence, fell silent—eating his meal as if he were back at Luxeuil under Benedictus' rule—it was Willimond who entered into easy conversation with his former queen. It was the everyday remembrances of life in Hwitstan that started them talking: the trees and fields that surrounded Finnsburg; the rivers and weirs and hills; the curve of the beach; the storms, and floods, and changes of season. For a time, that way, they avoided the more painful memories. But eventually Hildeburh's thoughts turned toward the people and events of their past, the various thanes and peasants they had both known. They spoke of the servants of Finn who had been most loyal: Beowlaf son of Beow; Finn's fast friend Aelfin; Guthman and Guthric who were hot of head and full of pride but true to the death; the faithful Froda, who did not fail in the end though it cost him his life. Though only distant names to Kristinge, they were people whom Willimond and Hildeburh had both known well. Peasants, too, they remembered: Lopystre and Lawyrke the fishermen, and others of their small congregation. They spoke at length of Daelga the poet, and of favorite songs that one or the other still remembered. And when their thoughts turned to Ulestan, Willimond recounted joyfully the old thane's last years and the peace he had found at Luxeuil.

If at first Kristinge was jealous over the easy relationship the other two fell into and the intimacy from which he felt excluded, his jealousy soon faded. He knew well enough that Hildeburh could not be blamed if even now she confided more readily in Willimond, whom she had known so well. So for a time he was content to sit silent and listen, learning what he could about his mother, and even growing to know Willimond in ways he had not known him before. Even when they spoke of Daelga and Ulestan, whom he had known well, he could not bring himself to speak.

Hildeburh departed before the morning was over, leaving the monks to their work. One full day had passed since their arrival in the village, and another was already partly gone. With the daylight hours already grown short, Willimond was eager to begin his work as a fisherman. "I hope to have a first catch before Fjorgest returns," he commented.

"How will you start with this new way of catching fish?"

"I am not without knowledge about the ways of fishing," the old monk replied defensively. "When I was a monk at Lindisfarne—long before you were even born—I caught many fish out of the sea with nets. And lest you forget, I also spent many years working the weirs of Hwitstan. That was my trade."

Kristinge laughed at him. "You know neither the river nor the trade," he said. "Nor even the type of fish to be found here. You will be lucky to catch anything all winter."

"I trust in Something greater than luck," Willimond replied.

Kristinge shrugged, and set off into the village with his former mentor to find the implements necessary for his new vocation: baskets, creels, ropes, and especially a net. As it turned out, fortune *was* with them. The second peasant they spoke with, a cowherd who was standing near the Great Hall with a half dozen scrawny cattle, pointed to a hut on the far side of the village. He mumbled the name of a trader, said a few incoherent phrases in a heavy Danish dialect that Kristinge could not decipher, and then said, very clearly, "bad fisherman." Following the directions, the monks found an old trader in his hut. The man, whose bald head and gnarled hands made him look thrice Kristinge's age, had tried the vocation of fishing one summer years before, thinking he had grown too old for the cold days on a seabound trading vessel. But he hadn't had the patience for it, and after a hungry summer had returned to his old occupation. Once they got him to stop talking about his travels, they discovered he was still in possession of a pair of disused woven nets and a few other supplies. "They might come in handy to one interested in that sort of work," the old many commented casually. Of course once he found that his guests were interested in *acquiring* the merchandise, their value suddenly rose. They bargained for a while, and eventually agreed to a price, namely all the coins remaining in Kristinge's purse.

What the monks acquired were a pair of nets, old and disused, plus an odd assortment of baskets, lines and hooks. Neither Willimond nor Kristinge had ever seen fishing line before, though they had heard of fish taken on hook and bait in the mountain lakes east of Luxeuil. The line was made of braided horse hair. "Three strands if you use feathers, and five if you fish deep," the old trader had explained, reciting the lore he had picked up from the Frankish fisherman who had sold it to him. Skeptical of their chance for success, Kristinge and Willimond nonetheless departed with the equipment in their possession. They labored through the remainder of the day, and by sunset were able to restore the nets to usable condition. Willimond also made another improvement. Fascinated by the thought of luring a fish using a hook and bait rather than simply netting it, he took the few hand-carved wooden hooks he had purchased to Fjorgest's metal-smith and convinced him to fashion some sturdier metal hooks out of brooch pins. By the end of the day, they were outfitted.

Hildeburh returned just as the sun was setting. She had brought with her two loaves of hearty bread and some salted cheese. Though the early darkness of late autumn had already fallen, neither monk was yet ready for sleep. They invited her again to join them for their evening meal, and they resumed their conversation where it had left off in the morning. Feeling less awkward than he had in the morning, and no longer content just to listen to the other two reminisce, Kristinge started questioning Hildeburh long before she had finished her bread. "Tell me more of your life here. Was it difficult to learn to live among the Danes?"

"Difficult?" Hildeburh repeated. "Perhaps you have forgotten that I am a Dane. That you are half Dane." Kristinge blushed, but Hildeburh was not looking at him. "Difficult? It is not so different. When your brother Finnlaf was young I used to tell him stories about his uncle Hnaef and his grandfather Hoc, and what a Danish village was like." She paused, and sighed a sigh that was already becoming familiar to Kristinge. "Difficult. Alas, there is little more to say but what I have already told you. My life has not been as exciting as yours. I am fed and kept warm, but I know little love here. My family is gone. God alone is my comfort." She fell silent a moment. Kristinge, sensing the melancholy turn his question had brought about, regretted having asked it. "I feel older than I ought to feel," Hildeburh finally said. "Finn made me feel young. Younger than I have felt until..." She turned to Willimond as if to add something, but she did not finish.

"He was a great king," Willimond agreed. "He bore the chieftain's torc proudly. Friesland has not been the same since Folcwalda's line departed."

Hildeburh nodded. And for the first time since their reunion, she and Willimond began to speak openly of Finn. Kristinge, knowing little about his father, could only listen as Hildeburh told both of her husband's love and of his pride; of the great battles he had won and how he had gained the loyalty of so many Frisian chieftains; of his last year of life and what happened to him following the death of his son; and finally of Finn's own death. Her voice was hushed and somber as she spoke, not only for fear of being overhead— Hildeburh did not speak Latin and so they conversed in the Frisian dialect which any Dane would have understood had they listened closely enough—but because the subject demanded it. And because it was the first time since Finn's death that Hildeburh had been able to speak about it. Willimond added a few words here and there, but mostly it was Hildeburh speaking. She wept as she told of their last few days together, and of standing with Daelga atop Finnweard watching the final battle. Of the deaths of her brother Hnaef and her oldest son Finnlaf, she would not speak. It was long past dark when she finally left the hut, promising to return the next morning to guide Willimond to the river where he would fish.

"You were quiet tonight," Willimond said after Hildeburh had left.

"There was little for me to say," Kristinge replied. "I did not know my father." He paused a moment, then continued. "Nor did I know my mother. It is different for me. For you, it was merely a long separation. You have not seen her for many years, but there are still many memories you shared." The twinge of jealousy started to rise, but he quelled it. "I have never known her."

"You did—" Willimond began to object.

"As queen, perhaps," Kristinge forestalled. "Even as part of the small congregation. But not as my mother."

Willimond acknowledged Kristinge's thoughts with a nod of his head. "She feels the same way about you, I think. But she wants to know you."

"Tell me about her. I want to know her."

Willimond leaned back on his mat. The fire was burning low. Kristinge prodded it with a long branch, and threw on another small log. "She watched you," Willimond said. "As much as she could, she kept her eye on you. And whenever you were not around, she asked me about you. But she was afraid. Afraid of getting too close to you for fear she might start to love you too much as a son she was not allowed to have. Afraid, perhaps, that her actions might reveal more than she was allowed to reveal—a fear she has again now."

Kristinge waited for a time, hoping Willimond would say more, but the older monk had fallen silent. Eventually, the younger monk gave up waiting. He pulled his covering over him and drifted to sleep dreaming of his days in Hwitstan.

As promised, Hildeburh met them the next morning ready to guide them to the river where Willimond was to fish. Kristinge, dressed in his heavy woolen tunic, was waiting outside with Willimond when she arrived. Hildeburh was silent at first, as she led them northward out of the village. There was a spark in her eyes that Kristinge had not seen the day before. Willimond looked the same way, though Kristinge was slow to identify what it was. After they had put some distance between themselves and the last of the huts, Hildeburh began to question Kristinge more about life at Luxeuil. They fell into easy conversation as he described for her the countryside of southwestern Francia. Never having seen peaks as high as those of the Vosges mountains, Hildeburh had difficulty even imagining them. He told her also of his tasks at the monastery, which he had earlier described briefly. Of his work in the fields she showed little interest in hearing. It was peasant labor. But about the copying of scripture and other ancient manuscripts, and his work translating, she was fascinated, especially his work as the scribe for Abbot Walbert. He told her how he had transcribed the Abbot's account of the history of Luxeuil and its founder Columbanus. Some of the stories of Columbanus were of such a miraculous nature that Kristinge had found them difficult to believe. To his surprise, however, Hildeburh had no trouble believing the tales of the Irish monk. When he told how the Lord had protected Columbanus from King Theoderic and his grandmother Queen Brunhild, Hildeburh stopped walking.

"He just walked out of the king's prison?" she asked.

"He not only walked out himself," Kristinge responded, repeating what he had heard from Walbert. "He struck the chains free from all the other prisoners as well, and then led them all to chapel where the jailer found them repenting of their sins and asking forgiveness."

"Like the Apostle Paul?"

Kristinge raised his eyebrows in surprise. "Yes," he answered, not mentioning that he had never thought of that.

"And Theoderic? What did he do?"

"There was little he *could* do. The hand of God was against him. He sent Columbanus back to Luxeuil with warnings—which the old abbot ignored, of course. There was also the time he was interrupted in his prayer retreat by a bear wandering into his cell..."

By the time he had finished his stories, they had reached the river. It flowed northwestward out of a gap in the hills. Where the northbound road met it, it was only about thirty feet across, cascading through a narrow ravine. A footbridge had been constructed above the river, but Hildeburh turned aside and kept to the south bank. She led them upstream another half mile above the ravine to where the river deepened and the bank was more accessible. The air had warmed considerably in the hour they had been walking, turning into the mildest day since their coming to Danemark. Along the riverbank the sun was melting the thin layer of powdery snow left the previous night. "This spot is where Jiorlic often comes," Hildeburh explained. "He claims there are fish here, though he brings few back to Heort. I wonder that Fjorgest keeps him, except that he is a chieftain's son and is too weak to survive long in battle."

Willimond responded by taking off his outer garment, setting down his basket, and going to the water's edge with his line. He stood looking at the water for a time, holding in his hand the long pole he had fashioned the day before. "Perhaps I should have brought a net," he commented, staring down at the pole in doubt. "I wonder if we could build weirs here."

"It has been tried," Hildeburh replied. "Too much ice and floods, I am told. There are weirs in a few smaller streams, but they provide few fish."

"But how do I use this?" Willimond asked, looking down at the strange implements in his hand. "The Danish trader was only able to pass on to me what he had heard from the Frankish trader before him. Which, judging from his lack of success, is not promising."

"You'll have to learn somehow," Hildeburh said, with an amusing smile. "And trust our God."

Willimond nodded. He had gathered an assortment of baits to use. In his basket were some small strips of meat, a few hardy insects which had not disappeared with cold weather, and some feathers. He held up a small handful of feathers and looked at them skeptically. It was the feathers they had been told to use. The other baits Willimond had brought of his own initiative. Neither he nor Kristinge had been able to imagine catching a fish on a feather. "Maybe they eat birds?" Kristinge had suggested.

"I think if anything had *worked*, he wouldn't have sold us the line," was Willimond reply. Now, while Kristinge and Hildeburh found themselves a dry rock several yards up the bank, Willimond hooked a small beetle onto his line. It looked like the most promising of all the baits. Extending his pole as far over the river as it would reach, he dropped it in the water. They all stared expectantly, thinking perhaps that a fish would immediately jump out and entangle itself on the line trying to get the beetle. But no such thing happened. The beetle floated on the swift current a few feet, then sank under the weight of the hook and line. A short time later, the line had pulled taut in the current and the beetle was up again dragging on the surface.

Kristinge watched for a time, curious as to whether the older monk would have any success. "Try casting your net on the other side of the boat," he jested, after several attempts failed to produce any fish. "It worked for Saint Peter."

Willimond ignored him and continued plying the water. Kristinge's mind began to wander. His thoughts had turned to Aewin and he was just wondering where she might be now when his mother's voice distracted him. He looked up quickly, thinking that perhaps Willimond had caught a fish. But the neophyte angler, who by this time had moved several yards up the river, showed no signs of success. Kristinge realized his mother was talking to him. "You have told me little about the Frankish court," she was saying. "I have heard of the Frankish kings. What was his mead hall like? Was it like Finnsburg? Or Heort? And what did you sing before the king?"

"It is a big hall," Kristinge replied distractedly. His thoughts were still on Aewin. "Much bigger than any I have seen in Friesland. As for the wealth, I cannot describe it. I think there is more gold in a single room of that palace than in all of Friesland." He paused as his thoughts drifted back to his visit to Paris. "And yet it is a cold place. They are not hearth-companions who drink together there. It is no *mead hall*." He continued his description of Clovis's wickedness, giving a brief account of their appearance in the great hall and of the songs he had sung.

"He was fearless!" came the voice of Willimond. Startled, Kristinge looked up. Still with no catch, the older monk had taken a rest from his labors and was now standing a few feet away listening to Kristinge's story. "Your son has left out the best parts of the story," Willimond went on, as he sat down on the rocks beside them. Despite Kristinge's verbal objection, he gave several embellishments how

Kristinge had told the story of Daniel and the Babylonian kings, leaving the younger monk both embarrassed but also a little proud that his mother could hear what he had done from other lips than his own. Hildeburh's eyes grew wide as she heard of the danger her son had risked. "Alas," Willimond concluded, looking down at his fishing line in disgust. "I think I will have no such success as Kristinge had. I can see why the old trader was eager to be rid of this. I do not think man was intended to take fish on a line."

"Have you tried the feathers?" Kristinge tried.

Willimond shook his head. He sat there silently for a few moments, then shrugged, reached into his basket, and proceeded to tie a feather onto the hook. "It cannot be any less successful than what I have tried."

As Willimond returned to the waters edge, Hildeburh continued to question her son. At her prompting, Kristinge went on to tell of other nights he had played the bard, from his first song at Gundomer's estate on the night he had been given his harp again all the way until his landing on the shores of Friesland. Of Aewin he said nothing at first. Though memory of her returned often to his thoughts, he did not mention her by name. He said only that he had sung in the hall of Frotha. He did not say that he had sung the song Daelga had so long ago composed for Hildeburh herself. Only when Hildeburh spoke of her own remembrances of Frotha and his brother Froda, did Kristinge shyly mention Aewin and the two times he had seen her.

Hildeburh's eyes lit with a distant memory. She spoke in the soft melancholy voice reserved for things long lost. "A beautiful young girl. Not from the most powerful of clans, but she would have been a good wife to a chieftain. Fiery, if I remember. So was her brother." She turned to Kristinge. "You know she was to have been wed to your brother Finnlaf when she grew older. If—" She fell silent and did not finish the thought. "So many years have passed. She must have grown even more beautiful. I wonder to whom she was wed."

Kristinge did not say that he wondered the same thing. Of his hidden hope that perhaps...

A shout from Willimond caught their attention. Kristinge looked up to see him on his hands and knees scrambling in the rocks and mud at the edge of the river. Thinking the old monk had fallen into the water, he leapt to his feet to give aid. But before he had taken two steps, Willimond had arisen and was proudly holding aloft a small fish. Despite his drenched and muddy clothes, there was a huge grin on his face. "A feather!" he exclaimed. "It tried to eat a feather." He picked up his rod which he had cast aside, and brought his catch up the bank to be examined by his two companions. The fish had risen from the bottom of the river and greedily grabbed at Willimond's drifting bait, but the hook had not set very well. The monk had managed with his rod to bring it to the edge of shore where the fish had flipped off the line in the grass just inches from the water. Only a quick plunge had prevented its escape.

"I thought perhaps you had caught it with your teeth, like a bear," Kristinge joked, but he was impressed. "Like Bjorn. Half man. Half bear." He picked up the rod and examined the end of the line. The feather was only slightly bent, and the line undamaged. Somewhat baffled by why a fish would want to eat a feather, he handed the rod back to Willimond.

A short time later, Willimond managed to lure another fish into striking his hook but he could not bring it to land. Moving along the river several yards in both directions, he received several more such strikes before landing a second fish. No sooner had he the fish ashore when a stranger appeared from downstream. It was a short man, with skinny arms, a small face, and a long bent nose. Over one shoulder he carried a large sack of what looked to be fishing supplies. Kristinge guessed quickly enough that this was the fisher Jiorlic of whom Fjorgest and Hildeburh had spoken—the ungainly youngest son of some distant Danish chieftain who had banished his offspring to Fjorgest's care. In his right hand was a sword. From the mix of surprise and consternation on his face, Kristinge guessed also that he had been watching them and had seen Willimond's catch.

Jiorlic stormed down toward Willimond with his sword held threateningly before him. "What right have you to fish this river?" he demanded. "By my right, I claim whatever catch you have unlawfully taken for yourself."

Before Willimond could reply, Hildeburh had risen to her feet. "He fishes here by the command of Fjorgest," she replied sharply.

Jiorlic spun around to see who had spoken and was surprised to see Hildeburh there. He bowed, but only slightly. "I did not know you were with him," he said. "Nonetheless, I demand by right that he depart from this spot."

Hildeburh's face had grown red, but before she could speak Willimond interrupted. "I have no desire to take your rightful spot," he said, in a calm and humble manner. "I will gladly yield the river to you and move elsewhere. Our chieftain Fjorgest has truly instructed me to assist your pursuits in supplying Heort with fish for the winter. He told me as well that there was room on the river for both of us, and that I was to give you first preference."

Jiorlic, who apparently had expected a battle, looked baffled by Willimond's calm acquiescence. But he regained his haughty composure. "Then be gone. This spot is mine."

"May you be as blessed here as I was," Willimond replied. Before Hildeburh could say what was on her mind, he took her arm, gathered his belongings, and the three of them moved upriver past several bends in the stream, well out of sight of Jiorlic.

"You did not have to give way before that whelp," Hildeburh said in an offended tone when they had settled again. Willimond only shrugged and returned to his task. While he fished, the other two continued to converse. Though Hildeburh at first was unwilling to speak of her life among the Danes, if Kristinge questioned her enough she had no shortage of interesting tales to tell: descriptions both of joyous Danish weddings and also of their mournful hopeless funerals with their great pyres; the tragic deaths of some of the chieftains and great warriors who were their distant kin; the events that lead to the decline of the Hoclinges and the waning of their power; and also warnings gleaned from the few monks who had ventured to Danemark as missionaries and quickly found their martyrdom. Though Hildeburh herself was full of joy in the presence of her son and former friend, her tales were full of a brooding sense of tragedy which left Kristinge in a dark mood.

Fortunately the weather was beautiful, and Willimond met with success beyond what any of them had hoped for. By the middle of the afternoon, he had put seven more fish into his basket, though not without interference from Jiorlic. Thrice the jealous rival appeared from nowhere after Willimond had caught a fish and demanded that Willimond relinquish his spot on the river. However while Jiorlic with his nets caught nothing, the monk met with equal success wherever he went—all using his new fishing line with the hook and feather. Had he managed to bring to shore every fish that struck the hook, he would have gone home with several baskets full. But his tenth fish brought an end to the day. Late in the afternoon Willimond walked up to where Kristinge and Hildeburh were sitting on the shore talking. His eyes were wide open with awe.

"What is it?" Hildeburh asked.

Willimond held out his pole. The line was broken.

"A fish?" Kristinge asked.

"A leviathan," Willimond replied, finding his voice. "It must have been ten feet long. I did not known such monsters of the deep dwelt in rivers."

"A sturgeon," Hildeburh said. "They are prized not only for their flesh, but for their eggs and skin as well."

"Whatever it was," Willimond continued, his wonder still evident in his eyes, "I will need either a heavy net or much stronger line than this to bring one home. I don't even think it felt the hook. Just one snap of its head and the line was broken."

Willimond was hesitant to depart, but Hildeburh assured him he had already caught as many fish as Jiorlic did in a week. They started their walk back to their new home.

CHAPTER 10:

SONGS OF WINTER

That same afternoon, Fjorgest and his men returned to the village. The loud laughter of high-spirited warriors announced the band's arrival several minutes before the men reached the door of Heort. Thus it was that the chieftain found his bard and new fisher, eager to present their catch, already waiting for him at the mead hall. Seeing the basket full of fish, Fjorgest grinned in obvious satisfaction and slapped the two men on the back. "I see the gods *are* with you," he proclaimed in a loud voice. "The best meat, bread, and drink of Heort shall be your board if you continue provide us with such bounty as this."

"Shall we smoke them for winter?" Willimond asked.

"You will eat more than enough salted fish in the days to come," the chieftain replied. "Bring half of the day's catch to the smoke house, but let the rest be cooked now while it is still fresh. My hunters have also brought seal and mallard from the coast. Heat up the hearth fire. Let us have a feast!"

Willimond and Kristinge bowed and departed. "The God, not the gods," Willimond mumbled gruffly as they walked away, but Kristinge did not think he had ever before seen such a great smile on the older monk's face, especially when they walked past Hildeburh's hut and saw that she had been standing in the doorway watching the entire exchange.

"He *was* with you," Kristinge agreed.

It was not long before Fjorgest's instructions had been carried out. Willimond, who had already gutted the fish, brought some to the smoke house while the cook took the rest to prepare for the feast. Meanwhile the hearth was set to blaze, other food was brought from the storehouses, and a supply of mead and ale was set out in vats. By the time the stars were visible, the chieftain's hearth companions—his thanes, warriors, and retainers—had gathered. The mead hall had sprung again to life. As Fjorgest promised, the food was plentiful. Willimond and Kristinge sat next to each other on a bench not far from the fire, enjoying the rich board and the warmth of the blaze after a long day of work. Hildeburh sat across the hearth from them, now and then risking a smile at her son. The chieftain occupied his own bench with a drinking horn in one hand, a plate before him, and a content half-smile on his face. The seats nearest to him were inhabited by his closest thanes, whose faces Kristinge recognized from the treasure-giving of the earlier evening. Missing were the two visiting chieftains who had returned with their thanes to their own villages. But the hall was fuller than before, for many women— who were not always welcome in the mead hall, or who did not feel comfortable there—had joined their husbands and brothers. Wives beamed with delight at finally having their seafaring men home for the winter.

Anticipating Fjorgest's return and still nervous about his small repertoire, the young bard had struggled over three days to compose two new songs even as Willimond had worked to provide a catch of fish. Buoyed by his success a few nights earlier and anticipating his mother's presence again that night, he was anxious to present them. He was also glad for the women in the audience. It felt to him—even though he was still a stranger—more intimate. When he found that Sceaptung had not come to the feast and that he would have no competition, his excitement grew further. He ate only a little, eagerly awaiting his call.

And he did not have long to wait. Because of the skald's absence, it was still early when Fjorgest called upon him to entertain. Full of nervous excitement, he stepped to the hearth. Men and women both, with food and drink still in hand, quieted and turned to listen. The young bard began with an abbreviated version of Deor's Lament, a song he had sung for them only a few nights earlier but which he risked singing again, remembering the praise it had garnered both in Heort and among the Franks. His audience, friendlier and more relaxed than the first night, warmed at once to the song. He followed it with a well-known tale of Scyld Scefing—a favorite story of Hildeburh when she had been a young girl in Danemark. Absently, he almost introduced the song as for his mother and only caught himself at the last moment. Nervous at how close he had come to a possibly fatal mistake, he sang more quickly than he intended. Still, his audience cheered with delight when he was done. Though every person in the hall had heard some version of the tale a thousand times before, none of the Danes had grown tired of it. And the familiar story broke down a few more barriers between the bard and the unfamiliar audience.

Sensing the time was ripe, Kristinge followed the Lay of Scyld with a longer seafarer's tale that he was sure would merit the praise from any who had ever ridden a boat upon the seas. He had heard something akin to it only a few nights earlier from one of the traders who had led them to the village—a poor lyre-player, and one with no great voice, but a gifted story-teller nonetheless. Having just finished a sea voyage, Kristinge had been deeply moved by the song and had committed the first part of it to memory. Later he had composed a few new lines, and rearranged other parts for his own style. He sang it now.

> I sing a true song,   speak my own tale,
> tell of my troubles: how in toilsome days
> sorely I suffered   sorrowful times;
> how pains often bitter   planted in my breast.
> Through halls of cares   I was carried and held
> when wide rolling waves   whelmed me with fear,
> seized often my ship,   at night snatched its prow
> when tossing past cliffs.   And cold was torment.
>
> My feet were frozen,   by frost were bound
> in fetters so cold   where cares always sighed
> hot round my heart;   and hunger did tear
> my sea-weary mind.   Men dwelling on earth,
> lives full of pleasure   know little what falls:
> how I, wretched sad,   in winter remain
> of close kin bereft,   on cold icy seas.
>
> I hung near hoar-frost;   from hail-showers fled.
> No sound of voice   but the roar of the sea,
> storm beating stone-cliffs,   slap of the waves.
> While song of swans,   screams of eagles,

> gulls' lonely shriek,   and the gannets' cry
> replaced the mead-drink   and laughter of men.

Kristinge could almost feel the cold waves upon him as he sang, and could sense the loneliness of the seafarer. He gently plucked at the strings and in a forlorn voice told of his protagonist's long voyage and his exile away from men. By the time he came to the end, the hall was deathly silent and every eye was upon him.

> Yes, shadow of night   and snow from the north,
> with hoar-frost hard   and hail on the earth,
> bind fast the ground   in grain of cold.
> And he with life's joys   and few lonely tales,
> no bone-breaking sorrow   or bitter experience,
> proud and gay-spirited   in safety he waits
> in his lord's lofty hall.   Little does he know
> how I, weary, wander   without ever ceasing.
> on the rough brine road.   Yet I must remain.

> Why do I pursue   the seafarer's way?
> My heart gives no rest   unless I do roam.
> My thoughts are ever   wandering thence
> urging me forward   to follow the seas.
> They beat 'gainst my heart,   heedless of burdens,
> that I might make trial   of the tumult of waves.

Dead silence erupted into loud applause at the end of the song. Men and women alike lifted their mead cups, and eyes sparkled in the firelight at the tale. Kristinge's natural bard's intuition had not led him astray. This was the right song for these people. He had captured them again as he had done his first night among them. He could feel the air charged with anticipation. He felt the bard's spirit on him, and knew that all in the hall were his prisoners—at least for the time, until the spell was broken. He waited only a few moments while those present refilled beer and mead cups. His eyes scanned the crowded hall. Faces other than those of Fjorgest, Willimond and Hildeburh were beginning to appear familiar. The thanes seated at the chieftain's side, the scarred warrior with the wide toothless smile beside his plump wife—

Kristinge saw him then. Sceaptung had slipped into the hall some time during the song. He sat now in the same dark corner, away from the fire, the intimidating scowl still upon his face as he glared angrily at the bard. Kristinge looked away quickly. The skald's presence unnerved him, though he didn't know why. He wondered why Sceaptung had come, why he had come late, and if Fjorgest knew he was there. It was best not to worry about it, he told himself. He had many more songs to sing. He had composed another new song about a mighty smith imprisoned by an evil king; he planned to sing this now. Yet almost as if his eyes were drawn there against his will by some powerful force, he couldn't resist one last look toward the corner. It was then he noticed that Sceaptung had not come alone. Seated next to the skald were two other shadowed figures, also newly arrived. Dressed in heavy black robes and carrying strangely runed staffs, they looked darker and more mysterious even than Sceaptung.

Kristinge realized almost at once what they were. *Priests!* And not priests of his God. These were priests of the Danish gods. Of Asgard. Priests of Tiwaz and Woden. Of Nerthus, Freyr, and Freyja. Sceaptung had brought them. Kristinge was sure of that. And he could feel his own mood changing as he watched them. Long ago he had learned of these priests, both in Hwitstan and later in Luxeuil. He had heard of their secret rites and rituals—of the human sacrifices carried out at their hidden grottos, of their unholy power. Though Kristinge was warm from the fire and his own exertion, he shivered at the sight of them and what they represented. Now he had to struggle to turn his eyes away, and to shake off the same sense of fear he had felt three nights earlier.

Feeling a need for reassurance, the monk-turned-bard glanced over toward Hildeburh. It was like walking from utter darkness into bright daylight. Though she was oblivious to the presence of the skald and priests, the warm smile she focused on Kristinge was like fresh air. He let out a sigh as if a weight had been removed from his chest. He turned next toward Willimond, who also gave him an encouraging nod. Kristinge glanced again at the skald and priests. Only Sceaptung had his eyes open. The other two gripped their staffs firmly, moving their lips with strange mumbling expressions. Though it was impossible to hear any words from where Kristinge stood, he did not think he would like what they were saying. The red wood on their staffs had the tint of blood. The sense of darkness among them was powerful.

Utter darkness.

Darkness?

Kristinge looked once more at Willimond. There was a strange aura about the older monk. He was almost glowing. Darkness and light. The contrast was powerful. It hummed through him like the strumming of twenty harps. And as he stood there, a new thought began to run through his mind—a powerful image as much as it was a focused idea. A sense of battle. A struggle that Kristinge was in the midst of. Like the confrontation between the Abbess Telchild and King Clovis that he had witnessed weeks earlier, only more intense. The evil emanating from the priests was both stronger and more deliberate than that of the Frankish king's insanity. As if the blood from the sacrifices still dripped from the hands of these priests.

It was a startling realization, both frightening and eye-opening. And with that revelation came another thought—a thought still young, but with implications that were evident already. This *was* a battle. Not a rivalry between bard and skald, but between their gods. Sceaptung was there for his *gods*. He had heard Kristinge's final song the other night and had come tonight to oppose him—to contend against the God of that song. There flashed then through the young monk's mind the stories Hildeburh had told him of the human sacrifices made by the priests, and of the power they wielded over the people. Of martyred missionaries who had ventured to Danemark and never left—monks whose bodies were weighed down in the depths of some bog. They were images of terror. Yet strangely enough, Kristinge did not feel afraid. Perhaps it was the presence of Willimond and Hildeburh that reassured him. Perhaps it was the bard's spirit still upon him. He lifted his harp. He had not planned to sing this song. It was young and not fully formed, composed only that morning, fresh and untested. But it sprung now to his lips. The words formed up on his tongue as if growing with his thought. And his confidence soared with his voice.

Of the Shaper of Life   a lay I now sing,
A tale that is true   I will tell in this hall,
With fair words speak   of a wedding feast
When powerful magic   made potent mead-wine
And great high glory   of the God-son was seen.

The Maker of Mankind,   Middle-Earth's Chieftain,
Father-Spirit of life   once lived as a man.
He moved among mortals,   a holy Messenger,
To lead men to life,   the Son of the Lord.
He wanted to grant,   to give to earth's race
The high Heaven-kingdom   as an eternal home.

As a mighty chieftain   he chose twelve thanes,
Hearth-companions   to hear his commands.
The Protector of People,   the powerful God,
Wandered far by foot   with his followers.
Hill-forts he visited,   clans and their villages,
Chieftains in mead-halls,   merchants and peasants.
Wise men were eager   to hear his words.

To a wedding he went,   the wondrous God's Son,
His followers too,   twelve honored friends.
And his Middle-Earth mother   with the mighty One traveled.
A bride to be given,   a beautiful maiden,
At a great high house,   a rich guest hall.
Earls came from far,   nobles to the feast.
Warriors were merry,   the people with mead
Drank and celebrated   the day of the wedding.
Proud servants poured   wine from their pitchers;
They had good mead   to make the guests happy.
On the benches was bliss.   The sight was beautiful.

Then the wine ran out;   the wedding drink finished;
Not a single drop   for servants to bring
To the thirsty crowd   could then be found.
The vats were empty: the vast stores consumed.

For the guests it was sad   the celebration would end.
More greatly would grieve   the groom and his bride.
The great host of the feast   had failed in his duty.
On him shame would fall   if no wine could be found.

Then the loveliest lady   did not wait long,
The Middle-Earth mother   of Mankind's Lord
Went speedily and spoke   with words to her Son,
Told Him what happened   how the host had no wine.
From her Holy Heaven-Son   she asked for help.
She prayed for the people.   She knew of his power.
But the Ruler's son   his answer had ready.
To His mother he spoke,   "What is it to me?"

On earth was still secret   that He was God's Son.
"Why do you speak so   in front of strangers?
What is warriors' wine   and the wedding drink?"
He spoke of his kingdom: "My time is not come."
But His wise Earth-Mother   trusted well in her mind
Even after these words   that He would not refuse.
She spoke with servants,   warned them to silence,
Commanded they listen   and obey the holy Lord.

Six vats of stone   were standing there empty.
Very softly he spoke,   the mighty God's son
"Fill these with water   drawn from the well."
The servants obeyed,   those with the barrels
filled them with water,   spoke not of His words.
God's mighty Child   then choose that moment
To show his great power   among those people.
What was once water   He made into wine.

The drink was then poured,   drawn with the pitcher
And placed in the hands   of the head of the wedding,
Who after the host   ruled over the people.
As soon as he drank   his delight was great.
He could not refrain   but spoke to the crowd.

He said that most earls   the best wine serve early.
"When men are merry,   and drunk from the mead,
They serve cheap wine.   That is the custom."

"But Lo! This host   the best held for last.
To this folk he served   first the cheap wine.
When guests were full,   were drunk from the feast,
Then brought, of all wines   the best I have tasted."
Now again was bliss   for groom and for bride.
The host had heard   high words of praise.
And many a thane   was then made aware
That the holy God's Son   a great sign had performed.

When he was done, Kristinge bowed his head. Fjorgest tossed him a small gold ring while the gathered company cheered. "An interesting tale" the chieftain said in low voice and with a strange smile. "A god who changes water into good mead-wine? Now *there* is a god I would have visit my hall." He said no more, however, and if he suspected that Kristinge was speaking of a new god—the Christian God so disdained by that people—he gave no indication. After all, stories of gods walking the earth were common enough among the Danes as not to arouse any suspicion.

Sceaptung, however, was not so blind. As Kristinge sank to his seat, tired from his singing, the skald and his two companions stomped furiously from the hall.

Late that night, snow began to fall. Not the light flurries of October that left only fine white dust, but a heavy winter snow. When the storm subsided a day and a half later, and the clouds at last began to thin, the snow was above Kristinge's knees. The long Danish winter had begun in earnest. The season of travel was over. Trade ships as well as the infamous raiding vessels had returned home. Trader, hunter, and warrior alike were back with their families. The grain had been harvested and stored for the winter, fuel gathered and stacked for fires on the hearth, and what meat there was from the autumn hunts had been carefully smoked and salted. Only a few hardy hunters would continue to seek game and waterfowl during the winter months, hoping like Willimond to supplement the winter's reserves with fresh meat. Life in the Hoclinges village had slowed to a trickle like water along an ice-bound spring. The days had become short, the nights long, and the air cold enough that even with their heavy fur cloaks the two monks longed at times for the air of southern Francia.

Had it not been for Hildeburh's presence, Kristinge would have found the northern winter difficult to endure. To earn his board, he performed almost nightly in Fjorgest's famed mead hall, Heort, or traveled with him to nearby clan-villages. Though on most evenings he sang only a few songs for a small gathering of thanes, now and then the chieftain opened his storehouses for larger feasts. Then Heort would fill with guests: not only the warriors and their women, but wealthier traders and chieftains from other clans come to see Fjorgest—to receive gifts from the chieftain's hands or to give gifts to his thanes. Then Kristinge would sing long into the evening, exhausting his repertoire as well as his lungs. On these nights especially, the young singer wondered with some dismay how he had taken up the role of a traveling bard. More than once he grumbled at Willimond, blaming the older monk for his troubles. "Were it not for your unwanted meddling I would never have taken up this harp under the ridiculous pretense of barding. Who will long be fooled? I should be fishing at your side and sleeping in my own hut at night, not blistering my fingers and straining my voice for a hall full of drunken warriors."

Yet despite his complaints, Kristinge grew in experience and confidence. Rarely did he lack encouragement. Willimond, who was now more like a brother to him than a father, came to Heort as often as Fjorgest allowed to listen to his former pupil. While Hildeburh, who by right of birth had a seat at the mead hall whenever she desired, was there every night listening to her son. Her presence alone was sufficient to lift Kristinge from even the darkest of moods. Her expressions of delight—the obvious pride in her sparkling emerald eyes as she watched him perform—was for Kristinge worth more than any reward given by Fjorgest. When he saw her face in the midst of his audience, he grew bold. Though during the days he was full of doubts, ever questioning his skill and wondering how much longer it would be before Fjorgest grew tired of him or the skald succeeded in bringing about his demise, at night when the bard-spirit was upon him and his mother was near, he was fearless and confident.

Of equal importance, Kristinge also learned from Hildeburh many of the Dane's favorite legends: tales that she had heard since her youth and could recite nearly as well as any bard. There were tales of seafarers and wanderers; of famous battles; of great chieftains and smiths; of powerful swords, magic tools and enchanted ships. These Danish songs—added to the many he had recalled with Willimond's help from the days when the poet Daelga sang before Folcwalda and Finn in Finnsburg—served Kristinge especially well, and his repertoire continued to grow. Before long he was spinning new tales of his own making from these familiar legends and characters. Though he said nothing of the Danish gods themselves, others of their famous heroes found themselves woven by the young bard into new stories and adventures. The old story of Aurvandil, whose frostbitten toe the god Thunar flung into the sky to become a star, Kristinge spun into a tale of an angel whose bright light became the morning star and the hopeful promise of God's coming.

Some sung and others chanted to the gentle plucking of harp or recited with the meter and rhythm of a poet, the songs sprang to his mind as if they had life of themselves. Not many nights passed without him introducing a new lay of his own composition. And as his attempts met with success, he gained confidence, attempting ever longer and more elaborate tales. Some lasted far into the night or were spread out over several evenings—often, to his own surprise, growing during the telling. For the Danes, as Kristinge learned, were true lovers of story, ever eager to hear something new. Their appetite was insatiable. The longer the story the better.

It was his success with these new songs and the long-bred Danish love of story that fully convinced Kristinge that he was right to bring the Gospel to those folk in their own most beloved form. Thus it came to pass that on many nights, when his audience was particularly receptive, he would end his singing with a tale of a different sort: a tale drawn from the great heroes of his own faith. As the weeks passed, he told tales of David, Joshua, and Gideon. Of Samson and Noah he told as well. And tales of the God-son himself, and of his band of twelve thanes. Tales of water turning to wine, and of a executioner's tree coming to life such as he had already told. These tales he told, not in ancient Hebrew style, nor even as they might have been told six centuries earlier during the time of Christ, but in the Dane's own style adopting their rich northern rhythm and vocabulary for the greater lessons he had to tell. For Kristinge had not forgotten his conversation with Willimond on their first day in the Hoclinges village—the seed that had been planted many weeks earlier in the Frankish court of Clovis. Nor had he forgotten the success God had given him when he had sung to the Danes of the *Cross-Dream* and the *Wedding Feast of Cana.*

He had stumbled onto something powerful. Whereas a monk preaching of a strange god would long since have lost his head, a bard telling heroic tales was applauded. What warrior among the Spear-Danes could not rattle their shield in tribute to the great chieftains Joshua and David who led the Israelite clan to victory in battle against an overwhelming foe? And were not the Danish myths themselves full of tales of the gods walking the earth as men? Even a chieftain could praise a God-son who dwelt on earth as a man doing great works of power: healing the sick, making good mead-wine out of water, raising the dead, and calming the stormy seas by the power of his voice. Even Aurvandil, the star of hope, became in his songs a harbinger of the god-son, just as the morning star promised the coming of dawn. Only when he attempted to put into song any teachings on humility—the command to love one's enemies—did the warriors grumble and Fjorgest prove stingy with his reward.

Thus it was that though his new occupation was one he had taken reluctantly and only out of need, those first weeks among the Danes were good days for the young monk-turned-bard. Except for the bitter cold itself and the long nights, he had little cause to complain or to doubt that his God had blessed him. As Petrica and Walbert had said, and as Daelga had long ago prophesied, there was power in Kristinge's voice. It was not long before his reputation had spread to surrounding villages, and chieftains began to visit Fjorgest from afar. The only troubling thoughts he could not altogether escape were the recurring self-judgment that he was singing for the slayers of his father's kin, and the fear that he would one day meet the fate of Fjorgest's previous bard.

In all the clan, there were only three who failed to be pleased by the new bard. Kristinge had guessed on the first night in Heort that he was to have an enemy in Sceaptung as well as in the priests of Freyr whom he met a few nights later. As the days rolled by he saw that he was not mistaken. His songs did not go unopposed. Whatever else Sceaptung was, he was no fool. Kristinge learned this quickly enough. For the skald understood as few did—other than Kristinge himself, and perhaps Hildeburh, Willimond and the priests—that the new Christ-God was a threat to him. Not only was the skald's importance as a story-teller in Heort being challenged by a skilled new scop, but his very role as a spokesman for the gods. Kristinge was a threat to the gods themselves, and thus to any who wielded power in their names. When men ceased to believe in the gods whose history the skald told—if men no longer followed Freyr and Freyja, Woden, and Odin, and Thunar—then they would cease to follow their priests.

"Sceaptung will oppose me," Kristinge had said to Willimond after his second night singing for Fjorgest.

"Are you surprised?" Willimond had asked him.

Kristinge had thought back upon the stories he had heard so many times of Columbanus and the founding of Luxeuil. Columbanus had found enemies not only in the pagan king and queen, but even among Gallic bishops who sensed a threat to their own power. And there was Willimond and his tales of his early voyages with Aidan to preach the gospel to the Saxon kings, and of his later coming to Friesland. "No," Kristinge had answered slowly. "Wherever the Gospel is preached, it will be opposed. But perhaps that knowledge was in my head only. Never before had I experienced it myself." He then told the older monk what he had seen in the hall those first two times he had sung, of the priests and the skald, and of the enmity he had sensed from them.

"That I do not doubt," Willimond had replied. "Their is a spirit of darkness about them. They have already heard in your songs what Fjorgest has not, and have certainly guessed whom you serve. They will oppose you. *How* they will do it, I do not know. You can only pray."

Kristinge had said no more on the subject. The possibility of being martyred for his faith had never disappeared from his thoughts. He knew the histories of those few missionaries who had gone among the Danes. They were short histories. Few of them ever returned. But these thoughts had not prevented him from doing what he had done: from continuing to put into song the tales of *his* God. And in choosing song as his vehicle, Kristinge had unwittingly drawn the battle lines, though it had taken him many days after his conversation with Willimond to discover this. When Sceaptung realized that Kristinge could not be intimidated, and that through song he had so quickly earned a place in Fjorgest's hall, the skald had returned to his duties with a new zeal, investing an energy he had never before shown and an intensity which surprised even Fjorgest. Almost overnight Sceaptung's manner changed. For those who didn't know the reason for the change, it appeared almost miraculous. And it was effective as well. For Sceaptung knew the Danes as Kristinge did not. He knew what inspired them. And for all Fjorgest's complaints about the skald's croaking voice, he soon proved he could forge a tale that would hold his audience. He composed new tales of Odin and of the fiery Thunar—tales that despite his unimpressive appearance and dour expression became very popular among the folk. And the people could not help but hear the skald's message in these songs: *his* gods were the mighty warrior-gods and fertility-gods upon whom their livelihoods depended: the *true* gods of the Danes. Asgard would be unhappy, he warned, were the Danes to abandon them and serve other gods.

Kristinge noticed as well that the skald was often at Fjorgest's side, whispering in the chieftain's ear. This frightened him far more than the Skald's songs. Ever did the young bard wonder what they were saying, and how long it would be before Fjorgest turned against him. Would they not some day guess that he was a monk? Nonetheless Sceaptung's skill was so far surpassed by Kristinge's that for the time, despite the old skald's greatest effort, he could not displace the new bard. His only recourse was to make sure his stories about Asgard carried well into the night, leaving little time for his rival after him. This he did on more than one occasion. The effect, however, was only to lighten the burden on Kristinge. As for the priests who had appeared mysteriously that evening, they did not return for many weeks.

And if any other among the Hoclinges guessed at the battle that was being waged, they said nothing.

CHAPTER 11:
Long Nights

hildeburh **sat beside** her son one cold sunny morning. "Your stories are beautiful," she told him, with the pride only a mother can know. She was with him often now. Having grown tired of the imposed secrecy—of seeing her son only rarely and always in fear—she had worked out a scheme to spend time with the monks even when Fjorgest was not absent from the village. It was expected that a bard would be knowledgeable in letters, she had explained to them one morning about ten days after their arrival. And it was not unheard of for a Danish queen to increase her learning under the tutelage of a skald or bard. After convincing even Willimond that her plan was unlikely to arouse suspicion, she had obtained Fjorgest's permission to do just that. Thus had come about her freedom to visit Kristinge whenever she desired—which was often. When the weather was not good enough for fishing, she, Willimond and Kristinge would spend hours together sitting in Hildeburh's hut beside a small fire, sharing food and stories, or talking of their hopes. "Never have I seen the Gospel made so clear," she continued. "Or so beautiful. In time, I think you may win them."

Kristinge did not answer. He was not sure how much he could hope for. Just to be with his mother was enough for the time. And he felt almost as proud of her as she of him. She took her new role as student in earnest, showing herself both eager and able to learn. As one of the few in the village with both the time and interest for such pursuits, Hildeburh was a model student. She proved adept at Latin, surprising even Willimond with her talent. For his own part, when he saw that she was serious, Kristinge proved a good teacher. In this way, he grew to know his mother and to build just a few of the bonds he had never known. When the Christ Mass came, and time to celebrate the birth of the Lord, the three followers of Christ gathered in the monks' hut for a small feast, breaking bread and sharing wine together. It did not compare with the winter solstice feast in Heort a few nights earlier. Nonetheless, the event brought tears again to Hildeburh's eyes, as she told how long she had desired to celebrate the Mass with others. In those times, Kristinge felt such a surge of emotion that he thought he would burst. Yet the emotion itself he could not describe, for it was akin at once to both joy and sorrow.

Nonetheless, Kristinge's thoughts did on more than one occasion turn to Aewin. And they did so with increasing frequency as the winter progressed. His meeting with her again, after so many years, could only be wild coincidence, and little did he think he would ever see her again. Any wish that he might was foolish. Thus whenever he found his thoughts drifting toward her, he busied himself with other things. And there was no shortage of tasks to keep him occupied. When he was not tutoring his mother, he was most often at work composing songs. Or, when the weather was kind—Kristinge was less willing than Willimond to brave harsh conditions in pursuit of fish— he would travel with his friend, enjoying the solitude of the lakes and rivers and the chance to be away from the mead hall for a few hours.

It must be said that the older monk, in *his* new occupation, had met with as great success as Kristinge had with his harp. The new fisher was granted such bounty from the river that Hildeburh feared Jiorlic might try to interfere. "You do not know this *fosterling*," she said with such disdain in her voice that even Kristinge was taken aback. "He is petty and cowardly. It is no wonder his father sent him to Fjorgest."

"What can he do to me?" Willimond replied, with no trace of concern.

"He is a chieftain's son. He might pressure Fjorgest into dismissing you."

Willimond laughed. "As long as God continues to put so many fish in my basket, Fjorgest will not send me away."

"Do not be so sure," Hildeburh replied. "And even if Fjorgest refuses, Jiorlic might simply kill you one day and throw your body into the river."

Willimond, however, was not afraid. He continued at the task given him. He avoided confrontation, yielding to Jiorlic's demands no matter how unreasonable. And he was so successful wherever he went that nothing Jiorlic did was able to thwart him. In this way, the older monk eventually proved more successful at conquering his rival than did the younger monk did his. Before many weeks had passed, Jiorlic had given up his own nets and begrudgingly joined Willimond who was happy to teach his new companion what he had learned about fishing with a line. Despite Jiorlic's initial hostility toward the intruder, the two became good friends, often disappearing together for two or three days to the lakes to fish with lines through the ice.

During these longer trips Kristinge was not able to go with them, for Fjorgest would not let his bard be too long absent from the hall. Often Kristinge was asked to sit with Fjorgest beside the hearth or stand by him at the door, telling him of Francia and what he knew of the southern kingdoms. On occasion he was also called to travel with the chieftain to other clan-villages. With slow winter travel, they would be gone for three or more days at a time. It was when he was apart from Willimond that the time moved the slowest. It was then also that Kristinge's thoughts turned most often to Aewin, and to Frotha, and to his eventual return to Friesland. For he knew that he could not forever stay among the Danes. He had known this in his spirit from the moment he had stepped upon the Danish soil. Despite the joy of reunion, something still drove him on.

What made things worse was that after some weeks, Hildeburh took to joining Jiorlic and Willimond from time to time on their expeditions even when Kristinge was not with them. The first time she did so, Kristinge was gone with Fjorgest. When after three days he returned to the village, tired of being with Danish warriors and eager to see his mother again, he discovered to his dismay that she was nowhere to be found. She had disappeared with Willimond to the lakes. Though Kristinge admitted it to neither of them, he was jealous. When they returned late the next day, their baskets full of fish, he was terse with them both. Then, only a week later, Hildeburh disappeared again with Willimond and Jiorlic, leaving Kristinge alone in his hut for the day. His singing at the mead hall that night was rushed and gloomy, leaving nobody happy but Sceaptung.

"Where were you yesterday?" Kristinge demanded of his mother the next morning, though he knew already the answer.

If she heard the reprimand in his voice, she gave no indication. "With Willimond. I have missed his teaching these six years."

"I thought you did not like Jiorlic."

"Perhaps I misjudged him," she countered. Her voice was suddenly defensive. "But whether I did or not, I was not there to be with *him*."

Kristinge felt his jealousy grow. "Fjorgest will be suspicious," he warned. But that was not his real concern, and even as he said it he felt guilty for his attempted manipulation.

"I think not," Hildeburh answered, her voice now echoing some of the coldness in Kristinge's. "For one, I do not think Fjorgest cares what I do. I am not his wife. For another, it is no more strange my spending time with *him* than with *you*. You yourself have told Fjorgest he was once your tutor. It stands to reason, then, that he also should tutor me."

"But—" Kristinge started, but he could think of nothing to say.

"My son," Hildeburh then said more softly. "Do not begrudge me this. I have learned so much from him. Do not forget, it was he who first told me of Christ. It was he who taught me much of what I know. I have known him longer than I have known you."

Kristinge closed his eyes. "I am sorry," he said slowly. "I was jealous."

"Do not be. You are the only son I have left. But Willimond, too, is dear to me. Dearer than I can say. And wiser," she quickly added.

Something in her voice caught Kristinge off guard, but he couldn't identify it. "You need not convince me," he admitted. "I, too, have benefited from his wisdom. And his selflessness. Where I would be today were it not for him, I do not know. But I know better how Timothy must have felt for Paul."

Hildeburh nodded her head. "Perhaps Finn was wiser than anybody knew when he gave you into Willimond's keeping."

Kristinge pondered this for a moment, then slowly voiced his agreement. "I do not know whether it was human wisdom at work or not, but I have no doubt that the hand of our God was at work." Her words had struck close to home as he realized just how much he had come to rely on Willimond's support. And also on Hildeburh's. That dependency frightened him, and as the winter waned he found his peace diminishing and his thoughts ever turning southward. The passing of time among the Danes did not make him any more at ease in the mead hall, regardless of his success there. Exactly what it was that troubled him, he could not tell. Fjorgest especially was an enigma. Sometimes he was a gruff warrior chieftain who seemed perfectly capable of slaying his own thane—*or bard!*—in a drunken fit of anger. Other times, he was the generous treasure-giver who had interceded to save Hildeburh's life. And yet other times the sense that Fjorgest possessed some dangerous hidden knowledge was more frightening to the bard than his fear of being slain for displeasing the chieftain.

What influence the chieftain had on his mead hall, Kristinge could not tell. On the best of nights there was a certain fellowship in Heort that held just a taste of the fellowship Kristinge had known at Luxeuil. There was an aroma of something deep and profound and inviting—something Kristinge had a hard time identifying, but struggled to capture in his songs. Still, after his six years in Luxeuil the young monk found the pagan Danish ways rough and unwholesome, especially among the warriors. Their lives were centered on but two things: fighting and feasting. And their feasting was not confined to food; they treated their women like cattle. The men demanded complete loyalty and subservience from their wives, while they themselves thought nothing of taking concubines as freely and frequently as they wanted, sometimes right in the middle of Fjorgest's hall. Women caught in adultery were shaved, stripped, and driven from home and village, while men caught in the same act went unpunished. The hypocrisy and wickedness infuriated Kristinge. And not that alone. He found oppressive the entire warrior culture of the Danes, with its pagan rites, war-gods and fertility-gods.

"Do not be so quick to judge," Willimond reminded Kristinge one day when the younger monk was complaining. "They are not much different than the Frisian people—than the village of Hwitstan where you grew up. The warriors, I mean. Of course most of the folk here, the *peasants*, are just like peasants anywhere: too concerned with what they will eat tomorrow to have time for the idle pursuits that occupy the sword-bearers. But even the warriors are not so different here than they are in Friesland."

Kristinge did not believe it. Though he was barely fourteen years old when he had left, his memory told him that Friesland was not at all like Danemark. "But *you* were in Hwitstan," he said, as if that somehow made Hwitstan different.

"And now I am here," Willimond replied with a smile. Kristinge had no answer. "As for me," the older monk went on, "I find that my love for your mother's people is growing. It is a strange thing, too. For I thought I could never forgive them for burning my church and ravaging my flock—for the acts that were responsible for driving me from Hwitstan. But our God is a God of grace. He continues to teach me. Remember that all are lost apart from Christ, whether Gaul, or Frisian, or Frank, or Saxon. The need here is no more and no less."

As usual, Kristinge found it hard to disagree with his old teacher, but the words provided little comfort at the time. At least Fjorgest was a good chieftain, showing mercy and compassion on the villagers of his clan, and attempting as best he could to see that they were not too much overworked or underfed. Nor did he display the same behavior as many of his thanes. "In all of the time he was married," Hildeburh told Kristinge, "I don't believe he ever took another women—though as chieftain he had the power."

Kristinge nodded, but the knowledge did little to improve his opinion. Perhaps he had been in southern Francia too long. For on top of all else, he was unaccustomed to the northern winters. The days were painfully short, and the nights brutally long. The villagers spoke already of the lengthening days, but the change was imperceptible to Kristinge. Six weeks following the Christ Mass, the brief sunlight hours still seemed barely long enough to walk across the village, and the shadow cast by the noonday sun was nearly as tall as himself. Then came a time of especially bitter cold, that encompassed the village like a siege. When mornings came, Kristinge was loath to leave his small hut. He spent his hours wrapped in his cloak beside the embers of a dying fire, too tired to gather more wood and too cold to sleep. As winter progressed, he slipped more and more out of the discipline of his monastic habits. Only Willimond's presence and example spurred him on.

And ever as the days passed, Kristinge's thoughts turned more and more toward Friesland, only now, mingled with his thoughts of Aewin, came more distant memories: memories of the burned village of Hwitstan, and thoughts more remote still of his joyous youth among the Frisians. He saw too the dying face of Ulestan, and heard again his final words. Even at night he dreamed of Luxeuil and Jouarre, and listened to the strange words of Walbert, and Petrica, and Telchild, and Osanne.

A bright beacon in the darkness. *A voice crying in the wilderness.* A prophet? A bard?

Was Danemark the wilderness of which Osanne spoke? Surely not. His heart told him no. Friesland was his wilderness. Kristinge realized again that he had been avoiding his homeland. He had skirted it. Leaving Luxeuil, he had traveled through Francia instead of the more direct route across Friesland. Walbert's messages had been but a convenient excuse. For all his desire to leave Luxeuil, Kristinge had delayed his return to Friesland from the day he had set out. Even during his voyage along the coast, he had avoided contact. Why?

He had needed to find his mother first. That was true. But what now—now that he had found her? Would he stay here forever, in Danemark? As the bard of Fjorgest? Was he scared of what would happen in Friesland? Or was he simply afraid because he had not yet answered Walbert's question: *Will you return as a monk or prince?*

Though the days slowly began to lengthen with the promise of spring, and the worst of the winter cold passed, Kristinge's distress did not dissipate. Rather, his sense of uneasiness grew. And though he sought hard to ignore it, he could not. He could not even hide his unrest from his mother—though she gave him the freedom of silence: a freedom he gladly accepted. For after just a few weeks in her company, she already seemed to know him better than he knew himself. *Is that what it meant to be mother and son?* He wondered. At first, their time together had been full of conversation: of questions and answers and stories; of much to share, and little time to do so—or so Kristinge thought. But as the days passed, they felt less and less a need to talk. Kristinge would sit in the hut with Hildeburh, playing his harp and watching her struggle with Latin as he had long ago struggled under Willimond. Yet even then, in the moments of greatest contentment, his eyes were ever on the door.

It was two conversations that came late in the winter that finally propelled Kristinge toward his doom. The days had grown noticeably longer—along with the hair on what had once been a young monk's tonsured forehead. The river, which had frozen over during the dead of winter, was once again free of ice. Though the ground was still covered with snow, the daytime temperatures rose above the freezing mark. Fjorgest was already beginning to make preparations to depart for his coastal village, though the day of departure was still a few weeks away. "You will leave for Friesland soon," Hildeburh said to Kristinge one afternoon, as they sat alone in Kristinge's hut.

The comment took Kristinge by surprise. Until that point, she had refrained from asking his plans. "I do not know," he answered.

Hildeburh sighed. "Though I have often tried in the time you have been here, I cannot even begin to express the joy I have felt getting to know you, my son. And my pride, too. God has worked wonders in you life."

Kristinge blushed.

"And yet I could not hope to keep you here with me forever," she went on. "I would not want to. You are still young, and there is much for you to do."

Kristinge wanted to protest, though he knew in his heart that she was right. But he didn't have a chance. His mother didn't pause. "You have spoken of Father Petrica, and Abbess Telchild, and of the prophetess Osanne: what they told you concerning your call. Do you believe their words?"

"I do. I believe what I understand of them, anyway, though that seems little enough."

"You feel trapped."

Kristinge looked up in surprise. "Trapped?"

"By me," Hildeburh said solemnly. "You have found me. We have had our time together. Now you are ready to depart; your heart leads you on. Yet you do not want to leave me. You pity me."

"No," Kristinge objected. "That is not the case. I have no desire to depart. I would spend twenty years as your child, if I could."

"You were always my child, even when you knew it not. And you always will be. I told you how I watched over you from afar. I have known you long before you knew me."

Kristinge smiled. "So then it's my turn to watch you."

"Your eyes are southward turned. And I believe your heart is also."

There was a moment's silence before Kristinge sighed and

nodded. "That is true enough."

"Then it is only me that keeps you here."

"No."

"What, then?"

Kristinge looked down at his feet. He mustered his courage before looking back in his mother's eyes. "What you say is true enough, I suppose. I would never have come here were it not for you. And had I not found you, I would have left as soon as I could. Yet never have I felt trapped—save perhaps by the snow and ice!" Hildeburh's eyes told him to go on. He did. "I am afraid."

"Afraid? Of what?"

"Of what I will find in Friesland."

She looked confused. "Do you fear enemies there? Rivals? Your father had few—"

"No," Kristinge interrupted. "I fear the unknown. Not the unknown of the land and culture—the Frisii are still my people; I have not been away so long I have forgotten my roots. Rather, I fear what I will be called there for. I fear the aloneness. I fear the decisions. *I fear that everyone I will meet will know more about my life and fate than I do myself.*" He looked down at his feet again. It was the first time he had said this aloud—the first time he had admitted it even to himself. For a long time, there was silence.

"Did I ever tell you about my first trip to Friesland?"

Kristinge looked up. The question caught him off-guard. "No." Then, hesitantly, "Would you?"

Hildeburh needed no urging. Her memories came forth as if the event had but recently passed. "It was late spring. Almost Summer's Day. I was to be married on Summer's Day. It was a strange time in my life. I was young then. Younger than you are now. A girl of sixteen summers. Only the year before I had met Finn. He was strong and brave. The kind of man a young Danish princess dreams about being wed to. Yet there was something even more to him.

"Do you know what he did when he came to Hoc my father seeking a bride? He did what no other prince or king had ever done before nor has done since. All could have been arranged without my consent. Daughter of kings are given away like treasure to be used in bargaining. That is the way it is. I did not contest this. Yet Finn came to *me*. He walked with me, and talked with me, and asked me questions and answered those I asked him. He asked *me* if I would marry him. He did that *before* he spoke with my father. He treated me like a person. And I truly believe that if I had said 'no', he would never have bargained with Hoc for my hand—though my father certainly would have given me away with or without my consent.

"And so there I was, preparing to travel south with my father and brother to be given in marriage to a man I actually loved. And I was terrified. Yes, I knew I was leaving behind all I had. Leaving behind my family and village, my home. My land. My language. The Frisian dialect sounded strange in my ears. I didn't know if I would ever learn to understand the Frisian speech, or if I would ever make new friends. But that was not what terrified me. I was nervous, to be sure. But if anything, those challenges thrilled me. What terrified me was my love itself. I had no understanding of it. What did *love* mean? Why did I feel the way I did? What did it mean to *give* myself to a man? To Hoc and Hengest, my marriage was a treaty. They understood it all too well. But to me, it was a romance. A mystery. Something strange and foreboding. As terrifying as it was captivating. As the day approached, I think I nearly went mad with the excitement and fear that warred within me."

"And which won?" Kristinge asked. Something about her story had touched a nerve. She did, indeed, know him well.

Hildeburh laughed. Her emerald eyes sparkled in the light and her face beamed with an old memory. For a moment, Kristinge could see the sixteen year old princess inside her. "They both did. That's what made it so fun!"

CHAPTER 12:

THE SACRAMENT

Kristinge did not see his mother again for two evenings. She disappeared for two days with Willimond and Jiorlic, who were traveling to a smaller river higher in the hills to the east. Kristinge was no longer bothered by the time Hildeburh spent with his former teacher; he had ceased to begrudge her those days, knowing that in many areas Willimond was better equipped to be her teacher. Also, her recent words were still fresh in his memory, giving him more than enough to think about while she was away. When the priests of Asgard appeared in the village the morning after Willimond's return, walking alongside a cart pulled by a pair of oxen across the frozen ground, Kristinge gave it little thought. For weeks now, he had ceased to be troubled by the skald Sceaptung or his dark companions.

Then Hildeburh appeared at the door of his hut, her face white with fear. "You must leave. At once!" she exclaimed before they even had a chance to welcome her. Her voice was full of panic.

"Leave now?" Willimond replied, rising to his feet. It was the first rainy day of the year, and the snow on the ground outside was turning to white slush.

Kristinge stood also and walked toward the door where his mother stood. "Leave?" He echoed nervously. "What is wrong?"

"The priests. They have returned."

"The priests have been here before," Kristinge answered. "I do not fear them."

"You do not understand. This time, they have brought their *idols*."

"I do not fear their idols any more than I fear them," Kristinge said truthfully. But he sensed the distress in his mother's voice. He stepped toward her and put a hand on her shoulder. "You need not fear that *we* will bow—"

"That is the point," Hildeburh interrupted. "They *know* that Christians will not bow before their gods. They have learned that well. That is how they have found Christians in the past. They bring their great statues of the goddess Nerthus in their wagon, and all in the village must make a sacrifice to her image. If you do not make the sacrifice, then you are put to death. *You* become the sacrifice. They take you to their grove and never..." She didn't finish, but buried her face in Kristinge's shoulder.

Kristinge had not seen Hildeburh so distraught. He looked over at Willimond, but the older monk was pacing the floor. "Do not fear," Kristinge repeated, hoping to comfort his mother. "Our God can protect us."

Hildeburh lifted her head. "Do you not hear? That is what the others said: the missionaries. Now they are dead." She didn't pause. "You see? You *must* leave. I know you will not make sacrifices to their gods. I do not ask you to. By don't stay just to be killed."

Kristinge was at a loss. He had not expected this. He needed time to think. "But what of you?" he asked.

"Fjorgest has protected me in the past. He will do so again. But he might not protect you. The priests have great power, even over chieftains."

"Willimond?" Kristinge asked, looking for guidance.

The older monk was shaking his head slowly. "I will not leave. To run from their gods would be—would be as bad as sacrificing to them. If God takes my life—"

"But my son!" she exclaimed, her eyes pleading with Willimond.

Kristinge closed his eyes. *Her son,* he thought. Now he understood. She didn't fear for herself. Only for him. Yet what would he say? What could he do? Was Willimond right? Would leaving now be an act of fear—of giving in to the wishes of the priests? Even if he had already planned on departing? And what of his mother? How could she bear if he, too...

Kristinge was glad that he was never forced to decide: that he never had to make the choice of facing the altar for the sake of his God or fleeing for the sake of his mother. For Hildeburh, with her warning, had come too late.

Even as Kristinge, Willimond, and Hildeburh stood there in the hut, each silently awaiting some response from the others, Fjorgest appeared at the door. "Kristinge," the chieftain's voice commanded. "We will speak!"

Kristinge lifted his face. He looked at his companions. His mother was ashen and trembling. Willimond, though his expression was one of resolve, also showed fear in his eyes. "I will come with you," the older monk said.

"No," Kristinge replied, though in his heart he desired his old mentor's company more than anything. He was speaking softly, inside the hut, so that only Hildeburh and Willimond would hear. "Stay with my mother. I will go alone."

"Then we will stay and pray."

"May your prayers be heard," Kristinge said, and stepped out of the hut without looking back.

The chieftain stood waiting, a stone expression upon his face. "Come," he said, as soon as Kristinge stepped out of the hut. Without another word, he began walking northward toward the near edge of the village. The monk followed meekly. That their path did not lead toward the mead hall as he had expected did nothing to alleviate his fears. Perhaps the priests already awaited them outside the village. If so… Kristinge blocked the thought from his mind as best he could.

When they were well beyond the last hut in the village, Fjorgest spoke. "Winter is coming to a close. Will you stay at Heort as my bard?"

Like so much of the morning, the question caught Kristinge off-guard. *Will I stay?* Had Fjorgest brought him here to ask *this?* What of the priests? Surely, they had spoken to the chieftain even that morning. Kristinge was not prepared for this question. He was not sure how to answer. Was this a game? A test? "You are a generous king and gift-giver," he replied diplomatically. "But I had given thought of traveling southward."

"You will say good-bye to your mother, then?"

His mind still on Sceaptung and the danger awaiting him with the priests, Kristinge did not catch Fjorgest's trap. He answered without thinking. "I will say good-bye to her, though it will be hard. We have spoken—" He stopped suddenly, his face turning pale with the horror of what he had just inadvertently admitted. *My mother.* He turned his eyes from the road to face Fjorgest, even as his trembling legs prepared to flee. For now there were two crimes attached to him—not that he was the son of Hildeburh, but that he was the son of Finn, the heir of Finn's torc, and therefore also the heir of his blood feuds. And he was not sure which was worse in their eyes, to be a follower of Christ, or a son of Finn. But what chance did he have to escape?

Yet Fjorgest just stood there, his eyes fixed upon Kristinge with an almost humorous expression on his face. "Peace," he said. His gruff persona that he used with his thanes, or when standing at the door of his hall, was gone. This was his more subtle counterpart: the sharp and crafty Fjorgest. "You need not fear me. If I had reason to seek your life for this, you would already be dead. Long ago, I guessed who you were."

Kristinge held still, but his heart was racing. "Was I that careless?"

"You could have been more careful," Fjorgest said with a sly grin. "But you would not have deceived me forever."

"Does everybody know—everybody in the village?"

"No. I have not made my guesses known to any save you. In truth, there are not many left who would even care. Even I myself might not have guessed had I not years ago heard a rumor from Frisian traders that Finn and Hildeburh had a second son. But with that rumor in my mind, the guessing was not difficult. There were clues enough, anyway. You bear a striking resemblance to Hildeburh. And from your first day here, you reacted to each other in a way that would not be expected between a young foreign bard and a former queen. I have keen eyes for such things," he explained, still grinning. "It is a helpful gift for a chieftain to have, if there are rivals plotting for power. Besides, there was the question of what brought you here in the first place; we are not, as you may have noticed, on the middle of a trade route. So I was left with questions seeking answers."

"When did you get your answer?" Kristinge asked. Once again, somebody else knew too much about him. And if that was to be the case, he needed to get some information from Fjorgest. *And what of the priests,* he was still thinking.

"That Hildeburh is your mother? As I said, I guessed early on. Of course it was not confirmed until just now. But I was in no rush. You were not going anyplace, and I enjoyed your services as my bard. As to the other questions, I do not yet have all the answers. Who Willimond is, other than a superb fisherman, I do not yet know." He paused. "Yet his services, too, I have enjoyed."

Now Kristinge came to the question foremost in his mind. "Am I safe?"

"You speak of the blood-feud? Of the battle of Finnsburg?"

Kristinge nodded.

"Safe from me? Yes. You have not wronged me, nor has your clan. If anybody was wronged that day, it was Hildeburh: Hildeburh who lost both brother and son. As to who killed our lord Hnaef, I have heard tell it was your brother Finnlaf. That is what the Danes say. But I have made other guesses myself."

Kristinge's eyes lit up. "Then you know the truth. It was not my brother Finnlaf, but—"

Fjorgest silenced him with a sudden stern hand gesture. "I said I made guesses, but none that I would speak among my people. It matters little to me. I am a chieftain, and I hope to stay one until the day I die. Blood-feuds are convenient excuses for ambitious thanes and kings who seek to increase their power. I have no desire to bring such a feud against myself. And neither do I want to raise one against another. As for me, I am content with my power as it is."

So Fjorgest did know about Finnlaf, Kristinge thought, *though he was unlikely to say so.* Somehow, that knowledge helped him to relax slightly. But he knew his danger was not over. "And others? Are there any remaining who fought at Finnsburg? Any who might remember?"

"There are some, though few in this village. Hunlaf, Oslaf, and Guthlaf are dead, but they still have kin among the Jutes. And there are others among the Hoclinges that could be *incited* to anger against your clan."

"They do not know who I am, then?"

"I believe not. But if I was able to guess, they could as well. And if you stay long enough, somebody certainly will."

"Then I must go."

"That would be wise," Fjorgest said. "For you must know there are other dangers as well; there are worse things among my people than being the son of Finn."

"The priests," Kristinge breathed.

"It is good that you have seen them. You do a worse job hiding your religion than you do hiding your relationship to Hildeburh. And your Christ-god does not settle well with the Danes. If you drain the bogs, you will find more than one body of your so-called bishop-missionaries."

Kristinge nodded, but now he was on more comfortable ground. "I made no effort to hide my faith. I would tell any who would listen."

"And so you have done, craftily well, young bard. Given a few years, you might even persuade me."

"I would that I could."

For the first time, Fjorgest' face darkened. "I am not so easily turned from the gods of my people. Woden and Thunar are gods I can serve: warriors who lead their people in battle. I would rather hold Thunar's hammer Mjöllnir than bear the cross of your Christ."

"Would you?" Kristinge said. He pressed his king, now, taking risks he had before reserved only for his songs. The prophet's spirit was upon him. "You would follow Odin as well, the son of Woden? You would serve the great deceiver? Become yet another of his *berserkers*? Their ways are one, Woden and Odin. They use their servants, but give nothing in return. What have they ever provided for you, save war itself? Have you learned nothing yet of war's futility? Where is Hengest, your brother? Or Finnlaf, my brother? Where are Hnaef and his thanes? Or Finn and his hearthwerod? Where is Hoc?

Anger was building on Fjorgest' face, but Kristinge did not stop. "I tell you where they are. It is not *Valhalla*. Their corpses lie rotting in their graves, eaten by worms, as they themselves eat the fruit of their lives. This is where your gods will take you. This Odin that you serve will take you to your death. For myself, I would chose rather a God who speaks the truth. I would serve a God who would die for me, rather than a god who would kill me. Do you call it freedom becoming one of Odin's berserkers? Then I tell you that the servants of these gods, even you yourself, are in shackles. It is Christ alone who will set you free."

Kristinge fell silent. He could feel his heart pounding within him. Fjorgest was glaring at him. "Shackles?" he growled. His hand fell to the hilt of his sword. "Do not speak to me of your Christ. I did not save you from the hand of the priests to hear about your god. I saved you for one reason only: you are a worthy bard and you served me."

Kristinge did not reply. His boldness had fled as it had come. Once again, he feared for his life. For a long time, he just stood there staring at the ground as Fjorgest stood glaring like Odin himself. A light breeze swirled around them. Then Fjorgest's words sunk in. *Saved me from the priests?* He lifted his head. "Saved...?"

"Even this day, they have sought your blood. And had you brought your gods to us in any manner other than song, your blood they would have sought much sooner. I have spared you for a time—a time, I say. It does not sit well with me to bow down to every demand of these priests, or they will think too highly of their own power. I am chieftain of my people, not their slave. I wear no shackles! But I tell you that they will no longer tolerate you in our midst. They will persist—they will not cease to trouble me—until I give in. Then you will be in their hands." Fjorgest fell silent for a moment. His hand left his blade and his voice lowered. "I knew when I saw your shaven heads that you would be trouble. I should have run you through with my spear right then. Did you think we would not recognize two *monks?*" he spat the name. "That I would not know who you were simply because you wore no robes?" But despite his words, the anger in his voice had subsided. Kristinge knew the danger was passed. He breathed an audible sigh. He was surprised a moment later when Fjorgest laughed.

"I would rather lose you to a southward-bound ship than to a downward-bound blade. If the wrong person were to guess whose son you were, they could demand vengeance." He had dropped the issue of Kristinge's God as though it were a hot coal. "Yes. You will depart from here. And I will grieve the loss of a good bard."

Kristinge bowed his head. "Then I am more indebted to you than I thought."

"And I to you," Fjorgest said. But rather than explaining his answer, he turned and started back toward the village at full stride.

When Kristinge returned to his hut, Willimond was still on his knees. Hildeburh was not to be seen. "Where has she gone?"

Willimond rose slowly to his feet and turned to face Kristinge. The look on his face was both relieved and quizzical, but he asked no questions. "She has gone to Heort, hoping to plead your case before Fjorgest."

Kristinge sat down on his mat, still trying to digest all that had been said. "It is not yet necessary."

"Then she guessed wrong? The priests had not come for you?"

"No. She was correct. Had I known how dangerous my situation was, I might have fled weeks ago." He paused for a moment, but went on before Willimond was forced to question him further. "Fjorgest knows more than we had guessed."

Willimond stared hard at Kristinge for a moment. "He has guessed—"

"That I am Hildeburh's son." Kristinge finished. "Yes."

"And you are still alive."

"I am." Kristinge replied. He proceeded to tell Willimond some of the conversation—at least that part concerning his heritage. "I believe he even guesses that my brother Finnlaf was *not* responsible for Hnaef's death. He is shrewder than we guessed."

"Then you are safe?"

"From Fjorgest, yes. But he has suggested that there are others—relatives of the Jutes—who might yet press the issue of a blood feud if they learned who I was, and if it was to their advantage to do so. And he has also hinted that, if hard enough pressed, he might oblige them."

Willimond nodded his understanding. "Then he has done you a favor by telling you the truth, and giving you ample warning."

"He has. He has done me more favors than one."

"The priests?"

"The priests. They came for me."

"The Abbess Telchild told you that among the Danes your crimes would be more than one."

"She was right. The priests, I think, hoped I would be their next sacrifice. Thanks to Fjorgest, they have been denied for the time. All his reasons for doing so, I do not understand. It seems in part he was simply protecting a well-liked bard." Kristinge couldn't help but smile as he said this. Then he went on. "There is also something of a power struggle—a chieftain unwilling to yield too many demands to powerful priests. But whatever the case, Fjorgest has hinted that his protection is temporary. From neither the enemies of my God, nor the enemies of my father, will he long guarantee my safety."

"Then what will you do?"

"When the trade routes open in the spring," he replied, "we must depart. It is time to go to Friesland."

"From the day you left Luxeuil, your plan has been to return to Friesland. The search for your mother was only a detour."

"Yes, though it is also true that I have been afraid of that return. But now the time has come. It was Hildeburh herself who made that clear."

They were silent for a time before Willimond spoke. "When will you depart?"

It was only then that Kristinge noticed that, throughout the conversation, Willimonds been saying 'you' rather than 'we'. *Was it an accident?* "Fjorgest will be leaving with his war band in just a fortnight, traveling to his summer hall on the coast. He says that I ought to be able to find a southward-bound trade ship within another week after that. But why do you speak of what *I* will do and when *I* will depart? Surely we will be traveling together?"

Never before did Kristinge remember being so surprised as when he saw Willimond hesitate, and then slowly shake his head. The young monk jumped to his feet. "No!? You joke with me. It is unkind."

"I do not jest. I will not be returning with you to Friesland. I may never return."

"Never?" Kristinge objected. "But the church—your church? And the believers there? What will become of them?"

"The church I built was destroyed. Burned in the fire that consumed Finnsburg. You yourself have sat with me in its ashes."

"It can be rebuilt. And there are other villages. Other chapels. Other believers."

"My work in Friesland is done," Willimond said softly. But he was still looking in Kristinge's eyes. It was Kristinge who had to turn away.

"Done?" he asked, astonished by what he was hearing. He rose to his feet and started pacing around the small hut. He tossed up his hands and said again, "Done?"

"Done," Willimond repeated.

"But..." Kristinge began. He fell silent. He was dumbfounded. Taken by surprise. He had no more words.

"I said that *my* work in *Friesland* is done," Willimond went on after a pause. "But that does not mean that *God's* work there is done, nor that He is done with me."

Kristinge turned back to face him, and their eyes met again as he spoke. "But *you* began the work. You preached the Gospel—brought the word to the people there. Will you abandon—"

"Abandon what? What remains of what I began? Who knows. Little, it would seem. But it was God's work from the start. Always. Not mine. And now I am growing old. Too old for more traveling. Too old to ride from village to village, week after week." He held Kristinge's eyes as he spoke, but still he only hinted at what was on his mind. "It is time for somebody younger."

"You want me to go," Kristinge breathed, finally catching the look on Willimond's face.

Willimond sighed. "Yes. I would like to see you go. But alas, it is for God to send and not I."

"But where will *you* go," Kristinge asked, returning to his original question. "Back to Luxeuil?"

"No. I will not return there now. It was never my home, though I did grow to love the people there."

"Then where? Lindisfarne? Aidan is no longer—"

Willimond shook his head. "Not Lindisfarne. Not now. Perhaps a visit some day."

"Iona?"

Willimond just smiled and shook his head again.

"You're staying here?" Kristinge asked, with a sudden hint of insight. He looked around to make sure that nobody was listening and whispered, "Among the *Danes*?!" Had Willimond been serious when he had told him about growing to love the Danish people?

"Your mother is still a beautiful woman," Willimond said, without answering Kristinge's question. "And not so old, either. You know she was very young when she married your father. Only fifteen. We have spent much time together over the past few weeks. She is lonely, but the joy of the One is still in her. She says there is much work to be done here. She would like to have a church built. There are already a few believers among the Danes."

Kristinge's jaw had dropped as Willimond spoke. "You *are* remaining here!"

"God has many surprises."

"To shepherd the flock...?"

"To keep Hildeburh company," Willimond answered. "To help in the labor that she has begun."

Kristinge shook his head, still slow to understand what Willimond was trying to tell him—slow to put together the pieces: the numerous references to his mother Hildeburh. "It will be hard," he said. "The Danes are a stubborn, hard-hearted people."

Willimond smiled. "Hildeburh, your mother, is a Dane. And you yourself are half-Dane."

Kristinge blushed, embarrassed by his unintended judgment of his own mother.

Willimond went on. "Four times God has called me from my home. Four times I have followed Him. He has always been faithful. Now, I believe, He is going to give me a new home. But *home* will have a different meaning now."

Still Kristinge did not understand what Willimond was saying.

"Your mother and I are to wed," the monk finally said. "I know we are old," he went on, as Kristinge stared in astonishment. "But not so old. Ten or more years we might have together if God blesses..." he didn't finish the sentence. A moment later, Kristinge had wrapped in his warm embrace Willimond, the father of his heart.

Had Willimond been a young Danish chieftain, and Hildeburh still the daughter of a powerful king, their wedding day would have been a great celebration: a feast to mark an important time for the tribe. Years earlier, Hildeburh had enjoyed such a wedding. Dressed in fine many-colored garments, elaborate tunics, and jewelry of gold and bronze, she had been more than queen that day. With Dane and Frisian alike gathered for the occasion, the dancing, singing, eating and drinking had lasted many nights in the village of Hwitstan.

By contrast, the wedding of Hildeburh and Willimond was quiet. Though once a queen, Hildeburh was one no longer. Hoc and Hnaef, her father and brother, were long in their graves. And in the eyes of the Danes, Willimond was but a peasant. Yet the event was no less joyous for the participants. Fjorgest, in his typical gruff fashion, at first showed no interest in the matter. Hildeburh was no longer the daughter of an important chieftain to be given away as part of a treaty.

If anything, the new chieftain of the Hoclinges was happy to rid himself of any remaining responsibility for her. But on the eve before the wedding—perhaps by coincidence—there was a small celebration at Heort. In the afternoon, Fjorgest's warriors gathered at the small pond near the village for a rare series of games and contests. Some competed in a variety of skittles played upon the ice with bones, while others attempted racing upon the ice by strapping to their feet crude blades made of bone, and a few cast dice upon the ground wagering coins and fur. Later, there was a feast in the mead hall. With the spring approaching, Fjorgest was generous with the remaining winter supplies of cheese and grains, and thus the food was plentiful. Of course nothing was said about the wedding, but the chieftain took time to honor his fisherman Willimond and to pay him for his work with a handsome gift of furs. Though Willimond and Hildeburh appeared oblivious, Kristinge could not help but think that Fjorgest was honoring them with a wedding gift. His own gratitude for the chieftain increased.

The wedding itself took place the following morning, on a holy day: the Sabbath. It was only ten days after Willimond's announcement to his future son-in-law. The time had passed quickly. Kristinge performed the sacrament of marriage, joining his spiritual father Willimond and his natural mother Hildeburh, and administering to the two their first holy communion as husband and wife.

CHAPTER 13:

A STRANGER

When the wedding celebration of Willimond and Hildeburh was over, Kristinge plodded back to his hut alone. A strange mix of joy and sorrow washed over him. The joy of Willimond and Hildeburh—a joy obvious on both their faces as Kristinge led them in vows of marriage—*this* joy the young monk was able to share. Watching these two whom he loved come together was a wondrous thing. Yet he felt also a strange sense of grief, as if in some fundamental way he had lost them both. The implication of that loss struck him as soon as he arrived at his hut and saw that Willimond's few belongings had been carried away to his new home with Hildeburh. Kristinge was alone now. Though the sun was still up and the day far from over, he laid himself down on his mat and closed his eyes. All that remained for him in Danemark was to say farewell.

As he expected, Willimond and Hildeburh were not seen frequently during the next two days, and the few times that they did show their faces he avoided them out of embarrassment. It was not until the third day after their wedding that the newly married pair sought out their son. Knowing that the time of his departure had come, they had interrupted their new life together to bless him and say what words were to be said. They found him in his hut where they shared a mid-day meal. Feeling awkward around them now, Kristinge was at first silent. But Hildeburh was persistent and broke through the silence, and over the rest of that day and through the days following the three of them gathered frequently. They walked together along the river and through the familiar surrounding countryside, sometimes in silence but more often speaking of what lay ahead. They spoke of Kristinge's coming voyage to Friesland and what he would do there; of the work of Hildeburh and Willimond in Danemark among the Hoclinges; and of the Danish priests who were sure to oppose them. Somehow, though, Kristinge felt that he was now on the *outside*. When they asked him whether he would return to Friesland as a monk, bard, or prince, he answered only that he would return as a priest and seek to continue the ministry that Willimond had been driven from. He didn't share with them all the doubts he felt about the decision, or the struggles he had gone through coming to it.

The day of departure arrived a week after the wedding. It hadn't rained in many days, and the ground was dry enough for travel. Fjorgest announced that on the following morning he would depart for the coast. Kristinge packed his few belongings in his satchel, and went to bed in his hut for the last time. In the morning, Hildeburh and Willimond joined him for a small morning meal to help strengthen Kristinge for the long voyage ahead.

"You will not be traveling with me?" Kristinge asked once more. "As far as the coast?"

"We will come later in the summer," Hildeburh answered. "But not yet. Willimond said the fishing here is especially good now."

Kristinge nodded. He was glad. If they had come with him, it would only have prolonged their farewell. Still, he was heavy of heart when it came time to say good-bye. He did not know if he would see either of them again. He guessed he would not. Willimond, perhaps on some hidden cue from his new wife, stepped out of the hut leaving Hildeburh and Kristinge alone. Kristinge never forgot their final words, but etched them in his poet's memory. The last thing Hildeburh did was to remove from her neck a beautiful gold necklace. She held it in her hands for a moment for her son to see before she wrapped it around his neck. It was a two-sided coin. On one side was the familiar Friesland mark of a sea-bird on the trade winds. On the other was an owl.

"This was made for me by the jeweler Deomaer for my wedding day," she said through her tears. "A symbol of the union of the houses of Hoc and Folcwalda. I am part of a different union now. The coin is for you. Wear it well." She paused and a smile came even in the tears. "Think also of our old friend, Ulestan, who served us all so faithfully. The wise and steady one. The owl stone." Then she handed him also a smaller pouch of jewels and coins, the last remnant of her treasure from when she was the Queen of Friesland.

Kristinge absently dropped the pouch into his own purse, and then strode from the hut before his tears became too great. He wiped his eyes as he emerged. Outside, he found Willimond waiting for him. "They are starting out now," the older monk said, nodding toward a large band of rough warriors marching out the southwestern end of the village. A few children and wives straggled along, giving final hugs and farewells to husbands and fathers. It would not be a long separation for them; most of the families would follow the warriors to the coast within a few weeks. It was ritual for the warriors to go first.

"I can catch up," Kristinge replied. "They will not be traveling fast with so many."

"Fjorgest will not let them get too far without his bard," Willimond added, struggling to smile.

Kristinge did not smile, but shook his head worriedly. "Will I be safe among the Danes for another week? And how long will you and Hildeburh escape their priests?"

"God will defend us. As for you, I believe He has work for you to do in Friesland."

"Another prophecy?"

Willimond shook his head. "I am no prophet. Yet I do not doubt the words that have been spoken of you by others who *did* have the gift."

Others? Kristinge thought. *Daelga, Petrica, Osanne.* Too many. He chose not to think about it. "And you? Will He defend you as well? Danemark is far less safe for a Christian monk than Friesland is."

"'The Lord stood with me and strengthened me,'" Willimond replied, quoting from the Apostle. "'He delivered me from the Lion's mouth, and will deliver me from every evil deed and bring me safely to His Heavenly kingdom.'"

"To Him be the glory forever," Kristinge added.

The two monks embraced. Kristinge wanted to ask if Willimond would ever travel to Friesland—if they would ever meet again—but he was afraid of the answer. Lifting his bag over one shoulder and picking up his harp in his other hand, he turned and walked away.

The journey to the coast was slow. Fjorgest, despite his words, was in no hurry. They traveled by a roundabout route, far less direct than the one taken inland by the traders the previous fall, walking but a few hours a day and stopping many times at various villages where Fjorgest benefited from the hospitality of other chieftains. Thrice during this time Kristinge was called upon to sing in a strange mead hall, which he did serviceably well though without his usual excitement. Nevertheless, the spring air felt pleasant, and he enjoyed the travel and did not grow anxious at the delay. During his waking hours he had ample time to ponder his return to Friesland. He was no longer fearful, though he did not know his plans. The thought of returning to the hall of Frotha came to his mind more than once. Only a few months had passed since he had sung there, and he was sure he would still be remembered, and even welcomed. It was there also that he had last seen Aewin. But he drove from his mind the thought of her, reminding himself again that it was his brother to whom she had been promised. By now she was likely wed to another, with little memory of Finn's family. And none of Kristinge. Even if she did remember him, he was no longer the son of a king. In her eyes, he had never been one. He was only a traveling bard—or a monk, he was not sure—while she was close kin of a clan-chief. All these things he told himself in deciding against a return to Frotha's hall, but it did not keep him from thinking of her. Had he truly thought he might find her there, he might yet have gone to Frotha. But she was not of Frotha's clan. He had seen her there in passing. Where in Friesland she dwelt, he did not know.

In the end, Kristinge decided to return first to Ezinge. It was the village nearest to the ruins of Hwitstan. A village he had visited with Willimond on more than one occasion. There he would seek any survivors of the burning of Finnsburg, and also any believers who still remained from Willimond's church. What else he would do, or how long he might stay, he had no idea. And pray though he did, God had given him no new wisdom when they finally reached the Hoclinges' coastal village. Coming over a rise, Kristinge saw again the great sea: the swan road that would bring him back to Friesland. Little though he looked forward to more days in a boat, he understood once again why it inspired such mighty songs. A longing in his heart to stand upon his home soil was sparked.

That day there was feasting at Fjorgest's coastal hall. Food in plenty they had brought with them, and though good drink was lacking, the hunters who had gone ahead had brought in some of the season's first waterfowl. Like the swiftly lengthening days, this was a sure sign that winter was over. The warriors and traders both had reason to celebrate. It was in good spirits that Kristinge sang that night, performing the duty of a bard before Fjorgest for the last time. He sang four songs, starting with *Deor's Lament*—the very song that had earned him a place in Fjorgest's hall—and ending with the tale of the God-Son and the wedding feast. Such was his power as he sang that night, and so great was the spell of his voice, that when he finished singing the chieftain and his gathered warriors swore that the water in their mugs had turned to good mead.

Two days later, Kristinge purchased passage for Friesland with three south-bound trading ships. Fjorgest wished him well and gave him as a parting gift a gold brooch of Frankish craftsmanship. It was a miniature drinking horn. "If ever you return to Danemark, your harp will be welcome at Heort. A mead cup larger than this awaits you. May the gods be with you." A moment later he added, "And your own god as well."

Kristinge nodded and bowed, but no words came to his lips. The ship slid off the beach as the sun rose behind them. He looked back only once, overcome by the longing to see Willimond and Hildeburh a last time. But he knew they were not there, and his heart told him he would not see them again in this life. Not for the last time, he wondered what would become of the one whom he had long ago called Father, and the one whom he had so recently learned to call Mother. The tears of sorrow upon his face as he sailed away from the land of the Hoclinges bit his cheek more deeply than did the cold spray of sea water.

Nevertheless, he was glad to be traveling once again. Now that he was apart from his mother, he had no wish to linger among the Danes. His eyes were turned southward, and already thoughts of Friesland filled his head. For the first time since his departure from Luxeuil, he felt ready to return to Hwitstan. A strange sense of urgency was upon him. Fortunately, the shipmasters as well as the ships themselves—vessels akin to those which had brought Kristinge north in the fall, though a few feet longer—proved true to the Danish reputation for seamanship. With tail winds driving them, and seas less choppy than was the norm for that time of year, they traveled swiftly. The sailors, too, had been ice-bound for too long and were glad to be on the waters once again. Kristinge listened to their laughter and coarse talk, but he kept to himself. He made no effort to speak with the traders nor did he volunteer to entertain them with his harp, but instead occupied his time with thoughts of his return. The question posed months earlier by both abbot and abbess—the question for which he had felt no clear answer when it was asked—was once again fresh upon his mind: *With what cloak would he return to his homeland?*

Now, however, at least part of the answer had become clear. He would keep secret his identity as the son of Finn. He would not return as a prince, but was content to remain a fosterling. The winter in Danemark had convinced him of that. The lives of the chieftains were the lives of warriors. He had heard enough of their tales. Woden had enough berserkers. As a monk or priest he might return. Even as a bard. But not as a warrior. Not as a chieftain.

Yet even this decision did not set him at ease. He would have to do much better in Friesland than he had done in Danemark to prevent any from guessing who he was. He could not be careless. Other enemies his father had outside of Danemark. Kristinge had come to learn that. He had heard the tale of Réadban's betrayal of Finn. The chieftains Aldgisl and Réadban both sought the rule of Friesland, and would view any son of Finn as a threat to their own ambitions. That Kristinge had no intent of pursuing the torc would not matter to those two. He had not forgotten the warnings of Abbess Telchild. His ancestry was threat enough to them. He would risk the danger of being a priest, but not that of being an aspiring prince.

This thought at least was firmly settled in Kristinge's mind when, less than two weeks after his departure from the land of the Hoclinges, on a bright morning some time past the spring equinox but not yet summer's solstice, he found himself sailing along the northeastern shore of Hwitstanwic. When they rounded a point of land and the broad bay with its familiar wics opened up before him, his heart leapt with recognition. A short time later, the traders pulled onto the beach about a mile northeastward along the coast from where the old tower Finnweard stood. They waited only long enough for Kristinge to step out of the ship with his belongings before poling back out into the offing.

He had returned.

Kristinge stood there alone on the shores of Friesland and watched the three ships sail out of sight. Then he turned his eyes inland. With a sigh, he heaved his sack over his shoulder and carefully lifted his harp. The portent of the moment did not evade him. This was why he had left Luxeuil so many months ago. It was also what he had been avoiding. He was home. There was no chance to turn back. The ship had left. What *would* he do?

Standing on the beach, all of his thoughts of the past three weeks raced through Kristinge's mind. He had chosen the village of Ezinge as his destination in part for its proximity to Hwitstan. Ezinge had, as he remembered, a small chapel and a few disciples of Christ. Four years before their departure from Friesland, a young Kristinge had watched Willimond build that chapel. Whether it still stood so many years later, he did not know. Their disturbing discovery in Dorestad— the peasants who had abandoned their faith in the Christian God to worship again the idols of their people—had left him in doubt. Yet of all the places he might go, Ezinge was most promising. Willimond had spent much time with the few believers there, and their faith had been strong. Furthermore, to get to Ezinge he had to pass nigh to Hwitstan and he hoped once more to see the ruins of what had been his home. His initial plan had been to rest there for the night as he and Willimond had done months earlier. Now that he was here, the thought of a night alone amidst the burned buildings in the deserted village unsettled him. Furthermore he had not counted on being let off the ship on the opposite side of the river. Unless the old bridge was still in place, it would take more than an hour to walk upstream far enough to cross the river even in low tide, and another hour to walk back to the village.

No. Someday, he would return to Hwitstan, but not today. First, he must find shelter. And food. That meant finding a settlement. The quickest route to Ezinge from where he stood would be to travel along the north side of the Hwitstan river—the *Hunze* as it was known upstream further from the coast. If he remembered clearly, a long day's march might suffice to complete the trip to Ezinge had he started at Hwitstan. But much of the morning had passed, so that he had little hope to reach Ezinge before sunset; if all went well, he *might* be there by the middle of the next day. Then, if any of the disciples had remained faithful to Christ, he *might* find lodging as a monk. Otherwise, he would sleep by the chapel—*if* it was still standing. *If. If. If.* He laughed aloud at how uncertain even the next day was. He took one more look back across the bay toward the small hill upon which the tower Finnweard had once stood. Then he started up the beach.

Kristinge's walk took him over the dunes and along a low hill. Cold sand filled his sandals, but it didn't bother him. This was Frisian sand, the sand of Hwitstanwic. It felt right. Even the cool spring air coming off the sea behind him and blowing down his neck didn't trouble him. It was good to be back. His mind was already racing ahead to what he would find when he reached his destination—to the thought of living again among the Frisians. To the hope of seeing Aewin. The hope that perhaps she remembered him. That her response to his song in Frotha's hall had not been his imagination. He blushed at the memory of Frotha's warning, but it did not stop a hundred questions leaping to mind as he breathed once more the air of his homeland, and memories uncounted flooded over him. What would the days and weeks to follow bring?

Preoccupied with these thoughts, Kristinge did not at first notice the tower rising some distance ahead and to his left. Not until a loud gull's cry turned his head in that direction. Then he saw it. Atop a low slope away from the water was a tall stone structure. He stopped and looked more closely, thinking perhaps that his eyes had deceived him. He did not remember any buildings there. There had been no other villages this close to Hwitstan. Moved by curiosity, he veered away from the shore line in that direction to pass the structure more closely, though it meant a little extra work.

As he drew closer, Kristinge realized the structure was a watchtower, much like the older tower Finnweard that had stood between his village and the sea. It sat atop a hill, perhaps three stone throws from the shoreline. When he came to a point even with it, his curiosity overtook him completely. He turned left and started up the slope to investigate. His legs, sore from too many days cramped in a boat, protested at the climb but he persisted. A minute later, he found himself standing on a low hill surrounded by a few scattered trees. East, north, and west, the great sea was spread out before him like a blanket crusted with jewels. At present, however, he paid it little heed. He was looking up at a small stone tower, about twelve feet high. For a long moment he stared at it, wondering who had put it there. Then he remembered that Finn had built it years past to help guard Hwitstanwic. Slowly his memory came back. The tower Finnweard had been torn down after the battle, as he had already seen. But Finn had built five of these watchtowers: Finnweard, plus two others in each direction along the coast. This one—the middle one on the eastern side—still stood. More distant memories were now returning. Days playing upon the beaches, looking for sea-polished stone or chasing gulls along the sand. Watching the great ships set out to sea. Working the weirs in the river with Willimond and the other fishermen of the village.

On a sudden urge, Kristinge set his bag and harp down near the base of the tower and looked for a way to climb. Spotting an old wooden ladder lying on the ground on the other side of the tower, he went over to investigate. Unfortunately, the ladder did not look promising. The rungs were old and rotted. Kristinge turned back to the tower. The intervening years had not greatly damaged the stonework as they had done to the wooden ladder, and the walls still looked solid. Tentatively, he put his foot in a hole and reached up for a handhold. The structure held his weight, and no stones loosened. Casting one final glance up the wall over twice his own height, he took a breath and began to climb.

The climb was easier than Kristinge expected. The stone was as solid as it looked, and there were plenty of footholds and handholds. A minute later he swung his body over the low parapet and was standing atop the tower, in possession of a commanding view of the long flat coastline around Hwitstanwic. To the northeast, beyond the bay where his eyes first fell, he could see another hill upon which stood the next tower—little more than a gray speck rising in the distance just above the level of the trees, but still standing. It was clear now why Finn had built these watchtowers. Except under cover of fog or darkness, no enemy could approach Hwitstan from the north by land or sea without being seen many miles away. Realizing this, Kristinge was surprised that the towers had been left standing, and had survived the sacking of Finnsburg. Hengest must have known of the towers.

Had they been too far away and their destruction of Hwitstan so complete that they did trouble with them? He turned around. The ruins of Finnweard were just barely visible down the coast in the other direction. That was where his mother had stood with Daelga, watching the last battle of Finn.

A tear came to Kristinge's eye. He turned and looked westward out across the water. The bay was beautiful. The sun was already far enough to the west that it glittered brightly off the surface of the waves, causing Kristinge to squint as he scanned the far shores of Hwitstanwic. Only then did he become aware again of the sound of waves crashing on the shore below him, and the cries of the gulls screeching about him. One large dark gray gull flew over to land on the stone to his left, but veered off at the last minute when it realized that the tower was occupied.

It was strange, Kristinge thought, how much life was here. And how little. The village had lain vacant since the battle. Nobody had even attempted to resettle. Pondering these things, the young monk stood alone atop the tower much longer than he intended, gazing out across the bay and listening to the sounds of the waters, and the birds, and the wind whistling across the stone. Once again a memory of Aewin rose to his mind, and he wondered where she was and if he would again see her. Perhaps even now the winds were taking the Danish trade-ship along the shores to the village where she dwelt. The same winds that had so often taken Finn far down the coast. And Folcwalda before him. How many times had his father and brother sailed along these shores? Kristinge could picture them now. Friesland's last king, standing atop the hill overlooking the bay, perhaps with his arm on the shoulder of his elder son Finnlaf. Perhaps the two of them had even stood together atop the very tower upon which Kristinge now stood. Kristinge, the lost son. The forgotten son. The disclaimed son.

Not until another gull let out a loud screech close to his ears did Kristinge snap out of his daydream. How long he had stood there he did not know, but the sun was much farther to the west than when he had arrived. He had been lost in some distant memory of a summer's day long ago—the sound of young children playing along the beaches, looking for pieces of amber washed up upon the sand. He shook his head slowly as if trying to release the memory. Then he turned around to depart. It was time to begin the journey to Ezinge. Yet he couldn't help one last look. He turned back toward the water again. The low clouds along the horizon were beginning to glow red. The day had almost passed and he had traveled no more than a mile. He would be hard-pressed to make it to Ezinge by the following evening.

"So be it," Kristinge said aloud. He could begin his journey to Ezinge in the morning. This was as fitting a place as any to spend his first night alone in Friesland. He had seen some dry driftwood and a few dead branches with which he could build a fire. And he still had a loaf of bread and a flask of mead. There were sure to be springs about where he could find water, and he had not forgotten all he had learned at Luxeuil about wild roots and seeds. Abandoning his perch, he climbed down from the tower and set about gathering wood before it grew too dark. Since moving into his own hut with Willimond the previous fall, Kristinge had taken to keeping a tinder box. Building a small hearth with a few stones that had either fallen from the tower or still remained from its construction, he was able to start a small blaze. When he was satisfied with it, he leaned up against the wall of the tower and reached for his harp and the remainder of his food.

It was a cool evening, and the warmth of the fire felt nice as Kristinge stretched his fingers along the harp strings and caressed them. For some reason, perhaps just his sense of solitude, the instrument sounded strangely compelling that night. Though he had no audience, he was in the mood to play. He paused briefly for some drink and a bite of bread. The strong wine tasted good on his dry lips, and he took a second then third swallow. Then, with a second bite of bread still in his mouth, he closed his eyes and gave in to the harp and the impulses rising within him.

As if in answering harmony, the wind began a slow whistling through the chinks in the rock tower, and the trees creaked gently in the breeze. Before long, the quiet solitude of his playing had become a performance. Inspired by the sound of his harp—which on rare nights like this had a mind of its own—or maybe inspired by his return home or simply by the beauty of his surroundings, new melodies began to spring from Kristinge's fingertips. Melodies strange to his ears, yet mysteriously familiar. For a time, then, it seemed to him that he was no longer the player but had become the audience, and he was barely aware of the movement of his fingers. Only thrice more in his life did such a feeling ever come upon him. And though in the weeks to come bits and pieces of those melodies came back to him, he could not again create that moment nor could he remember most of the songs save as a fleeting memory or as one remembers a dream. Yet at the time, whether or not he would later remember the songs did not matter. Though no audience was there to hear him, he was immersed in song.

How long this lasted, Kristinge did not know. He had been playing for some time when he opened his eyes and glanced up from the strings. The fire had died down to a hot bed of coals with but a few flickering yellow and orange flames. And across the fire, a pair of white eyes glowed against the dark background. The sight startled Kristinge, and in the darkness of a strange place the worst possibilities jumped at once to his mind. Wild animals. A boar, or perhaps wolf. His hand froze, and he nearly dropped his harp. Or a bear. Resisting panic, he reached to throw more wood on the fire hoping the flames would scare the creature away. It was then he realized that the eyes were too high off the ground for an animal. They were more the height of... Even as Kristinge realized that it was a man, the stranger stepped forward into the light of the fire.

He was tall, with a heavy bear-skin cloak and a matching fur hood covering his ears. Where he had come from, Kristinge did not know. At the moment, it did not matter. Instinctively, he inched toward the wall, pressing his back against the stone in a defensive posture. The man was wearing a sword, and his right hand rested on the hilt.

Robbers! Kristinge thought, as he looked around for some defense. But he was alone and unarmed, and there was no place to flee. He'd rather have faced the animals. Though he knew there was little Willimond could have done, he wished his old friend was with him.

"Keep playing," the stranger said. There was in his voice a tone of command. Kristinge's obeyed. His thoughts turned to the treasure he had brought with him from Francia and Danemark. His mother's necklace was still about his neck for all to see. As for his gold, he had foolishly left it all in the purse at his waist. It was too late to hide it now. But the thought came to him of Luxeuil, and the two times during his years there when robbers had come down from the mountains and set upon the monks. And he thought of the love that had been shown by the abbot even to *them*—even after they had speared two of the monks. Still, Kristinge's hands were trembling as they returned to his harp. Obeying the stranger's orders, he began to strum it again, softly but continuously, as if his life depended on his obedience.

"What were you singing?" the man asked, taking another step forward and holding his hands out to warm them by the fire. His heavy accent was unmistakably Frisian. His face was also better lit now, and Kristinge could see his charcoal eyes beneath bushy gray eyebrows and a creased forehead. It was not, he thought, the face of a robber.

"Deor's lament," he answered, looking into the darkness on either side of the stranger. Was he alone?

"You are a bard."

Kristinge nodded, though it had been said as a statement and not a question.

"In the service of a king?"

"I *was* ," Kristinge answered, thinking back on Fjorgest. *I am no longer*, he almost added.

"Do you have any bread?"

The question caught Kristinge off-guard. He thought of the half loaf that remained from his dinner. It was all he had left to sustain him the following day. The thought of lying to preserve his remaining food crossed his mind. But his conscience would not let him lie. "Yes," he answered. He turned to pull the bread from his bag and realized it was sitting out on the blanket to his right, in plain sight of the stranger. He was glad he had spoken the truth.

The man sat down across from the fire. He reached over and helped himself to the bread. Again, Kristinge thought back on the stories of Columbanus' first winter at Annegray. Those months had seen a steady succession of robbers coming down from the mountains upon the undefended monks, only to find that the monks were even poorer than the robbers themselves. And *still* they gave of what they had. As Abbot Walbert had done in Kristinge's time, though raids from robbers were far fewer in those latter days and the population of the monastery much larger. "There is wine, too," the young monk offered, ashamed that he had been tempted to lie. He handed his wine-skin to the stranger who took it and drank.

"You are a stranger here, bard?"

It was funny for Kristinge to hear *himself* called the stranger. He thought about the question. Had he so lost his Frisian accent in just six years? Perhaps that was good. How much should he tell this man? "I have come from Danemark. I spent the winter there in the service of a king." As soon as he said this, he realized that it might be even less safe to come to this part of Friesland as a Dane than to come as the lost heir of Finn. He quickly added, "Before that I lived south in Francia."

The stranger was looking Kristinge over closely now, studying his face. "Francia and Danemark?" he repeated. "And yet you look oddly familiar to me." When his eyes fell on the coin that hung around Kristinge's neck, they opened in surprise or curiosity.

... made ... by the jeweler Deomaer ... symbol of the union of the houses of Hoc and Folcwalda ... His mother's words echoed in Kristinge's ears. Would the pendant be recognized as a mark of his identity? He quickly turned his eyes downward, feigning to concentrate on his harp while trying to hide his face from scrutiny. He wondered how he could remove the necklace or tuck it beneath his cloak without drawing more attention to it. With Willimond no longer with him, Kristinge felt far less confident; more vulnerable. His hands were trembling. Yet the man did not appear to be a threat. His questions were harmless enough. Perhaps it was Kristinge's imagination. The thought of Willimond had put him in the mood for some company.

"Where are you going?" the stranger asked before Kristinge had a chance to say anything.

"To Ezinge," Kristinge answered looking back up at his new guest.

He thought he caught a slight smile on the man's face. "Ezinge will be fortunate to receive you," he said. Then he explained. "Your playing of the harp is beautiful, as is the sound of your voice. A good bard is always well received."

"When I was playing earlier, I did not know I had an audience," Kristinge replied, changing the subject of conversation. "I was startled when I saw you, clse I would have offered hospitality sooner. If you seek a place to spend the night, you might rest by this fire. I don't have enough wood to burn all night, but it will keep you warm for a time. And I would enjoy the company."

"If I can listen to you play and sing more, then I will gladly accept your offer."

Kristinge nodded, all the while continuing to play his harp. And the stranger fell silent, content to listen. The young monk-bard had thought to practice some new songs to ready them for Ezinge in case the chieftain there was in need of a bard. With an audience, he was no longer inclined to do so. In a low voice, he instead sang a few familiar Frisian songs and then put down his harp. His fingers were growing cold and he wrapped them in his cloak. The man spoke no more, and Kristinge didn't have the energy to pursue a conversation. After a time, he rolled out his blanket and lay down. When he fell asleep, the stranger was still sitting across the fire.

When Kristinge awoke the following morning, he was alone. For a moment, he forgot all about his guest of the night before. But when he remembered him, and the booted footprints in the damp soil convinced him that it hadn't been a dream, his felt for his purse. It was still at his side, and nothing of his small wealth had been taken from him. More curious now, he rose and went in search of the stranger. He walked around the tower twice, looking for clues. More booted tracks led him a short distance down the slope to where he found signs of a horse having been hobbled for the night. But horse and rider were both gone now. Kristinge was not a good enough tracker to determine how old the prints were, but he guessed they had left at least an hour earlier. On foot he would never catch him. That was fine, though. Kristinge was content to be alone, though he couldn't help wondering who the stranger was. He walked back up the hill, packed up his belongings, and started walking south and inland.

As he expected, it took him nearly all day to reach Ezinge. Much of the land was still under water from the spring floods, and even the higher ground where he walked was wet and muddy. This made for difficult footing and slow travel. But despite the conditions, he did not risking straying far from the river knowing that the Hunze would eventually lead him to Ezinge. At present he was in no great hurry. And he was not sure he would be able to find his way to Ezinge if he wandered too far from the river. It had been many years since he had walked this route. So he plodded on. The sun rose higher on his left, and this day proved as beautiful as the last. Yet it was a strange walk. Despite the years that had elapsed since his departure from Friesland, and despite his uncertainty about the path, there was a certain vague familiarity to all Kristinge saw. This made the walk at once both enjoyable and also sad—a memory of years lost that could never be regained. He paused frequently to look around at this tree, or that hill, or some curve in the river familiar from his youth—trying if he could to capture the exact memory. And failing.

The terpen village of Ezinge itself he still remembered. It was a wide village, with a large number of pit dwellings sprawled haphazardly across the top a fifteen foot high terp, very unlike the orderly layout of Hwitstan and many other Frisian and Danish villages. Of course terps—the wide flat mounds, manmade over many years by the buildup of cow dung and clay—were common in Friesland, particularly near the coast. Though they offered only little in the way of defense against human marauders, they did provide a secure refuge from water above the oft-flooded surrounding plains. The Ezinge terp had been inhabited for many generations. Though most of the dwellings were newer pit dwellings, a few of the older timber and thatch structures remained in the center of the village, left over from an earlier period. These taller wooden buildings rose up above the surrounding houses, and it was these that Kristinge first caught sight of against the skyline as he approached the village a few hours past midday. He was still a long way off, but the glimpse of the village filled him with excitement and he picked up his pace.

Slowly the terp grew in size as he crossed the plain in a wide loop to avoid the floods. He lengthened his strides to match his eagerness. What would he find there? he wondered. One thing was first on his mind. For once it was not Aewin. Nor even thoughts of Finn, his father. It was the chapel he wondered about. When he reached the near slope of the terp, he turned without delay, following the old oxen-road—the *axwei*—around the northern edge of the village. He was almost running now, straight to where the chapel had once stood on the eastern edge of Ezinge. Though out of breath, he did not stop. Eagerly he climbed up one of many narrow paths from the axwei onto the terp, his eyes searching even before his feet reached the top.

Though many years had passed, the village was much as he remembered it. Except one thing. There was no sign of the chapel. His heart pounded. Of a dozen possible explanations, the most likely was that the chapel had been torn down, destroyed by the priests of Freyr out of jealousy for their own wooden gods. Six years was too long a time to have left it abandoned. In his heart, Kristinge knew that. He had feared it all along. Yet he felt his heart sink when he remembered the labor Willimond had poured into it. He stood there for a long moment on the edge of the terp, with the cool wind in his face, fighting down the instinct to turn around and flee. Where else could he go? It was just a building. He could build another.

"God give me strength..." he began. His prayer ended mid-thought, and his eyes opened wider in the sudden joyous revelation of a man reprieved. He started to run. There, half hidden behind two other huts and toward the center of the village, was Willimond's old chapel. The small wooden structure was still standing after all. Kristinge had failed to see it at first because it was not where he had remembered it. Either the terp and village had grown around the chapel in the intervening years, or else his memory had been wrong. He didn't care. He was so overjoyed to find the chapel still standing, he nearly sprinted to the entrance, his bag and harp bouncing on his shoulders as he ran.

At the door of the chapel, Kristinge stopped. He took a deep breath. Then, setting his belongings on the ground, he opened the wooden door and peered inside. The chapel was small. About eighteen feet long and twelve feet wide. Tiny compared with some of the buildings at Luxeuil and Jouarre. Smaller even than the church in Hwitstan. But it was a place of worship and prayer, and Kristinge did not begrudge its size. With a sense of reverence, he stepped inside. His eyes fell at once to the cross at the back. A peasant in Hwitstan had made it for Willimond to bring to Ezinge. His eyes on this symbol of Christ's humility, Kristinge dropped to his knees and offered prayers of thanksgiving for his safe voyage. And for the safekeeping of the chapel over those many years.

As he sat there then, praising God for His faithfulness, a strange feeling came upon Kristinge. He looked down at his garments, gifts from the Queen Balthild now stained and worn from the wear and travel but still rich and warm. And he thought of his old monastic robe. For the first time in many months, he was back in a house of God. He returned to his bag of belongings, and sorted through his few items of clothing. He stepped back into the chapel. Solemnly, he removed the heavy cloak given him by queen Balthild, and for the first time since his departure from Francia he donned once again his monk's attire. He rubbed his scalp. He would have to reclaim his tonsure, having given it up upon his departure from Paris. Nonetheless, it felt comforting to be back in his old robe. Wearing what he had worn for so long in Luxeuil, he returned to his knees with renewed inspiration. Then he prayed for the village of Ezinge, and for guidance in his mission there. And for Willimond and Hildeburh. And for Luxeuil and Father Walbert. And for all of Francia, and Friesland, and Danemark. He stayed on his knees until the sun was touching the horizon.

When he was finished, Kristinge rose again to his feet. It was then that he noticed how clean the chapel looked. The dirt floors had been swept clean of grass and debris, and the corners were free of cobwebs. There were no signs of deterioration in the building. Any holes in the wall had been filled with wattle. *Could it be that somebody was still using the chapel? Were there still believers in Ezinge? Or*—he shuddered—*was the chapel being used for other purposes?* It was time to find out. Turning around, he strode from the chapel. At the door he paused and looked down again at his belongings. After a moment's contemplation, he picked up his bag and set it inside the building, choosing to carry only his harp with him. If the chapel *had* been taken, then it was time to claim it back. With that in mind, he went in search of the village chieftain.

Though the day was waning, most of the village of Ezinge was still empty. The peasant farmers were out in the nearby fields, working the ground in preparation for planting—in those places it was not flooded or too soggy. From a few huts, Kristinge heard sounds of craftsmen at work. From one building he smelled the distinctive odor of baking clay and in another the sound of bellows being pumped. At the far end of the village from the chapel was a chieftain's hall. It was not as big as Finnsburg had been, but easily large enough for a few dozen warriors. Kristinge walked in that direction. He was almost there when he heard voices coming from one of the larger houses to his right. He turned to look just as three men parted the skin hanging on the doorway and stepped out of the house into the village.

They were traders, judging by their appearance. Or rather, as Kristinge discovered when he looked more closely, two traders and one of their peasant slaves. The peasant was carrying a big pile of woolen cloth—the *pallia Fresonica* for which the Frisian merchants were so famous. The traders were arguing loudly about whether to go straight to the fairs of St. Denis, or to try the markets of Dorestad first where Frankish traders from the south were likely to be at that time of year. When they saw Kristinge staring at them, they ceased their arguing. One of them looked as though he were about to shout something, but he stopped suddenly and peered at the young monk more closely, as if he recognized him. Kristinge, too, thought the trader looked vaguely familiar.

"A monk?" the man said in a distrustful voice. "You're not from Ezinge."

"No," Kristinge replied, trying to figure out where he knew this man from.

"I know you," the trader claimed. "Haven't I seen you in Ezinge before? Or Hwitstan?"

At the mention of Hwitstan, Kristinge almost froze. *Was his identity so quickly discovered? What would they do when they recognized that he was Finn's son?*

"You know this monk?" the other trader asked. "I didn't think you did much business with the monasteries."

"Not on the Isles," the first replied, turning away from Kristinge. "Only in Francia from time to time—near Paris."

At the mention of Paris the glimmer of recognition solidified in Kristinge's mind, and he was able to place the memory. This was one of the traders with whom they had bought passage to Danemark in the fall—the one whom they had let off in Hwitstan halfway along the voyage. "Yes, we have met," Kristinge replied, anxious to direct the trader's memory away from Hwitstan and toward Francia. "But not here. We met in Paris. I and my companion bought passage on your ships to Danemark."

"Danemark?" the second trader asked, in surprise.

The first trader looked back at Kristinge. He scrutinized him carefully. "Yes. I remember now. But you were not in a monk's robe then." He appeared proud to have remembered all that. "So you're still alive. Didn't think you'd ever return from *that* place."

Before Kristinge could answer, they turned and started walking again, content to have solved the riddle. He breathed a sigh of relief. But as they walked away, he could hear them speaking still. "Danemark?" the second one asked. "What did he want there?"

"Never said," the first replied. "But his way was paid with good coins. I don't question gold."

"Huh," the second one grunted, as their voices faded. "I wasn't with you on that trip, but I could have sworn he looked familiar too. But if..."

Kristinge lowered his head and turned around. He waited until the traders were gone before he resumed his walk toward the chieftain's hall. Though the spring air was well above freezing, there was already smoke rising from a hearth fire when he came to the door of the hall. That was a promising sign. Kristinge paused outside the entrance just for a minute, pondering what he would say when he entered. Had he been raised as the son of Finn, he would have known the name of the chieftain of Ezinge. But growing up as a young apprentice to the monk-missionary Willimond, there was not reason he needed to have learned it. If he had, he didn't remember it now. In any case, it was as likely as not that the chieftain had changed. Ezinge was small compared with Domburg and Dorestad, but it was big enough to have its own small war band. Anybody who led the war band in a successful raid—or a successful defense of the village *against* raiders—would earn the title of chieftain, replacing whoever had ruled before him. Since the chieftain would have owed his allegiance to some Frisian overlord or king, the rule could have changed hands six times in as many years. There was not much Kristinge could do but enter and hope—no, not hope, but pray for the best. Pray he did. Then he entered.

CHAPTER 14:
AELFIN, SON OF AELTAR

A familiar voice rang out from the interior of the hall. "Greetings, bard."

Bard? The voice caught Kristinge off guard. He had not come to Ezinge as a bard. He blinked in surprise as his eyes tried to adjust to the wood smoke and dim light. *How was it that he was already known as a bard?*

"I see you have your harp. That is good."

The young monk-bard stood there mute, wondering what to do next. He peered into the hall. *Who was speaking? Who recognized him? Who had known he was coming?*

"Enter, bard. Or do you prefer the cold?"

Kristinge shivered, but not from the cold. Despite the onset of evening air, he was sweating. He searched his mind for some clue about who in Ezinge might know of him. The voice sounded familiar. Where had he heard it before? At least he had been addressed as bard, and not prince. Nonetheless he was unnerved. He wanted to turn and run.

"I say again, Enter!" This time, the voice was firm and compelling. The command was not followed by a question. Still blinking away the sting of smoke in his eyes, Kristinge obeyed. Nervously he stepped forward, still wracking his mind. *Who knew him already, before he even entered the mead hall? And how?* His gaze wandered around the interior of the structure looking for some clue. *Had he been there before, years earlier? Was it possible that whoever had called him 'bard' knew also that he was the son of Finn?*

It did not take him long to search the hall. The small wooden building was rectangular in shape, just a little longer than it was wide with a low angular wooden roof supported by eight pillars running in rows along each side. Near the back center was a wide hearthstone surrounded by wooden benches. It was on the center-most bench, the widest of them, that Kristinge's eyes came to rest. There on the far side of the fire sat a richly dressed chieftain with a large glass drinking horn in hand and a knowing smirk on his face. It was he who had spoken. On either side of the him sat three thanes, also well attired. Two servants, less well dressed though by no means poorly provided for, stood behind the chieftain waiting for his orders.

Kristinge walked slowly up the aisle between the mead benches, and approached the hearth where the ruler of Ezinge sat waiting for him. Not able to see clearly in the fluttering shadows and smoky glow of the fire, he could not yet make out a face. When he reached the hearth he bowed, still wondering how this chieftain had known him. The concern left him more than a little nervous, but there was little he could do. He tried again to remember where and when he had heard that voice before. It seemed more recently than seven years past.

"What?" the chieftain exclaimed, when he saw Kristinge's monastic robe. "What is *this*? You are garbed as a monk? Are you a monk or a bard? Tell me!"

Kristinge flinched. So, he thought: monk or bard? He had been in Friesland barely a day and already he was pressed to the question: monk, bard, or... At least he had not been given the third option: king. Perhaps he would never have to face *that* choice. As to the other two, though he had no desire to verbalize his decision so soon, at least he already had some answer. Even as Kristinge pondered this, the chieftain rose to his feet. Kristinge saw him better now. He was a tall man, strong and broad of shoulder with legs that looked like tree trunks. He was no longer young. His graying hair and creased forehead were showing the signs of his age. However he was not yet so old that younger warriors would cease to fear him. The stern glance with which he appraised Kristinge's robe was alone enough to make the young monk back up a step. But it was his charcoal eyes and bushy gray eyebrows that gave him away. Kristinge's eyes widened in sudden recognition.

"I see that you are less talkative even than last evening," the chieftain answered himself. "But now you are the guest and not the host. Still, such silence is a strange trait for a bard. Stranger still for a monk outside his monastery." He laughed at his own slight on monks. "But as you showed me hospitality beside your fire, I can do no less for you." He motioned to the servants behind him, who handed forward a bronze mug of Frisian ale and a plate with some cheese and bread.

"I am honored by your hospitality," Kristinge finally said, relieved to have discovered how it was that he was already known. So it had been the chieftain of Ezinge whom he had entertained beside his fire the night before. Once again, God had provided in a surprising way. Kristinge was now all the more glad that he had not withheld the last of his bread. The question did not escape his mind as to why the chieftain had been traveling alone such a distance from his village, but it was a question he knew not to ask.

"I have been awaiting you," the chieftain went on, as he took his bench again and motioned for Kristinge to do the same. "You took longer than I expected."

Kristinge sat down and took a swig of the ale. It was strong and good, and made him realize how thirsty he was. He followed the first swig with a longer draught before speaking in his own defense. "I was on foot. I saw from the tracks that you had a horse."

"So I did," the chieftain replied. There was a hint of humor in his voice as he went on. "So you are a bard, a monk, *and* a tracker."

"I am no tracker. The hoof prints were unmistakable." Only after he finished saying this did Kristinge realize that the chieftain had been ridiculing him.

"Then that leaves bard and monk. Which is it?"

"I am a monk, first," Kristinge replied, as if the answer were easier than it was. And even in this answer, he felt trapped. "But I have been called a bard, and I will serve in that way when the need or duty arises."

"The need for a bard may arise soon," the chieftain replied, ignoring Kristinge's other answer. "Tell me first, what is your name?" He was watching closely as he asked this.

"I am Kristinge."

"Kristinge," the chieftain repeated with a slight nod. His eyes narrowed and his brow creased even further, as if he were dredging up some distant memory.

Again, Kristinge grew nervous. "Kristinge of *Luxeuil*," he added. It was a trick he had learned from some hunters in Danemark—disguising his scent with a stronger, different scent. He wondered if it would work.

"Luxeuil? I have heard of this place. A monastery. It is far south, beyond the lands of the Franks."

"*Among* the Franks. It is in the Vosges mountains."

The chieftain narrowed his eyes. "You do not look Frankish."

"I have mixed blood," Kristinge replied, risking as much of the truth as he dared expose at the time. Even that was foolish. How many could boast of a Danish mother and a Frisian father? He went on, again hoping to change the subject before the chieftain could ask any more questions. "And now already I must ask for your forgiveness. I should know the name of the chieftain whose hall I have entered, but I have not traveled through these parts in many years, and so I must confess my own ignorance. Yet if I am called as a bard, I would know whom I serve."

"I am Aelfin, son of Aeltar," the chieftain replied. The name sounded familiar to Kristinge, but again he couldn't place it right away. "And if your singing last night is a sample of your abilities, then I would have you sing for us this very evening."

As his earlier answer to Aelfin had indicated—and as he had told Willimond and Hildeburh even before his departure from Danemark—Kristinge had finally decided that when he returned to Friesland it would be as a monk, not as the son of a chieftain, nor even as a bard. Or rather as a priest, for what was a monk without a monastery? Yes, as a priest. As best as he could, Kristinge would fill the role vacated by Willimond seven years earlier. Had not Willimond himself passed on that calling? As to the prophecies that had been made about him by Osanne and others, he had pushed those from his mind. Still, he couldn't help but ask of Aelfin, "You are in need of a bard, then?"

"Ah. No," Aelfin replied, at once both relieving and disappointing Kristinge. "I have a very apt bard. So skilled is he that he feels no threat from traveling bards and minstrels. Dyflines is his name. An Irish bard with a gift of story. I have no desire to replace him. If you join us this evening, you will hear him yourself."

Another bard? Kristinge grimaced inwardly at the memory of Sceaptung. "Then I need not bring my harp?"

"Bring your harp. Unless you prefer to sing without it! I have told you. Dyflines fears no competitors. He will listen to you, and applaud you if you are good. And if you are not, he will show you such skill of his own that you might not lift your own harp ever again. But come, I have heard you myself and know that you have nothing to fear."

"Again, I am honored by your hospitality, as well as by your confidence" Kristinge replied, bowing his head.

"Still," Aelfin went on. "You have not told me what took you so long?" He picked up his drinking horn as he spoke, and took a long draught. Yet his eyes did not leave Kristinge as he waited for an answer.

"It is a long way on foot. Longer than I..." — he was about to say *remembered*, but he caught his own mistake and changed it quickly — "... expected."

"Yes," Aelfin said shrugging. But he demonstrated that he knew much of what went on in Ezinge, as a good chieftain should. "Yet once you arrived in the village, you were some time before you came here. Surely it did not take you all that time to find this hall?"

Kristinge answered without thinking. "I went first to the chapel."

"Of course," Aelfin replied slyly. "You are a monk first, and a bard second. But tell me, how did you know there was a chapel here?"

Already Kristinge had let his tongue slip and given away more than he intended. He knew it. What was he to say now? Any answer he gave would raise suspicions. Fortunately, he was rescued a moment later. For as he sat there fumbling for an answer, in through the door came a half dozen thanes and warriors, and with them another man who had to be the bard Dyflines. He was tall and lean, with deep red hair, wiry arms, and a four-stringed lyre held casually over one shoulder. He looked to be a few years older than Kristinge. He was laughing and joking with the thanes as if he knew them well.

"Greetings, O Great One," the entering bard said in a voice bordering on sarcasm, and with an exaggerated bow.

"Sit, and be silent, O Loud and Clumsy One," Aelfin replied, in a voice that would have sounded much angrier were it not for the smile on his face. "Or I'll silence you myself with my foot. And you know from past experience how hard is my foot and how well-made my boot!"

One of the warrior-thanes—one whom Kristinge later learned was a young cousin of Aelfin's named Maccus—lightly jabbed the back of Dyflines' locked knees with the butt of his spear, causing the bard to crumble to the floor, which he did with exaggerated dramatics. As Kristinge watched the display, he found himself drawn to this chieftain and his bard, a feeling he had never had with Fjorgest.

"Better get up quick," said another thane who had been sitting there silently all the while. "You've got competition tonight."

Dyflines sprang nimbly to his feet, but he did not appear daunted by the news. "Competition, friend Ceolac?" he asked, addressing the thane who had spoken. "Who will it be? Whom will we have the pleasure of hearing this evening? Have *you* learned to play the lyre?"

Of course Kristinge was the only stranger in the hall, and in a moment Dyflines was looking right at him. "A harp-player, I see. Unless the shape of your bag deceives me. Then it will be a pleasure indeed. Though I, for one, prefer the lyre." So saying, he spun his lyre deftly in his hand so that the neck rolled over his wrist leaving the instrument laying in his arms ready for playing. He strummed a few notes, then lifted it back over his shoulder and sat down.

It was not long before food and drink were served, and the small company of two bards, twelve thanes, and the chieftain Aelfin joined together for the evening meal. When the meal was finished, more drink was brought and the bards were called forth to sing. As the guest bard, Kristinge was invited to sing first. At Aelfin's request he started with *Deor's Lament*, followed it with the *Seafarer's Song* he had learned among the Danes, and ended with the *Song of the Cross-Tree*. The three songs were well-received, and even Dyflines' applause was sincere. When Kristinge was finished, Aelfin rewarded him with a small ring. The monk sang one more song then set down his harp and turned expectantly toward the other bard.

To Kristinge's surprise, Dyflines proved as good as Aelfin had promised. The Irish bard's songs were laced with a strong Celtic flavor, full of fanciful tales of dragons and gods and talking creatures. As if to prove his prowess, he ended with his own version of Deor's Lament, despite having only just heard it from Kristinge that evening. And though he lost a few words, he made up for the deficiency by spontaneously composing two new verses of his own. It was an impressive feat for a bard, and Kristinge returned the applause. If he had grown proud of his success as a bard in the hall of Fjorgest, then he was humbled now. He was in the presence of a *true* bard.

When the singing was finished, more mead was passed around. Kristinge had a second drink, but did not stay long to partake of more food. Something about the chapel drew his thoughts. A short time later he excused himself from the presence of the chieftain, departed from the hall, and returned there. With no place else to spend his first night in Ezinge, he unrolled his blanket on the floor. Yet even all alone in a strange village, there was a deep sense of calm on him that night. He was soon asleep.

If his first day in Ezinge had been busier than Kristinge expected, his second was more quiet. In answering Aelfin's question, Kristinge had chosen a path, at least for the time. Not that of a monk, as he had told the chieftain. He had given up Luxeuil. Even his tonsure had vanished beneath the winter's growth of new hair. Rather, Kristinge would follow the path of a priest—the call given to him by Willimond.

There was, however, one barrier to this choice. Kristinge had never been a priest. He had not been trained as one. He was a Luxeuil monk. Skilled in the weeding of gardens. Perhaps even in the study of scripture. He was a student. Once a novice. Later a brother. For a short time a traveling bard. Never a priest. *Where did he begin? Who was his model?* During his last two years at Luxeuil, he had on occasion traveled with Father Petrica to visit peasant villages in the mountains surrounding the monastery. He had watched his elder minister to the people there. Yet those trips had been rare, and Kristinge remembered little of them other than the miles of silent walking at Petrica's side. His thoughts took him back further, to the days of his childhood. Willimond also had come from a monastery. From Lindisfarne. He had trained as a monk. Yet he had become a true priest to the people of Hwitstan. He had been an apostle to all of Friesland. Had his years with Aidan trained him for such? Perhaps. But alas, Kristinge—as a youth of only fifteen summers—had given little thought to the possibility that he would one day be called to replace Willimond. He had immersed himself in the studies of scripture. In the learning of Latin, and the teachings of the saints. But he had paid little attention to the duties of priesthood. Would that Willimond or Petrica were with him now!

"Let no one look down on your youthfulness," the Apostle Paul had

written to Timothy. *"But in your speech, actions, charity, faith, and holiness show yourself an example."* Kristinge awoke from his night's rest with those words on his heart. *Example to whom?* he wondered, when he had pondered the scriptures for a few moments. How could one be called a shepherd who had no flock? Yet the calm that had filled him that night before was still there. He would leave that question to God. For today, he chose not to worry. After a trip to the river to wash his face and hands, he returned to the chapel to spend the day in prayer and fasting.

And so the second day passed in silence. And the second night was spent in the chapel. It was not until the coming of his third day in Ezinge that the new priest received his first visitor. He came during the hour that would have been Compline at Luxeuil. Kristinge was again on his knees in prayer at the front of the chapel when he became aware that he was being watched. It was nothing conscious. Perhaps the small room had darkened just slightly from a body filling the entryway. Or perhaps it was the barely perceptible sound of a person breathing. Or perhaps it was his sixth sense: an inexplicable feeling or instinct. At once both curious and a little afraid, he rose to his feet and turned to greet his guest.

It was Aelfin. The chieftain's large frame filled the entrance. Yet there was a hint of nervousness on the warrior's face. He appeared uncomfortable to be so close to the inside of a Christian chapel. His arms were folded across his chest, and his legs were spread in a stern stance, as if he were fighting to appear intimidating rather than intimidated. "I have told you before that I already have a bard," Aelfin said, starting the conversation abruptly.

The comment took Kristinge even more by surprise than the presence of the chieftain at the door of his chapel. The greeting he had received from Aelfin two nights earlier had been warm enough, and he knew he had not failed at the harp. Was he no longer welcome? Why? "I have served as a bard in the North for these past many months," Kristinge replied cautiously. "But I tell the truth that I came here as a priest, and not as a bard."

"I had not yet finished," Aelfin continued, his voice softening slightly. "It was my thought to tell you that though I have already a bard and I have no desire to lose him, I would still welcome you to stay in Ezinge. You have no small talent, and it may be that I will call you to sing for me from time to time. As for a priest," the chieftain went on, sweeping his right arm in a gesture to encompass the chapel and its few possessions, "I have no need for your new religion. The gods of our people have served us well enough in the past. But the chapel has been empty for many years now. The priest who built it was sent south some years ago—before I came to Ezinge."

Willimond! Kristinge almost spoke the name aloud, but he managed to hold his tongue.

"I know only a little of this chapel's history or of his, though there are some here who still remember him. You may stay here if you desire. My gods need feel no more threatened by your presence than does my bard."

Kristinge smiled inwardly. *If Aelfin knew the truth!* The God he served was a far greater threat to the gods of that place than Kristinge would ever be to Dyflines the bard. But he didn't say so. There would be time enough for that to become apparent on its own. Nor did he mention that he had *already* planned on doing just what Aelfin suggested: remaining as a priest. For Kristinge knew from the histories of Aidan and Columbanus and many others that it was always best to receive the blessing and support of the local rulers. Of course he knew also from Columbanus' story that even without the blessing of the king, the work of God would continue; God was greater than any earthly king. "Your offer is very generous," Kristinge replied diplomatically. "This is what I had hoped for."

"So be it," Aelfin said. "I will neither support nor hinder your work here."

He who is not for me is against me, Kristinge thought, but again he held his tongue. There was time. He knew that just for a pagan king to allow him to stay was no small thing. It was an important start. There would be time for God to change Aelfin's heart. He thanked the chieftain again, and then waited for him to depart. But Aelfin did not leave. Surprising Kristinge for the third time that day, he stepped into the chapel. Kristinge knew enough about the Frisians and their gods to know that the people had a certain fear and respect for their holy places: the shrines and groves where the gods were served and where the rites were performed. There was something healthy about this respect, he thought. It brought the Frisians and Danes with their pagan gods closer to the truth than those like the Frankish king Clovis who had abandoned religion altogether and embraced instead his lusts. Again Kristinge's thoughts drifted to the question of how to capture this sense of reverence and fear, how to capture the far-off beauty of their heroic ideals, and use it to tell of the true God and of the true Heroism of humility—the Heroism of the Christ on the Cross. As his memory drifted back over his days in Danemark and his attempts to tell the Gospel in the heroic verse and tradition of these Germanic people, he barely noticed that Aelfin had taken a seat on one of the two narrow benches in the chapel. Then the chieftain's voice caught his attention again.

"I have been in Ezinge only a small number of years. My people were driven from Domburg by the Franks four winters ago. We came eastward, looking for land away from the Rhine." He spoke in a distant voice, like one of the Chroniclers. A wandering monologue much different from the voice and manner he had used in his hall. "Ezinge had gone through some suffering itself in those days: raids, disease, poor harvest. Many of its buildings were empty, though a few had been filled by refugees from Hwitstan after the fight at Finnsburg." He paused for an instant and looked at Kristinge as he said this, then he continued. "It was mostly Saxons who lived here then. Descendants of the raiders who took the village generations earlier, though over the years they had mingled with the Frisian populace of Hwitstan."

At the second mention of Hwitstan, Kristinge sat down on the other bench and began to listen more intently. Though he was not yet sure what it was or why, there was something more than he had first thought to this visit from his new chieftain. He didn't know whether to feel nervous or honored.

"They had no chieftain," Aelfin said, continuing his unasked-for explanation. He stared out the open door as he spoke, only now and then casting a sidelong glance in Kristinge's direction. "When I came here from Domburg with my war band, leading the remnants of our people—those who had not stayed to live under Frankish rule—*I* was taken as the lord of Ezinge. There was no *real* war band here that could have opposed me then, but I would not have forcibly made myself chieftain as the Franks had done. The people took me by choice." He paused. "I have known much sorrow these past years."

Kristinge narrowed his eyes and shook his head in amazement. Was this a *chieftain* speaking now? A war leader? What solace did he seek? And what solace could Kristinge offer? Had Aelfin come seeking a bard? Or a priest?

"We lost our homes to the Franks," Aelfin went on, unaware of Kristinge's questions. "We fought at first, but too many of my people were lost and the enemy was too strong. In the days of Finn and Finnlaf, we might have held them off. Finn would have come to our aid, as his father had done before him. But their tale, too, is a tragic one. Now our land has no real king. No chieftain to bring us together. We have lost a great lord. And I? I have lost a great friend."

Finn and Finnlaf. The rest of the family that Kristinge had never known. And now never would. Their names stung like secret darts. *Was it his own history that Kristinge had returned to Friesland to face?* He was not sure. His own unresolved questions came bubbling to the surface like a salty spring, causing him for a moment to forget all about Aelfin's troubles.

A moment later, the tone of Aelfin's voice changed slightly, as if he were remembering some temporarily forgotten hope. His gaze turned back on Kristinge. "Yet all is not lost. I live. And Dyflines brings back some joy to my hall. Not all joy was vanquished with the losses of Hwitstan and Domburg. There is laughter in that Irish bard, and that is what a good bard should do, is it not? Yes. He is brash, and young, and full of life. Like I was, long ago." He sighed.

"You knew Finn?" Kristinge asked, barely hearing the comments about Dyflines.

"Indeed, I knew him. My father Aeltar was one of his thanes. And I was a thane of Finnlaf. A thane? Yes. A thane and a friend also, if I can be so bold as to call myself such. Finnlaf was a great prince. The day my father Aeltar died was made doubly sad because I had to leave Finnlaf's side and return to Domburg to be its chieftain. Alas! If I had been in Hwitstan to fight by his side at the end, gladly I would have died for him."

Kristinge found his eyes growing moist. In his youth he had felt nothing but joy at the prospect of journeying with Willimond to far-off Luxeuil, a center of learning and of pursuing the call of God, so he imagined it. And so it was, in a way. Yet though Kristinge had not known at the time, he too had been driven from his home, sent away like an exiled prince. Now he had to face that. His thoughts drifted back to the day he had ridden southward from Hwitstan, and for the moment the strangeness of his present situation—of an unknown chieftain speaking to him in such a way, confiding in him as one might confide in a priest or friend—drifted from his mind.

"But the Danes," Aelfin was saying. "*They* are not the *real* enemies now. It is the Franks. Every month, more of them are crossing the Rhine. If we don't stop them soon, Friesland itself will fall. We need a new king. If our chieftains do not agree on a Frisian king, they will get a Frankish one." All of a sudden, Aelfin stopped. He glanced sidelong at Kristinge with a strange look in his eyes. "The Franks, yes. And here I am talking to one!"

Kristinge fought down his thoughts of his lost father and brother, and brought himself back to the present. Aelfin was abruptly rising to leave. "No," Kristinge protested. "I am no Frank, nor do I desire a Frankish rule over us. I have met king Clovis, and would not be ruled by him."

At the mention of Clovis, Aelfin's eyes widened in surprise. "But you come from Francia, do you not? Are you not a monk of Luxeuil?"

"I am," Kristinge admitted, "but there are many monks at Luxeuil, and only a few are Frankish."

"Then where *are* you from?" Aelfin asked, a sly look in his eyes.

"I have lived in many places," Kristinge stammered out. "I have mixed blood."

"What mix, I wonder," the chieftain said, but he didn't wait for an answer. A moment later, he had stepped out the door and was gone. Kristinge did not follow him.

The weeks that followed as spring progressed toward summer were good ones for Kristinge. He settled into Ezinge. Not wanting to live in the chapel, preferring to preserve it for purposes more holy, he built for himself a small hut on the edge of the terp not far away.

Between the wealth he had brought from Balthild, what his mother Hildeburh had given him, and what he received now and then from Aelfin in reward for his occasional singing, he was able to keep clothed and fed. He enjoyed his role as part time bard, and soon developed a good relationship with Dyflines who visited him frequently to exchange songs and practice new compositions.

The role of priest on the other hand was much newer to him than that of bard. Nor was Kristinge merely a priest, but a lone priest in a pagan village. It was a task very unlike being a young monk in a large monastery. Yet on his very first Sabbath day in Ezinge, the lone priest discovered who it was that had kept the chapel clean during those many years since he and Willimond had last been in Ezinge. He had his second visitor. It was a poor peasant farmer named Dunnere. A short thin man with scraggly limbs and just a few puffs of gray hair, he nearly disappeared beneath his heavy roughly-stitched cloak that looked more substantial than its owner. Dunnere had no family. His only possession was an old goat he kept for milk and treated like a child. And he was lucky to have that. He had no family farm land. He tended his chieftain's cattle on the lands surrounding the terp, and also worked in the few flax fields the village kept. Like most peasants, he could count no higher than twelve—the largest number of cows he had ever watched—and so he wasn't sure exactly how many years he had lived. It was long for a peasant, he knew. But to Kristinge, it wouldn't have mattered if Dunnere was ten or a hundred. The new priest was overjoyed to find that he did have a flock in Ezinge, small though it may have been.

In the days following, Kristinge discovered more about the old peasant. Dunnere still professed a Christian faith some six years after Willimond's departure, but it was a faith full of superstition, heavily influenced by the Germanic culture that surrounded him. He had little understanding of the tenets which defined Christianity. His belief in God was based on one thing: he claimed to have been miraculously healed of a stomach illness when Willimond had laid hands on him in the name of Christ. This happened just a few months before the old priest had left for Luxeuil. Dunnere had not forgotten him. Nor had he forgotten 'young Kristinge', though Kristinge had no memory of him. Now Dunnere was determined to serve the God who had healed him. Though in Ezinge he was all alone in his faith, he had come to the chapel every seventh day—except for the few weeks when he was too busy with the flax harvest, for which he apologized—and cleaned it and recited the Lord's prayer. He claimed that God had promised him in a dream that a real priest would one day return to Ezinge, during Dunnere's lifetime, and had asked him to keep things in ready. And now he took Kristinge to be the fulfillment of God's promise.

Another prophecy? Kristinge wondered wryly. More people knew more about him than he knew about himself. But it no longer troubled him, and he soon grew to love the old peasant as he sought to build up his knowledge of the God he served.

Kristinge also grew in friendship with the thanes Maccus and Ceolac. Though some of the warriors disdained his company, speaking of him only as "the Christian priest" and accusing him of slandering the "true Frisians gods", as a bard Kristinge earned the appreciation of many thanes including Maccus and Ceolac. Kristinge also soon learned that Dunnere was not the only believer in Ezinge. There were a few others, all peasants, whom Willimond had led to the Lord. Without a priest, they had drifted away from their faith, but when they saw the chapel once again holding masses they were quick to return. Of course as long as the chieftain resisted Christianity, Kristinge knew there would be few additional converts—probably none among the warriors. But he also knew that God rejoiced for every lost sheep who was found, whether chieftain, warrior, or peasant. He remembered how in Luxeuil all labored together: peasant, merchant, and king. There were no nationalities. No classes. So he served the few as joyfully as he would have served the many.

Aelfin also spoke frequently with the new priest and part-time bard. Though it had been a comment made in passing, the Chieftain remembered Kristinge's claim to have met Clovis. Now he was interested in hearing more about the Frankish king and his armies. He did not hide his disappointment that Kristinge knew so little about Frankish battle strategies, or the size of their war bands. "What do you expect from a monk," he muttered. But his comment was made without malice, and it did not stop him from continuing his questioning. And the young monk-turned-bard-turned-priest soon realized that he knew more than he thought. In particular, his news of the present turmoil over the Frankish throne and his description of Clovis' illness excited the chieftain's hope. Aelfin kept returning again and again to the threat of Frankish invasion, and to the need for a united Friesland and a Frisian king.

"Maybe now," he said, referring to the instability in Francia, "Maybe *now* is the time for us to attack and drive them back from the Rhine. If we act swiftly, and if they remain divided, we may win. You say the new High King, Chlotar son of Clovis, is just a child?"

In this way, spring passed and Summer's Day arrived. There was a small celebration in Ezinge. Kristinge was called upon to join Dyflines in singing throughout the day as the villagers feasted on domesticated and wild pork, fish, and the remnants of the previous year's barley and flax. There was also plenty to drink. Kristinge followed the pattern he had set as a bard in Danemark, singing a mix of both common Frisian songs and his Germanic Gospel.

Many days he spent alone in prayer and in the study of scripture. Other days were spent at Aelfin's side answering questions, which to Kristinge's discouragement were only infrequently about his God. But he did not lose patience. On the Sabbath he led his small flock in worship, preaching to them from the Word and leading them in the Holy Communion. When one or another was sick, he would visit them and pray for them, anointing them with oil as he had seen both Petrica and Willimond do on occasion. Often his thoughts turned to his former teacher, and to Hildeburh. Wondering how they were doing, or worrying about opposition from the priests of Freyr, he would pray for them. To Luxeuil his thoughts turned at times also, though rarely did he feel any regret at having departed or any longing to return. Then his thoughts would turn to Aewin, and for a time he would forget altogether about Danemark and Luxeuil both, and wonder whether he would see her again. More than once he considered asking Aelfin about her, but he could never think of a way to pose the question that would not arouse suspicion, and so he held his tongue. Thus it was that the days rolled by.

It was not until midsummer that his worries began to arise. As days once again began to shorten and the fall harvest approached, Aelfin began to question Kristinge more and more about where he had come from. At first his questions were direct, and Kristinge, wary of them, was successful in avoiding them or in answering vaguely enough to satisfy the chieftain without lying or giving too much away. Later, however, the questions became more subtle, and Kristinge's guard slipped more than once. Dyflines joined too, and he was even wilier. As the weeks passed, the priest was slowly backed into a corner regarding his identity, and he began to suspect that there were rumors spreading in the village. His greatest fear was caused by Dunnere. The old peasant remembered Kristinge from before, and he didn't understand his priest's exhortations to remain silent about the matter. Of course Dunnere tried to comply. And Kristinge thought he might be safe, since the poor shepherd had little contact with Aelfin and his thanes. But the village was too small. The danger he feared was not far away.

Kristinge had been gone from Luxeuil for a year now. Nigh upon the autumnal equinox—the fall harvest celebration—he was again called upon to sing before Aelfin in his hall. He complied joyfully for he had recently composed a new song, the tale of Gideon, and was looking forward to the opportunity to perform it before the chieftain.

The hall was fuller than Kristinge had ever seen it when he entered that evening with his harp. All of Aelfin's thanes were present, and some other warriors as well, many of whom Kristinge did not recognize. This was a greater gathering than the hearthwerod of a local chieftain, though the significance of that observation did not strike him until later. Whatever the case was, the young priest-bard was not daunted by the size of the crowd.

Not until he saw *her*.

She sat across from Kristinge, one of three women in the hall that night, surrounded by a half dozen warriors from another village. Unlike the first time he had seen her the day he left Paris nearly a year earlier, she was now quiet and drew no attention to herself. Still, though shifting bodies obscured her from view, it took only one glance for Kristinge to recognize her: the hair as black as night—as black as her eyes—and the skin smooth and white. Her high, proud, forehead. The round shoulders and full lips.

Aewin.

How had she come here? Kristinge's heart leapt at the possibility. Had she come because she had heard rumor of Kristinge's presence in Ezinge? The thought was too much—too ridiculous—to hope for. But he could not help but wonder. Had she also guessed, as Frotha had, that it had been her for whom he had sung that night many months past when last he had seen her? Did she remember him from years earlier in Hwitstan? Suddenly, Kristinge began to sweat. He turned his eyes away quickly, hoping to avoid eye contact. But he couldn't help wondering if she noticed him. If she was looking at him.

It was a warm summer night and no fire was lit. For the bards, a small space had been left clear on the hearthstone. When he was called upon by Aelfin, Kristinge stood with his harp. Her presence had made him nervous. He thought about changing the song, about singing again what he had sung for her nearly a year ago in Frotha's hall. But he couldn't bring himself to do it. He couldn't even look at her. He performed the song he had planned. He sang of the mighty warrior-chieftain Gideon and his small band of thanes who won a great victory over the enemies of his clan. How the Creator-God and Lord of Gideon's people whittled the chieftain's war band down to only a small number of the greatest warriors, and then won the victory over a vastly larger foe so that the people would know it was the work of their God and not their own strength that had won them the victory. The song ended with Gideon attacking the enemy host from the surrounding hills.

> "High on the hill-tops,   lamps hidden beneath jars,
> there three hundred stood.   They knew no fear.
> With Gideon they waited,   watching below
> the feared Midianites,   the foreign murderers;
> The valley they filled,   that vast hateful foe,
> like locusts swarming   swallowing the land.
>
> But Gideon, he followed   the God of his folk.
> He lifted his torch.   Trumpet he blew.
> The great God he called   to guide his war band.

Then warriors shouted,   shields raised on high,
held up their swords,   and sounded their horns.
Gave a great cry,   called with their voices,
their jars they smashed,   shields then they clashed.
'Our swords for God,   for Gideon,' they shouted.
Led by their chieftain,   they charged down the hill.

Then the Lord Himself,   the Chieftain on high,
down in their midst   the mighty God came.
The Midianites heard   a horrible sound.
The camp was confused.   They cried out in fear.
And taken by terror,   each other they slew;
Those cowards killed   their own companions.
That foe then fled   Gideon's fierce attack.
Whelmed over in fright,   in fear ran away.
And Gideon won,   his war band conquered,
By God's own strength   stood 'gainst his foe."

The song went well, and Kristinge was pleased when he was done. Yet the mood in the hall was tense that night, and the response was less than he expected. Feeling that he had failed, for a moment he forgot about Aewin. Almost at once, Dyflines was called upon to sing. Kristinge returned to his seat and tried to listen as the other bard with his lyre stood on the hearth and began.

The first song that Dyflines sang was no surprise. It was *Deor's Lament*. Dyflines had sung it three or four times since first hearing it from Kristinge. And Kristinge had to admit that Dyflines now sang it better than he did. The Irish bard knew the rules and patterns of the poet's trade well, and he practiced far more than Kristinge. He was quick at learning songs, and just as adept at composing his own. He had already added five of his own verses to the lament.

No. That he sang this song tonight was not the surprise. Nor was it a surprise that he had composed yet further verses. It was the *subject* of this final verse that caught Kristinge's attention.

The flower of Finn,   the fair Hildeburh,
queen of all Friesland,   her fate was too great.

Her strong eldest son   struck down in his youth,
The life of Finnlaf   whom she had loved.
And bound too by blood,   her brother Hnaef,
In the same battle fell   on Friesland's own soil.
Yet more great her grief   did grow still when
in Hwistan was hewn   her own husband Finn.
          That has passed over;   so also will this.

Applause did not follow this song. Dyflines's singing had been too powerful for that. Battle-hardened warriors sat with their mead cups, glassy-eyed and silent, staring at the empty hearth. Not a single one was left unmoved. The bard himself remained silent for a time, lowering his lyre and sitting on the bench across from Aelfin.

But Kristinge could hardly appreciate the genius with which Dyflines had composed and performed the lament. He had been struck too hard. Not by grief. He knew his mother had suffered great loss, but he knew also that she now knew great joy. He knew better than any there how true Dyfline's words were. Hildeburh's grief *had* passed over.

Which was precisely what frightened Kristinge. How did Dyflines know? Deor's lament told of great heroes who had passed *through* tragedy and sorrow into joy and redemption. That was the pattern of the song. But for those sitting in Ezinge who knew about the tales of the fights at Finnsburg and Hwitstanwic, there was only grief. No joy. Hildeburh's son had died. Her brother had died. Her husband had died. Had Dyflines changed the pattern of the song? Or did he know something more?

Her strong eldest son struck down in his youth, The life of Finnlaf whom she had loved.

Then finally it struck Kristinge. Her *eldest* son?

CHAPTER 15:

ΠΕIR OF FIΠΠ'S TORC

Oyflines was a good bard. Perhaps even a great bard. He was too wise and crafty to use words lightly. Kristinge knew that. Yet the implications of the song were all too clear. To mention Hildeburh in the context of *Deor's Lament*—to refer to her *eldest* son—these things spoke a message a clear as daylight. Dyflines might as well have come right out and said, *Hildeburh had more than one child. It was the eldest son who died. The youngest lives. Now her sorrow has been turned back to joy; this too has passed.*

This could not be coincidence. Could everybody in the hall be blind? Kristinge risked a single glance in Dyflines' direction. The bard was not looking back. He gave no indication that he was even aware of Kristinge's presence, no indication that the song was sung for anyone in particular. A minute later he rose and began to sing again, lifting the mood of the company with an heroic tale of Friesc, a Frisian chieftain and mighty warrior of old. He sang loudly and energetically, strumming his lyre so forcefully that the strings appeared on the verge of breaking. Kristinge, however, was too shaken by the first song. He was not able to pay attention to the bard's singing for the rest of that evening. He had forgotten even about Aewin. Long before Dyflines had finished singing that evening, while mead still flowed and stew still stood warm by the fire, the young priest left the hall and wandered back to his hut alone. That night, he slept very little.

Despite all Kristinge's fears, however, the following morning dawned clear and bright, and the life of the village continued on as normal. Nothing had changed. Kristinge walked through the day's activities ready to bolt at any moment, like a deer walking past a den of wolves. But Aelfin did not appear at Kristinge's door confronting him with his identity and challenging him as a rival. In fact, nobody treated the young priest any differently than before. The song Dyflines had sung—his version of Deor's lament with the mysterious new verse about Hildeburh—was not even mentioned. Everything about the day was routine, except for Kristinge's jumpiness. And so by the middle of the afternoon he was beginning to wonder whether his fears had been unfounded, if the singing about Hildeburh *had* been a mere coincidence with a significance magnified only by Kristinge's imagination. By the end of the day, he was once again thinking about Aewin. And though he dared not venture into the mead hall, he spent the last two hours of the day wandering about the village hoping to catch sight of her.

Thus it happened that when Ceolac found Kristinge near the chapel late in the afternoon and told him that he was again requested by Aelfin in the hall that evening, the young priest could not resist accepting the invitation despite his persistent sense of waiting danger. The possibility of Aewin's presence alone was enough to draw him. When evening came, he retrieved his harp from his hut and went to the hall. And when the mead had been served and Aelfin called on him, he sang his two songs. The gathered company was large again that night with more faces Kristinge did not recognize. Unfortunately, the mysterious Aewin was not one of them. He still did not know from whence she came. Nevertheless, Kristinge sang energetically. Though he felt more nervous and self-conscious than usual, this night his songs were well received. He finished and sat down with a satisfied sigh, setting his harp beside the bench and readying himself to listen to the other bard. And when Dyflines started to sing—and there was yet no indication that anything was out of the ordinary—Kristinge became more convinced that he had been worrying for nothing. Though his sense of uneasiness had not left him, he tried to relax and listen.

The Irish bard began with another heroic lay about Friesc, which he followed with one about the great Danish hero, Beow of Old. Whether it was that the company was livelier than usual, or the crowd larger, or the mead stronger, Kristinge did not know, but the response to the Bard's first two songs was loud and energetic. The mood in the hall was festive and the spirit was catchy. By Dyflines' third song, a new tale about Weland the Smith, Kristinge was finally relaxing.

For his fourth song, Dyflines chose the *Lay of Folcwalda*. Though Kristinge had not heard it sung in many years, and though it had changed somewhat over the course of time and with a different poet, he recognized it at once as one of the old bard Daelga's poems. He started to grow nervous again to hear this particular song, especially after the previous night's song about Hildeburh. But a heroic song about Folcwalda was normal from a bard in Friesland. He knew that. And he liked the piece; it held more meaning for him now than it ever had before, for he knew now that Folcwalda was his own kin: his father's father. He forced himself to relax again.

Dyflines sang the long song in its entirety, ending with Folcwalda's death at the hands of the Franks after the *Battle of Domburg Isles*.

> "Now gone is our lord,   laid on the byre.
> Felled by his foes,   Folcwalda was.
> One final voyage,   one farewell too many;
> our king traveled south,   sent help when called.
> He sailed from these shores;   a ship bore him off
> to far off Domburg,   to his doom freely went,
> to gather Friesland: one folk, one king.
>
> Departed is our king,   cold now in death.
> Felled by his foes,   Folcwalda was.
> But Friesland he united   for Finn his son,
> the victory he won;   wise was our king
> though never to hall   or hearth did return.
> Great is our grief!   A good ruler we lost.
> For Hwitstan, Alas!   Long shall we mourn."

Though Kristinge had never known his grandfather Folcwalda, he had heard the tale of that last voyage many times during his days in Hwitstan. He was fighting back tears by the time Dyflines finished. He could hear some of the old poet Daelga in the voice of this young Irish bard, and he imagined Daelga's gray hair and ageless slate eyes hovering over a hearth fire singing of his former lord. But even more, Kristinge could see his own father Finn, and his brother Finnlaf, all of whom had died warriors' deaths.

When the song was over, Dyflines paused briefly. He turned toward Kristinge and gave a quick sly discomforting glance that made the young priest squirm in his seat—made him sense that something really *was* going to happen despite all the time he had spent assuring himself to the contrary—and then he began his next song. It was a song Kristinge had never before heard, but one he would not forget. For short though it was, it was a song that would change his life.

> From Hwitstan he went,   the wise thane Ulestan,
> from hearth, from home,   from hall and from king.
> A weary wanderer,   but he walks not alone.
> He went with God's man,   the good monk Willimond.
>
> No foe drove him forth.   No fear made him leave.
> He did not seek   that sorrowful way.
> One command he received,   one care from his ruler.
> To him was trusted   the highest of tasks:
> this boy to keep,   the king's own blood.
>
> Thus Ulestan did take,   traveling so far,
> the sad road south   with snow close behind.
> They promised to protect   the prince between them.
> And by God's grace,   by the good One's mercy,
> to joy and to peace   their path may still lead.
> And hope is held high   the third may come home.
>
> A king to Friesland,   Finn's son, Kristinge.

When the final words of the song had been sung, Dyflines stepped back from the cold hearthstone. With a satisfied grin on his face, he again looked over at Kristinge. He was not the only one to do so. In the stillness following the song, every eye in the hall had turned toward the youngest son of Finn who sat there in his monk's robe holding a harp and wondering what to do.

Kristinge breathed sharply and audibly into the silence, blinking back at the unblinking eyes. He was stunned. Trembling. Heat from an imaginary fire swelled around him, nearly causing him to faint. He swayed in his seat. A dozen thoughts flashed across his mind in rapid succession. It had happened to him in Danemark with Fjorgest.

He should have guessed it would happen here. He should have *known* he could not keep his heritage a secret forever. But how had Dyflines guessed? Had the Irish bard sung this of his own initiative? Or had Aelfin put him up to it? Was this the reason for the large crowd gathered there that evening? Had they *all* known *already*? Did *everybody* know more about Kristinge than he knew about himself?

But the foremost of all his thoughts were the questions: *What now? What would happen to him?*

Still watching Kristinge with an enigmatic grin, Dyflines lowered his lyre and sat back down on his bench. Throughout the hall everybody sat perfectly still, watching and waiting. Everybody but Aelfin. The chieftain had risen from his bench even as the bard had returned to his. He stepped deliberately and directly toward the young priest now. There was a stern set to his shoulders. The muscles on his bare arms glistened with sweat and bulged in anticipation of motion. The eyes of those present in the hall were now irresistibly drawn from Kristinge to this towering warrior figure. Though there was no fire in the hall, Kristinge could see a red gleam in the chieftain's eyes as he approached. The tension in the hall was as heavy as the coastal spring fogs. The gathered warriors were frozen to their mead-benches by the drama in front of them.

"Perhaps you thought we would not know who you were," the chieftain barked into the stillness, the gleam in his eyes growing as he spoke. Kristinge could not answer. He sat there mute. *No,* he realized. *I knew you would somehow know. Everybody knows.* Even as Kristinge thought this, Aelfin drew his great polished and sharpened broadsword from his iron-bound sheath. "Perhaps," he said again, "you thought you could escape your fate."

"Fate," came Kristinge's barely audible echoing whisper. *Fate?* he thought, into the ensuing silence. Was it fate that his life would come to an end just as had his brother's? And his father's? And his father's father's? By the sword. This, certainly, was not fair. He had not chosen the fate of the warrior.

Or had he? Had his return to Friesland itself been an acceptance of that path? Had he wanted all along to be discovered? He did not know. The silence deepened as Aelfin raised the blade with both hands. For just an instant then, as Kristinge watched his own death approaching, he was filled by a strange detached calm, frightening in its coldness. The thought crossed his mind how much better off he would have been were he back in Luxeuil. If he had never left there. He would have been better off, too, if he had stayed at Jouarre. Even in Danemark. There were a hundred thousand places he might be better off than sitting unarmed in front of a chieftain who suddenly saw him as a rival.

A rival? Kristinge's voice stuck in his throat. His calm disappeared. *No!* He wanted to protest. Not a rival. He had no desire for the torc. Not Friesland's torc. Not Ezinge's torc. He never planned on usurping Aelfin's place as chieftain. He wanted to tell Aelfin that. But he knew it didn't matter. He knew the Frisian code well enough to know that. A rival's *potential* claim was as much of a threat as his *desire*. Aelfin had no reason to spare him. Kristinge closed his eyes, and wondered what the cold metal blade would feel like on his neck. Would it end quickly? Would he feel anything? He had seen Frisian warriors die slow deaths from battle wounds. The thought terrified him. He hoped for a quick and merciful end.

But the end was slow in coming. When Kristinge could stand the tension no longer, he opened his eyes. And what he saw then, he did not at first understand. The chieftain of Ezinge had dropped down upon one knee in front of the young priest. He waited there now, holding his sword out in front in a gesture of homage.

"The king has returned," Aelfin said softly.

There was a murmur throughout the hall.

"The king has returned," he repeated, a little louder. This time, some of the murmuring took the tone of assent. A few of Aelfin's thanes rose to their feet, drawing their own blades.

"THE KING HAS RETURNED!" Aelfin shouted. His voice was joined by a dozen more voices as he shouted it a forth time. By the fifth time, half the hall had joined him. By the sixth, the voice was unanimous.

Kristinge did not know what to do. He did not know what to say. But his paralysis had been predicted by Aelfin. The chieftain knew what to do, knew what to tell him. He *knew* how to manipulate the gathering.

"Take the sword!" Aelfin said, speaking quietly but firmly against the growing uproar as he stared fiercely into Kristinge's eyes. It was not an offer, or even a suggestion. It was a command.

Overwhelmed and at a loss, Kristinge complied. He took the sword from Aelfin and held it in front of him, grasping it by the hilt with both hands. For the first time in his life, he found himself holding a weapon. The weight of the blade took him by surprise. He almost dropped it. He had to work hard to hold it up. *I never chose...* he caught himself repeating. But things were moving quickly now. *Too quickly.* Aelfin had risen to his feet. He raised his hands and gestured for silence. It came across the hall at his command. Then the chieftain spoke, his powerful voice filling the silence he had just created.

"The prophecy was true. Finn's son has returned. The rightful heir to the Frisian throne."

"The king has returned!" voices shouted again.

"Friesland has faltered for too long. The king's torc awaits an heir. And now the heir has returned—*the heir of Finn's torc!*"

Aelfin turned to Maccus who stood beside him. "Now," he said, holding out his hand and nodding toward his thane.

Maccus reached his hand into his cloak and pulled out a large silk pouch crusted with jewels. He handed it to Aelfin. Kristinge continued to look on, speechless and unable to guess what the bag held, though inwardly he thought he should have known. When Aelfin reached in and pulled out a large shining golden object, Kristinge's heart leapt.

"Finn's torc," came a hushed whispered from nearby, as Aelfin held up the heavy, soft, gold neck band. Kristinge recognized the torc, wrought by the jeweler Deomaer during the final year of Folcwalda's life. He had seen it many times in his youth, adorning the neck of Finn the king—the neck of Finn *his father.*

"Yes. Finn's torc," Aelfin repeated. He turned toward Kristinge and spoke to him, but with a voice loud enough that all in the small hall could hear. "Shortly after the battle of Finnsburg, when Finnlaf your brother was killed, Finn sent this torc to me for safe-keeping. Perhaps he guessed that his own doom was nigh upon him. I do not know. He told me then what I had long ago guessed but had kept to myself: that you were his son and the son of Hildeburh, the rightful heir of the torc and rightful ruler of Friesland. He told me too that he hoped you would one day take this from me, charging me to keep it for you until that day. I never saw Finn again. Just a few months later, he died at Hwitstanwic. And with him in his defense died many great heroes and loyal thanes whose names we will not forget."

Aelfin fell silent for a moment, allowing the memory of those names to linger. Then he continued, his voice growing louder as he spoke. "Daelga the poet came to Domburg just a few weeks after the fight. He told the tale of your going from Hwitstan, and the tale of Finn's final battle. It was the tale of the treachery of the three Geatish brothers whose names we will not repeat, but whose acts now have been avenged. He told these tales so that the truth would not be utterly lost. Then Daelga disappeared into the south and was not seen in Friesland again. For seven years I have held this torc, sharing the hope of Finn and the hope of Daelga. The hope that you would one day return. For seven years I have held the torc of Finn. Let it now rest on its rightful neck."

And as Kristinge stood there trembling, still holding the heavy blade awkwardly in both hands, Aelfin stepped forward. He pressed his hand firmly down on the young priest-bard's shoulder, indicating what he should do. Kristinge understood. The youngest son of Finn knelt before the chieftain, still holding the sword but letting the weight of the blade rest on the ground beside him. Nobody else moved as Aelfin took the torc in both hands and lifted it up. Then slowly, with all watching, he bent the soft gold band around Kristinge's neck.

"Heir of Finn's torc, the king has returned!"

Aelfin pulled Kristinge to his feet. It was as if he had raised Finn himself from the dead. The hall erupted. Aelfin's warriors filled the room instantly with loud shouts and the sounds of swords beating against benches. Kristinge grew dizzy. Suddenly aware of the significance of the torc about his own neck, for the first time that evening he noticed that three of the warriors also wore gold torcs. So there were other chieftains in the hall that night besides Aelfin. This event extended *beyond* Ezinge. Now Kristinge could feel it pulling him in too, like the pull of the Hwitstan river when he was just a young boy and would wade a few steps out into the strong tidal current to help Lopystre and Willimond with the weirs. He fought against the frenzy growing around him, fought being sucked in by it. He tried to remain calm, tried to understand what was happening, forced himself to look around. It didn't help.

These other chieftains came forward now, each in turn bowing before Kristinge as they placed their swords at his feet, symbolic of their vow of service to a new king. Aelfin spoke their names and the names of their clans, and the names of their fathers and fathers' fathers who had served Finn and Folcwalda before: Theoman son of Theofor, who ruled at Beowic; Wihtred son of Wihtlaeg who ruled at Aalsum; and Isernfyst who ruled another Saxon clan at Heorotburg. All nearby villages. Meanwhile the din in the hall slowly shifted from a loud clamor to the steady rhythmic beating of sword on wood. Once again, all eyes were fixed on Kristinge, waiting for him to speak. Once again, he knew not what to say. And yet once again, Aelfin rescued him.

"Let us celebrate the day! It is a time for rejoicing." The chieftain gave the order. Servants entered the hall carrying mead and ale, enough for all present, with plenty to spare. There was another loud cheer. For a few seconds, swords were beat against benches again. Then, as the sound of swords was slowly silenced and replaced by the sounds of drinking, Dyflines leapt for the second time that evening to the cold hearth. As always, his lyre was ready and so was his tongue. And for the next hour, his laughter-filled voice resonated through the hall, recounting tale after tale of Frisian heroes, and of the victories and achievements of Folcwalda and Finn, and the names of those who had died in battle at their sides, and of the founding of Friesland and the defeat all who had since tried to conquer it. And all were sung in such a way that Kristinge knew that he himself was the great hero being celebrated. And still he had not spoken a word, but sat there with Aelfin's sword resting on his lap.

And so the night swept past, like a strange, dizzying storm. And Kristinge just sat there at Aelfin's side, at once both keenly aware of every movement, and every ale cup filled, and every vow of service given him, and every gift given by Aelfin in his behalf, and also at the same time lost in a fog as if none of this were happening—as if he were watching it happen to somebody else, or distantly observing his own dream. Or was it a nightmare, magnified by the dizzying effects of too much mead?

Early the following morning, when the celebration was over and the late summer sun was just beginning to lighten the sky over the distance horizon, Kristinge was still sitting in Aelfin's hall. Around him, not a wakeful soul was to be seen. Aelfin was laying asleep or drunk at Kristinge's side. The other three chieftains also lay sleeping on benches, with a few of their closest thanes scattered around the hall nearby. The rest of the war bands had taken to the ground outside, as the celebration had overflowed the small building into the surrounding village.

A gentle breeze of a warm summer night wafted past Kristinge, enticing him to stir from his trance. He rose, and absently made his way toward the door, stepping over bodies while trying again to make some sense of what had happened. What *had* happened? he wondered. He wasn't sure he knew. He wasn't sure he even *wanted* to know. He remembered Aelfin speaking to him late in the night, some time after Dyflines had finished with the last of his songs. Kristinge had hoped to learn something from the chieftain then. Had hoped to hear some explanation. But he hadn't. By then, most of the warriors had been well on their way to drunkenness. And though the chieftain, himself half drunk, had displayed a tongue looser than usual, his thoughts had been turned to the past and not the future.

"When drunk, *I* slay no hearth-companions," he said, boasting of his worthiness to receive the service of his thanes. "Neither did Finn," he went on. "He was a good king." He took another long draught as if to warm his memories further, and then he began to speak about his days in Hwitstan and of the great fellowship that had once inhabited Finnsburg. He told of the day so many years ago when he had first met Folcwalda, when the great warrior-king had sailed to Domburg, in part to rescue it from Frankish raiders and in part as a veiled threat to its former chieftain Ecgwalda. He told how Ecgwalda had finally pledged himself to the Frisian king, sending a war band to Hwitstan under the command of his most trusted thane Aeltar. And how Folcwalda had told Aeltar to bring his young son Aelfin with him to Hwitstan. Thus Aelfin had grown up in

Finnsburg, and though some years the senior of the two, he had later become close friends with young Finnlaf. They had hunted together. Trained as warriors together. But they had not died together.

At that point, Aelfin's thoughts had become more sullen, jumping to the subject of his own troubles. He had no children of his own. No heir to *his* torc. His wife had died childless. After saying this, he had looked straight at Kristinge. *And Kristinge had understood that look.* "You are my son."

And all gathered had understood, when Aelfin gave gifts in his hall that night—gold rings, and armbands, and old swords and spears—that the gift-giving was in the name of Kristinge, the new prince.

Now all lay sleeping from the drink. Their snoring filled the air. Kristinge needed to get away. Tired as he was from a night without sleep, he needed to walk. Life in Luxeuil had not prepared him for this. Not even his childhood in Hwitstan, or his few months in Danemark prepared him for this. He wandered around the perimeter of Ezinge for a long time, following the axwei and letting his thoughts wander, watching the day dawning in the eastern sky. When the sky changed from gray to red, and then from red to blue as the first rays of sun pierced the cloudless sky, he stopped by the river Hunze and splashed his face in the water. It felt good. He did it again. He rose then and left the ox-path, wandering further from the terp past the cattle-herds tending their cows in the fields to the north of the village, and along the few flax and barley fields west of the village where the laborers were already at work. Some of the peasants who recognized Kristinge greeted him as he passed, but they looked at him strangely. At the time, he didn't fully comprehend why this was, thinking perhaps it was only the tired expression on his face or his wet unkempt hair from his dip in the river. But there was something else that they were looking at—something around the young priest's neck, and something that he was holding, things that were out of place.

Not until he stepped through the door and into the chapel did the significance of those expressions become clear. Kristinge's right hand still held tightly to Aelfin's sword. Kristinge the priest. And he still wore Finn's torc. But he didn't remember where his harp was.

The momentum of that night and the events set in motion by Aelfin would carry Kristinge through the next few weeks and into autumn. He hoped that first day to continue his life as a priest, doing what he had been doing since arriving in Ezinge, as if nothing had happened. Ignoring the torc that now lay hidden in a box in the corner of his hut with his remaining coins. Ignoring the sword, too *big* to be hidden, that stood *beside* the box staring at him like a strange reminder of the cross. But he soon found that he was unable to go on as he had. Aelfin had other plans for him.

Late in the morning, Kristinge was at the chapel praying and beginning his penance for the carrying of a sword. Aelfin, the after-effects of his drunkenness having nearly worn off, appeared at the door. When Kristinge became aware of the chieftain's presence, he grew tense. But he kept his eyes closed and his head bowed in prayer, hoping not to be disturbed further.

Aelfin entered. "It is good that you have taken off your torc for now," the chieftain of Ezinge said after a moment. "The time to wear it again will come soon, but for the present it is best to be cautious."

Kristinge's concentration was now completely broken. Still, he kept his head bowed and said nothing. He was not sure there would *ever* be a time for him to wear the torc.

Either oblivious of Kristinge's prayer posture or not caring, Aelfin continued speaking in a low and serious tone. "The celebration last night was good. The seeds have been planted. But you know that despite my bold proclamation, you are a long way from being king."

At this, Kristinge lifted his head. *A long way from—*

"Farther than a day's journey from here, nobody even knows your name." Aelfin laughed as if it were a funny joke, as if that detail were unimportant in his quest to make a king of Kristinge, his self-proclaimed foster-son. But the laugh was unconvincing. A moment later, he took a seat next to Kristinge. Then he stood up again, looking uncomfortable in those surroundings. "Come with me. There is much to discuss."

Kristinge nodded. There was much to discuss, much he needed to tell Aelfin. Still, he said nothing just yet. Where would he begin? He rose and followed Aelfin from the chapel. Last night there had been no time. No choice but to succumb. Today was different. He did not have to follow Aelfin's plan. How could he wear the torc? How could he carry the sword? It was the same question. He would speak to the chieftain. Soon.

But the chance never came. Aelfin did not lead the way back to his hall as Kristinge expected, but toward the northern end of the village. When they came to the edge of the terp and looked down the drop, there were Maccus and Ceolac waiting with four horses.

Kristinge looked at Aelfin. "Where—?"

"We will ride," Aelfin answered. "To Hwitstan."

Kristinge sucked in a deep breath. He had hoped to return again one day to his home village, but he was not sure now was the time. He looked down at the horses, two of which stood riderless. Among the Frisians, horses were more commonly kept for meat than for riding. Few even of the warriors could ride, especially among those of Saxon descent. And fewer still could fight on horseback. On his voyage south to Luxeuil many years earlier, however, Kristinge had learned to sit on a horse and not fall. He followed Aelfin down off the terp. A minute later, the four of them were riding north along with Hunze river heading toward Hwitstan.

For a time the entire company was silent. It was many minutes before Kristinge felt comfortable on the back of his beast, and he gave little heed to their surroundings nor did he have much extra concentration to devote to conversation. By the time he was able to look around, they were already out of sight of Ezinge. It was then that Aelfin began to speak. And for the rest of the afternoon the young heir of the torc said little. Perhaps it was the thought of Hwitstan that left him silent. Or perhaps it was just that Aelfin gave him little chance to interrupt. The chieftain spent most of the ride explaining in detail the current situation in Friesland so that Kristinge would understand what was needed in order for him to become king. With occasional comments from his two thanes, Aelfin went on to name the major clans of Friesland, and their chieftains; where the largest villages and best halls and beaches were; what sorts of weapons could be found and at what price; and many other things his newly adopted son lost track of.

"Though there is *some* need for discretion, we cannot afford to be overly cautious," Aelfin explained after describing to uncomprehending ears how large a war band they would need and why. "We must move with speed and urgency, or we will find we are too late."

"I do not understand," Kristinge finally said, interjecting a rare word into the dialogue. The whole idea of being king was still too new to him. He could not begin to understand all of what the chieftain was telling him. The need for urgency was the least of his concerns.

Aelfin took the comment in a far narrower sense than Kristinge intended it. He explained slowly. "There are many reasons for urgency, not the least of which are the Franks. I have said before that if we do not have a king soon, we will surely fall to them. With all the quarreling among our own chieftains, few realize how great a threat the Franks are. But I lived at Domburg too long to underestimate this enemy. Now Domburg has fallen and Dorestad is hard pressed. Remember that Francia is still a vast kingdom. Divided though it is, we are like a small clan compared to its power. If the Franks are ever united again under a strong king then we will be swept away. Unless we grow much stronger than we now are."

Maccus, who had been with Aelfin at Domburg, nodded his agreement. He bore scars from his battles with the Franks, and he did not hide the fact that he was eager to avenge himself. "The Frankish people have lived too long among the Romans. They have forgotten their virtue. We must teach them soon that the true warrior is to be feared."

When Maccus had finished, Aelfin continued where he had left off. "There is an even greater reason for urgency. There are others vying for the torc of Friesland. One is the chieftain Aldgisl. He is strong and ambitious, and at the prime of his life. Already he is the most powerful chieftain in Friesland. His war band numbers many hundreds. He will soon hold sway over all of us." He paused. "The other threat is Réadban"

At the mention of Réadban, Kristinge took a sharp breath.

"You have heard of Réadban then?" Aelfin asked.

"I have," Kristinge replied, but he did not explain. He did not say what he had learned the previous fall—that Réadban had helped bring about the death of Finn. The knowledge was still painful to him. That he had not even known Finn as his father when he died did not matter. A strange rush of anger and pride swelled up at the thought of that betrayal. Suddenly Kristinge was more interested in what Aelfin had to say.

"Réadban is older than Aldgisl. He is past his prime as a warrior. But as a chieftain he is still powerful. His ambitions know no bounds, and he is crafty as well."

What caused the question to pop unbidden into Kristinge's head, he did not know, but he asked it without thinking. "Does he still have sons? I heard they were dead."

Aelfin looked at him and nodded with approval, as if to acknowledge that it was a good question. "You have heard the truth. Réadban had two sons. Radbod the Young died a few years ago. He was strong, and savvy, and even more ambitious than his father. His ambition overran his strength. The elder son, Ultar, was more cautious, but in other ways more foolish. He is now dead also."

"Murdered in his own mead hall, or so we have been told," Maccus interjected. "A thing unheard of among Frisians."

"Though perhaps not so surprising," Ceolac said softly.

Aelfin did not respond. He waited a moment, and then continued. "Without sons of his own, Réadban may give his full support to Aldgisl. They are distant kin. If this happens before we are ready to act, then Aldgisl will surely rule Friesland unopposed. The one thing we have in our favor, though it is also a great danger, is that Ultar's infant son Rathbád still lives. Rather than support Aldgisl, Réadban may wait a few years and seek the kingship for his own grandson. Or maybe even for himself. We must hope for some sort of indecision and delay on Réadban's part. As I said, if he gives Aldgisl his full support before we can act, then we have little hope that Finn's torc will return to the neck of his offspring. On the other hand, if Réadban opposes Aldgisl openly, then there will be great trouble for Friesland. Though it might help *your* cause if those two weakened one another, it would be disastrous for our folk. We cannot continue to fight amongst ourselves." He paused as if to remember the direction of his thought. "Whatever happens between them, it is good that they do not yet know of your presence. By the time they hear of you, we must already have gathered a much greater war band."

"War band?" Kristinge asked, tasting the word for the first time.

"If you went to war for the torc today, you would have only a hundred thanes and warriors."

Kristinge's jaw dropped. "I would have..." He didn't finish. The thought of having a war band of his own was terrifying.

"A pledge of support from a chieftain is a pledge of his war band," Aelfin explained with a grin. "All warriors who serve a thane of yours, also follow you. Between the four chieftains who now serve you, you command a war band over a hundred strong, with six warships and twenty horses." Kristinge did not smile. He did not know if he needed to feel impressed or appalled. A moment later, Aelfin's smile faded also. "And alas, as I have said, that is far too few. Even Réadban alone, without the help of Aldgisl, could crush you easily. We must gather more support. Increase your army. We must call on the thanes who were loyal to your father."

"But those that were here last night—?" Kristinge started to ask. He still had not said what was foremost on his mind. That he was his own greatest obstacle to becoming king. That he was a priest, and not a ruler. For now, he was intrigued enough to listen to Aelfin.

"Not enough," The chieftain interrupted, slowly shaking his head. "They are important chieftains, and I do not doubt their loyalty. They would not take lightly the pledges they made last night. But they were hand-picked. I chose them because they knew your father and brother and were loyal to them. I tell you this not to discourage you, but so that you will know what is necessary. My own warriors and thanes were prepared for last night. They knew what was going to happen, and what they were supposed to do. It was carefully arranged to gain the support of these first three chieftains."

Aelfin's thanes Maccus and Ceolac rode silently on, eyes on the road ahead of them. But Kristinge didn't need them to speak in order to know that Aelfin had spoken the truth. The entire event had been arranged merely to *manipulate* the other chieftains? "Why—?" he started to ask.

Then chieftain stopped him with a hand. "Look!" he exclaimed Reigning his horse to a halt, he pointed ahead. They had just come around a bend in the river. In front of them, up a low hill to the left of the river, was Hwitstan. Or what remained of it. "We are here." The rest of the company stopped beside Aelfin. The conversation was forgotten at the first glimpse of their destination. Kristinge took a deep breath, unsure whether he wanted to ride ahead or turn and flee. He had returned to Hwitstan only once since his departure seven years past, walking with Willimond through the ashes of the old chapel at dusk on a late autumn night the year before. It looked different during daylight. Again he wished Willimond were with him. It was difficult to believe that a year had passed since their departure from Luxeuil.

After a moment of silent watching, Aelfin got their attention again. "Listen to me," he said in a low voice, his gaze fixed on Kristinge. The conversation was not over, and he would finish it before they rode the last short distance into the village. "Do not *underestimate* the significance of the past two evenings. Planned though it may have been, it is still a time to remember. You now have a war band. You have as your first thanes four good chieftains. But don't *overestimate* either. There is much to be done."

Kristinge nodded. "I understand." As frightened as he was, he was beginning to get caught up in the drama. The thought of Réadban wearing his father's torc was like a sharp spear in his side. The four of them rode up the slope into the ruins of Hwitstan.

As Kristinge knew from his previous visit, there was little left of Hwitstan. Few huts had survived the fires. And after seven years, even what little had remained was now rotting and fallen apart. Scavengers had picked over anything of value that had not been carried away during the raid. The sight was depressing. But Aelfin did not stop in the village. He kept riding up the small hill that separated them from the beaches of Hwitstanwic. Kristinge could smell the salt air now, and hear the surf washing along the shore. At the top of the slope, they dismounted. It felt good for Kristinge to be back on his feet again. Ceolac took the four horses and hobbled them to a pair of nearby logs. Aelfin, meanwhile, strolled toward the piles of rocks that had once been the tower Finnweard. Kristinge ambled along behind him, and found a seat on one of the boulders looking over the bay. When Ceolac joined them, he was carrying a large bag. Maccus produced a flask of beer, and Ceolac opened the bag to reveal the contents: a late afternoon meal of breads, cheeses, and dried meats.

"Come," Aelfin said. "Let us eat." They ate for a time in silence, watching the incoming tide creeping its way up the shore and listening to the gulls crying around them. A strange feeling came over Kristinge as he sat there. Once again he remembered himself as a child, playing along the beaches with the other children of Hwitstan during the summer celebrations, running up and down the sand, looking for sea-polished pieces of amber washed ashore by the surf. He could hear the poet Daelga's voice, standing atop the stump near the cooking pits on a warm summer evening, singing the long Frisian lays that put the younger children to sleep. He could picture Finn and Hildeburh, standing atop the tower arm in arm, like statues of marble guarding the village. Guarding all of Friesland! King and Queen. Frisian and Dane. He remembered Finnlaf, too, loud and brash but not unkind. He remembered even the young girl Aewin who had once visited the village. Now here sat Kristinge, the son of Finn, looking out across the same beaches. In the distance, he could still make out the gray spot of a second watchtower. Was he truly the heir of Finn's torc? For a moment, it seemed possible.

When Aelfin spoke, it was as if he had been reading Kristinge's thoughts. "Your father and your father's father before you were great kings. Chieftains like the mighty chieftains of old. Were Folcwalda or Finn alive to help you, you would have no trouble inheriting the torc. Friesland would be a place of hope." He looked out over the sea and after a moment continued. "Alas, as a foster-father I can not do as much for you. Of the thanes loyal to your father, most died with him at Hwitstanwic. Few are left who will support you simply because of the name of Finn. That is another of our troubles."

Kristinge nodded, but his thoughts were not on the size of Aelfin's war band or the number of his father's thanes who had survived. He was wondering what his father had *really* been like—wondering what it would have been like to have known him. When he turned back toward Aelfin, he saw that the chieftain had stopped talking, and was now staring at him with a very solemn expression. "Tell me what became of Ulestan?' the chieftain asked. "Did he not also ride south with you when you left Friesland?"

A lump came to Kristinge's throat at the thought of the old warrior. The owl stare. He fingered the pendant at his neck. His thoughts raced backward to Luxeuil, and the morning over a year ago when Ulestan had revealed to Kristinge who he was: the day that Ulestan had died. Slowly, the whole voyage south seven years earlier came back to him. And to his surprise, he found himself speaking of it to Aelfin, confiding to the chieftain for the first time what had driven him from the monastery. He told of the last few years of Ulestan's life, and how the warrior had died. He told how he had come to learn who he was. There were tears in his eyes when he finished.

"He was a great warrior!" Aelfin said. "He served his king well, as a loyal thane should do. And he served you well, also. His last duty was to protect you—to bring you safely to Luxeuil, and one day to tell you who you were. He has done well. He gave his life for you so that you could one day be the king. So that you could wear your father's torc as your father wished. And now you have returned."

Aelfin waited only long enough for the words to sink in. *As your father wished...*

"Would that Ulestan and more of your father's thanes like him still lived," the chieftain went on a short time later. "Yet only a few remain, and most of them you have now already met. As for the rest of the Frisian chieftains?" He lifted his left hand in an enigmatic gesture. "Six and a half years have passed since Finn's death, and with those years have come many young warriors into power: warriors who never received gifts from Finn, who never shared the mead-bench or fought at his side. And even among those of Finn's thanes who remain—even among those who *did* serve your father—some served him only out of fear or greed. To gain *their* support, you have but two choices. You can convince them it is in their own best interest to serve *you* now: that you are a treasure-giver worthy of their loyalty. Or you must be so strong that they have no other choice but to obey you. Now you see what stands against us. Until you are stronger—until your war band becomes much larger than it now is—you cannot rely on the sword to make yourself king."

"And yet I know well enough," Kristinge replied, "that *only* the sword will make a king in Friesland."

Kristinge was amazed to hear himself speak. Aelfin, too, was surprised. He looked his new foster-son in the eye, and for a moment they held each other's gazes. Then Aelfin smiled and nodded his heads. "You know more than I thought, young prince. You speak the truth. It is the sword that makes the chieftain, and no less the sword that makes the king. And that does not leave us much time. This autumn and perhaps the coming winter. Beyond that, we cannot hope, for Friesland is not a huge kingdom and word travels quickly. Traders sell information like they do wool, and there will be chieftains who will feign to follow you but whose swords are given to others. Thus it is. By next spring, Réadban and Aldgisl will know of you and your presence here, and they will know you are a threat to their own ambitions. If you are not strong enough by then, they will crush you."

CHAPTER 16:
WAR BAND

The small band spent that night on the ground near the old tower Finnweard. They built a small hearth with stones from the fallen tower, and roasted a large rabbit that had wandered too near Maccus' bow. Then, as they sat around the fire drinking wine from a shared skin, Aelfin and his thanes began their plotting to win for Kristinge the high torc of Friesland. They knew from the start that if their campaign was to succeed, they would in short time need to secure the aid of several more chieftains. The next two would be the most difficult, for they had as yet little to offer except the name of Finn. Once Kristinge's war band had grown more substantial, however, others would follow. But whom to approach first? Ceolac, Maccus, and Aelfin all had different ideas, and long into the evening they argued about various chieftains. Their strengths and weakness. Their might in battle and the sizes of their war bands. Their loyalty. Whether they had known Finn. Whether they were thought already to be loyal to Aldgisl or Réadban.

Kristinge—though their planning affected him the most—said nothing. Despite his reticence, there was growing inside him a small spark of belief that Aelfin's plans might actually work. The visit to Hwitstan and the ruins of the hall where Finn had once ruled had not been without affect. Might it be that Kristinge, one day, could bear the torc of his father? With one ear to the conversation of the moment, and another to voices long gone past, the torc-heir fell asleep.

The next morning, they arose early to return to Ezinge. As they rode, the three warriors continued their talk of how to build up Kristinge's war band. They had agreed to speak first to a young chieftain named Eomaer of a small coastal clan. His predominant traits were two: a youthful impetuousness, and a hatred of Aldgisl. For the young heir, however, the vague dreams of the previous evening had faded. In the reality of daylight, miles away from the ruins of Hwitstan, the hope of becoming king was both more remote and less desirable. Thoughts of wearing his father's torc, he told himself, were utterly foolish. He was a priest, not a chieftain. A monk, not a warrior. And yet... And yet he could not altogether shake loose the idea. What had Ulestan really died for? Was it so that Kristinge could return to take his father's torc? His arguments that he should reject the plan at once were not convincing. Whatever he told himself, he did not *feel* like a priest. Once again, he heard Osanne's voice. *You will build no church.* He could not keep the words from ringing in his ears.

Once back in Ezinge, Kristinge returned to the chapel to spend the day in prayer, but it was a distracted prayer and he soon gave up and returned to his hut. The following morning, Aelfin came once more for Kristinge. His foster-son was in the chapel, trying again to focus his thoughts on prayer with only a little more success. This time, Kristinge was not disappointed at the interruption. He felt the desire for distraction.

"We must begin," Aelfin said. He ordered the confused Kristinge to remove his monk's robe, and to don his torc and the richer clothing he had received a year ago from queen Balthild. With a lofty air to his voice, as if it were some important occasion, he explained, "You must begin to wear things more befitting for a king. The people of this village, at least, must come to see you as their chieftain or you will never succeed in the broader realm."

Kristinge obeyed. He guessed well enough what the chieftain had on his mind. Kristinge was to be seen by the villagers walking at Aelfin's side, wearing a king's torc. Aelfin was planting an image. He was seeding it first in Ezinge with simple peasants, later to grow and spread through the realm. At first Kristinge was tempted to resist the plan—to resist being drawn into an idea to which he had not yet agreed. Despite the chieftain's anxious presence at his side, he returned to his hut at a slow walk, trying as he went to think of what he might say and how he might refuse. He worked unsuccessfully to formulate some plan of his own. Even as he unpacked the cloak from his bag of possessions, he searched for an excuse not to put it on. But no plan formed. When Kristinge held the cloak in his hands and examined it for the first time since he had come to Ezinge many weeks earlier, memories of Balthild and Telchild swelled in his mind. His thoughts flashed back to his brief visit to Jouarre and Paris, to his meeting with the abbess, and then the king, and finally the queen. And then to the memory that he could not shake.

You will build no church.

He heard it as if she was still beside him, her strange wild eyes burning his forehead as she clutched his face with her vice-like grip.

No church. No church. No church.

Kristinge closed his eyes, as if it might drive the memory away. But it only made it stronger.

... just a voice crying in the wilderness. You will build no church. Just a voice. In the wilderness. No church.

Fleeing the voices of his past, Kristinge threw off his monk's robe, donned his coat and trousers, and ran from his hut. Aelfin was still waiting outside, toying nervously with the large broadsword at his side. Yet despite his impatient expression, he said nothing about the delay. Perhaps he guessed something of Kristinge's thoughts and did not yet want to press the young priest too far. Whatever was on the chieftain's mind, as soon as his recently proclaimed foster-son stepped out of the small hut, he took him by the arm like a bear grabbing a cub and began to march around the village. As they walked, Aelfin spoke loudly about Ezinge and Friesland, and what it meant to be a chieftain. He spoke of their plans for when Kristinge was king, stopping now and then to talk to one or another of the villagers, and making known to all in Ezinge of his adoption of Kristinge as a foster son. Kristinge, in between his frequent hearty slaps on the back, alternately felt ashamed and proud of the display. He said hardly a word, however. Whatever he may have felt, he had little choice in the matter. Whenever there was a lull in Aelfin's talk, the voices of Telchild, Balthild, and Osanne rang in his ears.

Later in the morning, when the tour of Ezinge was complete, they returned to the hall and continued their discussions where they had left off on the previous day. As the day progressed, Aelfin began to move from his general strategies for making Kristinge king to the specific details of his plan: a plan, he confessed, that had been forming in his mind since the night he had met Kristinge at the watchtower on Hwitstanwic, and guessed him to be the son of Finn. To help himself forget about Osanne and her strange unnerving prophecies, Kristinge paid greater attention to the chieftain. He gave careful note when

Aelfin began to list the names of other chieftains who might still be loyal to the family of Finn, or who might for some other reason follow Kristinge—any who might readily take Finn's heir as their king, and who were known *not* to be following Aldgisl or Réadban. They would begin with these chieftains, and as their support grew along with the size of their war band, they would reach farther and farther into Friesland and take greater risks.

"But will these chieftains follow *any* king?" Kristinge asked once. He was thinking not only of the Frisians, but of the Franks, Angles and Saxons as well. They were kindred races who prized freedom, and would not easily bow before anyone. Kristinge had learned enough of these peoples and their histories and he knew the chieftains were the proudest among them. Friesland had been many years with no real king, and would surely resist one now.

"They followed Folcwalda," Aelfin answered.

"It took him many years to win Friesland's torc. And *he* was a mighty warrior: a *real* chieftain."

"They will take a king out of fear."

"Fear of me?" Kristinge asked, incredulous at the idea that anybody would actually fear him, and even more appalled at what it would mean if it were true.

Aelfin studied Kristinge's face before he answered. "Fear of the Franks. I tell you again, if we are not soon united, then we will surely collapse."

"But me?"

There was a look of worry on Aelfin's face. "If it is not you, it will be somebody else—Aldgisl, or another of Réadban's kin. Or Réadban himself, the betrayer of Finn."

Kristinge said no more; Aelfin's final words struck him like the blow of a fist. Not altogether unwillingly, he let the chieftain continue with his plans. Aelfin was not one to be questioned too often. Within two days, messengers had been sent to a dozen Frisian chieftains, beginning with surviving kin of Finn and Aelfin and also the former thanes of Finn who were still alive.

During these days, they also began a new aspect of Kristinge's preparation: his training with a sword. It was Maccus and Ceolac who took this responsibility. The arrived at Kristinge's door early in the morning, and nearly dragged him to a field a short distance from the village, out of sight of the working peasants. "I am a priest, not a warrior," Kristinge protested, but Ceolac and Maccus ignored him.

"You are a warrior now," Maccus said. "As you have said yourself, it is the sword that makes the king."

"And Aelfin has commanded it," Ceolac added.

Reluctantly, Kristinge submitted to their instruction. In relative privacy on the far side of a grove of trees, away from the village, they had their young trainee doing nothing but repeatedly swinging a heavy stick against their shields which they held up to his blows. Ill-used to such exertion, Kristinge was drenched in sweat and gasping for breath within minutes. They did not let him rest, however, until more than an hour had passed. When he was so exhausted that he collapsed, they gave him a short break to drink some water. But they were not easy trainers. Soon they had him going again, this time holding the shield while the two of them battered it. "Strength and stamina make the warrior," they repeated whenever he stopped. "The one who rests in battle during the day does not survive to see the mead hall in the evening."

Thus did Kristinge labor throughout that morning. And for many mornings after that as Aelfin's most trusted thanes took the duty of turning the young foster-son into a warrior. Each morning it was the same. They pulled him from his hut early in the day, and took him away from the village to teach him what they knew. After a few days, they switched from heavy sticks to real weapons. They taught him the proper way to grip a sword for great two-handed strokes, and how to wield it with one hand when holding a shield as well. They taught him where to strike an enemy—how to levy a blow at an opponent's arms or skull, or to cut at his legs—and also the defensive strategy of swinging his blade in wide circles to protect himself when tired or outnumbered. Others weapons in addition to the sword, they taught him too: the Danish spear, the heavy Frankish throwing ax, and the Swedish battle-ax. Both the uses of these weapons and the defenses against them they taught, each day driving Kristinge a little harder and longer until slowly he began to grow more comfortable with the weapon in his hands, and to gain some strength in his arms.

"You are doing well," Maccus said one day, after an especially grueling morning. "Those thin arms of yours are finally growing some muscle."

Though compliments from the two thanes were not easily won, Kristinge did not feel any satisfaction. His hands were covered with calluses, his arms and legs with bruises, and his body with sore muscles. He took little pleasure in his training, nor delight in the results. Had this tutelage under Maccus and Ceolac been the sole aspect of his preparation, he might have forsaken the torc after one day. But there were other aspects of Aelfin's plan to make him king, and not all were so unpleasant.

At the chieftain's insistence, Kristinge had begun dwelling in the mead-hall with the thanes and warriors of his new hearthwerod. It was, as Aelfin pointed out, his duty as well as his privilege to sleep with his warriors beside the hearth. It was in the hall, at the side of Aelfin his foster-father, that Kristinge took his part in that intimate fellowship: the sharing of mead, and the giving of gifts. Gifts given in his own name. Given by the hand of Aelfin to win for Kristinge the loyalty of his thanes. Men who previously would not have deigned to speak with him were sharing his mead cup and receiving treasure from his hand. And it was not an unpleasant task. There was a hierarchy in the Frisian society, and a priest was near the bottom. But a warrior—one who slept in the mead hall—sat near the top, with the chieftain and his kin the highest among them. Wearing the torc of Finn, Kristinge received greater esteem than ever he could hope for in a monk's robe. Christian priests, where they existed, were barely above slaves. Neither did bards, esteemed though a good one might be, hold the status of a warrior. Even the pagan priests, though they wielded power in the clan, were beneath the warriors. The honor of a priest was a distant and fearful respect. In Ezinge even more than in Danemark, the priests of Freyr and Woden were seldom seen. They were cruel dark men whose power came from fear. But now Kristinge had nothing to fear from them. Thus despite his initial misgivings, he was growing accustomed to his new role. As he had noticed in Danemark, there was in the fellowship of the mead hall something that he had missed since his departure from Willimond. It was only a shadow, perhaps, of the deeper fellowship at Luxeuil—as Luxeuil itself was only a shadow of something else. But for a short time a shadow is better than nothing.

Thus the days wore on toward winter as Aelfin and those who had joined his plot nervously awaited word from the chieftains to whom messages had been sent. With each day that passed, the danger grew. So did Kristinge's doubts. Though the sword-training, as grueling as it was, gradually grew easier with his increased strength and conditioning, there were other costs which were harder to weigh. A few nights after Kristinge had begun to sleep in the mead hall, Dyflines took ill. Without consulting Aelfin, Kristinge retrieved his harp from the chapel and sang for the gathered company. It was the most enjoyment he had felt singing in many weeks. And it was a mistake. The songs went well enough. Kristinge could tell that. Yet though Aelfin said nothing about it that evening, he was clearly not pleased. The next night, Dyflines was still sick. Again Kristinge took out his harp and sang many songs for the gathered warriors. This time, Aelfin was even more sullen. The following morning they spoke.

"It would be good to leave aside the harp for a time. Leave aside your barding." Aelfin's voice was not unkind, but it held an edge that was not quite gentle.

Kristinge sensed it was a command more than a request. He tried to smile as he responded. "Has my voice lost its beauty? Or has my harp gone out of tune?"

"Neither, my *son*," Aelfin said, stressing the last word but failing to return the smile.

"Then what? My choice of songs? Name what you would hear and tonight you will hear it."

Now Aelfin's voice grew stern and his face red. "I will hear *nothing* from you this night."

Disregarding the chieftain's stern response, Kristinge protested. "But Dyflines still lies in his hut. I spoke with him last night. He groans like a dying man—though he knows well enough that it is nothing serious: just a stomach ailment that will pass soon enough."

"One night without a bard will not destroy the fellowship of the hall. And there are reasons why it is best for you not to sing."

"I am listening," Kristinge said, gesturing with his open hands to indicate he was ready for an explanation. Though he found it difficult to think of Aelfin as a father, since his being named as foster-son he had grown far more bold with the chieftain than he would have been as either a priest or a bard.

"It is not fitting for a king—or future king—to *entertain* his warriors like a common bard or minstrel. It will ruin—" he began. Then he quieted himself for a moment, seeking some way to better explain, though Kristinge already guessed what the issue was. "How will your people follow you as *king* if they see you as a *singer of songs*. A king is to be served, not to serve. To be entertained, not to entertain. Warriors must follow you into battle. A king is a wielder of the sword, not the harp."

"Then I will make a poor king," Kristinge replied softly. But he said nothing else about the subject. At Aelfin's insistence, he laid aside his harp and played it no more. Yet it was only with sadness that he forsook altogether his role as bard.

Still, his service as bard and poet he had given up by a conscious decision. His duties as priest were also soon enough forsaken, but this decision was not as clear. It was more that the duties were slowly and unwittingly pushed aside and forgotten than that he chose to abandon them. Yet as the year rolled onward, more and more of his time was spent at Aelfin's side, and less was spent in the chapel or with his flock. The chieftain was forging ahead with his plans, and for the time Kristinge did not resist.

Just eight days after the first messages had been sent by Aelfin, a band of twenty thanes and warriors were seen riding up the Hunze river from the west. Spears and Frankish-made swords glittered in the sunlight as they approached. While they were still some distance off, a warning reached Aelfin. The message quickly spread through Ezinge. It was a tense few moments then, for nobody knew who these warriors might be.

"Raiders?" Ceolac asked as he rose beside Aelfin and donned his sword and shield.

"Raiders we can fight. I fear more a Frisian war band of Aldgisl's men. Then we would be hard-pressed. We are far from strong enough to face him if he has found out so early about our plans. I had counted on at least ten weeks, and hoped for the whole winter."

"What would he do?" Kristinge asked.

Aelfin only shook his head grimly as he walked out the door of the mead hall toward the western edge of the village. A group of his thanes followed, while runners were sent to gather the rest of the war band if necessary. By the time the chieftain's company reached the edge of the village, the riders were nearly there as well. At the sight of so many horses and mounted warriors, the horse-fearing Saxons of the village grew nervous and afraid. Even the Saxon *warriors* appeared fearful. However Aelfin and some of his Frisian thanes could ride well enough that they were not daunted by the large number of horses. "Do not fear," Aelfin said calmly, when he had seen the size of the approaching war band and counted that there were only twenty. "We have more than forty warriors in Ezinge, and some ten horses. If there is hostility, we can easily defend the terp even against twenty mounted warriors. Horses will not serve much purpose attacking up the side of a terp."

When the small war band arrived at the bottom of the village, Aelfin went to the edge of the terp to meet them, with Ceolac, Kristinge, and ten others warriors at his side. The rest of his war band continued gathering in the village.

It was a proud-looking war band, fresh and well-armed, that faced Aelfin from the bottom of the terp. "I have come," came a sharp voice from the lead rider, as if that pronouncement alone were the most important thing in the world at that time. It was a young warrior. He had a smooth, youthful face, with long blond hair braided down his back like the Germanic chieftains of old. His eager eyes scanned the top of the slope for somebody worthy of responding to him.

"Welcome, Eomaer," Aelfin replied. "It is a proud band of warriors that has followed you from afar. You bear the many leagues of travel as if they were but a few. There is strength in your youth."

Kristinge breathed a sigh of relief. Though he had not before seen Eomaer's face, he recognized the name from earlier conversations. Eomaer was one of the chieftains to whom Aelfin had sent a message. He ruled a small clan of horsemen at Dronrip. He had lived only eighteen years—young for a Frisian chieftain—yet his confident manner showed no signs of the uncertainty of youth. In fact, Aelfin had told Kristinge much of Eomaer. He was already a formidable horseman, and that was unusual among the Frisians. For though there were a fair number of horses in Friesland, they were kept more for food than for transport. A horse worthy of bearing a rider was not common. Thus the gift of a horse from a chieftain to a thane was a worthy reward indeed, like the gift of a great broadsword. Most chieftains possessed only a small number of prized mounts for themselves and their thanes, and even those few were seldom if ever ridden in battle. Frisian clans like Eomaer's that could send thirty mounted warriors into battle were almost non-existent: so rare that some claimed Eomaer was descended from the Huns.

Of course Kristinge knew the stories of the Huns. He had heard of them not only from the bards of Friesland, but even in Luxeuil where the great histories were written and kept. Two hundred years earlier, Attila and his vast eastern hordes had swept across the continent eventually carrying their invasion over the Rhine and deep into Francia. It was their prowess on horseback along with their strange dark faces that had struck the most fear into their Germanic enemies. Their equestrian feats had left behind not only a wide trail of devastation, but also an indelible mark among the white-skinned folk of the north. The Saxons, who had *always* feared horses, had come to hate them more. But a small number of their Frisian kin, Eomaer's ancestors among them, had paid close heed to the battle skills of these ruthless invaders. Fanciful tales abounded, of course. Some claimed that a band of Huns had remained in the north, and that their blood ran in the veins of Eomaer's ancestors. Other tales told of Frisian children who had been taken captive in raids, had grown up among the Huns at home on horseback, and had later escaped and returned to their own people. Whatever truth there was in these stories, Eomaer and his war band were esteemed for their riding skills. "Are we welcome then? Or must we spend all day staring up at you?" the young chieftain replied.

"You are welcome in my mead hall. Come to the southern end of the village. There you will find the path more suitable to your horses."

While they waited for Eomaer to lead his war band into the village, Aelfin spoke softly to Kristinge. "Dronrip is not far from here, though I wager they spent more than two days in travel and came at a leisurely pace. They do not look like men who have ridden hard."

"Have they come in response to your message?" Kristinge asked.

"That is my guess, though I know not what that response will be. Whatever the case, we will find out soon enough."

"But he is not against us?" Kristinge queried further.

Aelfin did not answer directly. "I do not believe he has come out of fear of the Franks, as we hope others will. Dronrip is not yet threatened by Frankish invasion. It is not coastal, nor is it close to the Rhine. His clan has not yet encountered Frankish raiders or war bands. Besides, Eomaer is not one to do anything out of fear."

"Then why? He is too young to remember Finn."

"Yes. He was not yet born when Folcwalda died. He may have some memory of Finn, but he was too young to have fought beside him. Still, he would not have come if he were not interested. He may yet join our cause."

"Why?" Kristinge asked again, his curiosity as persistent as his doubts. He still had little faith in Aelfin's vision. Little reason did he have to believe that anybody would take a monk from Luxeuil as king. If he really *had* believed he could one day be king of Friesland, he might have resisted Aelfin's scheme more vigorously.

As the riders crested the terp and approached from the other side of the village, Aelfin explained. "Eomaer's father died at the hands of Aldgisl's uncle. It was during a battle in Geatland when they were serving rival lords. There is a blood feud between them now. As the chieftain of a small tribe, Eomaer knows he has little chance to avenge his father's death. He has no power to exact the weregild. His only hope to do so is in the service of a rival king of greater power."

Kristinge was not convinced. "But why *me*? Why would he serve a son of Finn?"

"As I said, in you perhaps he will see that chance to avenge his father. We must count on that. Besides," Aelfin added. "I have met him. He is ambitious. Do not forget that you are the grandson of one of Friesland's greatest legends and the son of another. That is worth something. He may have come here just to meet you."

That made Kristinge thrice as nervous as before, but it was too late to do anything about it. A moment later, Eomaer reigned in his horse a few feet away. At his command, his warriors dismounted. They left the horses in the care of servants and followed Aelfin and Kristinge into the hall.

Inside the mead hall, a feast was prepared for the whole company. Bread and salted fish were served along with ale and some smoked game. Then, while the war bands from Ezinge and Dronrip shared food and the mead cup, Aelfin and Eomaer talked together along with their few closest thanes and Kristinge. Though Kristinge said very little, he had the strange sense that he was being carefully watched— weighed on the scales and examined like a piece of merchandise. And he couldn't help feeling that he was going to be found wanting. Yet when Dyflines had sung—a carefully chosen selections of songs in praise of Kristinge's Frisian and Danish ancestors—and gifts had been given by Aelfin, Kristinge found Eomaer approaching him with his offer of allegiance and service. He had won another thane to his war band. A thane who commanded skilled horsemen. Aelfin's plan was bearing fruit. As he had guessed, the young chieftain Eomaer was eager to oppose Aldgisl. The final decision was made when he heard that Kristinge's war band had already grown to over a hundred well-armed warriors.

As Eomaer knelt and offered his sword, Aelfin smiled and nodded to Kristinge who had already been instructed what to do when such occasions arose. He took the hilt in his hand as offered, reversed the blade, and handed it hilt first back to Eomaer thus accepting his offer of allegiance. What happened next, however, took even Aelfin by surprise. When Eomaer had risen to his feet, he spoke again. "My sword and my loyalty I offer you first. What I offer with it is of no lesser value." His eyes narrowed as he spoke, as if to judge Kristinge by his response. "As a sign of my service, in my father's stead I give you my sister to wife."

Kristinge's jaw dropped. *Wife? This cannot be.* His moment of success had turned into catastrophe. He could not take a wife. He could less take a wife than lead a war band. He was a priest.

Aelfin was taken by surprise also, and for an instant was speechless. But the chieftain of Ezinge recovered quickly. He embraced Eomaer in a great warrior's hug. "You are truly rich to give such gifts."

"Then you accept?" Eomaer asked pointedly.

No! Kristinge wanted to say. *I cannot. I am a monk!* But he couldn't speak. For inside he knew he had another reason as well. His thoughts were still on Aewin.

"Accept? We accept with great honor. Your sister shall be like a daughter to me, even as Kristinge has become my son. It is a great day for our clans. In your father's place, you have done well for your people—and for your sister. They shall be wed this very winter, when Kristinge once more takes upon his neck the torc of Friesland."

They shall be wed? This winter? Kristinge almost fainted. Though he knew this was the way among the Frisians, he could not believe it was happening to him. He did not even know Eomaer, no less his sister. How could he be wed to a strange woman? How could he be wed to *any* woman? He was a priest. He had spent six years training to be a monk. Had he remained in Luxeuil but another year or two, he would have taken his vows. And monastic vows or not, he had devoted his life to the service of God. He could not wed. What would he do? What would he say?

He barely heard the remainder of the conversation. Only that Eomaer promised to return within the fortnight with his sister, so they could seal the betrothal. All Kristinge's own plans crumbled.

CHAPTER 17:
BATTLE

Aelfin sat in his customary bench beside the fire, a horn of some warm beverage in his hand. "It is necessary," he stated. "It is impossible!" Kristinge replied, angrily venting his frustration on Aelfin. Four weeks earlier, he would not have thought of speaking to a Frisian chieftain as he now was. But standing at the edge of the terp looking out over the river Hunze as it flowed unrepentantly to the sea, he was feeling the need more than ever to pull some shred of control back to his life. His years at Luxeuil and the discipline of monastic life still clung to him, despite all the turmoil that he had been thrown into and the months that now separated him from monastic life.

"It is already done," Aelfin. His voice was calm. "We have accepted—"

"Change it. I cannot wed. I am a priest."

Aelfin's voice took a sudden stern turn that make Kristinge question his own presumption. "You!" the chieftain said, pointing his finger like a spear at Kristinge's chest. "*You* are a Frisian chieftain, the bearer of a torc, and soon to be the king. This wedding has been arranged. It will happen." He paused to let the words sink in, then added in explanation, "It is necessary to secure your power."

Then I don't want any power, Kristinge wanted to reply, but Aelfin's stern glance warned him against such a comment. "I have never even met her," he argued instead, changing his tactic since his foster-father thought little of priesthood and gave no heed to Kristinge's training as a monk.

"Have you learned nothing?" the chieftain replied in exasperation. "You are a chieftain now, not a peasant. What *you* think of *her* means *nothing*. A wedding is a treaty between tribes, not an act of sentiment. Your taking his sister to wife is your best guarantee that Eomaer will follow you loyally. And not just Eomaer. When others hear what has happened, when they see you gaining power and taking another chieftain's sister to wife, they will join also. This is the best thing that could have happened. It is a stroke of luck beyond my foresight. I only wish I could claim it was my idea."

"Then why now? Why Eomaer? Why not wait?"

"It is *convenient*," Aelfin answered, grinding the last word between his teeth. Then a grin spread across his face, and he slapped Kristinge on the shoulder. "Are you afraid of a woman?"

Kristinge blushed. "I don't..." he stuttered. "I never..." *Was he?* "No," he answered firmly. "But why Eomaer? He knows nothing of me. And I know nothing of her—of *him*."

"Ah, Eomaer," Aelfin said with a knowing look, apparently finding something in Kristinge's questioning that he could understand. "He is a bold one. I confess that his proposal surprised even me at first, though were I in his shoes I might have done the same. He is not the most powerful chieftain in Friesland. His clan is small, as is his war band. Perhaps I could have done better and wed you to a powerful Danish princess, as Folcwalda did for Finn. Or even to the daughter of a rich Saxon chieftain. That would have been a treaty indeed. Yet I do not take Eomaer lightly. One day he may be your most worthy thane. And it is good that other chieftains see that those who follow you are not unrewarded. It will be a good marriage."

Kristinge could only shake his head. How could he make Aelfin understand? There were some things Kristinge could go along with. What harm did it do to sleep within the mead hall rather than alone in his hut? What harm was there even in carrying a sword? He had not used it on human flesh. And even if he had, tales of Irish monks proficient with the sword were not unheard of. *But betrothal?* It was not a matter of politics. He wasn't waiting for Aelfin to find him the daughter of a more powerful chieftain. He could never touch a woman.

Nevertheless the days passed, and the appointed time for Eomaer's return approached all too quickly. Kristinge grew more afraid. Despite the warnings of Aelfin, he began to think of excuses he might give—any reason to escape the betrothal. Even on the day that Eomaer's war band was spotted approaching up the Hunze river from the west, Kristinge continued to resist the plan, casting one argument after another on the chieftain's deaf ears. When Aelfin did not listen, Kristinge grew desperate and considered fleeing Ezinge.

His inclination to do so was strong. Only under stern warnings did he stay at Aelfin's side—stern warnings and the realization that he could not escape even if he did flee, for there was nowhere for him to go.

"This is not done to satisfy the lusts of a chieftain," Aelfin reminded Kristinge. "If you want that satisfaction, as a king you will have power to claim it as often as you want. You need not lack women." Kristinge stood gaping, appalled, as Aelfin went on. "But this woman—this marriage—is for your clan, for all the Frisian people."

Kristinge was unconvinced. He stood at the edge of the terp watching the war band from Dronrip approach—and sulking like a prisoner.

"Return to your hut and put on your torc. And the sword as well." Aelfin commanded. He looked Kristinge in the eye. Then, as if reading Kristinge's thoughts, he turned to Maccus and Ceolac. "Go with him, and see that he returns quickly."

Kristinge obeyed under coercion, but he did not hurry. He trudged back to his hut. Under Ceolac's watchful eyes he placed the torc around his neck, then strapped the huge broadsword across his back. Neither felt comfortable. *I will not marry,* he told himself. He had been foolish to follow the chieftain's plan as far as he had. If Aelfin did not say something to Eomaer, Kristinge would. Even if it cost him Eomaer's allegiance. Even if it cost him the torc—a torc which he had not pursued in the first place. Angrily, he followed the two thanes back to the edge of the terp.

Eomaer's company had arrived, covering the final distance across the western fields while Kristinge was at his hut. The war band was at the bottom of the terp now, making their way around the axwei to the cattle ramp at the southern end of the village.

I will not... Kristinge started to say.

The words never left his mouth. Looking down the steep slope, his eyes widened suddenly in recognition. For it was then that he saw her. He blinked and looked again. His eyes had not deceived him. She rode in the middle of the company, behind Eomaer and surrounded by two dozen warriors. She was the only woman among them, but she sat tall and straight, bearing herself with a warrior's posture. Her black hair unfurled behind her like a banner as her horse moved along the edge of the terp into the gentle south breeze. In the warm afternoon air, the smooth white skin of her shoulders and arms was bare beneath the blue sky. And her gentle curves were visible even beneath her loose-fitting tunic.

Kristinge's jaw dropped in recognition. *Could this be the one he was to...?* His heart began to pound within him, and his hands grew sweaty. Was he to be betrothed to *her*, the vision that had haunted him for so long? The girl he had known as a child. Had sung to by the side of the river so long ago, and again more recently in Frotha's mead hall. The one whom he had seen in Paris. Hoped that he had in some way helped in a moment of her need. The one whom Hildeburh had many years earlier sought to have wed to Kristinge's brother. She was older now, as was Kristinge. She must be nearly twenty years of age. Well beyond the age when the daughters of chieftains were wed. And yet she was not wed. *Not wed?* No. Not *yet*.

"Look well upon her," Aelfin said softly. "Aewin, sister of Eomaer. She is one of the most beautiful women in Friesland. Convenience treats you well, for you do not do poorly in this treaty. Were I younger..."

Kristinge was no longer paying attention to Aelfin. *Aewin*, he breathed. Then it was true. His eyes had not deceived him. And at the realization of whom he was to wed, Kristinge's resolve to escape dissolved. All his former arguments against marriage vanished. After all, had not Willimond wed Hildeburh? Kristinge had not thought that *their* marriage was wrong. Did not the monastic rules only apply to one under the authority of a ruling Abbot? Was the life of a monk the only way to serve God? The Apostle Peter had been married. He must have been, because the holy scriptures mentioned the mother of his wife. And Peter was the rock upon whom the church had been built: the apostle for whom Luxeuil was named.

Kristinge's head continued to whirl. There must be some reason he ought still to resist. Striding across the village to meet the guests at the other end, he tried half-heartedly to remember all the arguments he had so recently given Aelfin. Yet he could think only of Willimond and Hildeburh, standing before him as man and wife. It was the thought of Willimond more than the Apostle Peter that swayed him. And so when Aewin reached the top of the terp, and her eyes searched for and found Kristinge, his feet turned to clay and his heart melted within him. *How could he have known it was her?* Shifting the sword on his back, Kristinge tried to stand tall next to Maccus and Ceolac who flanked him on either side. He was glad for all the work he had done building his muscles these many days. Though Acwin's black eyes were still proud, he could see that her glance was admiring as she gazed upon him and saw the torc around his neck. Did she recognize him? Did she see him as a the heir to the torc? Or as a bard who had once sung for her? As a monk in Paris, eager to help but too weak and afraid? Or would she see him still as the young boy from Hwitstan? For the first time, Kristinge was truly glad to be wearing his father's torc. The celebration in the mead hall that evening might prove more joyful than he had expected.

Greetings were given on the open terp at the edge of Ezinge. Kristinge stood speechless as Aelfin welcomed Eomaer, his sister Aewin, and the proud warriors of Dronrip with them. The two companies then made their way to the mead hall where their greetings were exchanged again, more formally. Aelfin gave a more proper speech, but Kristinge heard not a word of it—not until Eomaer stood forward and presented Aewin, first to Aelfin and then Kristinge. "When the winter snows have melted, they shall be wed. Then our clans will be brought together as one."

For the first time in Kristinge's brief memory of her, Aewin blushed. She approached the chieftain's bench and lowered her head in deference. "It is my honor," she said. "The fame of your mead hall, and of your generosity in giving gifts is known far and wide, as are the name of the children of Folcwalda," she added, turning to Kristinge.

The young chieftain Eomaer presented Kristinge with a gold-brooch which he placed on a chain around Kristinge's neck. "This is a token of the coming betrothal. Wear it well and know the value of the greater gift you will receive in the spring."

In the spring? Kristinge groaned inwardly. *It is too long to wait.* He trembled as he bowed his head in return, still unable to speak.

Aelfin in return gave to Aewin a silver crown of Danish design, to be worn now as a token of the betrothal. And then the feast began. It was a feast that surpassed any the hall had seen in the months since Kristinge's arrival—perhaps the greatest feast in Ezinge in many years. Even the feast in which he had been given the torc and named as a foster son of Aelfin did not equal this. Gifts were given that night in plenty. From Aelfin's hand and in Kristinge's name, many young thanes in Eomaer's war band received gold and battle-tested weapons of great worth, as did Aelfin's own thanes. Eomaer, too, though it was not his hall and he had less wealth, gave gifts in his manner. Many thanes were richer when they left that hall than when they came. But Kristinge was oblivious to it all. For Aewin was seated on the bench beside him, her body lightly touching his so that he felt the warmth of her side and could think of little other than that touch.

When a little later she quietly placed her hand upon his, the last of his fears fled away along with his resolve against marriage. And that was the last he remembered clearly of the evening.

"My Lord!" came the urgent voice.

Kristinge opened his eyes and looked around. It was morning. The hall was crowded with sleeping warriors. He looked for his betrothed, but Aewin was nowhere in sight. He remembered now. Later in the evening, after Daelga's singing, she had left the mead hall to spend the night with the women of Ezinge.

"My Lord," the words were repeated more loudly. The unfamiliar voice was coming from nearby. Kristinge rolled over. Behind him, a young peasant of no more than ten summers was shaking Aelfin. The chieftain groaned. When he opened his eyes and saw who it was that had interrupted his sleep, he reached for his sword as if to strike him. The boy jumped away, terrified. "Raiders! Raiders!" he shouted quickly. "They have taken the cattle and killed my cousins."

Kristinge saw now that the boy had cuts across his hands and was bleeding from his left shoulder as well. He turned back to Aelfin. The chieftain was already on his feet. His anger at having been woken by a peasant was gone, replaced by a different passion and urgency. "Speak to me!" he growled. "When did they come?"

"This morning, early. At first light."

Aelfin and Kristinge both looked to the door of the hall. The sun was already above the horizon. The raid was at least an hour ago. If they had come by boat, they would be long gone down the river.

"How many?" Aelfin asked.

The boy looked confused. He lowered his head.

"How many raiders?!" Aelfin shouted. "Did you see them?"

The boy nodded.

"Can you count?"

The boy shook his head no. But before Aelfin had finished cursing, he stammered, "As m-m-many as there are c-c-cows in the East field."

"About fifteen, if I remember," said Ceolac, the first of the warriors to be up and alert.

"Did they come by boat?" the chieftain asked.

"From the woods," the boy answered. "From the sunrise."

"Eastward into the forest," Ceolac guessed. "Renegade robbers from the Jute villages eastward."

Aelfin snarled. "Maccus," he summoned. "Ceolac." The two thanes were on their feet. Despite the mead they had consumed the night before, they had already begun to strap on their blades in anticipation of a coming battle. They looked almost eager.

"Can we catch them?" asked Maccus who had also heard enough of the conversation to know what was afoot.

"I do not know," Aelfin answered. "They did not come by boat, but they have a long lead on us." He turned to the peasant boy. "What have they taken?"

"They killed my cousins, and my uncle is badly wounded also."

"What have they *taken?*"

"All the cows."

"My lord," interrupted the young chieftain Eomaer, who had walked up behind Aelfin. "We have horses. The raiders will be leading their plunder. Possibly on foot. They will not be swift. We can catch them."

Aelfin looked at Eomaer for a moment, then nodded his head. "We go at once. Let the men of Dronrip ride with Eomaer, and those of us who can sit astride a horse will join him. Come, we pursue this band of raiders."

At once, more than a dozen warriors were on their feet rushing toward the door of the hall. Others were lacing their boots, or searching for weapons. Kristinge sat watching as Aelfin reached the door ahead of Maccus, Ceolac, and Eomaer. Then the chieftain stopped suddenly and turned as if something had just dawned on him. When his eyes came to rest on Kristinge, Kristinge froze. "Come," Aelfin said, a gleam in his eyes. "This shall be *your* war band."

Kristinge hesitated. Other thanes were looking at him. He could see the impatient expression in Aelfin's eyes. To hesitate now would be a sign of fear in front of the warriors—warriors who would one day be asked to follow him. And what would Aewin think? Kristinge jumped to his feet and grabbed his sword. A moment later, he was out the door and chasing the others across the village. All of his tutelage under Ceolac and Maccus was to be tested.

It took little time to get the horses out of the stable and ready. Before Kristinge knew what was happening, more than twenty thanes and warriors were riding down the cattle ramp and onto the fields east of the village. Eomaer and Aelfin were in the lead, with others of Eomaer's thanes close behind. Maccus, Ceolac, and Kristinge, less experienced on a horse than those from the Dronrip war band, followed in the tail of the pack. They rode hard to the edge of the fields where the raid had taken place. There they stopped. Two young peasants lay still on the ground, dead or nearly dead. An older man, still clutching his staff, sat leaning against a tree groaning from countless wounds. Kristinge recognized their faces, but did not know names. He turned away. Behind him, he could see women making their way from the village, the sounds of their weeping already audible from a distance. But Aelfin did not delay to wait for them. The tracks of the raiders were not difficult to follow. It was a large band, and they were leading many cattle.

"They are moving swiftly, but on foot," Eomaer said, looking down at the tracks.

"We are fortunate they have not come upriver by boat," Maccus responded. Though not a warrior, Kristinge understood the comment. The most effective raids came by ship, moving swiftly and silently upriver, attacking then disappearing with the currents long before any response could be mustered. These were the Viking raids, of which the Danes were masters.

"They could not have taken this many cattle in boats," Ceolac said, shaking his head at Maccus' comment. "These raiders were not interested in gold and silver. They came for food."

"Whatever else they thought," Aelfin cut off the conversation, "they did not expect that we would have a full mounted war band in the village this night. Come. Let us make them regret that mistake."

They put their heels to their horses' flanks and were soon off. The trail took them through the small wood beside the river and into the fields and low hills beyond. As Aelfin had said, the raiders did not expect to be pursued on horseback. The pursuers had not ridden long, perhaps an hour, when they caught sight of the first straggling cow left behind by the raiders.

"They know we are coming, else they would not have left one," Maccus interpreted.

"Then they cannot be far ahead," Aelfin said. "Be ready."

Aelfin was right. They came over a low rise and saw the band of raiders a short distance ahead still making their way down the back side of the hill. The chieftain turned to Eomaer. "Kristinge shall lead the attack. You take some and ride ahead to see that they do not escape us."

Eomaer nodded. He called eight of his warriors by name, and they veered off to the right. Aelfin turned to Kristinge, who was now realizing that there truly was going to be a battle. The terror of that realization had not yet overcome the thrill of the chase, but soon would. "We outnumber them and are better armed," Aelfin said loudly so that all could hear. "The battle will be swift, and our victory complete." Then he spoke to Kristinge. "When we approach, they will have to turn to face us. When they do, we dismount and attack."

Kristinge nodded blankly. His hands were feeling cold and wet. He reached for the hilt of his sword but couldn't get a good grip. Ahead, the raiding band had abandoned the cattle and were fleeing as fast as they could. Already, Eomaer was passing them on their right flank.

"Give the command," Aelfin said.

Kristinge took a deep breath. This, he reminded himself, was what he had been practicing for with Maccus and Ceolac. "To the attack!" he called.

His voice was not as loud or authoritative as he would have liked, but the warriors responded. Urging their mounts forward once more, they charged down the hill. In moments they were upon the fleeing band of raiders. When they were but a dozen yards away, the raiders finally turned to fight.

"To your feet!" Aelfin shouted, reminding Kristinge of the command he should have given. Kristinge slipped from the side of his mount, and nearly tumbled to the ground on legs that had been turned to rubber. With him were fifteen warriors from Ezinge. Another nine were now past the raiders and had turned to attack from the other side. The enemy numbered only thirteen. They were clustered in a haphazard half-circle, with a wild array of old spears, axes, and swords. Hungry men, perhaps, but not trained warriors. They were shouting to one another in a heavy Jutish dialect.

Then the clash began. Attacking downhill, the Ezinge war band bore into the outnumbered host like an avalanche. Kristinge, however, had no time to watch. He found himself face to face with a terrified youth of no more than sixteen summers, tightly gripping an old chipped battle ax. For just a moment Kristinge stood paralyzed, as the human features of the young man burned into his memory. When the ax came swinging at his exposed arm, he almost didn't step back in time. The second swipe was closer, and Kristinge had to leap out of the way to avoid a gaping wound in his chest. It was enough. He knew the rules of battle. It was kill or be killed. In the first few seconds he had almost been a victim. He looked at his opponent more warily now, knowing what another mistake could cost him. Trying to remember what Maccus and Ceolac had taught him, he raised his own heavy broadsword and brought it slicing down toward the chest and midsection of his opponent just as the young man stepped in for another attack. It was a well timed blow. Kristinge's blade was much longer than his enemy's ax, as were Kristinge's arms, giving him a double advantage. How the young Jutish raider escaped the blow, Kristinge did not know, but his sword sliced only through thin air leaving him stumbling off balance. The youth was immediately back on the attack and Kristinge struggled desperately to get out of the way. Suddenly, he was fighting for his own life. The ax came sweeping toward his head. Lurching to his left, he rolled away from the blow as it hummed past his shoulder. Rather than fighting against his own momentum, he instinctively spun his body all the way around with a great blind two-handed sweep of his heavy sword. Guided perhaps by blind luck, he felt the blade connect, but knew not what he hit for the motion sent him tumbling down the hill and crashing into the legs of another warrior.

Terrified, Kristinge struggled to regain his feet. He looked up to see Maccus staring down at him with a broad grin. The sounds of fighting were already over. Kristinge rose slowly to his knees, then stood. Behind him his own opponent lay on the ground clutching his belly, unable to stop the bleeding from the huge gash across his mid-section. Kristinge pulled his eyes away. He surveyed the battle field. Thirteen raiders lay defeated on the ground. Not a single member of his own war band had fallen. Only one warrior from Dronrip had received a small wound on the head, not from an enemy weapon but from stumbling into a rock. The battle was over.

It was Aelfin who raised the victory shout. Others joined, until the blood-stained hill resounded with their jubilant sound. Before Kristinge knew what was happening, he had been lifted over the heads of the warriors and set again upon his horse.

"Hail the battle-leader!" Aelfin shouted.

"Hail the battle-leader," the war band echoed.

"Hail the new chieftain."

"Hail the new king."

The shouting lasted only a few minutes. The real celebration would wait for their return to Ezinge. The warriors soon turned to their work. The booty from the battle was small, for the raiders were not rich. As Aelfin had guessed earlier, this was a band of hungry robbers, not a well-trained war band. Their purses yielded but a few coins, and few of their weapons had any worth. Only two swords were of value. The others would be cast aside, or the metal forged anew for other purposes while the bodies of the fallen enemies were left to the beasts. It took longer to gather the cattle that had been scattered by the fighting. Kristinge, who had more experience with such matters than any of the warriors, started to help but Aelfin would not let him. He set him atop his horse while others did the work. Fortunately, the animals had wandered only as far as the edge of a nearby wood. When the old matriarchal cow was roped, the rest followed.

It was an hour or more after the battle before all were ready. The victors traveled more slowly on the way back to Ezinge. The horses were tired from the hard ride earlier, and the company was no longer in a hurry. Nor did the task of leading the cattle speed their travel. It was after midday when they arrived back at the village. To Kristinge's surprise, there was already a celebration waiting for them at the mead hall. Aelfin had sent word ahead with two of Eomaer's riders, and all of Ezinge knew in advance of the victory. Still, it was many minutes before Kristinge realized that he was the returning victor, the honored hero. All were talking about the great two-handed blow with which he had felled the leader of the enemy war band. By the evening meal in the mead hall, Dyflines had already composed a song which he sang to the cheers of the warriors.

Had not Aewin been there throughout it all, watching her newly betrothed with appreciation, Kristinge might have fled the celebration before it even began. He knew nothing of the battle, and was under the impression that he had almost been killed, not that he had won a great fight or done anything to change the battle's outcome. As for the foe he had faced, it had been but a young man and not a war-leader. But these things mattered nothing to Aelfin or Eomaer or even to Dyflines. It was fodder for the chieftain's plans, and inspiration for the poet's songs. And so the feasting continued, nearly matching the night before, and the two war bands were happy. And Kristinge, once again finding Aewin at his side, forgot for the time about the battle and the face of the dying Jutish boy.

The next day, to the disappointment of the torc-bearer, Eomaer and Aewin left to return to their clan-village. They promised to return before the next moon, and that Eomaer would encourage other chieftains to follow Kristinge. Two near-kin he had, who ruled clan-villages southward along the coast would almost certainly follow Kristinge. Neither had any great love for Aldgisl, and less had they for Réadban. "Wigmaer, especially, would be a worthy one to have at your side," Eomaer said, as he stood beside his horse at the bottom of the terp. "He is wise, and has given me good counsel since my father died. And a good warrior too. I do not think he has yet sworn his allegiance to any. He is my mother's cousin, and though some years my elder has been a friend since youth. He would not disdain to hear a word from me." He turned to Aelfin. "Added to the messages already sent by you, perhaps my word would prove enough to sway them toward Kristinge."

"If he is as worthy as you are," Kristinge replied before Aelfin had a chance, "then he is indeed a good—" he paused. "A good chieftain." Almost he had said *a good thane*, but he could not yet think of *himself* as a king, and thus to call somebody his thane—especially one who was already a chieftain—did not come easily off his tongue.

Eomaer smiled and bowed. Then, in a single fluid motion, he mounted his horse and prepared to ride homeward toward Dronrip. Aewin paused a moment longer. She looked toward Kristinge, but her proud eyes were clouded and he could not guess her thoughts. She had said little to Kristinge those past two evenings, and even now she spoke no words of goodbye. He offered her his arm to lift her upon her horse, but whether she saw it or not, she did not take the offer. In a motion as graceful as her brother's she swung herself astride her mount and turned it southward. A minute later, the company was out of sight. And Kristinge, though he had known her but a few hours and had not had even a moment alone with her, stared long after her. He missed her almost at once.

The days that followed went well for him and for Aelfin's plans. Perhaps it was that the story of Kristinge's victory spread—growing in color and embellishment as it traveled outward from Ezinge—or perhaps it was just the timing of the earlier messages sent out by Aelfin that had come to fruition. Within a few days the chieftains in Wijnaldum and Wieuwerd, cousins of Eomaer, imitated Eomaer's example and promised their swords to Kristinge's service. And in the week that followed, a number of other chieftains of small villages joined as well. Kristinge's war band was growing and so was Aelfin's ambition. New messengers were now sent out to villages more distant, with the word that Finn's torc had returned to Friesland and now sat on the neck of his rightful heir. Even Kristinge began to grow excited by the signs of success. By the first light snowfall of autumn, he had at his command over three hundred warriors including fifty horses and trained riders. Never having gone to war he had little real idea of how large a war band that was, but Aelfin told him it was substantial.

"You are now the third most powerful chieftain in Friesland," he said with a broad grin.

Kristinge thought back on Luxeuil, and the many monks who were descended from chieftains. Many he had known from ruling families among clans and tribes across the north. Sons of Irish warlords, and Saxon kings. Offspring even of the rulers of the Franks. He wondered what they would think of him now. Some of them, he knew, had made lifetime vows of monastic life. But others had been sent to Luxeuil only to be educated. One day they hoped to return to their people, perhaps to rule. *Was it such a bad thing, aspiring to be king?* Kristinge wondered.

As promised, Eomaer returned a fortnight after his departure, but to Kristinge's disappointment he did not bring Aewin with him. Snow had fallen the day before, and this time it had not melted. The land was covered by an ankle-deep white blanket. Eomaer was worried by the weather. "Travel will grow difficult soon," he said, when he had warmed up beside the hearth fire and shared the mead cup with Aelfin, Kristinge, and a number of their thanes.

Aelfin nodded. Kristinge saw that he, too, was worried. His words were slow in coming, but when they came they revealed the cause of his concern. "We are not yet enough."

"And once the snow sets in, we will hear from nobody else until spring."

"But what of the three hundred?" Kristinge asked.

"Still too few," Aelfin repeated. "We count enough to make Aldgisl or Réadban wary. That is all. Not enough to oppose them. Only enough to attract their attention. And perhaps their anger."

"Have they yet heard of Kristinge's presence?" Eomaer asked.

"I do not think so. If they had, they would be in Ezinge already with their war bands at our throats. That is one blessing of winter. Travel is slow for them as well as us. Perhaps no word will reach them until spring, and even if it does they will likely wait before they respond. Still, it is only a question of time. Word travels through Friesland. With each day, the risk grows greater. Careful as we have been, there will be some chieftain who receives our message who has sworn his fealty to Aldgisl. Then Aldgisl will hear soon enough of what we do. Or when the traders begin to travel, they too will bring rumor of our doings."

"Should we wait a time?" Kristinge queried. Aelfin's words had made him nervous. It was the first time he had seen the chieftain's confidence falter. "Should we abandon our plans?"

Aelfin frowned and shook his head. "It is too late."

It was Eomaer who broke the mood with a laugh. "Let them outnumber us two to one. Finn's torc shall not be taken from Kristinge's neck while I live. We have thanes among us who can fight three of Aldgisl's hired warriors."

Others threw in their words of agreement, and Aelfin joined Eomaer's optimistic laughter. He called for more mead and commanded his bard Dyflines to liven the evening with songs. But Kristinge knew that the chieftain was worried. Perhaps it was that worry that he carried to bed that night, or perhaps it was thoughts of Luxeuil that brought the old voices once again back into his head. He did not know, but the nightmare he had that night left him shaken.

He stood on a hillside, Finn's torc glittering brightly on his neck. He was the king now. The chieftain of all Friesland. Behind him was his war band. Ahead lay the enemy. A vast sea of Frankish knights and warriors with Clovis at their head, a half-crazed grin on his face and his still unclad mistress in his arms. Kristinge drew the huge broadsword from his iron-bound sheath. He lifted it high over his head and gave the command to attack. His army surged forward.

Down the long hill Kristinge charged. His hair, long now and bound in braids in the manner of Germanic chieftains, flopped against his neck. Behind him raced his war band. Ahead stood the waiting enemy. The warriors on both sides screamed with delight at the oncoming battle. The scream grew louder. It became a piercing wail. Still they rode on. The distance between the armies did not shrink. The sun beat down on them. Summer changed to autumn and then to winter. It was cold now. They were riding through the snow. The icy metal of Kristinge's blade burned his hands, but he could not let go.

Suddenly the gap narrowed. The armies came together. The waiting was over. Kristinge glanced over his shoulder to urge his men on. And to his horror, he found that they were gone. His war band had disappeared. Only Aelfin was still with him. The old chieftain's hair was now white with age—as white as the snow around them. He, too, knew that they

had been abandoned. Yet he did not stop. "It is too late," Aelfin cried.
"Too late." He charged past Kristinge, flinging himself headlong into the
vast Frankish army. "A king is a warrior," he cried just before he was
engulfed.

Kristinge watched Aelfin fall. He tried to turn and flee, but he
couldn't. His legs would not move. A Frankish warrior rose in front of
him, lifting his huge ax. He towered over Kristinge like a giant, only his
face was the youthful face of the young Jutish raider whom Kristinge had
killed in battle. He could see the boy's eyes now, full of fear and hatred—
just as they had been before. Terrified, Kristinge looked at his blade.
Though he had not yet swung it, it was already dripping in blood. The
blood poured down the blade, staining the snow beneath him. In horror,
he looked back at the enemy. The youth had disappeared. In his place stood
Willimond. Only Willimond was dead, slain by the sword in Kristinge's
hand.

"No!" Kristinge cried.

It was too late. Willimond had slumped to the ground. Kristinge
lunged toward him.

Though the hall was cold with the early morning air, Kristinge
awoke in a sweat. He was still in Ezinge. It was early November. The
fire on the hearth had burned down low. Around him, warriors were
sleeping peacefully, untroubled in their dreams. Did killing no longer
bother them?

Kristinge sat upright on his bench and tried to shake off the
effects of the nightmare, but he was still trembling. He could hear
Aelfin's voice. *A king is a warrior... Your war band is now three hundred*
strong... It is too late.

Too late? The words rung in his ears. Feeling the need to be alone,
Kristinge arose and went outside. Perhaps the cool air would refresh
him. He walked toward the bounds of the village. Though the dim
gray of dawn was making itself known in the east, the sky was still
bright with stars. Aurvandil was there among them. Earendil, as the
Christian Saxons called it. He stared at the stars for a time, as he stood
there at the edge of the terp, but it didn't help. The dream had faded,
only to be replaced by the memory of the Jutish raider now lying dead
in a field. For the first time, Kristinge wondered about him. Where

had he come from? Had he lived in the woods, wild and hungry? Or had he come from a distant village? Perhaps a family. A mother, or father, or even wife awaiting him in some distance place, hoping for food. Who would miss him?

His own people had died, too, Kristinge reminded himself. The raiders had killed folk of Ezinge and stolen their cattle. They were outlaws. But the thought did not comfort him. He could not help but remember another day—a day many years past, but still fresh in his mind—when raiders from the mountains had come down upon Luxeuil. A young monk just tonsured, Kristinge had been at work in the fields outside the wall of Annegray that afternoon. It had been late in the day, but early in the planting season. Twilight was upon the field when he had heard the cries. Loud voices. War cries shouting in a strange tongue. An uncommon sound in a Benedictine monastery. He should have guessed at once what was happening. But it had been many years—since before his own time at Luxeuil—since raiders had last come to the monastery. Thus it was that their coming had taken the monks by surprise, and it was several seconds before Kristinge understood what was happening. A band of robbers, twenty or more, were charging from the woods on three sides. Armed with spears and bows, and some with swords, they were attacking the monastery. And the monks, unarmed, fled before them. But the those on the far edge of the field had not run fast enough. Before they were able to reach protected enclosure at Annegray, four of their number had fallen, one struck down by a spear through his belly before he had even turned to flee.

On the attackers had rushed, their war cries soon mingled with the terror-filled shouts of the monks. But what had the monks found at the gates of the old Roman fort? Not a band waiting to defend them, but Abbot Walbert and Father Petrica. Unarmed. But they were not fleeing. Abbot Walbert had not even commanded the gates to be shut. His arms outstretched, he was going *out* to meet the raiders. "Stop," came his voice as a dozen monks stumbled past him. Kristinge came to a halt at his side, but Walbert was looking out at the swiftly advancing marauders, hot on the tail of the last few monks. "Stop!" he said again. To Kristinge's surprise, the raiders listened. So much authority was there in the abbot's voice that even they had stopped a few paces away from him. Around in a circle they spread themselves enclosing the gate of Annegray, but as of yet none approached closer than ten feet.

"What is it you want?" Petrica had asked them in their own tongue. "We have no treasure here."

"Food," they had demanded. "Do not lie. We have heard you have a great store laid up for winter."

"Food we have, and will share, but you needn't come at us with weapons," Petrica replied. Even as he said this, some of the younger monks of Annegray had appeared behind him, wielding various farming implements which in desperation they had hoped to turn into weapons. Though poorly armed, with all the monastery gathered they outnumbered the raiders at least two to one. And Ulestan was among them, holding in his hands a long-handled hoe. Had it come to battle, the raiding party would certainly have gone home far smaller than they had come even if they won the battle. They would have to think twice before attacking, Kristinge had thought. Which was good, for ill could the folk of Luxeuil afford to give away their dwindling winter stores.

But Walbert's thoughts had been different. "Put these things away," he had commanded his own monks. "Are you children to have to be told this? Put down your weapons and see to the fallen." Without a further word to the monks, he had turned back to the raiders who at the sight of the weapons had begun to edge forward. He repeated what Petrica had told them. "Little enough food we have, and our folk eat but scanty portions. Yet what we have we will share with you. But put away your weapons."

Kristinge still remembered his thoughts at those words. Walbert had not lied. Little food they had, and it would be many weeks before the first spring crops would arrive. He had not thought he could survive on rations any smaller than those he already received. Yet a short time later, the monks were carrying a large portion of Annegray's winter stores out to the raiders. Even as they did, the other monks returned from the field carrying their fallen companions. Three of the fallen were only superficially wounded. One, however, lay near death with a spear protruding from his side. Brogus was his name. His face was pale as he lay moaning in his agony, and Kristinge had been sure he was about to die. At the sight of him, many of the raiders had lowered their heads. Walbert had cast one look of reproof at them, as a parent might to a wayward child, and then—to the amazement of the monks as well as the raiders—he had reached down, pulled the spear free, and pulled Brogus to his feet. And Brogus had just stood there. He pulled his hand from his belly, and found not only that the bleeding had stopped but where the spear wound had been was now only a scar. He was fully healed.

Seeing the sight, many of the raiders had fled without even taking their food. "Demons!" they had cried. And "Witches." Others had fallen on their knees as if Petrica and Walbert were gods themselves. Yet when Petrica preached to them of the true God, many came to Christ. Never again did any of them come back to rob Annegray or Luxeuil.

CHAPTER 18:
EAST WINDS

The memory of Luxeuil brought Kristinge no comfort, and in the weeks that followed, his dream returned to him many times, though not always in the same form. Sometimes he saw himself standing at the bow of a warship, riding the waves onto the beaches where an enemy army awaited him. Other times he was astride his horse, waving his sword and shouting war cries in a strange language. Sometimes Eomaer was in his dreams also, crying out for vengeance, laying across Kristinge's knees the ancestral sword of his father's family and demanding retribution against Aldgisl. And the sword was already dripping with blood. Always the dreams ended with the face of the slain lad, and with Willimond, Petrica and Abbot Walbert looking with sorrow upon the scene.

He told nobody about his nightmares. Whom would he tell? Yet the dreams disturbed him greatly, continuing to trouble him long after he woke. A heavy guilt began to weigh him down. Many weeks had passed, however, since Aelfin had placed the torc around his neck. In that time, he had grown accustomed to its feel. He had grown used to the idea of being king; to sleeping in the mead hall; to the giving of gifts and the fellowship around the hearth; to the voice of Dyflines. He could even see himself riding from village to village, wearing his torc, visiting his thanes and dispensing fair justice when necessary. He could see Aewin at his side...

A king is a warrior, Aelfin's voice kept repeating over and over again. With each dream, the blood on his sword thickened. Soon, it was running down his arm. But now Kristinge had begun to build up a defense. He thought of Balthild and all she had done for Telchild and the monasteries at Jouarre. And she was only a queen—a former Saxon slave-girl. Kristinge thought also of Clovis and his insanity, and the wickedness he had done as king. Then he thought of all the great things a Christian king could do for Francia or Friesland. He thought of all the thanes who might bow their knees before God if their king were to lead them. And so in his waking hours he put his dreams aside and devoted himself more diligently to Aelfin's tutoring in the ways of a chieftain.

He was glad when, a week after Eomaer's visit, the young horse-chieftain returned with his sister Aewin. Two days earlier, another storm had brought the level of snow halfway to their knees, and a biting north wind was promising more harsh weather. The riders were cold when they arrived late in the evening after the sun had dipped below the edge of the horizon. Aewin was shivering uncontrollably, and though she did not complain, Kristinge could see she was in pain. He sat her by the fire, then disappeared to his hut where he grabbed his warmest blanket and returned at a run. He wrapped the blanket around her, and as he did so he let his hands rest on her shoulders for a moment, unsure if he had the right to do so. Their eyes met and held.

"I told her not to come," Eomaer was saying. "She would not listen. She is a stubborn one."

Kristinge took a seat beside his betrothed and turned to listen to Eomaer's words, wondering what had brought him to Ezinge—though he was by no means unhappy about the result.

"And her brother is not stubborn?" Aelfin replied with a smile. Eomaer growled. "What has brought you?" Aelfin went on with the questioning.

"No good news." Eomaer replied. Aelfin's eyes narrowed. Kristinge leaned forward also, as he continued. "Traders came up the coast just a few days ago—"

"By boat?" Maccus asked in surprise. It was well past the season for travel on the seas.

"By foot and wagon. They were returning home, bringing with them rumors from the south. Rumors of the return of Finn's son."

Aelfin let out a sharp breath. "Then word has reached the corners of Friesland."

"It would appear so."

They did not talk much more that evening. Eomaer's war band was exhausted. Some had already collapsed, and others were coughing harshly. It had taken them two full days of travel to make the trip, much longer than usual because of the weather. And Kristinge could see that it had cost them. Yet it was not Eomaer's message that troubled him most, but Aewin's condition. He spent much of the evening seeking to take care of her, bringing hot stew and warm drink to help revive her, and making sure Aelfin's servants kept the fire blazing. She barely moved, and her breathing was shallow. That night, she fell asleep with her head on Kristinge's lap as he prayed fervently for her health.

Though no snow fell that night, the next day dawned windy and bitterly cold. It was the time of year when the distance to the North Sea was not great enough for the inhabitants of Ezinge. Icy blasts of sea air whistled through the village as if the terp were an island. Yet this morning Kristinge did not mind. After hours of care, he had finally fallen asleep with Aewin's head upon his lap and for the first night in many days had slept with pleasant dreams. It was she who awakened him. He opened his eyes to find her standing above him—a heavy fur cloak on her back and a mischievous smile on her face— trying to pull him to his feet. "You're bett—" he started to say in a loud and joyful voice, but before he could continue she put her hand over his mouth and silenced him. The warriors on both sides stirred at the sound, but remained asleep. Aewin's eyes, meanwhile, were beckoning. Kristinge looked at her closely. A long warm night's sleep behind her, she looked refreshed and full of energy. As far as he could tell, she had suffered no lasting ill effects from the cold that had afflicted her the previous day. He was overjoyed to see she had recovered. He glanced around the hall. The warriors of Ezinge and Dronrip still slept along with their chieftains.

Come with me, Aewin silently mouthed, and pointed toward the door. Kristinge's sleepiness fled at once, and he obeyed without question. He rose, grabbed his own cloak, and followed. Quietly so as not to wake any of the sleepers—though Kristinge had no idea where Aewin was leading him—the two of them stepped toward the door of the hall. Outside, the wind was howling, and they could feel its cold draft through the chinks in the door and wall. Aewin was unperturbed. Kristinge saw now that she had on heavy fur leggings and warm boots in addition to her cloak. She pulled her cloak tightly about her and stepped outside, Kristinge still following.

"Where do we go?" Aewin asked, once they were outside.

The question surprised Kristinge. He thought he was following *her*. He glanced around the village as he thought for a moment. Wherever it was, he didn't want to be in the wind for very long. On an impulse, he reached out and took Aewin's hand, again wondering as he did so whether it was presuming too much. Aewin did not resist. Despite the cold air around them, a rush of warm blood flooded through Kristinge's veins at the feel of her hand in his. For a moment, all he was aware of was that touch—as if his entire body had slipped down into the fingers of his right hand. He led her across the village to the chapel. He had not been there for many days, but could think of no other place to go. Inside it was cold, but out of the wind. Aewin pulled her fingers from Kristinge's grip and sat down. Suddenly, Kristinge felt awkward. This was the first time he had been alone with her. No, he remembered, not quite the first. Twice before he had talked with her alone. Beside the river near Finnsburg long before, when she had told him of her promised betrothal to his brother. But that was long past. He doubted that she would remember that day as he did. Not knowing what to day, he sat down on the bench opposite her.

Aewin looked shyly down at her feet, then up again, then again at her feet, before finally looking into Kristinge's eyes. "That was you who saved my life in Paris," she said.

Once again, Kristinge was taken by surprise. She had seen him? And remembered? "I didn't exactly save you," he replied. *I did nothing,* he thought, but he did not want to confess this.

"Queen Balthild said it was you."

"Me?" Kristinge stammered. *Queen Balthild?* he wondered.

"Balthild is a gracious and generous queen," Aewin went on. "She spoke with me again after your ship departed. At her invitation, I visited her palace. We talked long about many things. When I thanked her again for her help that morning, she said she came to my aid because of you—because she saw you step forward to help me, though you bore not a single weapon and did not even know me. She was inspired by your courage."

Kristinge did not know what to say. He had not felt much courage. Only fear.

"You were dressed as a monk then," Aewin added, looking sidelong at Kristinge as she did. Then she shivered and again pulled her cloak tightly about her shoulders, but Kristinge did not pick up on the hint. After a moment of his silence, she spoke again, once more astounding him. "And in Domburg you were there again. It was me to whom you sang that night, was it not?"

Kristinge nodded in embarrassment. Had he been that obvious?

"It was a beautiful song. Never before had I been so moved by a bard." She paused. "Would you sing that song to me again?"

Flattered by the request, Kristinge ran to his hut to find his harp. He returned at a run. Despite his fears, Aewin was still waiting for him. The harp, cold from the weather and suffering from disuse, took many minutes to tune. The time was magnified by Kristinge's impatience. But finally the strings were ready. His voice cracking at first with nervousness, he sang to her the song one more time. When he was done, Aewin rose from her seat. She paced across the small chapel twice, then sat down—this time close by Kristinge's side. She slipped her hand under his arm as he strummed gently on the harp, happy to have the instrument in his hands once again and happier yet to have Aewin at her side.

"Tell me who you are," she said.

The words were spoken so softly that Kristinge barely heard. When he realized what she had asked, he stopped his playing. It was a big question, and he was not sure how to answer. *Who am I?* He wondered.

"When I saw you last autumn, you wore the cloak of a monk and were sailing away from me. When I saw you next, you were a gifted bard singing love songs to me. Now you wear the torc of a chieftain, and my hand has been promised to you in marriage. But I remember long ago a young man—a boy—in Hwitstan who entertained me with his singing while my father visited Finn. For a time after I saw you in Frotha's hall, I mistrusted my memory and thought it could not have been the same. But now I know it was you, and I know also that you remember me."

Kristinge blushed again at how easily she read his mind, and even more at how long he had foolishly and hopelessly clung to the memory of her. Or had it been hopeless?

"Who are you?" Aewin asked again.

Kristinge began again to strum his harp softly as his mind sought for words to answer. Who indeed was he? The question Aewin had asked cut to the heart of what had plagued him for so long. It was the question that had driven him from Luxeuil. He had thought the question laid to rest, but now he understood that it was not. He wished that somebody else could answer her. What would Willimond say? Or Hildeburh? Or Petrica? Or even Telchild? But none of them were there. He was alone with the question. Could he answer Aewin any more than she herself had already said? Had she already told him who he was better than he could have told her?

A long silence followed, through which Aewin sat patiently, watching Kristinge's fingers move over his harp. In the end, all he could think of was to tell his story. "I am the son of Finn," he began. "Though I lived most of my life without that knowledge." In a voice more rhythmic and melodic than he intended—more like a bard telling a heroic epic than a man speaking of his own life—he told Aewin his story. Not merely the tale of how Aelfin had schemed to make him king, but the tale of his life. For he could think of naught else he could answer. No truth, except the story. Back to his earliest memories his thoughts stretched. To the days of Finn and Hildeburh whom he had known only from a distance, and to his childhood along the wics of Friesland. To his labors on the weirs with the fisherfolk of Hwitstan and his training in Latin at the side of his monk and foster-father Willimond. He told of his memories of Aewin herself, and how he had never forgotten her. And he told what he remembered of the death of his brother Finnlaf and that terrible battle, and what he had learned from Ulestan. And so his tale continued, and Aewin listened intently, as he spoke finally of his departure from Hwitstan and his six years at Luxeuil, of his voyage through Paris to Danemark and his reunion with Hildeburh, his mother, and of his journey back to Friesland. He blushed as he told how Aelfin had recognized him, and had contrived to return to his neck the torc of his father. Only when the tale came to Eomaer's offer did he falter and fall silent.

By that time, the sun had risen high in its winter arc across the southern horizon and the wind had grown more brisk. But no interruption came and not a word did Aewin speak until he was done, save to press more closely against his side. "I am sorry," Kristinge apologized. "I did not mean to speak for so long."

But Aewin's eyes glowed more brightly. "Never has any man so confided in me," she said. "Not even my brother. And yet there is much still I would ask you."

Kristinge laughed. "Is there anything I have not already said?"

"This place. Luxeuil you have named it. I have heard little before of these *monasteries*. Even the name sounds awkward to my ears. Queen Balthild spoke of one near Paris, but I could not fathom what she told me, so strange and foreign does it seem to me." Again Kristinge laughed, and Aewin blushed. "You make fun of me for my lack of knowledge," she complained

"No," Kristinge objected. "I laugh at the thought of a monastery. Though I spent six years of my life there, words do not come easy as I try to explain what a monk does. It sounds odd even to my ears. But I suppose there is one thing at the center of it all. We are there to learn the teachings of Jesus."

"Jesus," Aewin repeated. "That name, too, I have heard from Balthild. From the time I first heard his name, I have wanted to know more of him."

Kristinge's heart leapt, and as he went on to tell her more, he learned that her words had not been not empty—that she really was eager to learn more about the God whom he served. Nearly as eager as he was to tell her.

It was not until they were interrupted by Eomaer and Aelfin that Kristinge realized it was already past midday. They had spent the whole morning together talking. "We searched the whole village for you," Aelfin said, but the tone of complaint in his voice could not hide his delight and finding Kristinge and Aewin together. If he had still been worried that Kristinge might carry out his threat and flee the village to avoid the marriage, his fears were now relieved. "Come," he said. "It is time to return to the mead hall." Kristinge nodded and rose. Stepping again into the cold wind that still ripped across the terp, he took Aewin's hand and returned across the village to the warmth of a hall fire and the fellowship of the hearth.

As Kristinge discovered upon entering the hall, most of the warriors of Dronrip had recovered from their ride. They sat around the fire, drinking from mead cups and eating dried fish while speaking with the warriors from Ezinge of weapons, and food, and family. Kristinge sighed, and released Aewin's hand. He wished suddenly that Aelfin's plan was completed, the torc firmly about his neck, and that they could be wed without delay. But she would soon be departing, he knew, and he doubted whether the torc would ever rest upon his neck.

"How long will you stay with us?" Aelfin asked the younger chieftain. If he had been speaking to anybody else, Kristinge might have thought his foster-father was concerned about his winter stores and was anxious to be rid of a guest. But he knew that Aelfin liked Eomaer and was glad of his company. Like Kristinge, the older chieftain had grown to like the younger despite his impetuousness. "You would do well to rest here a time. The windstorm has not abated."

"No, it has not," Eomaer agreed. "And not all of my men have recovered." Even as he spoke, loud coughing erupted in one corner of the hall, followed by more coughing elsewhere. "Were it the raiding season, I would not like to be away from my people so long, leaving them unguarded. Half of our war band is with me. But I do not expect any raids upon the village now. I think they are safe. Perhaps we will stay until the winds die."

At those words, Kristinge's heart leapt with joy. In his heart he had prayed that Aewin might stay for one more day. As it proved, his prayer was answered thrice over; Eomaer remained in Ezinge three more nights and days, and Aewin with him. They were joyous days for Kristinge. And for Aewin also. As often as they could, they would go together to the chapel and talk, just the two of them. And neither Eomaer nor Aelfin hindered it, save when they wanted Kristinge to join them in their counsels. For they were busy talking of war bands and weapons, and the treaty of marriage was a thing already agreed upon in their minds to which they needed give little more thought.

Even less thought did Kristinge give to talk of war during that time, except when he was pressed hard by Aelfin to give some answer. Instead, his mind was occupied with the task of getting to know Aewin. Having already told her much about himself, it was his turn to question her about her past. At his prompting, Aewin told of the death of her mother in childbirth when she was still very young, and of the death of her father in a faraway battle; of being raised by an old aunt and taken care of by her own brother; and of being trained as a sword-maiden until recently when Eomaer had decided she should be wed to a chieftain. She told how she had rebelled against his command until she found out it was Kristinge.

Kristinge laughed, and shared with her that he had responded the same way. But behind his laugh he wondered. *Why? Why were you willing to marry me? You knew nothing about me.* Yet these questions he was afraid to pose, for fear that in pondering her answers Aewin might turn away from him. Eventually, Aewin's questions led them back to conversations about Luxeuil and the God worshipped there: the God Kristinge preached. By the end of their three days, Aewin was ready to trust in Christ. Alas that Aewin and Eomaer departed the next day and Kristinge was once more alone with his thoughts.

"Winter is upon is," Aelfin said, continuing his pacing around the fire. In one hand he held a large drinking horn from which he was taking frequent swigs. In his other hand was his sword, a new one he had acquired from Frankish traders after giving his old battle-tested blade to Kristinge. He was tapping the sword on the benches beside him as he walked and spoke. "It is early in the year for this snow. Autumn has passed far too quickly."

Theoman and Wihtred were seated nearby, listening and nodding their heads in agreement. The first two clan-chieftains to cast their swords with Aelfin and accept Finn's son as king, they now came to Ezinge frequently to plot with Aelfin how to secure the torc. With them were a half dozen of their trusted warriors along with Aelfin's own thanes—Kristinge still did not think of them as *his* thanes—who preferred the companionship of the mead hall to their own cold huts. The young heir was seated near the fire between Maccus and Ceolac, trying to pay attention to the conversation, but feeling out of place. He was thinking more about Aewin than about plans for battle. He wished she were with him that evening. Though he had known her only briefly, he already missed her. In their short time together he had spoken more deeply with her than he ever had with Aelfin. He looked toward the closed door of the mead hall, half hoping that Eomaer and his company might arrive at any moment. But outside it was dark. A foot of snow lay on the ground and more was falling steadily. Winter had arrived, and Kristinge was not likely to see his betrothed soon.

Aelfin came to a halt a step away from Kristinge. "Just two more weeks would have been enough," he complained, angry at the weather for its uncaring interference. "But now—?" He lifted his sword and tapped the air, then took a big swig, draining the mead in his horn.

But now? Kristinge lifted his head as the unfinished question died away into the stillness of the hall. What do you mean, *but now?* The way Aelfin asked that question—the suggestion that the plan was now in danger of failing—caught Kristinge's attention, drawing his thoughts away from Aewin and back to the issue at hand. But now *what?* He wanted to ask, his heart suddenly beating faster. *Are you saying we won't be enough?* Yet he dared not ask the question. Not in the mead hall. Aelfin would say little in front of his thanes. And even if he would, Kristinge was afraid of the answer. It didn't take much to guess what the chieftain was worried about. As the weeks had passed, the former monk had learned much from his new foster father: the names of chieftains of the many clans in Friesland; the sizes of their war bands; the number of days of travel between their villages; which clans were at war with one another. All useful information, Kristinge thought, *if* he was one day to be king. But that possibility was doubtful now. For of greatest import, he had learned about his rivals Aldgisl and Réadban. "They will be swift to respond to any threat to their own power, real or perceived," Aelfin had said. "Réadban especially. He is ruthless. He is as bad as the Franks. He will waste no time killing you if he perceives that you are a rival to his ambitions, or those of his family. And he is powerful."

He will waste no time killing you. Those words had not been missed by Kristinge, who from the start had understood Aelfin's sense of urgency. It was not the *urgency* that bothered him. As long as the chieftain was confident, Kristinge had been able to keep his fears at bay. But now there was something more than mere urgency in the chieftain's concerns. Aelfin was visibly worried. The overwhelming confidence he had shown even two weeks earlier was conspicuously absent as he paced around the mead hall. It was this that now made Kristinge afraid. Very afraid. All the anxiety that he had managed to suppress since his betrothal to Aewin came bubbling to the surface. Kristinge knew too clearly that he was caught up in Aelfin's plan, whatever happened: no matter how little he had contributed to the planning; no matter how little he had *wanted* to be a part. His tension mounted as the chieftain paced around the fire spilling his doubts like bad mead. *What if the plan failed?* He wondered. *What would happen?* More than his betrothal to Aewin was at stake. It was his life that was in danger. And what part *had* he played? he asked himself. He had been dragged into the scheme with no warning, without his consent, even against his will. He fought down a sense of resentment against Aelfin, and remembered that he was betrothed to Aewin because of the torc about his neck. "What must we do?" he asked in as calm a voice as he could muster.

Aelfin didn't answer. He paced around the fire again. Then, ignoring Kristinge's question, he turned in the direction of the other two chieftains. "We must assume Aldgisl and Réadban have heard of Kristinge's presence by now."

Kristinge bit his lip. Once again Aelfin was addressing the other chieftains as if he weren't present. He knew why. Kristinge had no experience in the gathering of war bands and the making of kings. There was little he could contribute to the conversation. He was merely a tool. Knowing this did not help. It made matters worse. He could feel his anxiety turning to anger as his sense of helplessness increased.

"What does Aldgisl know about *him?*" Theoman asked, nodding toward Kristinge.

"He can only *guess* how big our war band is," Aelfin answered. He still said nothing about the visit from Eomaer. Kristinge wondered if the other chieftains also felt manipulated by Aelfin, and if they guessed that Aelfin knew more than he was saying. But he held his tongue.

"That is good," Wihtred said. "Let him be in doubt."

"But he now knows of Kristinge?" Theoman pressed.

"Yes," Kristinge answered, but the three chieftains ignored him.

Wihtred shrugged evasively. "We must *assume* that Aldgisl and Réadban know of Kristinge's presence here. That they know or will soon know that he is the son of Finn, and that he now wears his father's torc. They will know also that he has begun to gather a war band—that a son of Finn commands many warriors. They will know that Kristinge is a threat."

"Me?" Kristinge blurted out, unwilling to sit there any longer and be spoken of—to be used like a tool without any say. "Why am I the threat? It is *you* who have gathered the war band!"

Aelfin spun so quickly that half the remaining contents of his drinking horn splashed onto the ground near the hearth. "*WHAT?!*" he shouted over the hissing of his drink on the hot stones. An angry grimace appeared on his face. "Are you saying this was all *me*. Is it my torc I seek to secure?"

Kristinge did not answer. In his heart, he knew he had gone along with Aelfin's plan from the beginning. He had offered little resistance. He had never said no. Yet he still felt that he had never really been given a choice. For a long moment, all were silent. Kristinge was aware of the curious expressions of the thanes scattered around the hall as they glanced back and forth between him and Aelfin. Aelfin, too, became aware of the audience. He looked around him at the gathered chieftains and warriors, then back at Kristinge. He relaxed again. What he said next was exactly what was on Kristinge's mind.

"*You* know as well as I that even if what you have said is true, it will matter nothing to Réadban or Aldgisl. A son of Finn is a threat to them even if you had *no* war band. But the fact is, the war band exists. And if Réadban and Aldgisl have not yet heard of it, they will soon."

Again, Kristinge did not reply. He could not deny the truth of what Aelfin had said. He was a threat to any who desired the rule of Friesland. This was no longer a game. He was trapped. Perhaps that was what angered him.

"Even that is beside the point," Aelfin went on, not giving Kristinge any more time to think about what had already been said. "You were raised in Hwitstan. You have lived among the Franks, and have met their king. You have even lived among the Danes. You know that a chieftain is a warrior. It was not wealth that made me a chieftain. It was my strength." He clenched his fist around his sword as he spoke, his voice still intense. "It was my sword. It was leading my people in battle. It was protecting them—finding new land and a new village when we were driven from Domburg by a stronger foe. The moment I cease to do these things, I cease to be a chieftain. And what is true of a clan chieftain is ten times true of any who would rule a whole kingdom. Why do you think the Frankish kings have lost their hold on Francia? Because Clovis is a weak—" He didn't finish his sentence. "If you want to be king, you must be first and always a warrior!" Suddenly Aelfin's face lifted. A new idea was working its way through the chieftain's head: a new glimmer of hope. And Kristinge was almost afraid to hear what it was. "Ah," Aelfin exclaimed, lifting his sword and drinking horn in the air. "More drink. Fill your horns. Yes. Let us celebrate again."

"My lord?" Maccus asked.

"I have forgotten for a moment what this was about. Now I remember. And the memory tells me all we need."

"Tell us, that we may remember and rejoice with you," Theoman replied.

"Let us first share the mead cup," Aelfin ordered.

If nothing else, Kristinge had learned that Aelfin was skilled in raising the excitement of his followers. When the mead jug had been passed and all had taken a long draught, Aelfin sat down and began to speak. "Listen to me," he said. "From the beginning it was the accursed Franks we have feared. We need to unite Friesland to drive them from our land, to push them over the Rhine—as far across the Rhine as our strength allows. The war leader who can do that will surely be king."

Theoman spoke. "This I believe is true. Though my village has suffered little at the hands of the Franks, I know that all of Friesland fears them. Not only our traders, but many of our coastal villages have suffered at the hands of Frankish raiders and robbers, especially along the Rhine. If we lose the Rhine and the Meuse both, we will lose control of our trade and our wealth. We must regain Domburg, and control the Rhine."

"Yes," Aelfin said. "Then let us raise up Kristinge *not* as king. Not at first," he added to their surprised looks. "But as a war leader to lead a Frisian war band against the Franks along the Rhine. The step from there to king will not be a great one, but it can wait."

At the mention of his leading a war band, Kristinge began to grow nervous. Was his nightmare to become a reality? He was glad when Theoman spoke again. "But Kristinge is no warrior—"

"He has already led a war band into victory," Aelfin replied before Theoman could finish his protest.

Theoman shook his head. "You forget to whom you speak. I have heard your cleverly crafted tales, and I praise you for your savvy. But I know also that Kristinge, even if he did lead the attack as was claimed, did not defeat a host of trained Frankish warriors. He defeated a small band of poorly skilled and poorly armed raiders." He turned and bowed his head toward Kristinge. "I mean no insult, and do not challenge either your courage or your wisdom. I say only that you have not been raised as a warrior, and a few weeks of sword training with even skilled teachers such as Maccus and Ceolac will not make you one in so short a time."

"Yet *you* serve him," Aelfin said, cutting again to the heart of the issue.

"I do," Theoman replied, turning back to Aelfin. "I serve him not because he is a warrior, but because he is the son of Finn and because I loved Finn. And because I see in him some of the same wisdom and vision that was in his father and grandfather. The blood of Finn and Folcwalda is thick in his veins, as is that of Hoc whose name has still not been forgotten. But you know as well as I that the number of chieftains who will serve Kristinge for that reason is the number of chieftains gathered in this room. Though I serve him out of loyalty for his father, I am skeptical that you can make him king simply because he is the heir of Finn's torc."

"That is my point. Indeed, that was my idea from the start, though I had forgotten it."

"But it is even less likely that he will succeed as a warrior," Theoman protested. They were once again talking as if Kristinge were not present.

"With training, it is possible to *make* him a warrior," Aelfin replied. "He is still young. And he is strong. Whatever you may think of the battle, Kristinge stood his ground and slew his opponent." Kristinge cringed at the memory, as the face of the slain youth rose again to haunt him. "But you speak wisely," Aelfin continued. "No. I do not propose that Kristinge actually *lead* us into battle. He leads us in name and figure only, riding at our heads. You, and I, and Wihtred will lead in actuality. And our own thanes as well," he added, looking around the hall. "They are worth ten warriors each. Remember also that Finn may be dead, but he is not forgotten. There are still many who would rally to a battle against the Franks in Finn's name even if they wouldn't accept his son as king. If we promise a victory over the Franks, then Kristinge's name—the name of Finn's son—will draw the war bands, which is something I fear we could not do without him. He will ride to war with us, but the three of us will lead. And if we succeed, then it will be no great matter to make him king. And we his chief thanes," Aelfin concluded, with a gesture of his arms encompassing all in the room.

CHAPTER 19:
MONK, BARD, PRIEST, KING

Kristinge did not sleep well that night. Doubts and misgivings about what he was doing returned in full force. Were it not for Aewin, he might even have sought again to turn his path from the one laid out for him by Aelfin. But now he found that his love for her had grown, and he was afraid that if he lost the torc he would lose her as well. Furthermore, Aelfin was right: it was too late. Even if he gave up the torc and left Ezinge, Réadban and Aldgisl would pursue him. He had to continue on, following the path of his ancestors. Nevertheless, despite this realization, the next day Kristinge felt the need to be alone—to get out of the mead hall and the company of warriors. He walked through the fresh snow to the chapel. It was not the Sabbath, but he wanted to be alone to think and pray.

The chapel was cold as it had been a few days earlier when he had come with Aewin. He sat on a bench and pulled his cloak around his neck. And for a long time, he just sat there and stared at the cross hanging at the back of the church.

A king is a warrior, he heard Aelfin's voice repeating. *You are king because you lead your people in battle.*

"Is that so wrong?" he said aloud to the cross. "What of David? Was he not a man after God's own heart?"

The cross remained silent. But Dunnere entered the chapel a short time later. Kristinge had not spoken to him in many days. Weeks, in fact. When Dunnere saw Kristinge sitting there, he turned to go.

"No!" Kristinge protested. "Stay." He cursed silently when he realized he was still holding his sword. He had tried to make a point of never bringing it into the chapel. How had he forgotten so quickly?

Dunnere appeared nervous, but he obeyed Kristinge's request and entered. He sat on the bench near the door and looked at the ground by his feet. Kristinge sensed at once that something was amiss, but he didn't know what. He prompted the peasant with a few questions that were answered briefly. They spoke of the fall harvest, the amount of snow on the ground, and the abundance of game in the woods that winter.

"How is your goat?" Kristinge asked after a time.

Dunnere looked at Kristinge in surprise, then shook his head. "Dead," he answered.

"Dead?" Kristinge was shocked. The goat was not only Dunnere's only companion; it was his livelihood. What would he do without its milk? "When? Yesterday in the storm?"

Dunnere stared at Kristinge for a moment before he answered. "I do not know how to count days. She got sick shortly after the equinox feast."

The equinox feast? Kristinge calculated in his head. That was over eight weeks earlier. Eight weeks. Could it be? Had he so lost track of the happenings in the village? Of the lives of his flock? Or was it no longer *his* flock? Was he no longer priest and shepherd? Dunnere rose to depart, but at the door he turned around one more time. He voice was soft. "I brought her to you, hoping you might pray for her as Willimond once prayed for me. But I could not find you in the chapel. And I was afraid to go into the hall. I am just a peasant."

Kristinge nodded, accepting the reprimand. It was all he could do to apologize. He would buy Dunnere another goat. He promised himself he would do that. But when he lifted his head to tell Dunnere, the peasant was gone. A feeling of helplessness welled up inside him, then. He tried not to think of Dunnere, or of how he had failed him. But the look of betrayal in the peasant's eyes had been too much. "If I was king, I could help," he told himself out loud, but his words were empty. The fireless chapel seemed much colder.

Kristinge did not return to the hall that night. He slept in his old hut. In the morning, he went directly to the chapel, where he spent the day in prayer. How many others had he failed, he wondered.

Aelfin found him there late in the morning. "You are troubled," he said. Kristinge did not reply, but glanced at the sword leaning against the wall. Aelfin followed the glance and saw the weapon. "It is only for a short time," he promised misjudging the real problem plaguing Kristinge. "If we defeat the Franks and drive them back from the Rhine, you will surely be king. You will never need fight again. For now, however, you would be wise to grow more used to the feel of the sword in your hand, and how it swings. Continue to strengthen your arms so they will not grow weary of the weight when battle is upon you. Your thanes will protect you in battle, of course. You need not fear. Yet the more you look the part of a warrior, the better. I have sent word that your war band is to gather at the very start of spring, the moment we can travel. The time for caution is now past. In your name, I have sent word throughout Friesland that you will lead a war band against the Franks."

"In *my* name?" Kristinge asked, his voice giving away his frustration.

"It is *you* who will be king," Aelfin replied, with a hard glint in his eyes.

Kristinge met the gaze, looked away, nodded, and fell silent. There was much he could do as king, he reminded himself. He thought of various sites where he would begin monasteries. The first monasteries in Friesland! Then he thought of Aewin. And the goat he would give to Dunnere.

"Perhaps you will be the Gideon of our people," Aelfin went on, referring to the tale Kristinge had sung on the same night he had received the torc. Then the chieftain laughed. "But do not try to make *our* war band any smaller. I am not sure your god will give us the victory, or that my people are willing to trust him to try. They are too used to trusting Woden."

A victory over the Franks in the name of Christ, Kristinge thought. *Yes, that would convince the Frisians that his God was real.*

"Come," Aelfin finally said. "Your servant Eomaer awaits you in the hall. His war band has been traveling for some days, riding through the snow over forty miles to come here. It was a long journey and they are tired. We have fed them and warmed them, but now he wishes to see you. He has news of Francia."

"Eomaer?" Kristinge asked, jumping to his feet. "Is Aewin—?"

"She did not come. It is a long ride in the winter. But fear not, the day of your betrothal approaches quickly."

Though he did so more slowly than he would have if Aewin had come also, Kristinge rose and followed Aelfin back to the mead hall to resume his duties. The news from Eomaer was good. He had been busy during the past few weeks, and had gained more followers for Kristinge. He had thirty-five new warriors from a neighboring clan that occupied the coastal villages north of Dronrip. Moreover, it was a warring clan that had many fast ships. They would be ready in the spring to carry Eomaer's horses by sea. "It might be possible," the young chieftain explained, "to come at Domburg from the south by horseback." Kristinge nodded. He still had little idea of battle strategies, but he did have a good idea of the lay of the land. He tried to envision Eomaer's plan. "There is more good news," Eomaer went on. Kristinge nodded for him to continue. "Clovis is dead."

Kristinge was slow to grasp the strategic significance of that announcement. An image of the insane ruler surrounded by his brothel came to his mind. Then he thought of queen Balthild. What this would mean to her? Aelfin, however, had already risen to his feet. "What? Clovis is dead? When? Who has succeeded him in Neustria and Burgundy? Who is king of the Franks?"

Eomaer turned from Kristinge toward Aelfin and answered the questions. "I do not know exactly when he died, or how. Word travels slowly this time of year. I myself heard from traders only a few days ago. They did not know how he died. Only rumors. Some say disease. Others say he was poisoned by a servant. Others say he was killed by his own queen."

"It was not his queen," Kristinge said softly, but nobody heard him.

Aelfin sat back down. "Who now rules?" he asked, repeating his earlier question.

"His son, whom they call Lothar—or Chlotar the third—has been proclaimed the King of all Franks. Yet he is just a child, not even ten years old I am told. One named Ebroin, a thane of Clovis, has been named Mayor of the Palace of Neustria. He will hold the real power there."

Ebroin? The name sounded familiar to Kristinge. It took him only a moment to place it. He had met Ebroin at the palace. However that was not why he remembered the name. Abbess Telchild had also mentioned him. Ebroin was the one who had violated Osanne. And now he ruled the Franks. That was more reason to fear them. More reason, perhaps, to go to war. Kristinge could think of three people who would not be happy to have Ebroin in power. *Osanne, Telchild, and Balthild.* Here were their names again. For weeks, Kristinge had avoided thinking of them. Now the memories were returning once more. He barely heard the rest of the conversation. Eomaer and Aelfin talked briefly about the death of Clovis. They both saw it as a good omen. It meant an opportunity to attack the borders of Francia while there was confusion and discord. Then conversation returned to the strategy for attack. Where would they bring the battle against the Franks? And how? Would they settle for regaining Domburg? Or should try to drive the Franks back all along the Rhine? Eomaer, though still young, had many ideas, and Kristinge could tell from the way that the older chieftains responded that they respected him. But Kristinge understood little of the art of war; even had he been able to pay attention, he could not have followed their strategies. After a time, his thoughts wandered from the queen, the abbess and the prophetess to the poor peasant Dunnere and his lost goat.

Later, when the fire had burned low and the guests slept, Kristinge quietly questioned Aelfin. "Why has Eomaer changed his heart so quickly?" he asked, avoiding the real questions on his mind. "I thought he had no interest in a war against the Franks, but only in avenging his father's death against Aldgisl and extracting the weregild."

Aelfin smiled. "Eomaer is young. If he lives, he may well be your mightiest thane. And that may be just what he is thinking. Remember that the names of Finn's thanes are still remembered in the same breath as Finn." That was all he said.

Over the following three days, there was a celebration in honor of Eomaer. It was another attempt by Aelfin to insure the future loyalty of this thane. And perhaps also it was intended to raise the spirits of Kristinge. This it did, though only for a short time. With Eomaer, Theoman, and Wihtred present, along with Isernfyst, Kristinge had his own hearthwerod together in Ezinge. For the first time he really felt like a king, and some of his unease vanished. That night, as mead and beer were brought from the winter stores, he gave gifts to his thanes. Meanwhile, at Aelfin's orders, the best hunters in Ezinge had been sent into the woods for fresh game. Perhaps motivated by a desire to miss as little as possible of the celebration, they returned early on the second day with rabbit and venison. Fish were also taken from the river. And, in keeping with the festive mood, the weather turned warm and along the axwei and beside the huts the snow melted away under blue skies. The spirits of the gathered war bands were high as the celebration continued, and Aelfin once again sounded hopeful. Talk turned to the building of a larger mead hall for Kristinge's growing number of thanes. Perhaps even a move to a larger village.

Even Kristinge was in a good mood, succumbing to the atmosphere that surrounded him. He had grown to like the impetuous young Eomaer, even as he had grown in a short time to love Eomaer's sister Aewin. In Aewin's absence, he and Eomaer spent much of the celebration talking together. In the young horse-chieftain, Kristinge could see the makings of the ideal Frisian warrior. Intent. Fearless. Ambitious. Strong and confident. Kristinge was almost frightened by how compelling he found him. The older chieftains, on the other hand, were far less compelling and more enigmatic. Wihtred and the Saxon Isernfyst spoke infrequently, and Kristinge guessed little if anything of what they were thinking. There was an impenetrable darkness about them. Theoman spoke more often and more directly than the other two, and reminded Kristinge of Aelfin, though with fewer different sides. Aelfin himself was difficult to predict or comprehend. At one moment, he was a character from Deor's lament: a quiet, lone warrior remembering better days when he was a chieftain at Domburg and the served a great king. This was the Aelfin whom Kristinge had first met upon the watchtower at Hwitstanwic. Yet in the presence of Dyflines the bard, the chieftain was once again a young warrior, glorying in battle, and looking forward to victories to come. Still at other times Aelfin was the wise and kind father figure—though Kristinge could never truly think of him as father, a role that he still gave in his heart to Willimond. Finally, when in the presence of other chieftains, Aelfin was a careful plotting warrior, planning the conquest of the torc of Friesland. That was the Aelfin that Kristinge knew best, and the one who scared him most. To that Aelfin, Kristinge was only a tool. *He leads us in name and figure only, riding at our heads,* Kristinge could still hear Aelfin saying to Theoman. *You, and I, and Wihtred will lead in truth.*

Unfortunately, the celebration could not last all winter. It ended after three days. Eomaer and Isernfyst with their war bands departed first. "I will bring Aewin soon to be with you," Eomaer promised as he rode from the village. Kristinge bade him fare well, and with cheerful countenance urged him to keep that promise. But as soon as Eomaer was gone, Kristinge felt empty and knew that it would not be soon enough that he returned with his sister. Worsening the gloom, on the following day Theoman and Wihtred also left for their own villages. Once more, Kristinge was left feeling lonely and isolated. Winter solstice was just a few days away, and the nights were once again long; bad memories of his long winter in Danemark returned. And now that Eomaer was gone, Kristinge's sudden friendship with him did not keep him from pondering the young horse-chieftain's motivations. Three reasons kept surfacing: revenge, glory in battle, and honor as a thane of the king. Among the Frisian warriors, those were virtues. But all three of those motives frightened Kristinge.

Nine gathered in the chapel for the Christ-Mass. Kristinge looked forward to the event with great eagerness. Unfortunately, Dunnere was not among those present. Kristinge was worried about him, but he said nothing. He would look for him later, he thought. He read the Gospel accounts of Jesus' birth, and preached a homily to those present. They broke bread together. Then the peasant believers departed and returned to their huts, and Kristinge went in search of Dunnere. He was not in his hut. Where else in the village could he be? Kristinge wandered from place to place, but his search proved to be futile. He descended off the terp and walked around the axwei, where a well-worn trail spared him from the crusty snow. The old peasant cow-herd was not to be found. After a second trip around the village, he gave up and returned to the mead hall fearing his peasant friend was dead.

Aelfin was sitting in the hall beside the fire. There was a slight frown on his face. There was *always* a frown on his face when Kristinge went to the chapel or led his small congregation in a mass. However the chieftain said nothing, and the duty of leading mass, if nothing else, Kristinge had not forsaken. "The days are too short," Aelfin grumbled. "And the nights are too long."

Kristinge, having failed to find Dunnere, was worried. It was four days past the winter solstice. He knew the days would begin to grow longer. But he was in no mood to try to cheer the chieftain. Never before did he remember such a dreary Christ-mass.

"Is your sacred holiday over?" Aelfin asked, in a mocking voice. "Have you finished enlightening the poor peasants?" He usually spared his foster-son from the worst of his disdain for the Christian religion. Today he did not, despite the presence in his hall of some of his thanes whom he hoped would one day serve Kristinge as king.

"It is the birth of the Christ," Kristinge replied.

"You have not spared me the story," Aelfin said. "Your Christ was born a peasant in a barn, was he not? Sleeping in the hay with the sheep dung?"

"He was."

"And did he ever wear the torc of his people?"

"Not on this earth." *Not on this earth*, Kristinge said again to himself. *Not on this earth*. Suddenly, he could hear Willimond's voice. *Do you really desire your father's torc? Have you learned nothing about the Frankish kings? Nothing from their treachery? Their short-lived reigns?*

Aelfin shrugged, as if that was all that needed to be said. He lifted his drinking horn and put it to his lips, but it was empty. He picked up his sword from beside him and banged it against his shield. One of his thanes rose and filled his horn from a nearby canister of mead. Nobody spoke for a time. "Where is that rogue Dyflines?" he growled. Kristinge did not remember having heard the chieftain in such a sour mood before. Was it the strong drink? Or was there something else amiss?

"Shall I fetch him?" Ceolac asked.

"No. Let him freeze," Aelfin replied, still growling. "The cold sends his lyre out of tune anyway." A moment later, however, he changed his mind. "Go get him. We could use some song in this dreary place. But warn him I will not be easily pleased this night." Ceolac disappeared. A short time later, he returned with the bard. It was rare that Aelfin told Dyflines what to sing, but tonight he made an exception. "Sing to me of the gods," he commanded.

The bard nodded. He worked with his lyre for a few moments, tuning the strings and allowing the wood to warm to the temperature of the room. Then he began to play. He sang an old tale of a battle between the god Thunar and the giants, and of Thunar's eventual victory by his great strength and cunning, despite being thrice outsmarted and made a fool of. By the time the long song was over, Aelfin's spirits had been lifted. In fact, to Kristinge it appeared that the population of the mead hall had doubled, though it may have been only that those thanes and warriors already present drew closer around the fire to listen to the talented bard. They had also grown louder and more boisterous. Whatever the case, it was a different mood after the song was over than before. Almost a different company. All except Kristinge whose mood had slunk further.

"Sing more," the warriors requested.

"Give me more to drink," Dyflines replied with a smile. His mead cup was filled, and after he had drained half of it he picked up his lyre again. He then sang another long tale, this one about the god Odin who once came to Friesland in human guise as a bard, and was given lodging by a warrior named Raeban. When Odin revealed his identity the following morning, he gave a gift to Raeban, claiming it to be a payment for the warrior's hospitality. The gift was a powerful sword which could never be broken by human hands and which gave its wielder the strength of ten men. With the aid of this sword, Raeban then went on to become a powerful chieftain over many tribes. Yet in doing so, he slew his own father and his three brothers and earned the hatred even of his only son whom he eventually also slew. In the end, Raeban was driven away from his own tribe and became a lone warrior—a *berserker* in the service of Odin—until he was finally killed by Odin himself.

It was a new story, one that Dyflines had only recently heard or composed and was singing in Ezinge for the first time. And it was exactly what Kristinge needed to hear. When Dyflines was finished, he stepped forward, and before the Irish bard could protest had taken the lyre from his hands. Though Kristinge had never before sung to the lyre in front of others, in private he and Dyflines had exchanged instruments more than once—though not in several weeks. He knew something of how to get a pleasing sound from it. And tonight, there was no turning back. The prophet's spirit had come upon him as it had at times past. He gave himself to it. Ignoring the fierce warning glance that Aelfin shot him the moment he picked up the lyre, Kristinge began to sing.

Lo! We have heard it told how once it happened, in a past generation of mankind, that the world's Creator, the Chieftain of mankind, the God-Son Himself, came to Middle-earth. It had been declared of old by wise men and bards that this should happen: that the Lord of the Heavens, a mighty Warrior, should come to earth to redeem the clan of mankind.

Never before had a warrior, a chieftain of chieftains, chosen his own place of birth. Yet the God of the earth, the Son of the Lord, the mighty Maker of all who ruled an army of ten thousand angels, took the form of a baby. He came among men in Middle-earth in this guise: not as a ruler but as a small child. Jesus they named him, Mary his holy mother and Joseph his father, both in the line of great kings of old. He lived among men as a peasant, one of lowly birth, a worker of wood. This mighty chieftain wore no chieftain's torc. He became instead a bard: a speaker of truth. Words of wisdom he taught. He did not deceive men, the children of men. He told men how to have life. The mighty chieftain became a giver of gifts to his thanes, his loyal followers, and the gift he gave was Life.

This Lord of Heaven had the power over all mankind. He was a chieftain whose mead-hall was all of Middle-earth. He had the right to take life and give life, but he slew no hearth-companions. He did not take the lives of men, but gave his own life. Lo! The Eternal One Himself, the God-Son who fashioned the world like a carpenter fashions wood, gave his own life on a cross-span of wood. Instead of wearing a torc like a man, he chose instead to hang upon a rood. He whose war band had a hundred thousand angels, whose thanes were the god-angels Gabriel and Michael, waged no war against man. His enemies, liars and servants of the chieftain of darkness, took his life. They buried him. Men and women mourned. His mother lost her son, the offspring of her womb. Ten hundred thousand angels would have come at his call, a mighty war band to take him from the rood and defeat his enemies. Yet the Chieftain of man chose instead to die for man. He desired no berserkers. He wielded no magic sword. His sword was the Word of Truth.

In the tomb they laid Him, the Prince of all people, in the darkness he was bound for the burial. He who made the earth was swallowed by the earth, but the earth could not hold him. Lo! He rose again, survived the perilous journey to the nether world and returned. He who made life took life again to his body. We have heard of His many marvelous works, His miracles before the race of man, but no greater work did He do than this. The great Warrior Chieftain won His battle. The Lord of Victories returned to His thanes and proclaimed His Name. Near and far over Middle-earth he declared his ordinances to men, uttering in words what they should do, and promising another Helper. Then He left this earth, the Chieftain who had walked among men, and went to take again His torc in the Heavens.

We have heard tell of these deeds from trustworthy men, have heard how the great God himself walked among men; his guise was truth and humility. We have heard tell also that the God of Hosts, the Chieftain of all Chieftains, will return as a great warrior with a flaming sword. He will call his thanes and raise his war band, and his enemies will be destroyed. Glorious will be his gifts to his warriors, his thanes and people in that day.

Dyflines gave Kristinge a silent nod of approval: a word of encouragement between two bards. But there was no applause after the song. Kristinge returned to his own hut that night. In the back of his mind lingered the knowledge that Aelfin was angered. He did not care. For the first time in many months, he felt calm. He knew well enough that his *situation* was not resolved. Yet he had come to a resolution, and with it—at least for the moment—had come peace. Fear of what he would face on the morrow was there, but was held in check. For now, he would not worry. Tomorrow would look after itself.

He had not slept in his hut for many nights. Not for weeks. It was cold and dirty. He had not had a fire in there since winter. There was no wood. It did not matter. Shrugging these thing aside, he put on his warmest cloak, piled his blankets on top of him, and slept peacefully for the first time in many weeks.

CHAPTER 20:
RÉADBAN

Réadban sat astride his horse, anxious and impatient, a host of memories racing through his mind as he leaned forward eager to continue his journey. Long ago he had heard the rumor that Finn had sired a second child, a son raised in secret and sent southward to be reared in a Frankish monastery far away. At the time Réadban had given the rumor little thought. A strange and unlikely tale it had seemed then, come at a season when he was busy with more pressing concerns. Yet it held the ring of truth, and in the intervening years it had returned to gnaw at him. After all, such things were not unheard of. Many a Frisian chieftain had fostered away a younger son to be raised by a distant relative, or a clan lord of another village. It would not have been beyond Finn, Réadban thought, to send his own son away to Francia to hide as a cowardly monk. And now, had the rumors proved true? *Another son of Finn?* In the past two months, more than one trader had brought that curious story to Réadban's hall: that Finn had still a living heir, and that the heir had returned to Friesland and was raising a war band. A son named Kristinge, taken as a foster of the chieftain Aelfin. This was news that tugged at Réadban like the pulling of a scab off an old wound. Thirty years had passed since the day of Finn's wedding, the famous marriage celebration of Finn and Hildeburh, the day that was to bring hope to all of Friesland. Réadban scoffed at the thought. Finn was a fading memory, he told himself. A failed and soon-to-be-forgotten chieftain.

Yet for all his disdain for his former king, and for all the years come and gone, Réadban still remembered Finn's wedding day as if it were yesterday. He could recall the scene at the tower; he relived it in his waking dreams. With strong oaths, he had challenged the stronger and more skilled Finn to a fight. But the battle never happened. *Mercy?* Finn had *spoken* of mercy. He had not made Réadban fight the duel to which he had sworn, but had instead released him from his oath. Perhaps in doing so, Finn had even spared Réadban's life; Finn was a great warrior and there were few who could have stood alone against him in his prime. Yet that was not *mercy*. In front all his own thanes, before all who had heard him issue his challenge, Réadban had been forced to bow before Finn and acknowledge his own wrong. His *wrong*! It would have been *better* to have died. Yes he had suffered this humiliation before Finn, and he had not forgotten it. He had vowed to carry his hatred for Finn and all his offspring to his dying day. Long had he plotted his revenge, and long had it been in coming. But come it had, at last. Fate had been good to Réadban, that day; the gods had blessed him. Finn did most of the work himself, bringing about his own demise. Finn and the Danes. It was a convenient war. A misunderstanding that Réadban could not have conceived of better: the death of Finnlaf and Hnaef at each other's hands and the ensuing feud between the tribes. All Réadban had done was take advantage of the opportunity given him. When the time had come, he had influenced the right chieftains and made sure that Finn was unable to raise the war band he needed to stand against the Danes. Oh. It was good that Réadban had *not* died, for then he could never have tasted that sweet morsel of revenge.

And yet even that was not enough, Réadban now realized. He had not been able to *watch* Finn die; he had not *seen* Finn's humiliation. Réadban's part in bringing about Finn's death had been *too* small. No. The revenge was not complete. *And now? Could it be true? Could a son of Finn really have returned? Did he now have an opportunity to finish the revenge long desired?*

Réadban turned his horse and looked back across the valley, as if worried that some unforeseen catastrophe might still upset his plans and rob him of his rightful vengeance. But his war band was still there, four hundred and fifty strong! The warriors were spread across the open field taking their midday meal during a brief rest from the march. He smiled, still confident in his plan. The sudden attack on Ezinge would never be expected, not now at the onset of winter. Aelfin and Kristinge would not be prepared. Though Réadban had heard no trustworthy report as to the size of Kristinge's war band, other than the names of a few chieftains who had thrown their sword in with him, he knew that Ezinge was a small village; its puny war band would not stand a chance against a host as large as the one he now led. This would be another easy conquest, made that much sweeter by the thought of destroying Finn's son and the last of his loyal thanes. Nobody would remember the name of Finn.

And that was but the first step. The broader implications of the victory did not escape Réadban, for the schemes playing through his mind went well beyond his own revenge. He was leading only a part of the forces he now commanded from Dorestad. His war band had grown greatly in the past year. Ten more noble Saxon thanes had recently taken him as their lord and gift-giver, and with them came a hundred Saxon warriors: mercenaries perhaps, but hale warriors nonetheless, and fighters who had been proven in battle. With these following him, Réadban was now the strongest chieftain in all of Friesland. Stronger even than Aldgisl. Réadban cast a sidelong sneer of contempt at the other chieftain beside him. Aldgisl, a younger kinsman of Réadban's wife, was leading only thirty mounted warriors as part of the host moving toward Ezinge. Young in his power, Aldgisl was cautious but ambitious. It was at Réadban's own advice that the younger chieftain was biding his time. He smiled at the influence he wielded over his rival. "Keep your eye on Friesland, but let your power grow," he had told him. And Aldgisl, in his trusting foolishness, had listened, and brought only a token part of his war band to Ezinge. "My war band is easily a match for the task," Réadban had promised. "The more warriors we bring, the more we will have to feed."

Deferring to the wisdom—so he thought—of an elder kinsman, Aldgisl had reluctantly consented to the small number. "Agreed," he replied. "But I shall come with you, for I am curious to meet this new threat: this son of the legendary Finn."

Réadban smiled as he thought back on the conversation. Little did Aldgisl know that his greatest threat was not a son of Finn but the chieftain at whose side he rode. That he was riding to his own doom as much as to the doom of Finn's heir. For Aldgisl still looked upon Réadban as a loyal thane: a kinsman, no less. After all, Réadban had lost his own two sons. Radbod the Young, who might have made a good king, had died many years earlier. While Réadban's other son, Ultar, was too weak and foolish to ever hope to rule. Even Réadban had conceded that Ultar's death in battle the year before was no great loss. Yet their deaths had only temporarily dissuaded Réadban from seeking the torc. In his advancing age, he had pledged himself to support Aldgisl's claim to the torc. But he had secretly recanted of that pledge many months earlier. As his own power had grown, so had visions of the Frisian torc. He was not so old that his neck could not bear the weight of a larger torc than that of Dorestad. And Ultar's child Rathbod still lived. At the age of four, Rathbod was already a small boar. He could be made into a warrior one day, a king even. No. Réadban would not sit idly and watch Friesland's torc sit on another's neck. And now, the opportunity to do something had finally presented itself: the chance to eliminate two rivals with one swift stroke. By the time Aldgisl knew better, it would be too late.

If only Réadban were still fifteen years younger, he lamented. But then he turned his eyes back northward and turned his thoughts to the task at hand. Enough of his plotting against Aldgisl. He would first see the son of Finn humiliated and killed. And *then* he would worry about the other. It was Aldgisl who gave the signal to move on. And for the time, Réadban allowed him the vanity of thinking he led the war band. Winter's first assault of cold and snow had come early, but little snow had fallen in the past two weeks, and the unusually warm December weather had melted or evaporated most of November's snow. They were keeping a much better pace than Réadban had expected. They would have no trouble with their supply of food. In four days, before the first of the coming year, they would be in Ezinge. Then the last of Finn's sons would drink the bitter dregs prepared by his father, and Réadban would at last have his due.

At the southern edge of Wieuwerd, four men—three on horseback and one on foot—gazed silently out from the top of the terp across the flat frozen ground toward the southwest. Treothrym, a tall hardy warrior with angular cheeks, long brown hair, and a heavy beard, sat astride a bay mare. Beside him on matching chestnuts were his two younger brothers, Tredswar and Hyse, the latter an unbearded youth. The three brothers were similar in face and feature, though the younger two were not as large as Treothrym. Beside them stood Wigmaer, the chieftain of Wieuwerd. On foot, his head was just above the level of their knees. He was fairer of skin and lighter of hair than the other three, and just a few years older than Treothrym. All four had sheathed swords across their backs. Far away to the southwest, Hyse had just caught sight of something moving, but against the glare of the setting sun it was hard to make out what it was. "*Something* is coming, certainly," he said, breaking the silence.

"Is it a rider?" Treothrym asked. His eyes were not as good as his brother's.

"More like a war band," Hyse answered. "It is spread out over some distance."

Wigmaer was troubled at that report. "Then it is good I have three more worthy warriors beside me tonight."

"Do you think they are raiders?" Tredswar asked.

"I do not know," the chieftain replied. "Who else at this time of year would be crossing the frozen ground with a war band?"

"Franks!" Hyse said, alarmed.

Treothrym shook his head. "We are too far north. If they had crossed this far into Friesland we would have heard word before this."

"Then who?" Hyse asked, still scanning the horizon. "Surely not Danes—not at this time of year and not on foot."

Nobody answered. The four of them waited in silence as the dark spot grew closer and larger. Soon, they could all see it with little trouble. "It is a war band, without doubt," Wigmaer said.

"And a large one by the look," Treothrym added. "Our courage may be hard pressed on this evening." All of a sudden, Treothrym and Wigmaer looked at one another as an intuitive realization dawned on them simultaneously. "Aldgisl!" Treothrym breathed.

"Or Réadban," Wigmaer answered. "One and the same."

"Tiwes' curse. So they have heard." He turned back to toward Hyse. "Brother. Can you see any markings?"

"They are still a long distance off," Hyse replied. He paused. "But yes, I can make out something. The lead rider is carrying a lance with a banner. It may just be the reflection of the sunset, but it appears red. It is much too far away to see the crest."

"How many are they?"

Hyse scanned the approaching war band again. "It is difficult to count, but by my guess there are three hundred or more. They move slowly. Most are on foot. There are a few on horseback near the front."

"On foot," the chieftain mumbled, half to himself. "Yes a band that large would have to be. That is our only hope." He turned at once toward the three brothers on horseback, and in an urgent tone gave the command. "Leave at once. Bring word to my cousin Eomaer of what you have seen. Tell him all you know."

"Should we not wait and see?" Tredswar asked. "Count their numbers and determine who it is so we might know more to report?"

But the oldest brother was already spinning his horse as he answered for Wigmaer. "If it is Aldgisl or Réadban, we must get word to Eomaer at once. We cannot afford to be waylaid." Yet despite his words, he delayed a second longer, looking once more at the chieftain. "If he attacks you, our swords might be of service here. Shall we not stay and fight at your side instead? I can send Hyse with a message for Eomaer."

"We will fend for ourselves. If it is Aldgisl, I think he may not attack me. He will be interested in Ezinge only, and the rival who is seated in the mead hall there. That is why Eomaer must know of this. He will want to go to Ezinge himself. Tell him we will follow if we can and come up behind this army. Tell him also: if it comes to battle, we are with Finn's son."

Treothrym nodded. He lifted his spear in salute. A moment later, he and his two brothers were galloping through the village toward the northern edge of the terp, on their way back to Dronrip, praying to the gods as they went that the moon would be bright that night. They had many leagues to travel, and though they were uncommonly good horsemen for Frisians, they knew they would be hard pressed.

Sword strapped across his back, the chieftain stood by the door of the mead hall looking glumly out at the village of Ezinge as his foster son approached. Kristinge saw him standing there and swallowed hard. He had spent much of the morning in his hut wondering what he would say. When he had grown too cold there, he had wandered over to the chapel and spent time praying over the same question. Finally, late in the afternoon, he had stirred up his courage and risen to his feet. He approached the mead hall slowly, but directly. Aelfin nodded a silent greeting when Kristinge arrived, then motioned for him to step into the hall. Kristinge, also remaining silent, complied. He stepped inside. Once within, he took a quick instinctive glance around him. He was surprised to find the hall empty. Not even Ceolac or Maccus were there. Had Aelfin sent his thanes away? Why? Did he not want them to hear?

"Come join me," the chieftain said aloud, once they were both inside. Without waiting for an answer, he stepped past Kristinge and started toward the hearth. Kristinge followed. They walked to their usual benches beside the fire, which burned brightly as if recently tended. "Sit," the chieftain commanded. Again Kristinge obeyed. "Are you hungry?" Aelfin asked.

The question took Kristinge off guard. He was prepared for a confrontation. He had expected Aelfin to waste no time in raising the issue of the previous night's song, and of Kristinge taking again the role of bard against the chieftain's wishes. In short, he expected to be chastised. He was glad for the reprieve. "Yes," he mumbled in answer. He had not eaten all day.

Aelfin produced a loaf of bread and handed it to him. Kristinge ripped off a small piece and with it broke his fast. He set the rest of the bread down on his lap and closed his eyes. The longer he waited, the harder it would be. He slowly he reached into the large purse at his side and removed his father's torc. "I cannot wear this," he said softly. He cringed. It wasn't what he intended to say. At least not with those words. The truth was, he wasn't sure *what* he wanted—what he could or could *not* do. But he needed to say something. He could not let Aelfin control the rest of his life. He needed some control. Even if it meant losing...

No. He would not think of Aewin. He knew well enough what it would mean to forfeit the torc. And he loved her. But he could not possess her. He would not want to. And she? She would not be given to him if he did not wear the torc. Yet he could not wed her at that price.

Aelfin did not answer at first. Nervous at the silence, Kristinge sat and fiddled with the torc for a moment, oddly sad at the thought of parting with it. The torc was all he had from his real father. But he held it out to Aelfin and repeated his statement. "This is not for me. I cannot wear the torc. I am no chieftain."

"You are no chieftain? Or you are no warrior?" Aelfin finally queried, challenging Kristinge's comments. He made no motion to take the torc.

"You have told me yourself many times that they are one and the same," Kristinge answered, still holding out the gold band for the chieftain to take.

"Not—" Aelfin started to answer, but then he fell silent. He tried a different tact. "It is your Christian religion. It has made you afraid." He spoke with more than a hint of contempt in his voice.

"Afraid?" Kristinge was surprised by this accusation. "Of what?"

"You tell me."

It was a cunningly simple response, but it achieved its purpose. Kristinge's jaw dropped as he tried to think. *Afraid of what?* He was now on the defensive. Was he truly afraid? Was it only fear that drove him away? Perhaps. For a moment he could not answer. He pulled his hand back, setting the torc upon his leg. What was he afraid of?

"You have seen yourself that you cannot hide," Aelfin went on. "Wherever you go, you will always be Finn's son."

Kristinge nodded. Aelfin was right about this. His identity had found him at Ezinge. It had found him in Danemark. Even in Luxeuil it had found him. He turned the torc around in his hand, looking at the soft polished gold. He had already grown so used to it that his neck felt naked with it off. He almost put it back on. Then he thought again of Aelfin's statement. *It has made you afraid.* Yes. He was afraid, but not of battle. He was not even afraid of death. He was afraid of throwing away everything he knew to be important in order to grasp what was only fleeting: the torc. His own forbidden fruit. Good to look upon, it would make him a chieftain among men with war bands to rule; it would make him like a god. *It would win for him the hand of Aewin.* "I will not be your warrior," he said. His denial was stronger and his voice harsher than he intended.

Aelfin tensed as if accused. "Not *my* warrior?" he replied. "I do not ask for myself. I ask in the name of all Friesland. You will be our Chieftain." His eyes flashed with a challenge. "You will be our David, our battle-leader. You will be a Gideon like the tales you have told us from old. Surely your god has honored these men."

A month earlier, perhaps, this argument might have swayed Kristinge. Indeed, he had used the argument on himself. He had thought all too often of David and Gideon; of Samson and Joshua, and a dozen other warriors and chieftains who had been chosen by God to lead Israel in battle. These men of God had done no wrong in being warriors, had they? Yet that was not the point. For Kristinge knew also that the argument did not hold in his case. Perhaps Friesland *did* need a great leader to defend them against the Franks: a single king who would unite the land and lead the Frisian people in battle. Kristinge did not doubt that. But what he now realized was that there were a hundred men more capable than he of accomplishing that task. Aelfin, Eomaer, Theoman, Wihtred, Isernfyst. Even Ceolac or Maccus. Any warrior in the mead-hall was more capable than Kristinge. *Unless.* Unless the hand of God was upon Kristinge to lead the people in war. But there was no indication that it was. And many indications that it was not. Moreover, the Frisians could not even be *called* God's people. No more than the Danes or the Franks. That was the thought that kept returning to Kristinge. These were his people. But they had no special claim on God.

"I am not a warrior," Kristinge finally replied, with a heavy sigh. "I am a monk. Perhaps a priest, though at that of late I have failed. I am called to be a shepherd. To lead men to life, and not to death. I will neither be a *berserker* nor shall I make them. I will not wield a sword. I am not Gideon."

As he spoke, Kristinge could see Aelfin growing more tense. "Then tell me why not?" the chieftain shouted, angrily slamming his fist on the bench beside him.

Kristinge did not expect Aelfin to understand, but he explained anyway. "A peasant named Dunnere lost his only goat." As Aelfin stared at him, wide-eyed and uncomprehending, Kristinge went on.

"Dunnere, who faithfully came to the chapel and prayed for seven years, even when he was all alone. Dunnere who has been a more faithful and humble servant of God than I have been in the past few months. His goat died. His livelihood. His family. It died. It died, and I did not even notice for *ten weeks*." It was clear from the look on Aelfin's face that he had no idea what Kristinge was talking about. To him, a peasant was a peasant and a goat a goat. "There are more important things than leading a war band in battle," Kristinge finally said, unable to think of any other way to explain. "There is more to being a servant of God. More to being a shepherd."

"And there is more to your decision than you could imagine," Aelfin replied, rising to his feet. Kristinge looked up at him. The chieftain's face was calm again. There was even a hint of a smile on his face. That worried Kristinge more than the anger. "Perhaps you don't realize this," he said, starting to pace around the fire. He whirled toward the young priest. "It is too late!"

"Too late?" Kristinge echoed reflexively. He had heard that before.

"Too late. Messages have been sent all over Friesland. You *cannot* withdraw. As surely as the spring follows the winter, you have declared a war on Aldgisl and Réadban. Do you think, once they hear of your presence in Friesland, that they will allow you to live? Perhaps— perhaps, I say, though not likely—they *might* have let you live *if* you had returned as a monk only. But you have taken your father's torc. You have begun to raise a war band. When word reaches their ears, you will have but two choices: to raise a war band to lead against the Franks and then to stand against Aldgisl himself—to raise a greater war band than he has—or to stand and face your own death at his hands. There is no other option. It is too late."

Kristinge did not respond. He knew the truth of Aelfin's words. Even Kristinge, who still knew so little about the world of Frisian chieftains and warriors, knew that this chieftain's assessment could not be far wrong. It really was too late for him to turn back. In his many weeks of silent acquiescence, his weeks of blindly submitting to Aelfin's plan, he had been digging himself deeper and deeper beneath the hard soil of Friesland. He was right where the chieftain wanted him, in a situation where he could not refuse. That was why Aelfin was smiling. Kristinge slumped forward on his bench. The torc was still in his hand. He put his other hand on his head. *Did his own plans really mean nothing in the end?* Though his eyes were shut, he could sense the chieftain walking back to the bench. He heard him filling a horn with wine. Then a second. *Of course it was too late. He had known that. Why had he thought otherwise?*

"Drink," Aelfin said, making the kindest offer he knew how. Kristinge looked up. He took the drinking horn from his foster father's hand and took a sip. It was a strong batch of mead that curled his tongue in his mouth. He sipped more. "Do not speak again of your doubts," Aelfin said softly, after Kristinge had drained the cup. They were again seated side by side. "Today I was able to empty the hall that we might speak alone. I might not be able to do so again. Even if you doubt, you must at least *appear* confident. Your thanes will not follow you if they sense that you are not leading. Even the most loyal will leave you if you waver for too long. That is why your father failed in the end. Why more did not rally to his call when the Danes brought the day of his doom. Because he doubted."

Kristinge nodded. "You are right. I must not waver." But his response that followed made Aelfin's jaw drop. "Though the cost be high, I must do what I have been called to do. I must follow my God where he leads, even though that be through the valley of the shadow of death. I cannot wear the torc of Friesland."

The two of them stared at one another a long moment, as if gauging the determination of the other. Then Aelfin rose to his feet, an incredulous look upon his face. "Are you a fool? Have you not listened?"

"I have listened well," Kristinge answered in a soft voice. "All that you say may be—it *is* certainly true. I knew that well before I came."

"Then you will throw away your life?"

"He who follows the Lord Most High does not throw away his life," Kristinge replied.

"May the gods take you!" Aelfin cursed. "Do you think it is your life alone? Many brave and loyal warriors have given their allegiance to you. If you recant now, Aldgisl will kill them all. They knew that, but they placed their trust in you. Their only hope—your only hope and my only hope—is that you have a war band large enough that Aldgisl will not attack you."

Kristinge felt the full weight of the burden Aelfin was putting on him. He knew there was a danger to others as well. For a moment, he fought the urge to blame the whole situation on Aelfin, whose plan he had followed from the beginning. But he knew that he had willingly taken part. "I will take the responsibility upon myself alone. If there is a death to be paid, I will pay it."

Aelfin's face grew as red as the fire. Kristinge could see hot rage rising within him. For the moment, he feared for his life as much from Aelfin as he did from Aldgisl. "You do not understand Aldgisl and Réadban—you do not understand any *chieftain*," Aelfin began to fume. "Can you have been raised in Friesland and know so little of our ways?" He was shaking a fist at Kristinge. Kristinge began to feel defensive, wanting to give way to the urge to blame the chieftain. His caution left him, and he rose to his own feet to face Aelfin. Their faces were inches apart.

Yet before either could say another word, there was a loud shout from the entrance of the hall. They both turned toward the door in time to see two men burst in. It was Ceolac and Maccus, Aelfin's chief thanes. As they approached, the two combatants stepped back from one another and sat down.

"My lord," Maccus said, nearly out of breath.

"Speak," Aelfin said through his clenched teeth.

"It is a war band," Maccus panted. "A large one. Coming this way."

"How far away?" Aelfin asked, jumping to his feet. He reached to see that his sword was still there.

"I do not know," Maccus answered, still trying to catch his breath. "Large enough... large enough to attack. And all of your war band is still gone. We are the only warriors in the village."

"Are the gods against my every move?" Aelfin asked. "How long 'til they arrive?"

"Moments. They were coming hard across the ground from the west. They approach like raiders, making straight for the terp. We did not stay to count them, but came here right away."

"And our war band?"

"We do not know," Ceolac spoke this time. "They have gone hunting the boar, as you commanded."

"Get them back," Aelfin ordered.

"It is too late. They will not be back on time. And if we leave now to find them, you will be alone."

"Yet what can four do against so many?" Aelfin asked. Never had Kristinge seen him appear so frantic.

"More than two can," Maccus answered, his eyes narrowing as he gripped his sword.

"We will not leave your side," Ceolac confirmed.

Aelfin looked like he was about to object, but he caught himself. His warrior's instinct began to take over. His chieftain's calm returned. "So be it. Then let us go to meet our guests." He grabbed his heavy cloak, unslung the sword from his back, and started toward the door. Maccus and Ceolac followed, with Kristinge at the end. "And why are you still here, if the rest of the war band has followed my orders and gone after the boar?" Aelfin asked as they walked.

Ceolac shrugged. "We sensed we would be needed."

"If this is an enemy," Aelfin said, "then for your loyal disobedience you may have earned the right to die at my side." With that, they were out of the hall and striding across the village to the west side of the terp.

By the time Kristinge reached the edge of the terp, the approaching war band had already arrived. They did not bother riding toward the gradual cattle ramp on the southern end of the village, but had dismounted and were leading their mounts right up the steep west side of the terp. Kristinge, unaware that an enemy would not attack a village this way, was surprised to see that Aelfin was sheathing his sword. However when he turned back to look again and saw the foremost warrior just reaching the top of the terp, he realized why. It was Eomaer. Kristinge had not at first recognized the young horse-chieftain for he was dressed against the cold in a heavy cloak that nearly covered his face. Yet he was still armed for battle. On seeing who it was, Kristinge looked behind for a sign of Aewin, but instinctively he knew she would not be there. He could see from the expression on Eomaer's face that his visit was not one of pleasure.

Eomaer did not delay, or bother with the customary greetings. While his warriors began to look after their horses, he approached Aelfin along with six thanes. Treothrym was among them. Their faces were red from cold and wind, and they had the look of men who had ridden hard for many hours.

"We knew not that it was you who approached," Aelfin then said. "For a moment, we feared enemies."

"Do not sheath your blade," Eomaer replied. "They enemy you seek is not far behind."

At this, Aelfin's eyes narrowed. "Come," he said. Without further word, they walked back toward the hall where the fire still burned.

Once inside, Eomaer greeted Aelfin and Kristinge in a way more customary among chieftains, and as his thanes dispersed around the fire and began to warm their hands, he spoke his mind. "Alas. The news I bring is not good," he began, and the tone of concern in his voice was unmistakable. Kristinge did not know whether to be relieved that his confrontation with Aelfin had been interrupted, or worried about the news that Eomaer was bringing.

"We listen," Aelfin replied steadily.

"We have ridden hard from our village to get here. Strong horses have tired themselves to the point of death that we might come quickly."

"Speak your message," Aelfin said again.

Kristinge took a step backward, trying to distance himself from the conversation, but he was listening keenly. Eomaer gave him one sidelong glance and then went on. "It is a war band. A large war band. My thane has counted more than three hundred."

Aelfin's eyes widened at the news. "Three hundred? Where?"

"West of here, and inland. Near Wieuwerd. They come in this direction."

"Franks?" Aelfin asked.

"I do not know for sure who they are," Eomaer replied, "but I believe they are Frisians."

"How far away?"

"As I told you, we rode here as hard as we could, fearing the worst. The war band was south of Wieuwerd three nights past. With so many warriors at this time of year, travel will be slow. Yet if they are coming this way, then I guess they will arrive tomorrow by midday."

Aelfin nodded. He did not look at Kristinge, but his next word was what was on everybody's mind. "Aldgisl."

And so, Kristinge thought. *It was, indeed, too late.*

"That was my thought also," Eomaer said. "Did we not already suspect such?"

"Yes. Yes, but little did I think he would move against us so soon. Are you sure it is he?"

"I have not seen this band, but little do I doubt it is Aldgisl. And I know of no other reason for his coming here in the middle of winter with a war band of such size save to dispense with a rival."

"Odin take them all," Aelfin cursed again. "Thunar strike them."

"I fear it is we who will have to do the striking," Eomaer replied. For the first time, he looked around the hall. When he discovered it was empty, he turned back to Aelfin in surprise.

"Your war band? Your hearthwerod? Where is it?" First the first time, there was a hint of fear in his voice.

"They are not far away," Aelfin replied. "They hunt a boar that appeared in the woods yesterday. But I fear even with all my war band and yours that we will not be enough. Are you sure Aldgisl has three hundred with him?"

"I am sure of very little," Eomaer replied. "We know not for sure even if it is Aldgisl himself."

"Tell me what you *do* know," Aelfin said, unable to hide his frustration and impatience.

Eomaer nodded. "I had sent three of my thanes—Treothrym and his brothers; trustworthy warriors all of them," he said with a glance in Treothrym's direction. "I had sent them with a message to my cousin Wigmaer, the chieftain of Wieuwerd. On their second evening there, they were standing on the edge of the terp by chance looking southwestward when they saw the war band approaching. They did not wait to see who it was for fear that they would be detained, but took their leave of Wigmaer at once to bring word to me. Neither did I delay. Already their trip to Dronrip cost us time. The route from Wieuwerd here is more direct."

Despite all that had happened—not only his decision to abandon the torc but the danger now pressing hard upon him—Kristinge felt himself again swept up in the excitement. He *almost* wished he was still wearing the torc. He watched Aelfin closely. The chieftain made no response at first. Kristinge could see him calculating in his mind.

"How many are with you?" he asked after a minute's pause. "Twenty?"

"Thirty on horse. For reasons of haste I could not afford to bring any on foot, nor was I willing to leave my village altogether undefended, little though we could have done against so many if they chose to travel north instead of east. For the same reasons, Wigmaer could not yet send any to our aid. However he sent word to reassure us of his loyalty. If he is able, he will send a war band to follow Aldgisl's. Then if it comes to battle, he may fall on them from behind. But we can not count on that." He paused, then added, "I fear for my cousin. If Aldgisl has reason to believe he has pledged his loyalty to a son of Finn, he will bear the first brunt of their assault."

"Perhaps," Aelfin said. "But I fear more for us. If Aldgisl is coming here, there is little reason for him to waste time attacking Wieuwerd. If he eliminates us—if he can kill his rival," he added, with emphasis and a nod that Kristinge was sure was directed toward him, "then he need not worry about the others. Any battle he wages against Frisians will weaken his *own* war band if he one day becomes king."

"May Thunar strike me down if I let Aldgisl become king."

For the first time since he had made his decision, Kristinge realized another implication of his rejecting the torc. He was Eomaer's one hope to redeem his weregild: to seek his revenge upon Aldgisl. At that thought, Kristinge felt at once saddened that he was abandoning his friend, and also again convinced that his decision to refuse the torc was right. He would not be an instrument of revenge.

"I do not say Aldgisl will be king," Aelfin was saying. "Only that a future king would want to avoid attacking his own chieftains unless necessary."

"But will Aldgisl think in this way?" Eomaer asked. "A victory against us may weaken Friesland as a whole, but it would strengthen his own claim for the torc."

"Aldgisl, I think, will not risk unnecessary battle. Yet I know Réadban less well. He cannot be trusted. He is both more crafty than Aldgisl, and also less predictable. They were more savvy than I gave them credit for. I thought to have all winter to raise a war band. They have not given us the chance."

Eomaer nodded. He spoke with the voice of doom. "You have less than a day."

"We will do what we can. Do you have horses to spare? Have you sent word to Theoman, Wihtred, or Isernfyst?"

"Isernfyst, no. It is a waste of a messenger to send word that far north. And my horses have reached exhaustion. If we try to run them more in this cold, they will die. Even now, I fear for them. They need food. But I have sent word to Theoman and Wihtred, as well as to my cousin Aescholt. Still I fear it will do little good. By the time word reaches Theoman in Beowic, he will have no time to send his forces by foot. Wihtred has less far to travel. He may be able to reach us with help by late tomorrow."

Aelfin nodded. "You have done well. We will see that your horses are well taken care of—if I can get the Saxons in this village to touch them."

"I had not finished," Eomaer went on. Despite his young age, he spoke to other chieftains as equals. "Aescholt may be of some help yet. He should have received my message yesterday. If he can get his ships as far as Hwitstanwic, he may be able to bring help up the Hunze. It will be a rough voyage in the winter seas even inside the isles, but he is one to try."

"Then we stand at sixty men," Aelfin said. "We can count on no more."

"Will it suffice?"

"If it comes to battle, we will be hard pressed. But defending the terp, we might do it. If we can hold out long enough, they may have difficulty with their supplies. And perhaps more help will come before all is over."

"Come then, let us plan."

They turned to Kristinge, who until that point they had left out of the conversation. Kristinge was aware of their eyes upon him, but he did not take his own gaze off of the fire. It had burned down over the course of the two conversations. Just few flames now flickered up from the coals. "Think well what you do," Aelfin said softly. Only he and Kristinge knew of what they spoke. "And if your god can hear us, now is the time to call on him."

Now, indeed, was the time to call upon God. *What* to ask Him, however, was another question altogether.

CHAPTER 21:
REVENGE

As night was falling, Aelfin's war band returned from the hunt, successful. They brought with them not only the large boar that was the object of their pursuit, but two deer and several ducks. Knowing nothing of the news that awaited them, they were loud with enthusiasm as they strode through the village proudly displaying their spoils. It was only a few minutes, however, before word had spread among them of the war band approaching Ezinge. Then the sound of celebration died away. And though the mead hall was crowded that night with the combined war bands of Aelfin and Eomaer, it was not the jubilant company of hearth companions to which Kristinge was accustomed, nor even the over-rowdy throng of warriors feisty with too much celebratory mead. Instead it was a sober gathering facing the prospect of an imminent battle against great odds, with Kristinge not the least heavy-hearted among them. Fortunately, knowing that the warriors would need their strength on the morrow, Aelfin made sure all were well fed. Opening Ezinge's winter stores, he brought out an abundance of food to share among his men. Plenty of good beer, roasted grains, and dried fish augmented the fresh boar, venison, and duck. Nobody went hungry. And when the meal had been consumed, Dyflines filled the men with song nearly as hearty as their food. In this way, despite the fears that pervaded the hall, spirits were kept from sinking too low.

Aelfin and Eomaer joined their men in listening to the first few of the bard's songs. As the singing continued, however, the two chieftains with their most trusted thanes removed themselves to a quieter corner of the hall to speak of Ezinge's defense. Kristinge, who could not shake his sense of obligation to the warriors gathered there—his own responsibility for the situation they found themselves in—sat nearby the chieftains and listened silently but intently to their discussion. The news that Eomaer brought dealt a blow to his plans, and he was again unsure of what to do. For all his assurance when he had spoken with Aelfin, he still had not completely forsaken his desires: the allure of the Frisian warrior's life that had led him to go along with Aelfin's plans in the first place.

"You know battle better than I," Eomaer began at once, before his older and more experienced comrade had a chance to speak. "Stay on the terp and lead your war band in the defense of the village. The slopes are steep and a few men can defend much space. Let me ride from the mound with my mounted band. With our speed and mobility on the flat fields, we will keep an army even as large as Aldgisl's off-guard." He grew more excited as he spoke. Despite the obvious danger to himself, there was a sense of eagerness in this young chieftain: the eagerness that both frightened and intrigued Kristinge. "A skilled mounted warrior is a formidable foe," he concluded with a confident tone that belied the desperation of their situation.

"Is Aldgisl's army on foot?" Aelfin asked.

Eomaer didn't answer at first, but when Aelfin pressed him with the question a second time he admitted the answer was no. "Not entirely," he explained. "It was reported that there are a small number of horse soldiers among them. How many, we do not know. I have told you before that we saw only from a distance. But," he added, looking around proudly at his warriors who were seated in the hall, "none in Friesland are as skilled as these on the back of a horse. One of my men can outfight any two other Frisian on horseback. And any *five* on foot. Let us roam beyond the axwei and we will see that Aldgisl has little strength to attack Ezinge. Don't let thirty horses be wasted."

It was a bold boast, but Kristinge did not doubt it. He looked at Aelfin for his response. "No," Aelfin answered firmly. "I do not doubt your skills, but the plan is too dangerous. You would be outnumbered not five to one but ten to one."

"Every course of action we take is dangerous," Eomaer replied. "If we live through tomorrow, it will only be with the blessings of the gods. And by the gods, even Thunar would not want to face my men on horseback."

Kristinge found himself smiling at young Eomaer's confidence, and praying that God would spare his life. Even Aelfin was smiling. "Perhaps you would live through the battle," he acquiesced. "But who would stay within the village? Thirty men will not be enough to defend the entire terp. And we cannot afford for our war bands to be separated. If Aldgisl has brought three hundred warriors, he can easily surround us. We would be separated, and once Ezinge fell then Dronrip would soon follow."

Eomaer still did not concede, but pressed his argument for a few minutes longer. However when both Maccus and Ceolac entered the debate taking Aelfin's position, Eomaer finally relented. It was agreed that they would all remain on the terp and take a defensive posture. "A waste of horses," the young chieftain grumbled uncharacteristically.

"Not so," Aelfin replied at once. "Your horses will be needed *within* the village to reposition warriors to the weakest areas: wherever fighting grows fiercest. It is *their* horses that will be wasted since they are of no use attacking up the side of a terp. This is where our one real advantage lies: that they will have to attack up the terp. Defending the top of such a steep slope gives a warrior as much advantage as being on horseback. For that reason alone, sixty might hope to hold out against three hundred. If only we had a walled burg, then we might hold out against thrice three hundred!"

At the promise that his horses might still be of use, even if only within the village, Eomaer appeared more content with his role in the battle. Planning continued. Aelfin reviewed that the terp was steeply sloped around most of its three sides. The most vulnerable position—the crucial location to focus their defense—was the ramp on the southern end of the village. There the assault would be fiercest and the defense the strongest. "If it looks as though we can keep the ramp free of assault, and if more help comes by river, then perhaps you will have the opportunity to ride out from the village before the battle is over," Aelfin finally agreed. "When Aldgisl has been defeated, I will give you the honor of pursuing his fleeing war band and exacting submission from them."

At this, Eomaer's smiled broadened further. It was as if the battle was already won in his eyes. When the planning was over, Aelfin once again joined the rest of his thanes in drink, making a point of encouraging each warrior in person while they listened to the last of Dyflines' songs. Eomaer followed Aelfin's lead and moved among his own men with words of courage. By this time, the cloudy sky had long been dark and the night was well advanced. Despite the crowded hall and the promised troubles of the coming day, the warriors found places to rest. Aelfin's thanes, at least, had seen their share of battles, and they knew the warrior's discipline of sleep as well as fight. Well fed by food and song, and fatigued from their hard day's work, they put aside their fears and slept well that night. The long winter nights of Friesland did have their blessings.

Blessings to some, at least. Unfortunately not all in Ezinge shared the benefits of the many hours of darkness. Despite his own exhaustion Kristinge was unable to sleep, but instead lay awake thinking of what lay ahead of him—of what he needed to do. And his thoughts gave him no peace. Every course of action troubled him. He could find no escape. After a time, therefore, he turned to prayer, petitioning his God for strength and wisdom. Yet even his prayers were confused and incomplete, lacking the focus that his years of monastic discipline ought to have given him. In the end, he could only trust that his God could hear him nonetheless, and he took comfort in the words of the Apostle Paul: *though we do not know how to pray as we ought, the Spirit Himself intercedes for us with moans too solemn for words.*

During the night, the clouds parted and colder air more in keeping with the season came blowing down from the north. When the following day dawned, there was a deep chill over the village. Had servants not kept the hearth fire burning all night, there would have been ice within the hall despite the heat generated by the extra bodies. Nevertheless, before the sun had finished cresting over the low hills to the east, Aelfin had already positioned his scouts along the western edge of the terp. The ever eager Eomaer volunteered a company of five to ride out from the village and bring advanced warning when the enemy approached, but Aelfin said it was unnecessary. "We will see them soon enough—sooner than we wish. For now, let us rest and take sustenance." The chieftain ordered a large cauldron of barley and venison stew, along with plates of bread, dried fruits and nuts, to be set out by the hearth so the warriors could break their night's fast and fortify themselves for the coming battle. Soon the hall was full of warriors moving about and talking, often loudly as if the volume of their voices might drown the fear of battle. Oddly, it was in the midst of this commotion that Kristinge's exhaustion finally overcame him. He broke his sleepless night's fast with a hunk of the hearty bread and a long drink of cold water, and shortly afterward drifted off to sleep on a bench in the back corner of the hall. Despite the noise in the hall around him, he was blessed with a stretch of untroubled sleep that lasted through the morning.

When Kristinge awoke, the angle of sunlight at the door of the hall told that it was already midday. He was surprised to find the hour so advanced, and leapt from his bench to see if the village were already besieged. But though Aelfin and Eomaer were not to be seen, most of the warriors still sat in benches around the hall sharpening and testing their weapons while speaking in low voices of battles past, glories yet to come, and families left behind. The mood in the hall was tense, but there was yet no sign of any enemy. Kristinge, afraid to leave the hall for fear that he might have to face Aelfin, remained near the fire keeping to himself in silence.

It was two hours later when the watchmen first spotted the enemy war band approaching. Daylight was already fading from the sky when the lead riders became visible far across the fields to the east of Ezinge, near to the downstream portion of the Hunze river. Within moments, both Aelfin and Eomaer had been notified. They returned to the hall and told the warriors that the time had come. "Be brave," Aelfin said. "There is glory to be won this day for the warrior who shows his strength and courage." Then, already dressed and armed, the two chieftains hurried to the eastern end of the village. Kristinge donned his warm cloak, and pausing only briefly to check that Finn's torc was secure in the purse at his side, he followed. His sword he left behind.

Before half the enemy army had emerged from the distant trees, all of Ezinge had gathered on the edge of the terp to watch their approach. It was then that Kristinge realized it was not only the warriors of Ezinge who were armed; Aelfin had armed many of the peasant villagers as well. Kristinge's heart felt heavy at the thought that they all might be going into battle on his account: that they might *die* on his account. He looked for Dunnere among the untrained peasants, but he didn't see him. Nonetheless, his resolve quickened. There was no time to speak with Aelfin now, nor did he have the courage. He would have to act on his own.

"Thirty on horseback," Ceolac announced when they were close enough for him to count. "I see two standards. There are two chieftains among them: two wearing torcs."

"Aldgisl and Réadban," Maccus guessed. "They have come together to dispose of us and claim the torc. Yet both, I think, would be happier with a *king's* torc of their own than with a chieftain's. Maybe we should just let them fight one other."

Nobody responded to Maccus' last comment. At the name of Aldgisl, Eomaer eyes narrowed and his steely grip on his sword tightened. Kristinge saw this, and wondered how his young friend would respond to his plan. There was no time left to warn *him* either. No time to tell anybody. He wondered who would be most surprised. When Eomaer had arrived with word of Aldgisl's approach, Aelfin had assumed without asking that this news was enough to convince Kristinge that it was too late to turn back— enough to dissuade him from abandoning his torc. "There will be other chieftains among them as well if this war band numbers three hundred," Aelfin said. "Aldgisl had no easy task to raise and feed a war band of that size at this time of year, though he already holds great sway over many lesser chieftains. This must be a federation."

"It numbers *more* than three hundred," said Ceolac who was still looking at the approaching army and counting. Just now, the last warriors were coming into view.

"How many?" a number of voices asked at once.

"Four hundred or more."

Both chieftains could be heard drawing their breath sharply. But Eomaer's eyes were flashing as he spoke. "This is a good sign."

"Good?" Kristinge mumbled, looking at him in surprise

Aelfin, Ceolac, and Maccus also waited for an explanation. "How so, young friend? Even against two hundreds we would have earned ourselves enough glory in victory."

"Wieuwerd is safe," Eomaer explained. "Aldgisl cannot have waged a battle against Wigmaer, defeated him, and readied his troops to move again in such a short time. Not with the whole of his army."

"Then Wigmaer is safe," Aelfin said.

"It would seem so."

"And he will come to our aid?"

"If Woden is good to us," Eomaer replied.

Kristinge knew that the hopes of Aelfin and Eomaer rested on Wigmaer and the other chieftains allied with them. If Theoman, Wihtred, and Aescholt arrived with their war bands soon enough to bolster Ezinge's defense, and at the same time Wigmaer brought an attack against Aldgisl's rear, then they stood a chance of winning and driving the enemy away even outnumbered as they were. For this was their home territory. They held the defense of the terp. However despite Eomaer's proud words, without the help of these other chieftains the sixty in Ezinge had little hope of standing for long against Aldgisl's four hundred.

All fell silent then as they watched the army advance, seeming to grow larger as it spread itself out over the village fields which were now frozen and lightly covered with snow. First came thirty on horseback, keeping together in a little pack near the front left flank. Many of them wore battle helms. These were thanes and nobles; they would fight with broadswords and perhaps spears. Following them, the four hundred foot soldiers came in a less orderly fashion, carrying spears, axes, and all manners of weapons. At the end of the train were a half dozen carts pulled by pairs of oxen over the hard ground. Weapons and supplies, Kristinge guessed. There was no doubt that this war band came for battle. They marched across the flax fields like locusts, only *these* locusts were bent on the destruction of the village itself and not just its grain. When Kristinge saw for himself the size of Aldgisl's host, confirming Ceolac's count and far exceeding Eomaer's, his heart began to pound harder. He had never seen an army this big. Even at the largest celebrations of his childhood he never remembered seeing so many warriors gathered at once in Hwitstan. It dwarfed even the Danish raiding bands that he had left in their coastal villages the previous spring.

That it *was* Aldgisl and Réadban whose war bands now approached Ezinge was confirmed soon enough. Aldgisl was a tall warrior with a heavy dark red beard nearly matched in color by the bronze boar on his helmet. Aelfin, who had in the past ridden into battle at his side, spotted him first and pointed him out to the others. "If it comes to battle, let your blades seek first *his* neck."

"No. *That* one is mine," Eomaer claimed, giving no consideration to the fact that their war band was outnumbered by four hundred to sixty and that only by the wildest turn of fate would he even be alive on the morrow.

Réadban they also spotted soon enough. He was a little smaller than Aelfin, and much older. He wore no helmet over his graying head, but at his side carried a heavy black shield, like the Frankish infantry shields. There was a hushed silence over the defenders atop the terp as Réadban and Aldgisl drew closer. Kristinge could see the men around him counting the approaching warriors, and shaking their heads in dismay. A few turned back toward the village, as if to make sure their wives and children were hidden in their huts. Or perhaps to see them for the last time. The enemy warriors were close enough now that their faces were visible: a whole sea of them. When the advancing army came to the base of the terp, they began to spread out along the axwei on the eastern edge of the village.

Eomaer motioned to the few archers whom Aelfin had set up with their bows. "Should we take a few now and give them warning not to stand so close to the terp?"

Aelfin shook his head. "Let us speak with them first and hear what they will say."

"By the gods, you will not surrender!" Eomaer cried.

Aelfin shook his head. "We may yet escape this battle, but not by surrender. Mostly, I hope to delay. The longer we wait, the more chance of the others arriving to aid us." Even as Aelfin said this, as if in response to his wishes, Aldgisl and Réadban began to make their way around to the southern end of the village where the horse path onto the terp was. Six other warriors rode with them.

"Come," Aelfin said. "We will go to greet them. A meeting will buy us some of that time we hope for." He turned to a young warrior beside him, one whom Kristinge guessed had never seen battle. "Bring us four torches before it grows dark."

The young warrior appeared eager to comply, and dashed off at once to the hall. Then while the rest of the two mismatched armies stared at one another, Aelfin, Eomaer, and Kristinge walked briskly to the southern end of the village along with Maccus, Ceolac, Treothrym, and a dozen other of Aelfin's and Eomaer's strongest thanes. They stopped at the top of the ramp and watched as Aldgisl, Réadban and their thanes rode their mounts halfway up the path. When the two pairs of chieftains were fifty feet apart, Réadban stopped and lifted his hand. His men obeyed the command to halt. Another moment of silence followed while the leaders of the two armies faced one other, each measuring the other's resolve.

It was a tense few seconds. Until that moment, Kristinge had naïvely assumed that if he carried through with his plan, it would be enough to save Ezinge. But now, as he sensed more fully how little love existed between the two sets of chieftains, he realized this was not the case: that no matter what words were spoken that night, battle was the likely outcome. Understanding this, he began to tremble.

"I see we have been expected," Réadban finally said with a tone of proud sarcasm. He did not bother with the usual formality of exchanging greetings: a formality that was customary even among enemies. Astride his horse, his head was almost level with the top of the terp, and there was a look of haughty confidence on his face. As he spoke, his piercing eyes glanced furtively around the party of warriors facing him, as if looking for somebody in particular.

Kristinge felt Réadban's disdainful look as it rested upon him momentarily and then disregarded him and moved on. He shuddered briefly at the hateful touch of those eyes, but pushed it from his mind. He was focusing every ounce of concentration he had on the situation in front of him, bringing to bear everything he had learned so that he could pick his moment. *Réadban had spoken first, and not Aldgisl.* he noted. His thoughts were all still at the conscious level, not yet intuitive. *What did that mean? Was not Aldgisl the leader of this war band: the one who aspired to be king?* In the past fifteen months he had learned far more about the Frisian and Danish chieftains and the life and dealings of their societies than in the entire previous six years at Luxeuil put together. He had learned more about the Germanic warrior, about warfare and diplomacy, and about political ambitions and aspirations. He wondered if it would be enough for the trial he now faced.

"If you come seeking battle against fellow Frisians, you will find more battle here than either of you desired," Aelfin replied loudly enough for all to hear. "Why do you bring such a large war band to the edge of my village, and approach me wearing a battle helm? When proud warriors surround my village in battle attire, I do not invite them to my mead hall."

The formal duel of words had begun: a duel that might last many minutes or many hours. It was Aldgisl who spoke next, but he did not answer Aelfin's question. It was not the *duty* of Frisian chieftains— especially of those who sought to be king—to answer questions from inferiors. Kings *asked* questions. "Is it true that you have raised a war band against me?"

"There is a war band gathered and ready to fight the Franks," Aelfin replied. But he gave no more ground. "Do *you* stand against us?"

"You think to win back what you so easily lost in the past?" Réadban was speaking again, taking the reigns of the conversation back from Aldgisl, but also sidestepping Aelfin's question as Aldgisl had done. There was a challenging tone in his voice: like his glance, one of undisguised disdain and hatred. "Hah," he added, before Aelfin could respond. "Why would we believe you could succeed now, where you *failed* before?"

Kristinge's eyes opened wider. There could be no doubt that this was a deliberately intended insult. He did not need years of experience to know that Réadban was recalling the day when Aelfin had let Domburg fall to the Franks. He was not just testing Aelfin but *deliberately* seeking to provoke a battle. *But why?* he wondered. *What had Réadban to gain from a fight?*

In loyalty to their chieftain, Aelfin's thanes dropped their hands to their swords. If Réadban *was* trying to provoke a fight, he was following the right path. Aelfin's face turned red, and his voice rose close to the level of shouting as he gave his reply. "We seek to do what has long been needed: to drive the Franks far from the Rhine and take back all of Friesland. If *you* knew less cowardice, the war band behind you would have traveled south long ago, instead of north to harass your own folk: your blood kinsmen and fellow Frisians."

"It is a worthy goal," Aldgisl said, interrupting the words between Aelfin and Réadban with a comment that took them both by surprise. "Why indeed should the Franks be allowed on Frisian soil? Why should we not drive them far over the Rhine? Gather a war band and sweep through Domburg." He smiled. "It is a battle that might even make a king of a chieftain. For with such victories kings are made." He looked squarely in Aelfin's eyes as he said this.

"A king?" Réadban asked with mock innocence.

"It may be that there is one who already has claim to this kingship," Aelfin replied boldly. "One whose father and father's father wore Friesland's torc and ruled us all."

"Then rumors are true," Réadban said, his own voice now also rising to the level of shouting. Again his eyes could be seen glancing around. Only this time, Kristinge knew for whom he was looking. He felt exposed.

"Do you stand against us?" Aelfin asked again, ignoring both Aldgisl's correct assessment of their real motives and also Réadban's comment. "Do you force us to bring our battle against you, instead of against our proper enemies?"

Kristinge, who had never seen Aelfin appear so haughty and angry, began to despair further. The situation would be out of his hands before he had a chance to act. But again Aldgisl interrupted the shouting between Réadban and Aelfin. His voice was calm and controlled. "Must we yell at each other like enemies? Or shall we come together as Frisian blood-kin?"

It was strange. Kristinge got the impression that under other circumstances he would have liked Aldgisl. But his hopes for peace were still dwindling. Aelfin did not back down. He was seething. If he had a bigger war band, he might have begun a battle already. Réadban had done his work too well. "When a chieftain brings a large war band to my village and approaches with insults and battle helms, I do not invite him into my mead hall until I hear more of his purposes."

"There are only eight of us," Aldgisl said. He lifted both hands off his horse. "The war band waits behind us. Their orders are to remain until we return. If you *still* fear us, we will come to you unarmed."

"We fear nobody," Aelfin growled, though he made no motion to accept Aldgisl's proposal. Kristinge could see him pondering what to do. He guessed the chieftain's thoughts. *Did he really have a chance of winning a battle against such a large foe? Or was he forced to back down and let Réadban's insults go unchallenged.*

Eomaer leaned over and spoke softly to Aelfin. Only Kristinge and Maccus were close enough to hear. "Do not let them come up here. It is a ruse. They wish to spy the village and survey our defenses. Do not let them know how many stand against them. Let them feel some doubt."

Aelfin nodded. Without taking his eyes off Aldgisl, he replied to Eomaer's question with a question of his own. "What then shall we do? Would you have us go down among them? Aldgisl is a man of honor, but I do not trust Réadban. The path that brought him his torc is still wet with blood, even of his own kinsman."

"Have them send their horses away," Eomaer whispered. "We will meet them on the ramp."

Aelfin looked approvingly at Eomaer. Ignoring the situation for a moment, he spoke. "You are wise. I hope we live through this day that we might fight side by side again. Together, we might well defeat the Franks." Then he looked back toward the enemy and shouted. "Send your horses away. We will come down to you and talk."

Réadban appeared about to say something, but Aldgisl reached out his hand and held him. "We will do as you say."

Réadban pulled his arm free from Aldgisl's grasp, but he did not gainsay the other's words. Aldgisl dismounted first, followed by Réadban and their thanes. At Réadban's order, one of them led the eight horses back down the ramp. When the horses were gone, Aelfin stepped forward. Eomaer went with him on one side and Kristinge on the other. The three of them were flanked by Maccus and Ceolac. Five other warriors followed behind as they started down off the terp.

The two parties met in the middle of the ramp where horse, cattle, and oxen were led into and out of the village. Though oft in battles past many of them had fought at one another's sides, now the two groups stood staring at one another from four paces apart like blood enemies. Though no weapons were drawn, no onlookers would have mistaken this for a friendly meeting. Eomaer in particular was looking at Aldgisl with fire in his eyes.

But again Aldgisl showed why he was worthy of making the claim at kingship. Before either of the other three chieftains could speak, he began. "Folcwalda was a king worthy of his torc. He ruled well. His thanes had no cause to rebel, and his enemies no cause for pride.

His hands were rich and generous, and those who served in his hall were fortunate. Finn too was a good king, served by loyal and proud thanes." At these words, Réadban began to grind his teeth and clench his fists. Kristinge saw that he did not share that opinion. But Aldgisl continued to speak, looking around at the warriors facing him as he did. "I have heard that even Finnlaf was held in as high praise as his father and father's father before him, though his life's days were cut short."

All were amazed to hear Aldgisl lift praise for Finn's kin. Yet none were more surprised than Kristinge himself, who looked upon Aldgisl with new admiration, as one who finds that a past enemy is no longer an enemy but a friend. "You knew my father?" he asked, speaking for the first time.

At the first sound of Kristinge's voice, the eyes of all of Aldgisl's party turned toward him. Aldgisl's gaze was careful and calculating. *Did he see Kristinge as the son of a legend, or as a rival of the torc?* "I knew your father only as a young child knows a great hero."

Lured off-guard by Aldgisl's praise and kind words, Kristinge did not expect what was coming. The situation was far from defused. "A son of Finn?" Réadban said. He laughed a tight, mocking laugh. "We heard of only one son of Finn, and he lies dead. His body was given to the byre."

"*This* is Finn's son," Aelfin said, his temper beginning to flare again.

"Did Finn leave bastard sons across Friesland to make their false claims one by one?"

Aelfin had withstood the insults against himself, but at this insult against his former chieftain, king, and gift-giver, he could no longer restrain himself. He reached over his shoulder and grabbed the hilt of his sword in two hands. Before Kristinge could breath, it flashed from its sheath. The others were not slow to follow. A sudden look of fear crossed Réadban's face as he jumped backward and fumbled to draw his own blade. Yet before Aelfin could get to his foe, Réadban's thanes had stepped between them. Again Kristinge feared then that all was lost.

"Hold!" Aldgisl shouted before the blades crossed. His voice was stern and commanding as he spoke to Aelfin. "By your word we sent our mounts away and waited for you without our war band. If you strike one blow, then our band will not leave a single soul alive in all of Ezinge, nor a single building untouched by the torch. Nor," he added, turning to Eomaer, "will I leave Dronrip standing. Think not that I do not recognize you, Eomaer son of Eodan, leader of the horse-folk. It was said that you still sought the weregild from me. So there are two chieftains here. Seventy men to defend against four hundred?"

He had read the situation all too well. His words were no empty bluff. And for a second long moment, he and Aelfin stood facing one another. Finally Aelfin spoke. "We will honor our word." Whether spoken in true honor, or only in fear of Aldgisl, Kristinge did not know. Aelfin continued. "But see that your *servants* speak with greater honor of the king they once bowed before. The next time a word is spoken against Finn, we will not refrain from spilling the blood of the one who speaks it, even if it costs us our lives."

"I do not doubt you," Aldgisl said. Without looking at Réadban, he reprimanded him. "My thanes will show more self-control."

Now both Réadban and Eomaer were taut as a bowstring. But whereas for the first time Réadban's face showed a hint of fear, Eomaer's eyes had only Aldgisl's blood in them. Neither was pleased to show restraint. Yet Aldgisl and Aelfin were directing the stage now. "Now that I see Kristinge," Aldgisl went on, "I have no doubt that he is the son of Finn and Hildeburh."

A few breathed a sigh of relief. Kristinge was not one of them. *Where was Aldgisl leading? Did he really intend to relinquish so quickly his claim on the Frisian torc? Now that Kristinge himself had decided he would not wear it, was it being given back to him? Was God telling Kristinge something?*

His questions were answered with Aldgisl's next sentence. "Yet know well, Kristinge son of Finn, and Aelfin son of Aeltar, that *blood-bonds do not make a king!*" His voice was forceful and his intention could not be doubted: he had no plan to concede the Frisian torc to Kristinge. And though Kristinge knew the danger to his life had just increased ten-fold with Aldgisl's words, he nonetheless felt a strange sense of relief. "Do you not represent our two greatest foes?" Aldgisl continued, for the first time showing his own emotion and intensity. "Was not your mother Hildeburh the Dane? Even if Finn's blood gave you some portion of a claim, you hold also the blood of Hoc and Hnaef in your veins. And now you come to us from the heart of Francia, from the land of our greatest enemy, and make claim on your father's torc?"

"No," Kristinge answered, his voice barely a whisper against Aldgisl's indignant question. "No," he said again. "I make no such claim."

CHAPTER 22:
BETRAYAL

*T*here was a loud crack as a sheet of ice shifted on the nearby river. Across the fields at the edge of the wood, a crow cawed loudly. A second replied. At Kristinge's utterance of denial, a stunned silence had fallen across the warriors and chieftains gathered there in confrontation. Among both parties, eyes opened wide in surprise. Voices froze. Stares were fixed upon the young man who had spoken—the young man who suddenly became strangely cognizant of the myriad of everyday sounds around him: the soft bleating of goats, the chill wind whistling through the village, and the waters of the Hunze tumbling beneath the broken ice.

This calm lasted only a few seconds. Then the expected pandemonium erupted.

"Kristinge!" Aelfin barked. "Have you lost —"

"By Tiwar," Réadban cursed simultaneously. "Do you think we are fools? Do you dare—"

A dozen other voices also broke out, some shouting at Kristinge, some at each other, some in surprise, and others in anger; all essaying to drown each other out. But Kristinge was barely paying attention. He was watching the cold, distant winter sun dipping below the horizon. Not many days had passed since the winter solstice, and the light was fading rapidly. It would be dark soon, and Kristinge knew that the moon would be but a tiny sliver. He wondered who would be watching it in Luxeuil that evening.

"Silence," Aldgisl shouted in a voice that boomed louder than them all. "*Silence!*" It was unclear at whom the command was directed: Aelfin, Réadban, or the whole gathering. Yet there was something compelling in the chieftain's voice: an authority that made him difficult to refuse; even Aelfin obeyed. A silence as icy as the wind fell once again. When all had turned their eyes on Aldgisl, he opened his mouth to speak. "Do you tell us—" he began.

He never finished the sentence. Four lights appeared at the top of the ramp: torches. Suspecting an attack or ambush from the village, the warriors under Aldgisl's command stiffened and moved toward defensive stances. Kristinge looked over his shoulder to see what it was. Then he remembered Aelfin's earlier command to the young warrior. Two youths descended the ramp, each carrying a pair of brightly burning torches. They spoke no words, but holding the lights high they took posts on either side of Aelfin's company while all stood watching them, momentarily transfixed by the flames. Kristinge looked briefly upon the nervous faces of the two men, and then back at Aldgisl and Réadban. In the torch light, the glaring faces of the chieftains were once again visible. Aldgisl turned back to Kristinge and began to speak again. "Do you make *no* claim on Friesland's torc?" he demanded in a voice that was steady but charged with emotion.

"I make no claim," Kristinge replied, without flinching from Aldgisl's gaze. He reached into his purse and removed the gold torc that he had earlier removed from his neck. For just a moment, he grasped the cold metal in his hands; it was heavier than he remembered. *Did he really want to do this?* Ignoring the lingering trace of reluctance, he held Finn's torc in front of him as an offer.

If Kristinge's words had not been enough to convince his companions of his intentions, this action was. Eomaer stumbled backwards as if struck. Kristinge saw the motion from the corner of his eye; he winced and tried not to look in the direction of his one time friend, but he could feel Eomaer's gaze burning into his cheek, and could not help but glance in that direction. The expression on the face of the young horse-chieftain said all that needed to be said: the now gaunt eyes that were normally so full of life held a gaze of such deep hurt that Kristinge could not bear to look at them any longer. They were the eyes of one betrayed, looking at his betrayer. *How soon until the hurt turned to anger?* Kristinge wondered. On the other side, Aelfin had a similar look on his face, though he was not taken as much by surprise. The older chieftain's hand reached momentarily toward the torc, and then clenched and withdrew as if by great strength of will they were held back. Kristinge bit his lip. *What could he say to them?* He turned back toward Aldgisl. He could not afford to address Eomaer and Aelfin now; he could not yet offer his apology. For he guessed well that not all was over with Aldgisl and Réadban; the crisis was still unresolved. Perhaps it had just grown worse.

"Is this true?" Aldgisl asked again. He appeared as surprised as the rest. It was clear that he did not understand Kristinge's motives. *Could anybody understand?* Kristinge wondered. *No. No Frisian chieftain would ever comprehend why another would give up his torc.* For the first time since the confrontation had begun, there was doubt written on Aldgisl's face. Yet he did not lose control. He made no move to take the torc. Instead, his penetrating gaze searched Kristinge's face for some sign of a hidden plot. For some malice. "Do you truly release all claim to this? Before all who are gathered here?"

"No," Réadban shouted, answering the question before Kristinge could. At the sight of the torc, he had regained his composure and taken a step forward as if he too meant to snatch it from Kristinge's hand. All eyes turned to him now. "It is a ruse," he went on, a hint of desperation in his voice. "A trick. This piece of gold means nothing. If you take it, their jewelers and craftsmen will forge another later. We have heard. He has already raised a war band against you. Does not Eomaer's presence here testify to that?"

Réadban pointed an accusing finger at the young chieftain as he spoke, but Eomaer didn't notice. Kristinge could see he was still too stunned; his hopes of deposing Aldgisl and exacting the weregild on the kin of his father's slayer had been snatched from him. Kristinge feared that nothing he could say would ever assuage for Eomaer's sense of betrayal. He turned back toward Aldgisl and Réadban. "It is true," he admitted.

If Kristinge's willing forfeiture of the torc had surprised Réadban, this next confession surprised him even more. The chieftain's eyes widened for a moment, while his followers once more gripped their swords and readied for battle. In their understanding, this was a confession of guilt: Kristinge had admitted that he was an enemy of their lord. The monk had to explain quickly—had to explain in a way that Aldgisl and Réadban might understand, though in his heart his explanation was more for Aelfin and Eomaer than for any others. "It is true that I raised a war band. Though Aelfin also speaks truth that our battle was destined for the Franks, and not for fellow Frisians." Kristinge did not give anybody a chance to interrupt. "I returned to

Friesland seeking the father I had not known: Finn, son of Folcwalda, the warrior. For a time, it seemed to me that wearing his torc was the one way I might honor him. Now I see this is not true."

"Lies," Réadban hissed. Despite the cold air, the torch light showed his face was damp with sweat. "You seek to buy time. We have come upon you too soon and too suddenly, before you were ready. When spring comes, you will be at our throats."

Aldgisl just stared at Kristinge, still seeking some understanding. "Do you have no defense against these accusations?"

Suddenly, however, Kristinge was at a loss for words. What else could he say? He knew that Réadban's indictment sounded all too likely. "*This* is not true," he mumbled. "I have given up the torc."

"Already you have earned your death," Réadban went on, ignoring Kristinge's plea. "You and all who have cast their swords with your plot." He turned to Aldgisl. "Let us burn this village down. Put them to the sword and byre."

"You would be hard-pressed, cowardly fool," Aelfin growled. As angered as he might have been at Kristinge's decision, he would not take threats from Réadban. He took an intimidating step toward him. This time, Réadban did not back away from the blade. And still Eomaer said nothing. He was staring icily at Kristinge now: the same icy stare that he had previously given to Aldgisl. Kristinge let the weight of the torc—and the weight of his decision—pull his arm down. His held the torc dangling at his side.

"Listen," Réadban said to Aldgisl. "Even now he threatens you. As long as a son of Finn lives, and there are rebel chieftains such as these willing to follow him, he is a threat. Let us put him to death."

Aldgisl stood still for a moment, as if in thought. Then he nodded his head. "Réadban speaks wisely and again proves his worth. As long as Kristinge walks freely in Friesland, he is a threat to the unity of our people."

"A threat to your ambitions," Aelfin corrected, quietly but clearly. His eyes had narrowed to a hard slit.

Aldgisl only shrugged, as if Aelfin's words were of no account whether they were true or not. The look of doubt that had briefly appeared on his face was now just as quickly gone. The calm assured smile had once more returned. Aelfin started to open his mouth to add to what he had said, but then he shut it again. Kristinge knew what he was thinking. Had Aelfin not told Kristinge many times? It was the might of the warrior that made the chieftain—*and* the might of the warrior and his war band that made the king. For all Aelfin's pride and strength, there was no gainsaying Aldgisl, and no arguing with what he said next. "While I rule the largest war band, my ambitions are one with those of Friesland. You will give me the torc and return to the village. Tomorrow we will decide what your fate and that of your followers shall be."

Kristinge nodded. He started to lift the torc once again in an offer. But before he could step forward, he felt a hand on his shoulder. Aelfin was not as ready as Kristinge to accept Aldgisl's terms. He and his men made no move to budge. For a moment, the chieftains stared at one another. Yet at Aldgisl's final words, a smile had returned to Réadban's face: a sly grin that frightened Kristinge. "The largest war band," Réadban mumbled softly, repeating Aldgisl's words as if reminding himself of something. He looked once more at the torc in Kristinge's grip, then at Aelfin. When he spoke again, his voice was loud and clear. "Though your village is surrounded by a war band six times as big, you do not cease to threaten us and hurl insults upon us. But I am not one who does not know mercy. After all, it has been shown even to me. Did not Finn spare my life after I swore allegiance upon his blade and acknowledged my wrongdoing?"

What has Finn to do with this? Kristinge wondered, but he only mumbled aloud, "Finn?"

Réadban continued. "If you turn Kristinge and the torc over to me and swear your fealty upon my sword, then I will let you live and leave your village unharmed. For the good of Friesland, this offer I will give once and only once to all who have bowed before Kristinge. If you do not accept, then your lives are forfeit."

Kristinge understood at once that it was his own life being bargained for. Nevertheless, he breathed a sigh of relief. He did not want to see Aelfin or Eomaer die on his behalf: to see all of Ezinge ravaged in his name. If his sacrifice could save their lives, he would pay that price. He had made up his mind some time earlier. He closed his eyes and bowed his head. Then he started forward. Again Aelfin's hand came down on Kristinge's shoulder like a vice. "Do you think we are so easily frightened that I would give up one I have named as my son so that you could put him to death?"

Kristinge looked at Aelfin in surprise. *You would still protect me as a son? Even now?*

"I will not suffer that his life be taken from him," Aldgisl said, stepping back into the conversation. "Only that he not be free to stir rebellion among Friesland. He will be kept safely in my custody."

"Being a prisoner is one with death," Aelfin said fiercely. "You will not take him."

"Think twice," Aldgisl replied sternly. He had no reason to veil his threats now. "It is your *own* life that you speak of now."

"Perhaps. And perhaps yours also. Many lives will be spent if you seek to take Ezinge from us. Think not that we stand alone."

Réadban had not stopped grinning. "Do you speak of Wigmaer the weak? He will not come to your aid."

At the mention of this name, they once again had Eomaer's attention. "Why does the name of my cousin come from your lips?"

"Do you think we know so little of your plans?" Réadban went on, ignoring Eomaer. "Do you think that we would come here without knowing against whom we stood? We know those who have cast their ill-chosen swords with Finn's whelp. Wigmaer will not be coming to your aid."

"If you have taken Wigmaer's life, I will follow you to the ends of the earth and give your bowels to the wild boar," Eomaer replied, his eyes blazing with the red of the torch light. "Whatever injury you have given him, I will take from you threefold."

"No harm has come to Wigmaer," Aldgisl said. "We have simply left a token of our army behind in Wieuwerd to see that we were not followed." Then he turned back to Aelfin. "And so you see that before the battle has even begun, it has turned against you. You are a worthy warrior and chieftain, Aelfin. I have fought at your side more than once in the past, and would do so again. If you give Kristinge to me now, you will fight with me again, against the Franks. Even Domburg may be restored to you. But if you stand against me, then not the smallest hut will be left standing in Ezinge." Then he turned back to Eomaer. "And you, bold chieftain. I have heard that you have claimed the weregild against me for the death of your father. Know that I did not fight against him that day, nor did any of my kin. We took no part in his death. I owe you no debt. Know also that I have heard of your prowess on horseback, and though you have sought my life, my offer extends to you as well. I would rather have you beside me than against me. And you will see that I am not a poor treasure-giver."

Kristinge could hear Eomaer grinding his teeth. To his left, Aelfin too had fallen silent. Their hope of help from Wigmaer was gone, and Kristinge knew their chances of standing alone against Aldgisl and Réadban were slim. And at the mention of fighting the Franks and recapturing Domburg, even Aelfin's normally inexpressive face had revealed his sudden interest. *Would that temptation be to strong to resist? How strong of a bond did he feel toward Kristinge? Would he change his mind?*

"I will never bow before Aldgisl," Eomaer growled softly.

"I do not ask you to," Réadban replied. He had stepped forward now, and spoke in a loud and haughty voice. "It is me to whom you will swear your fealty."

Aldgisl turned sharply toward Réadban, a look of surprise upon his face. "What—?" he began to ask. However all eyes were turned toward Réadban now, including those of Kristinge who was trying desperately but unsuccessfully to make sense of what was happening.

Réadban did not hesitate. "It is I who will wear the torc. I will rule Friesland, and none other. As for promises for the safety of Kristinge, I make none. You are not in a position to demand promises of me. Wigmaer will not come to your aid. You have no other hope but to bow to me. It is *my* war band that surrounds you now. Aldgisl is but a token thane: another who will also soon bow before me. The torc belongs to *me!*"

Réadban's final words were spoken with such virulence and certitude that they were met with only a stunned silence: a silence even deeper than that which had followed Kristinge's proclamation a few moments earlier. Goats ceased their bleating. The wind fell still. The river itself seemed to stop its constant rushing in response to Réadban's proud words. Even the crows were silent.

Bewildered, Kristinge could only shake his head in a mixture of fear and confusion. He knew not what to think of this sudden turn:

what it would mean to his own future, as well as to that of Ezinge and Friesland. Though he had never before met Aldgisl, he had instinctively trusted him. Réadban, on the other hand, he trusted less with each passing moment. He had not been prepared for this. The strange peace he had felt since the start of the confrontation now faded to a deep uneasiness. *What did this mean?* He looked to Aelfin for some sign of understanding: some hint about what was to be done next. But Aelfin was as taken by surprise as any of them. Any of them except perhaps Aldgisl who appeared like a man caught naked in a blizzard.

"YOU?" Aldgisl sputtered, absorbing what Réadban had said after an initial moment of shock. "YOU!"

Réadban only grinned wickedly back at him. When Aldgisl saw that Réadban was serious, he took a step backward. His hand went at once to his sword, and he glanced around him as if waiting for his thanes to turn and stand with him against this *new* adversary: this conspiracy against him. And then came Aldgisl's second sting. Only one of the warriors on the ramp went to his side; the others stayed with Réadban. Aldgisl was cornered and outnumbered, and he realized it at once. Nor was there anywhere he could turn for help; Aelfin and Eomaer were not about to step to his side to defend him against Réadban. His look of surprise had become one of fear. His face grew pale. Whatever words of challenge and anger had formed on his lips died suddenly, or were suppressed in discretion.

Then it was that Kristinge guessed what was happening. It was not difficult to conjecture even without Aelfin's help. It was Réadban's thanes who had come up the ramp, not Aldgisl's. Either that, or more of Aldgisl's thanes in addition to Réadban had just betrayed him. But that was almost unthinkable! No. Though Aldgisl had spoken as one in authority, it must have been Réadban's war band that had come to Ezinge. *Then why had Aldgisl come with Réadban?* The answer was clear. Because Aldgisl had not expected this betrayal. He had trusted Réadban. He had been taken by surprise. He had come to take the next step toward his receiving the torc of Friesland. Instead, he was to watch it torn away from him.

Réadban gave Aldgisl a last, icy calculating stare, then turned back toward Aelfin. All Aldgisl could do was to stand and watch, and await his own fate even as Kristinge awaited his. "This is my offer," Réadban said. "Give Kristinge to me now along with the torc, swear to me your service, and you may live as my thanes. Resist me, and you will die. For I warn you: if you refuse to turn over Kristinge and the torc, Ezinge will burn in the morning. I give you until then to consider."

Aelfin and Eomaer did not answer, but Kristinge could guess what they were thinking. They had no choice left. No hope. To fight Réadban was sure defeat. And what reason did they have to risk their lives to protect Kristinge? None. Nor did Kristinge want them to. He would not be the cause of their deaths, nor of the destruction of Ezinge. He gathered his courage and prepared to speak. *I will go.*

Once again, however, before the words were out of his mouth another sound was heard from nearby: a horse galloping along the axwei at the base of the terp, mingled with some urgent shouting. As if given a sudden reprieve from the many dramas being acted out upon the torch lit ramp, everyone turned and waited to see what news would be brought. The rider stopped at the base of the ramp where the other horses were being held. After a word of consultation with a warrior there, he dismounted from his horse and started up the ramp on foot. In the darkness, it took him a moment to find his chieftain. "Lord Aldgisl," he spoke.

So this was one of Aldgisl's men, Kristinge thought. *And the messenger knows nothing of what has taken place.*

"Speak," Aldgisl said with a sideways glance at Réadban. "I trust your words are urgent." Once again, the younger chieftain was back in the picture. As Kristinge would learn, Aldgisl was never one to be underestimated.

"In front of these?" the messenger asked.

Perhaps Aldgisl guessed the nature of the message, and for that very reason, finding the tables suddenly turned against him, he chose to let the messenger speak. "Speak," he repeated. "Let everyone hear."

"A war band approaches, my lord," the messenger said nervously.

"*What?*" Réadban shouted.

"From Wieuwerd?" Aldgisl queried.

"No, my lord. They come upriver, from Hwitstanwic."

"How many? Is it a large war band?"

"Three ships."

Theoman and Aescholt, Kristinge guessed. *From Wijnaldum and Beowic.* He had been taught well by Aelfin; three ships meant sixty or more warriors. They had received Eomaer's message and were coming to the aid of Ezinge. Though Kristinge's own plans had not changed with this news, somehow the information brought with it a rush of excitement. He could hear the Ezinge warriors stirring around him, and knew they guessed the meaning of the message as well as he did. Hope rose in his heart.

"How far away?" Réadban asked urgently, the grin gone from his face.

The messenger looked at Aldgisl. When Aldgisl nodded his permission for him to speak, he turned toward Réadban. "They have come as far up the Hunze as they may—as far as the ice flows allowed—and now they continue on by foot. They are no more than an hour's march away." He didn't stop there, either. Though his voice was trembling, he went on. "There is more."

"Then speak!" Réadban shouted.

The messenger was afraid; he didn't like being the bearer of bad tidings. "There is another war band approaching as well. They have come by foot from Aalsum, and are yet three hours' march away. They have stopped for the night. Your rear guard spotted them."

"And this band?" Aldgisl asked in doubt. "Its size?"

"Thirty-five."

There was a short, silent pause, as yet another piece was added to the strange puzzle. It was Aelfin who spoke next. His voice was strong and confident. "Close enough that they will be here by first light in the morning, whether they continue to travel now or not. And so, our help is not as far away as either of us thought, nor is your enemy as weak as you might have guessed."

"We will attack you now!" Réadban replied, his voice sounding desperate once again. "We can deal with these other rogues when they arrive."

Now it was Aldgisl who turned on Réadban. "Are you a fool? Attack up the slopes of the terp in the darkness? These warriors know the village by heart. You would be fighting blind. And the others might fall on your back at any moment." His words had an effect.

Réadban was clearly disturbed by the news. His confidence was shaken. And there were other thoughts on Aldgisl's mind as well. Not having forgotten his own situation, he turned to the messenger and to the other thane who was loyal to him. "Give orders to my war band. We will depart at once." Without waiting for an answer, he turned and started down from the slope.

Réadban stood still for just a moment, his fists clenched tightly at his sides. Then he turned to his own thanes and began shouting orders. "Surround the village. And keep watch. When the other war band arrives, don't let them get to Ezinge. Keep them at bay. Fight if you must, but make them fight us outside the village. Don't let them add to the defense. We are still a match for all of them." Then he turned and saw Aldgisl striding down the ramp. "And don't let Aldgisl escape!"

But it was too late. Aldgisl broke into a run. Before Réadban's men could move, the other chieftain and his two thanes had already sprung upon their horses. Réadban's guards at the bottom of the ramp, not knowing what had transpired, made no move to stop them. In moments, Aldgisl was disappearing into the darkness.

Aelfin did not give Réadban time to ponder. "And so," he said. "All is no longer as it was. Even as our numbers grow, yours shrink. Some of your prey has already slipped from your grasp."

Réadban turned back toward Aelfin, his eyes glowing red with anger. Kristinge could see him struggling to appear calm as he spoke. "Merely thirty men: a token number from a token chieftain. Even without Aldgisl, we stand at four hundred, far outnumbering you. And as you can see, not even Aldgisl may stand against me now." Nevertheless, he was gritting his teeth in frustration that belied his words.

"I see well enough," Aelfin answered him confidently. "I know your thoughts. It is a dangerous game you play. Perhaps you have moved too early. Perhaps not; perhaps even Aldgisl can't stand against you. Yet I guess that you are not altogether sure of yourself, or you would not have waited so long to reveal your own ambitions. Can you risk a war against me now? You cannot attack tonight, and yet if you wait until tomorrow our war band grows. Then you will face us four hundred against two hundred. Though you still outnumber us, the odds are no longer so great, for we defend the terp. If you surround us and siege the village, then you will have enemies attacking you from behind. Yet if you let our allies into the village, then an army of that size could defend against you all winter long. And we would have food while your supplies dwindle. And what of Aldgisl? Will he sit idle?"

There was no reply from Réadban. He was still clenching his fists, glancing back and forth between Kristinge and Aelfin. For the first time that day, Aelfin had the upper hand. Or at least an even hand. Kristinge wondered what he would do with it—wondered what his own fate would be. "We have a war band. Two hundred strong, ready to fight," Aelfin went on. "Yet we would rather fight against the Franks than against you. You have offered me a bargain, and now I offer you one. If you spare Kristinge, then we will fight with you against the Franks. If I guess rightly, Eomaer may accept *your* over lordship, though he will never take Aldgisl's. Give him the task and men to find Aldgisl, and I doubt he will fail you. Then *you* can lead us against the Franks. The victory will be yours. And Aldgisl has spoken rightly: by such a victory a king could well be made."

Kristinge could see the thoughts churning in Réadban's head, as he weighed his ambitions against his thirst for revenge. Aelfin concluded the offer, his voice once again growing stern. "The torc we can offer you in more ways than one. But know this: that I have named Kristinge as my son, and many chieftains have sworn their fealty to him. If you kill him, then we are bound to avenge his death, even if we all die. Friesland will destroy itself, and the Franks will conquer us."

Kristinge knew then what a sacrifice Aelfin was making. He knew that Aelfin felt betrayed, and wondered that the chieftain didn't just turn him over to Réadban and be done with him. He wondered also if Eomaer would be so eager to agree to the same bargain. He knew that the bargain Aelfin was making held risk to both parties, for what could they give as proof of their word? Why would Réadban trust Aelfin and Kristinge not to continue to raise their war band, and bring it against him in the spring? Yet for the first time that evening, Kristinge had hope that not only the lives of his friends would be spared, but his own as well.

"You will feed my war band," Réadban said.

"For one day and one night," Aelfin replied.

"And give gifts in your hall."

Aelfin smiled. "No," he answered slyly. "It is you, as our new over-chieftain, who will give gifts in the hall."

Again Réadban gritted his teeth, but Aelfin had him. He turned once more toward Kristinge. Kristinge held his breath. He could see Réadban's fierce grip on the hilt of his sword as he faced his choice.

It took only a moment. The lure of the torc was too strong. Though he was clearly disturbed by the decision he was forced into, Réadban chose to accept Aelfin's offer: to give up his vengeance against Finn's son and his attack on Ezinge in order to gain the support of Aelfin and Eomaer in the greater contest he would soon face against Aldgisl. "There will be food for us in the morning. At first light, I will come to your hall with a hundred of my warriors. The rest will remain camped on the axwei. The armies of the other chieftains will also remain outside the village. If they accept my rule, and will follow us into battle against the Franks, then they will join us in the hall and receive treasure from my hand." Without waiting for a reply, he turned and strode down the ramp. As soon as he was at the bottom, he could be heard shouting orders to his men. "Where is Aldgisl?" he was shouting. "Find him. Track him down. Whatever happens, don't let him get away."

Kristinge closed his eyes and breathed a sigh of relief. He wondered whether Aldgisl would escape or not. He hoped he would. But for now, he was content that he had escaped.

"Come," Aelfin said. He and Eomaer turned and started back toward the hall. Kristinge followed, along with the thanes and torch-bearers.

CHAPTER 23:
FLAMES IN EZINGE

Eomaer was barely able to wait until they were back within the confines of the village and out of earshot of the enemy army before blurting out the question on his mind. "Will you really swear allegiance to that cowardly old fool?"

"Réadban is many things, but 'coward' is not one of them," Aelfin replied, each word slowly and deliberately enunciated. "Has he not just proven that? As to whether he is a fool, that is yet to be seen; when these events have run their course, then his wisdom or foolishness will become evident."

"By Tiwar," the young chieftain swore in reply, "I'd as soon cut off Réadban's head as serve him with my blade and acknowledge him as lord; I'd give my service to the Franks themselves rather than bow before him."

Kristinge was walking a few strides behind the two chieftains, only half-listening to their conversation. His own thoughts were drifting back to Luxeuil as—for the first time since leaving there some sixteen months earlier—he considered returning. He wondered if he would still be welcomed. But Eomaer's comment caught his attention. His stopped in his tracks and lifted his head. Had he heard right? In the torch light ahead, he could see Aelfin bristling at the mention of the Franks. Kristinge took a few quick steps and caught up.

"Curse the whole lot of them," Eomaer went on, his voice growing louder and angrier as he continued. "I should have cut them down on the ramp while I had the chance: an opportunity I will not again let pass."

Kristinge winced. He knew Eomaer well enough not to doubt that he meant what he was saying. Suddenly, Kristinge was feeling less secure about the peace he thought he had bought. He could imagine Eomaer, in a hot mood, riding out at night and raiding Réadban's camp just to provoke him into battle.

"Then likely you will bring about your own death," Aelfin replied.

"Ha," Eomaer laughed. "I do not fear Réadban. If he wants battle, let him have it. Theoman and Aescholt are nearby. And more help comes from Wihtred. By midday tomorrow, our numbers will have more than doubled. Do you think Réadban will even dare attack us now? He will have enough trouble with Aldgisl, I think. He has made himself vulnerable. He will not risk a battle. But if he does? Let him. The tables have turned."

"You judge Réadban too harshly. You underestimate him." Kristinge was again surprised to hear Aelfin defend Réadban. Until that moment, he had never heard Aelfin utter a single good word about Réadban. Had the possibility of recapturing Domburg so completely swayed him? "I say again that he is no coward, whatever else he is. He has just stepped forward in front of Aldgisl and made claim to the torc. That was a bold move."

"Bold? Cowardly, I say. It was done at a time when Aldgisl's war band was far away."

"It was a bold move nonetheless, and risky."

"Then why was he so afraid of Aldgisl escaping?"

"It surprises me, friend Eomaer," Aelfin said, suddenly changing the subject, "to hear you defending Aldgisl."

"And it surprises me, *friend* Aelfin," Eomaer replied in a low, threatening voice, "to hear you taunt me. I would fight even you, if I thought it would give me opportunity to seek the weregild: an opportunity to fight Aldgisl."

Again Kristinge stopped short at Eomaer's words. It was getting worse by the moment. He half expected a fight to break out in the middle of Ezinge. Réadban would not even *need* to attack. Fortunately, Aelfin only laughed in response. "Perhaps with Réadban wearing the torc, you will again have the chance. If Réadban becomes king, there will be no love shared between him and Aldgisl."

There was a moment's silence as Eomaer pondered this. When he spoke again, the threatening tone was gone but the anger was still audible in his voice. "Then you will help to make Réadban our king?"

"I will see what the morrow brings. It may be, as you have so shrewdly pointed out, that as our war bands stand in the morning we will have much more to bargain with than we did today."

"Now you are the Aelfin I have known," Eomaer said. "And thus there may be battle after all!"

"I said only that I will wait to see what the day brings, and whether our bargaining position has changed with the light. Yet it would seem that Réadban is now our best hope to defeat the Franks and drive them from the Rhine."

"Then that was all you hoped for from the beginning."

"What I once hoped for, you have heard. What may now come to pass, who can say? I know I am too old to be threatened, and too young to be afraid. Remember also that Réadban may be *your* best hope to avenge your family on Aldgisl, and was that not all that *you* hoped for from the beginning?"

They were now back at the mead hall. Word was sent throughout the village that there would be no battle that night. Sentries were posted in plenty, but most of the warriors returned to the hall or to their homes, told only to sleep with their swords at hand.

"Then I have no need of this?" said Dyflines, stepping from out of the dark shadows near the corner of the hall. Kristinge saw that he had strapped a fine Frankish broadsword around his waist. Where the bard had obtained it, Kristinge did not know, but he looked as one who had really meant to use it had the need arisen.

"We have greater need of your harp," Aelfin answered. He started into the hall. Eomaer followed him, along with the thanes that had been with them on the ramp.

Kristinge, glad for the opportunity to be safe within the mead hall once again, and thinking about the warm fire and some mead, waited for the last of the warriors to precede him and then stepped through the door. The thought of listening to Dyflines cheered him. He could use a song to break the tension. Yet had he thought even for a moment about what had just happened, he might have been more reluctant. At least he would have been more prepared for the greeting he received. But he was not. The events of the day had left him little time to think.

"STOP!" Aelfin shouted angrily. For an instant, Kristinge didn't realize to whom Aelfin was speaking. He instinctively obeyed, coming to a frozen halt just two steps inside the hall as he glanced over his shoulders wondering if one of Réadban's warriors had sneaked up behind him. But Aelfin was looking right at Kristinge. "You have no place here," the chieftain went on. Beside him, Eomaer was also glaring fiercely at Kristinge. "Tonight you have forfeited your right to stand in this hall. This is a place for warriors. For thanes, and men. For the chieftain and his hearthwerod. You are no warrior. No man of honor. And I have no need for a bard who knows so little the value of truth. Nor do I need a Christian priest. Be gone, and do not set foot here again."

Kristinge was too stunned to speak. This was the man who had named him as a foster son. The very same one who just moments ago risked much to protect him.

"Shall I drive him from this place with the flat of my blade?" Eomaer asked, when Kristinge did not budge. He took a step in Kristinge's direction. Kristinge backed out through the door, his jaw hanging down.

"Wait!" Aelfin said. Kristinge stopped. He was trembling. "The torc. This, too, you have forfeited. You are no son of Finn's. Give it to me."

Kristinge did not dare resist. With a shaking hand, he reached back into his purse and pulled out the gold neck band one more time. It was the last he was to hold on to it. He handed it to Ceolac, who stood beside him. Ceolac walked it over to his chieftain, and placed it on his neck. "It fits you well, my lord," the thane said.

"So it does," Maccus added. "Perhaps that is where it ought to stay."

The warriors watching the scene started to turn toward the fire, but Eomaer was not finished with Kristinge. The torc was not all that *he* wanted back. Still brandishing his blade, he stepped toward the former monk. Kristinge winced and tried to pull away as strong quick hands reached for his neck. He was not quick enough, and felt a sharp tug and a sting of pain. Then Eomaer stood in front of him holding in his hand the pendant he had given Kristinge months before: the token of betrothal to Aewin. "This, too, you have you forfeited," the young chieftain said, then he turned his back and stalked away leaving Kristinge alone.

Kristinge did not hear what went on between Aelfin and Eomaer after that, nor did he hear any of Dyflines' songs that evening. Rough hands fell upon his shoulders, and a moment later he found himself on the ground outside the mead hall. Though he had been in the warmth for only a few moments, the outside air felt more cold and hostile than it had that day or many days past. Taking one last envious look at the light visible around the edges of the door, he turned and walked back toward his hut near the chapel. It would be a cold, fireless night. Yet the icy chill of the winter air was the least of the stings that bit into him. The chill in his heart was far deeper. For he knew beyond a doubt exactly what it was that Eomaer had taken away from him. It was not the pendant. It was Aewin herself. There would be no wedding.

It was early morning. Dunnere was returning from the woods across the fields on the southwest side of Ezinge. He was leading a pair of goats, and gazing heavenward as he praised the Creator for His great blessings. He was only a few steps out of the trees when he saw black smoke spreading out into the sky above the village. A second later, the odor of burning wood reached his nostrils. He lowered his eyes from the skies back down toward the ground. Beneath the thick dark smoke that hung low in the cold winter air, an orange flicker shot out from a building near the southern edge of the terp. It was followed by another. Ezinge was in flames.

Dunnere stared blankly for just a moment before he understood. Flames in the dead of winter could mean only one thing. Stricken by sudden fear for his clansmen and village, the peasant started running toward the village, forgetting for a moment the two goats he had been leading. However he had taken but a few steps when he slowed, then stopped. *Could mean only one thing. Raiders. A war band. A battle. And Ezinge had lost.*

Dunnere's eyes opened wide. *Lost?! What would he do when he arrived?* He did not know. He felt panic rising within him. What if the enemy was still sacking the village. There was no use in going *toward* the village. If he was to run, it would be in the other direction. Yes, run, he thought. Escape. He turned back toward the woods to flee. Then he saw the goats and remembered what he had been doing. No, he thought. Do not flee. Walking back to his cares, he stooped to picked up the two ropes which held them. He looked again toward the trees and the safety they represented, but he resisted the temptation. He turned back around and faced the village. After a few moments' thought, he went onward. After all, God had sent him with a purpose. Anyway, how would an old peasant survive alone in the woods in the dead of winter? More slowly this time, leading the two goats on their short ropes, Dunnere began forward again. He scanned the land around the terp now, looking for signs of a raiding party along the axwei, and occasionally lifting his eyes to the sky where the smoke was still rising. By the time he reached the base of the terp a few minutes later, his legs were trembling. Yet he kept on. God had sent him on an errand. The Lord would not fail him. He must not fail the Lord. Dunnere's strong, wiry old legs carried up the steep bank, with the goats climbing right behind him.

When he reached the top of the slope, Dunnere scanned the village. To his relief, there was no sign of fighting. No enemy. *Why the smoke then?* He skirted around the side of a small hut, keeping his eyes open for danger. He had taken only a few steps before the source of the flames came into view. Then Dunnere's heart sank deep into his belly. For what he saw was worse than an enemy war band. It was the chapel. His small church was in flames.

Where is Kristinge? He wondered. *Why is nobody putting out the flames?* Once again, Dunnere dropped the ropes and began to run, leaving the goats where they were. And once again, he took only a few steps before he stopped. The scene was in full view now. There *were* men at the chapel, but they were making no effort to quench the fire which by this time had nearly devoured the small structure. *What?* Dunnere murmured. *Could it be? Did his eyes deceive?* No. He was not deceived. It was Aelfin, the chieftain. Beside him, a dozen other of his thanes and warriors looked on at the scene. *What were they doing?* Leaving the goats where they were to wander around the frozen turf foraging for food, Dunnere started trudging forward. Then came the sight that almost stopped his heart altogether. Crumbled on the ground beside the fire was Kristinge. All around him, Aelfin's warriors stood with swords drawn. Aelfin had killed the priest.

No! Dunnere shouted. Not pausing to consider the danger to himself, he ran toward the scene as fast as his old legs could carry him. *What had they done to his priest? Why had God—?*

Dunnere stopped near the edge of the half-circle just a few paces behind the thane Ceolac. Nobody noticed the old peasant or the tears streaming from his face. Almost involuntarily, his eyes fell upon the still form of Kristinge. *Wait? What was this?* Praise be to the God. Kristinge was not dead. He was bruised and dirty, but his eyes were still open and streaming tears as he watched his chapel burn to the ground. Glad to see that his priest was still alive, Dunnere now looked at him more closely. Thankfully he did not appear badly injured. Yet the pain in his eyes was clear as he stared at the sight of his chapel in flames: the chapel that Willimond had built many years earlier.

Why? Dunnere wondered.

A moment later came the heavy voice. "You have made your choice. Serve your weak god." It was the chieftain Aelfin speaking. "You have no part in Ezinge. No part in the mead hall. No fellowship with the hearthwerod of a chieftain. Today, you are no longer my son—"

"But the chapel—" Kristinge pleaded.

"We have our own gods. They have served my people from time without count, and they will serve us still. Your god has no place among the strong. Be gone, and return not to Ezinge except on pain of your own death."

Kristinge didn't respond at once, but just lay there, staring. A big scarred warrior—one whom Dunnere had heard named Maccus—put his booted foot in Kristinge's side and nudged him roughly. "The chieftain has spoken. Rise and be gone." The thane Ceolac was a little more kind. He reached down and helped Kristinge to his feet.

"Where?" Kristinge asked.

"Go find your god," Ceolac answered.

The despondent Kristinge took one last look at his chapel in flames. Then a push from one of the warriors propelled him from the spot. Dunnere reached out and caught him as he stumbled forward. He led the young priest from the fire and the harsh angry faces, and started walking toward the edge of the terp where the goats were waiting. "Are you hurt?" he asked gently.

Kristinge shook his head, but he was limping. "My harp," he mumbled. "Cloaks and scrolls." Dunnere didn't know what Kristinge was talking about until Kristinge leaned them both toward his hut. Understanding now, Dunnere waited as Kristinge gathered his few belongings: a pair of cloaks, his treasured harp, and a few parchments of holy writing.

"Be gone!" Aelfin shouted when they emerged. Still leaning on Dunnere for support, Kristinge lowered his head, and without a word started walking.

"I thought they had killed you," Dunnere said.

At first Kristinge didn't answer. When he spoke, his voice was broken. "I have lost all. All. The chapel—Willimond's chapel—burned. And Aewin... Aewin. What have I done?"

Dunnere did not know of whom Kristinge spoke, but now was not the time for questions. "Wait for me at the bottom of the terp," he said into the priest's ear. Kristinge nodded absently. Dunnere looked at him closely to see that he would be able to walk alone. Then he started back across the edge of the village to where he had left the two goats. The goats had not wandered far. At that time of year, beneath the crusty snow, there was little grazing to be done atop the terp. The old peasant grabbed the two ropes and hurried back to the ramp. Kristinge was only half way down; Dunnere caught him by the time he reached the bottom. He did not ask what had happened. The dealings of chieftains was not his business. Yet in his heart he wondered if he once again had his priest back. They walked silently for a time, heading southward across the fields toward the edge of the wood. When they were some distance from the village, he spoke. "The goat is for you." He hoped his words would encourage Kristinge.

"What?"

"The goat. It is for you."

For the first time, Kristinge lifted his head and looked Dunnere in the eye. "I do not understand," he said. Then he lowered his head again, as if he were ashamed even of Dunnere's gaze.

"God gave me two. One for each of us."

"God—?" Kristinge started to ask.

"He called me into the woods two days ago. He told me to keep walking and that I would find them. He said one was for you, that you would soon be needing it."

Kristinge nodded, but showed little surprise. "He was right."

"I've already tasted their milk, you know," Dunnere went on, his former cheerful demeanor returning. "It is fine milk. As long as she is with you, you will not want for good drink."

Kristinge raised his head again. This time he stopped walking. "This is for me?" he asked, as if he had not heard a word Dunnere had said.

Dunnere stood watching Kristinge for a moment. "Have they injured you?"

"Just a few bruises. I will heal."

"Yes. The goat is for you." He handed one rope to Kristinge. "And see?" he pointed. "God gave one for me also. It is bigger than the one I lost. She gives even more milk."

Kristinge shook his head once in amazement, then turned and started on. "God is good," he said, though his voice gave no indication that he really meant it.

"He is," Dunnere replied, in a more convincing tone. "He has showed me something else, too. Not so far away as the goats were. Just a morning's walk. Come with me."

Kristinge obeyed. They walked together throughout the morning, speaking little. Though Dunnere did not know what had happened, he did not bother the priest with his questions but gave him some time of silence. The air was once again unusually warm for winter, and they loosened their cloaks. When the sun had reached its highest point on its winter arc across the southern sky, the peasant produced from his pouch a loaf of bread and some wine. They shared the meal in silence. Then they continued their march. It took longer than Dunnere expected to reach their destination. Kristinge was walking very slowly, and Dunnere did not think he ought to disturb him by increasing the pace, so he patiently walked alongside. Yet when he saw the goal in a small cluster of trees ahead of them, he could not contain himself any longer. "See?" he asked. "It is here. God led me here, and told me I was to bring you—that you would know what to do."

Kristinge lifted his eyes and looked. For a moment, his face lit up with surprise. Dunnere, who was watching him closely, was glad to see this. The priest was too young to be so downcast. Then Dunnere turned and looked alongside Kristinge at the scene in front of them. Ahead, in a small grove of elms and ashes, was a small hut like that of a hermit. The walls and roof were made of rough hewn wood, with clay daubing sealing the cracks. It had a heavy bear hide for a door. Kristinge looked questioningly at Dunnere.

"It is for you. I did not understand at the time, though now I do. God said it was for you." Dunnere hoped to see a look of joy on his priest's face in appreciation for God's provision, but Kristinge only stared ahead. "Come. Follow me," Dunnere finally said. Silently, they approached the building. They looked over the outside for a moment, and then entered. It was bigger than it looked: perhaps ten feet wide and twelve feet long. It was just tall enough for a warrior to stand upright in. Dunnere, who was small, had plenty of head room. The hut was sparsely though adequately furnished: a bench, a single table, a pile of straw for a bed, and a small stone hearth for a fire. There were a few shelves on the wall too, with some pottery jars. All were empty, Dunnere informed Kristinge, but they would come in handy. "I don't think anybody has lived here for many years?" he concluded.

"Who built it?" Kristinge asked, speaking for the first time since they entered.

"Don't know. Maybe God himself."

Kristinge just stood shaking his head. "Am I to be a hermit then?" he asked in a dismayed voice. Without waiting for an answer from Dunnere or God, he turned and walked out the door. Once outside, however, he did not leave. He sat down on the frozen ground nearby.

"If you don't mind," Dunnere said. "I'll stay here with you a few days. Help you get some wood. Maybe find some food. I saw plenty of rabbit tracks. They shouldn't be too hard to trap."

"A hermit?" Kristinge muttered.

In the end, Dunnere stayed for more than a week. For the first few days, the priest spoke little and Dunnere was worried about him. Before long, however, he was like his old self again. They gathered fire-wood together and explored the surrounding area until they had found a nearby spring and also some frequented game trails.

As Dunnere had suspected, despite the cold they had little trouble capturing small game to eat, and Kristinge remembered his old monastic skills at finding edible roots even in wintertime. They built a small additional shelter for the goats, but somehow the goats managed to find their way into the house every night and the two added bodies helped with the warmth. When Kristinge unrolled his small bag of parchments with the scriptures, Dunnere guessed he would be okay. He left shortly after that, but throughout the winter and into the following spring he visited the hut frequently. At first the visits were to make sure the priest was surviving well enough. Then they were just for the fellowship. They spent many Sabbath afternoons together.

Though the inside of his hut was but a few degrees above freezing, Kristinge woke in a sweat. The word of the prophetess Osanne were ringing in his ears. They had come back to haunt him. *You will build no church. One who comes after you will build it. You will build no church. No church. You are just a voice.* Yet for some reason the words no longer haunted Kristinge as they once had. So the prophetess had been right. He had not only failed to build a church; he had succeeding in getting one burned down. And now what was he? Monk? No. Not even priest. A hermit. He laughed at himself. *This* had never been in his plans. But perhaps it had been in God's plan from the start. Wide awake, he walked to the door. The moon glistened on the freshly fallen snow. Winter was not yet gone, but it was going. The snow was heavy and wet. It would not be long before it disappeared. He threw another log onto the embers of his fire, then pulled out his harp. After a time he began to sing.

> *I have a bothy in the wood*
> *None knows it save the Lord, my God*
> *One wall an ash, the other hazel*
> *and a great fern makes the door.*

The doorposts are made of heather;
and the lintel of honeysuckle;
and wild forest all around
yields mast for well-fed swine.

The size of my hut? The smallest thing.
Homestead amid well-trod paths.
A woman (but a blackbird clothed and seeming)
warbles sweetly from its gable.

It was early morning, and Réadban stood on the edge of the terp in Ezinge. Six months had passed since Finn's torc had come to adorn his neck, and nearly all of Friesland's chieftains now acknowledged him as their overlord. Only Aldgisl and a few of his most loyal thanes resisted. These lived in hiding: a small, outlawed war band, on the run. Their existence concerned Réadban, but for now Aldgisl and his band would have to wait; the king had other duties to attend to. It was the fourth time Réadban had returned to Ezinge since receiving the torc. Summer's Day celebration had ended two days prior, but that was not the reason for his coming. This time it was to gather his war band for his assault on the Franks. Time for the promised battle for which he would earn the allegiance of so many chieftains: the battle for which he had been chosen as leader. *For with such victories, kings were made.*

With the sun rising red behind him, Réadban cast a shadow that faded somewhere far in the distance, beyond his sight. Below him, where the shadow of the entire terp lay on the river plain surrounding the village, an army of six hundred stood awaiting his order. Among them were more than sixty well trained thanes, and as many horses. It was a formidable war band. Beside Réadban stood his chieftains, surveying the band for themselves. Aelfin and Eomaer were among them. It had taken a few days for Eomaer's anger to cool, and a few more after that for Aelfin to convince him of the wisdom of following Réadban. Actually, Aelfin alone might have done little to convince him had not Réadban himself earned Eomaer's support. The new king had given the young chieftain the duty of finding and capturing Aldgisl and his war band—or killing them: a task which Eomaer relished, though he had not yet enjoyed success.

"How many more will join us between here and Domburg?" Aelfin asked.

"Two hundred and fifty," Réadban responded. "We will number ten times what the Frankish war band in Domburg numbers by the time we arrive. We will sweep them into the sea. Then we will do the same all along the Rhine, as far as Susburg."

Aelfin nodded. There was a gleam of anticipation in his eye at the mention of recapturing Domburg. Another spoke, an older chieftain with a long braid of gray hair and once-blue eyes that had now faded to nearly the color of his locks. "It is the largest Frisian war band in the memory of any chieftain alive. You have done well, Réadban."

"Had we raised such an army seven years ago, the Danes never would have defeated Finn," Aelfin added.

At this, Réadban's eyes narrowed into slits. He didn't reply.

"Are you not concerned with Aldgisl?" Eomaer asked.

Réadban knew what Eomaer was thinking. He desired permission to abandon the battle against the Franks in order to carry out his own vengeance against Aldgisl. But Réadban could not spare him. His horses would be needed against the Franks. There were none in Friesland who could match the skill of Eomaer's men in doing battle from the back of a steed. Furthermore, if rumor was to be trusted, Aldgisl's band numbered fifty or more. They might prove too much for Eomaer, despite all his skill. Aldgisl was a crafty one. "No," Réadban answered. "The Franks are our concern now. We will need you with us." He didn't wait for Eomaer to argue. He drew his sword and prepared to raise it in the signal to march.

"Wait!" Aelfin said. Réadban turned to him. "A rider is coming," Aelfin explained, pointing southward across the fields.

Sure enough, a lone rider had appeared from the trees and was now approaching across the fields following a direct line toward where the chieftains were standing. Thinking at first he might be one of Réadban's scouts returning, they waited. When he drew closer, however, they saw that it was not a scout at all. At first nobody even recognized him. He rode a small dapple steed, unlike those usually seen in Friesland, and he sat upon it rather awkwardly. He had a thick beard, not yet long but with a wild unkempt look nonetheless. Along with the beard he bore a strange cut of hair: long in the back and short in the top front as if at one time he had shaved his forehead and was now letting it grow back. On his chest he wore a sleeveless bear-skin tunic. His feet were bare.

"Greetings, great warriors," the stranger's voice rang out when he had reached the bottom of the terp. To Réadban's right, Aelfin stiffened as if in recognition. Yet he said nothing.

"Who are you?" Réadban asked.

"Just a voice," the stranger answered.

Réadban was in good spirits that day, else he might not have been so patient. And there was more than that at work also; there was something about this stranger that was oddly compelling: an arresting power that caused even a king to stop and listen. "If you have something to say, then speak it. Else depart."

"He speaks like a Frank," one of the chieftains whispered in Réadban's ear. "Hear his accent? He is a spy. Do not let him leave."

"It is no concern," Réadban answered. "Even if we let him go, he will not reach Domburg far ahead of us."

"It is no Frankish spy—" Aelfin began.

Réadban wasn't listening. He had already turned back toward the stranger. "I am in little mood to waste time this morning. If you have a message, we will hear it."

"You have commanded me to speak my message, then?" the stranger queried.

"I need not be told what I said. Now you try my patience. Speak."

"Hear then my message: the God of all the earth says this to the king of Friesland, 'Do not rise up in pride against the Franks. Their time of destruction will soon come, but you are not the one who will bring it about. Be content with what you have been given, for if your feet cross the waters of the Rhine but once, they will never return to their home. This I say to you and all your descendants.' So speaks the God of the Heavens." So saying, the stranger turned his mount and began riding back toward the woods.

For a moment, Réadban stood there silently. Then, regaining his senses, he shouted. "Catch him. Do not let him escape. Bring him back to me alive." Nobody responded. Nobody knew to whom Réadban was speaking. He had to repeat himself two more times, shouting the names of four of his thanes who were already mounted before any of them would act. By this time, the stranger had already covered considerable distance toward the woods. His small steed moved surprisingly fast. Finally, four warriors broke from the ranks of the war band to pursue him. But somehow, their reigns tangled up in one another, and they were further delayed. Before they finally started galloping after him, he had already disappeared in the woods.

They stopped just a hundred feet away and turned back toward Réadban. "Lord?" they shouted up at the top of the terp. "Shall we continue?"

Now, however, Réadban had guessed the stranger's identity. "After him," he shouted. "And do no return to me until you have captured him." He did not turn quickly enough to see the slight smile on Aelfin's face.

It was late summer. The evening air was already cool. It would not be long before the first frost. A band of men were making their way through the woods leading their horses when one stopped. "Lord," he said. "I see smoke rising through the trees."

A well dressed warrior walked up beside the one who had spoken. It was clear that he was the leader of that band. On his neck and arms were a number of gold bands, and his fine tunic was fastened at his chest by a pair of heavy, ornate gold brooches. In addition to his costly attire, he was healthy and strong. He was in his mid twenties, with a clean-shaven and handsome face, friendly green eyes, and light brown hair. Across the back of his horse was a beautiful sword in an elaborately enameled sheath. This, too, was the blade of a chieftain. "There are no villages nearby," he answered, when he saw the direction the other was pointing.

"Shall we explore? I do not complain of where our path has taken us, but I will say that a night beneath a roof would suit me well."

"It will not be long before we sleep in our own hall once again," the chieftain answered. "And once more I will give gifts to those who serve me." Then he spoke more loudly. "And know that those of you have stayed at my side will not fail to be rewarded most richly."

Another voice replied, "We would have stayed at your side eight years, not just eight months. Whom else would we serve?"

"Hail, Aldgisl," the warriors shouted in unison.

Aldgisl smiled warmly at the loyalty of his true hearth companions. Now it was time to find a hearth. Veering slightly from their previous course, they began walking in the direction of the smoke. In just a short distance, they had come upon a small hut in the woods. Though there was nobody yet visible, it was clear that one lived there. There were two fires burning: one inside and one out in the yard. Over the later, a large wild boar was roasting. On a rope behind the hut, a nanny goat was tethered. "This looks promising," a voice said. "A feast prepared for us. Let us see what else we may find."

"No," Aldgisl replied. "I will go first alone. You know what it is like to live in the wild. We will not steal from another." He turned to the one on the right. "Herthor shall come with me. The others wait here."

Aldgisl walked ahead into the small open space in front of the hut. He was about to shout out a greeting when somebody stepped out from the hut. "Greetings, king," the man said first. He was dressed in a robe that looked like the monks' attire that Aldgisl had seen during his exile in Francia, only older and more tattered. And the man had no tonsure.

"Greetings, hermit," Aldgisl replied, guessing the reason and nature of his host's existence in the woods. "You are a holy man?"

"I am a servant of the living God and his Christ," the hermit replied.

"And why is it that you call me king?" Aldgisl answered.

The hermit didn't reply at once. "Where is your band? I have been waiting."

Aldgisl raised his eyebrow. "You saw us coming?"

"I have prepared a meal," the hermit answered, pointing to the boar on the spit. "It should feed you all."

Aldgisl looked at the spit. "This boar has been roasting for many hours. You can't have seen us coming..." He didn't finish. He could tell from the hermit's expression that he would receive no answer to that question. "Herthor," he said, turning to his thane. "We have been invited. Bring the others." A short time later, fifteen tired warriors came walking into view. They tethered their horses to trees, or hobbled them to large stones and logs, and then collapsed on the ground. Not one of them failed to notice the spit and what it held.

"King," the hermit said again. "The food is for you and your men."

Aldgisl did not wait for the monk's offer to be repeated thrice. He motioned for two of his men to remove the pig from the spit. They tested it, and found the meat well-cooked throughout. The rest of the warriors, tired as they were, wasted no time in carving pieces for themselves. The hermit meanwhile set out two large jugs of water. "I can offer you no wine, only good water."

"Then it is I who will offer *you* the wine," said Aldgisl, still curious as to who this hermit was and how he had come to cook the boar. He fetched his last skin of wine from his horse and presented it to the hermit. He also took a large gold ring from his wrist and offered it to him. The hermit took the wine and filled two wooden cups, but he refused the gold ring. "I will take no payment for what has cost me nothing. God has provided the food for you."

"Some day I will hear more about this god of yours," Aldgisl said. "As for the gold, it is no payment. Take it as a gift." When the hermit still would not receive the gold ring, Aldgisl tossed it inside the entrance of the hut. Then they drank wine together. A short time later, when Aldgisl had feasted on pork, he returned and sat beside the hermit once again.

"You have come to be anointed as king," the hermit said, before Aldgisl could say a word.

Aldgisl narrowed his eyes. "You know me, then?"

"I do," the hermit replied. "We have met, not long past."

Aldgisl searched his memory. He had rarely been in that part of Friesland, and had no recollection of having met a hermit there. But another question was more pressing in his mind. "King?" he asked. "Then you have heard the news?"

"I have heard little news in the past nine months. Only what the peasant Dunnere brings me, and he pays little attention to the dealings of chieftains."

"Then why do you speak of me as king? What do you know of Réadban?"

"God has told that you will be the next king of Friesland. I was told to anoint you when you came—if you are willing to receive an anointing from a servant of Christ. If you are not, then the torc will not rest long on your neck."

"It harms me little to receive your anointing," Aldgisl answered, but he was more afraid than he was willing to admit.

"Then kneel."

Aldgisl looked around. His men had begun to listen to the dialogue. They were all watching him now to see how he would respond. Aldgisl took a step back, as if to walk away. Then he stopped. With a shrug, he stepped back forward and dropped to his knees before the hermit. The hermit took a small clay vessel from the bench at his side and held it over Aldgisl's head. "In the name of the Father, and of the Son, and of the Holy Spirit I anoint you king of Friesland." He let fall from the vase a few drops of aromatic oil on Aldgisl's head. "Now rise," the hermit went on. Aldgisl obeyed. A strange feeling had come over him: a presence at once both calming and terrifying him. What strange power did this holy man have? He was not like any of the priests of Tiwar or Woden whom Aldgisl had ever met.

The hermit spoke again. "Your reign will last many years. When a man of God comes from the north, you must receive him into your hall. He will be the bearer of good news to you and your people. Only do not seek war against the Franks. Be humble and content."

The hermit lowered his hands and sat back down. The short ceremony was over. Aldgisl did not know what to say. "Réadban is dead," he said in a soft voice. When the hermit nodded his understanding, the newly anointed king continued. "They took Domburg quickly, but by the time they had pressed two day's ride to the south the Frankish lords had already raised an army. Réadban's war band was destroyed, and along with him fell many good Frisian chieftains."

The hermit hesitated a moment before asking, "What of Aelfin?" And Eomaer?"

Aldgisl wondered how the hermit knew those names. He now felt more nervous, as if he should recognize this man. But he answered the question. "They live still. Eomaer escaped on horse. And Aelfin did not ride to the battle; he was wounded in the first battle and remained in Domburg. I am glad, for he is a good chieftain: one of the last alive who served Finn."

Finn! Aldgisl suddenly narrowed his eyes. He stared long and hard at the hermit. *How indeed had he known the names of Eomaer and Aelfin?* Suddenly, he jumped to his feet and drew his sword. Seeing this, a few of his men reached for their own blades and looked nervously around, as if expecting a sudden ambush from the woods. Aldgisl, however, was not looking into the woods but straight at the hermit. "Your hair has grown since we met in the cold of winter, young hermit." He held his blade in front of him. The hermit raised his head and met Aldgisl's gaze. There was no fear in his eyes as he looked up the edge of the sword. "And so again I meet the son of Finn. All was not finished at our last meeting, young Kristinge."

"Was it not?" Kristinge asked. "Then finish what remains to be done."

Aldgisl raised his sword. With a quick, skilled flip, he reversed it in his hands and held it hilt first toward Kristinge. "You have anointed me in the style of your god. Now anoint me as a Frisian chieftain."

The hermit took the blade in his hands. It appeared awkward in his grip, but he touched both of Aldgisl's shoulders as the chieftain knelt before him. As he did, he searched far back in his memory for the right words. "Rule long and well, Aldgisl king of Friesland. Slay no hearth-companions in anger or drunkenness. Serve your thanes well and they will serve you well. May this blade never break at your side, and may Frisian soil always be rich beneath your feet."

Aldgisl rose. The hermit Kristinge handed back the blade, anxious to be rid of it. Then he disappeared momentarily into the hut. To Aldgisl's surprise and to the delight of his company, when he returned he was carrying a harp. And for the rest of the day, the young hermit was once again a bard, and not a single man in Aldgisl's war band failed to acknowledge his skill.

When the long summer evening approached, Aldgisl departed, leaving the hermit Kristinge with many thanks for his hospitality. Kristinge stood in front of his hut and watched until the last of Aldgisl's warriors were out of sight. He was about to turn when a strong pair of hands slipped around his waist. He jumped in surprise, but then settled down without resisting the grip that held him firmly.

"How long must I stay in hiding? Are you ashamed of me?" The voice asked.

Kristinge sighed. He turned and faced Aewin. She gave him enough room to spin, but kept her arms around his waist. "I only worry about Eomaer—"

"That he will still come and take me from you?" Aewin finished. "Do not fear. He could not keep me from you before, and he will not succeed now. I have chosen to be your wife."

Though he had taken Aewin as his wife more than three months previous, Kristinge still felt his heart pumping with excitement to hear those words. He leaned forward and kissed her on the lips. "Réadban is dead. His war band was defeated by the Franks."

"I heard."

"Why did I not know you would be listening?"

Aewin shrugged.

"Then you heard also that your brother survived, escaping the pursuing Franks on horseback?"

"I heard."

"I am glad. Though I fear he seeks my life—" He couldn't finish the sentence.

"You did not betray him," Aewin comforted.

"Perhaps I did; perhaps I did not. But he feels betrayed and will not easily forgive."

"Then be content that I, at least, am yours," Aewin said with a smile.

"I am content," Kristinge replied. Arm in arm, they stepped back into the hut.

hISTORICAL ANÒ LITERARY NOTES

Most of the main characters of this book are my own creations. In particular, Kristinge son of Finn and Hildeburh, was born in my imagination, as was Aewin daughter of Eodan. The same is true of nearly all of the other Danish and Frisian characters in this story: Fjorgest, Aelfin, Dylfines the bard, Eomaer the brother of Aewin, Maccus, Ceolac, and so on. The only Frisian exceptions are the chieftain Aldgisl and the infant Rathbod.

Willimond has as inspiration two historical figures: Wilfrid and Willibrord, late seventh and early eighth century missionaries to Friesland. Also, Willimond's mentor Aidan was a real person, the "Apostle of Northumbria" and the founder of the famous monastery at Lindisfarne (or *Lindisfarena* as it was known in Old English). However, Willimond himself is also an imagined character.

Some readers will recognize Finn and Hildeburh as literary figures from the poem *Beowulf*. While it is likely that the *Beowulf* poet himself based them on historical figures, not much is known about them other than what the *Beowulf* poet puts into the mouth of Hrothgar's bard (who sings a poem within the poem at a celebration in the mead hall Heorot). The only other source we have about the fight at Finnsburg (which happened six years before this tale and forms its backdrop) is what can be gleaned from one other source, the fragmentary poem known as "The Finnsburg Fragment."

Nonetheless, every story must have a geographic and historical setting. My tale is set in northwestern Europe in the mid-seventh century during the waning days of the Merovingian Dynasty. I have sought to paint an accurate portrait of this historical setting and some of its famous figures. Many of the places, events, descriptions, and characters in this novel are based on historical and archaeological (as well as on literary) sources. For example, from references to a few historical events—the slaying of Grimoald by Clovis, followed not long after by the death of Clovis himself—the reader familiar with early Medieval Europe may even narrow the period of this novel to the years 656-658 ADE.

The Irish monk Columbanus—whose shadow hangs over the early part of this story though he does not enter it—founded the three neighboring monasteries of Luxeuil, Annegray, and Fontaines. He was a famous and important figure in Merovingian Francia, and the sketch I tried to draw of him relies on historical sources. To say that his latter relationships with the ruling kings and queens of Francia were tumultuous would be an understatement.

Saint Walbert was a Frankish nobleman who gave up the military and aristocratic life and eventually became the third abbot of Luxeuil in 628. He remained abbot for forty years (through the time this story takes place)—though he often lived a hermit's life—and was responsible for bringing the Benedictine Rule to Luxeuil.

Similarly, the abbess Telchild and her brother Agilbert were also real and important figures of the day, and both were buried in crypts at the monastery at Jouarre—another real place: a combined monastery and abbey which had close ties to Columbanus and Luxeuil. Agilbert eventually left Francia for Britain where he was consecrated as bishop, but his inability (or unwillingness) to learn Old English (and perhaps his contempt for the language and its people) seems to have been an impediment to his success there. At the famous Synod at Whitby in 664, Agilbert took the part of Rome against the Irish monastic tradition in the debate over the correct calculation for the dating of Easter. Though he appears only briefly in my tale, I did seek to depict him with a slightly less generous and gracious personality than his sister Telchild (also known as Theodechildis) about whom actually very little is known. There was also a real princess named Osanne, who ended up at Jouarre. (I have no reason to believe she was a visionary prophetess, but I'd like to think she might have been one.)

All of the Merovingian kings and queens named in this book, as well as the various Mayors of the Palace, are also historical figures: Clovis and his wife Queen Balthild, Ebroin, Childebert, Sigibert, Dagobert, Chlotar (or Lothair), and Grimoald. Clovis was indeed believed to have been insane, and by all accounts he was at least as hedonistic as portrayed in this book, while his wife Balthild (who really had been a Saxon slave girl, though perhaps of noble lineage) was a great benefactor of the abbeys around Paris and indeed was a saintly figure. She founded the Abbey of Chelles (where she was eventually buried). After the death of her husband she gave up her title and spent the rest of her life caring for the poor and sick.

Much less is known about Friesland (or Frisia) and its people than about Merovingian Francia. But something *is* known about two of the earliest missionaries to the Frisians. In 678, a monk named Wilfrid (who was actually Agilbert's spokesperson for the side of Rome at the Synod at Whitby, and who also studied for a time at Lindisfarne) was traveling from England to Rome (after apparently being expelled from Northumbria). He was blown off course, or perhaps shipwrecked, and found himself in the Frisian town of Utrecht where he was taken in and harbored by a Frisian king named Aldgisl. He stayed in Friesland for some time preaching the gospel to the Frisians. According to some sources, Ebroin—who by that time was functionally ruling Francia—hated Wilfrid and sent messages to Aldgisl to have Wilfrid captured or killed. Aldgisl refused.

Wilfrid did not stay long among the Frisians, and he was not very successful in winning converts. However in 690 a disciple of Wilfrid named Willibrord followed in Wilfrid's footsteps and ended up spending most of the rest of his life in Friesland. He founded several churches, achieving at least moderate success and eventually becoming known as the "Apostle to the Frisians".

Unfortunately the Frisian king Aldgisl, who was supportive of the church, was succeeded by one Rathbod. Rathbod appears here, but only as an infant grandchild of the treacherous Réadban. There is some indication he might have been a child of Aldgisl, but it is not at all clear. I have made him a more distant relative instead. Whereas Aldgisl supported the missionary endeavor, Rathbod was a pagan who hated both Christianity and the Franks. In 716 he burned many churches, drove Willibrord out of Friesland, and rebelled against Frankish rule. He died in 719, some sixty years after this story takes place.

The sources upon which I based my portrayals are many. They include a number of scholarly articles describing archaeological finds. One, amazingly enough, was particular to seventh century Friesland, describing especially its jewelry. The very narrowly focused article "Seventh-Century Jewellery from Frisia: A Re-Examination" by Ruth Mazo Karras (appearing in the journal *Anglo-Saxon Studies in Archaeology and History* 4, 1985) proved very interesting. Almost all of the Frisian villages mentioned in this novel are actual archaeological sites with relics from seventh century Frisian life. I have attempted to describe buildings, jewelry, weapons, clothing and even the layout of the villages of both the Danes and Frisians as accurately as possible.

Others sources were more general to the Germanic peoples of the early Middle ages and discussed everything from jewelry and coinage to weapons and religious artifacts. I also drew from a number of more general (less technical and more readable) books. My favorite was *The Birth of France: Warriors, Bishops, and Long-Haired Kings* by Katherine Scherman, but I also gathered bits of information as well as a more general sense of the time and its peoples from several other sources including: *Everyday Life of the Barbarians: Goths, Franks and Vandals* by Malcolm Todd; *Christendom: a Short History of Christianity and its Impact on Western Civilization* by Roland Bainton; *The Church Under Siege* by M.A.Smith; and *Christianity and the Celts* by Ted Olsen.

I am particularly indebted to the late Professor Robert Farrell of Cornell University who introduced me to Old English Language and Literature, helped me through my first translations of Anglo-Saxon poetry, gave me an introduction to medieval archaeology and pointed me to many sources, and helped me gloss certain words such as *wic* using hints of older meanings. In many ways he helped inspire this book.

I'm thankful also to numerous lectures on early medieval Europe from colleagues at Middlebury College and elsewhere over the past two decades. The scene of the land bequest to the monastery at Luxeuil in Chapter 1 is based on real practices of the day. Nobles and landowners might have been wealthy and powerful, but they were not always educated and in many cases could not read. As a result, a mere legal document with words on paper was worth much less, and thus the need for ceremonies with memorable events to mark the event of a land grant—and give it legal weight.

My older brother Willard Dickerson III—who has a Ph.D. in medieval history from Cornell University and was studying for that degree at the same time I was studying Old English Language and Literature and medieval studies (also at Cornell)—also pointed me to several sources. Though his period of interest was several centuries later, he provided considerable assistance: talking with me about the writings of Bede, and finding good books for me.

The Songs and Poetry

A word or two should also be said about literary as well as historical and archaeological sources. Kristinge, the protagonist of this story, is a bard (as well as a monk, for a short time a king, and later a hermit). He sings many songs throughout the story: in Francia at the estates of nobles and in the palace of Clovis, later in the Danish mead hall of the chieftain Fjorgest, and eventually back among the Frisians in Aelfin's hall in Ezinge.

A small number of those poems are my compositions, but the majority are either translations of, or are adapted from, medieval poems in the Old English language—many of which have Danish heroes and presumable earlier Danish or Norse sources. In both my own original poems (such as the heroic lays of Folcwalda and Ulestan) and in my translations, I sought to keep the style of Old English poetry by including its alliterative scheme, style of imagery, and especially its metrical form: each line is composed of two half lines of two stressed and usually two unstressed syllables. Consider, for example, the line:

> From Hwitstan he went   the wise thane Ulestan
> from hearth, from home,   from hall and from king.

Both of these lines have a triple alliteration. In the first, all three stressed syllables, all beginning with the "w" sound: "Hwit-", "went", and "wise". The final stressed syllable would be "Ule-". In the second line, the alliteration and stress is on the "h" sound of "hearth", "home" and "hall." (The two unstressed syllables per half-line is a loose rule; multiple syllables such as "-stan he" may blur together as one, or may simply be ignored.)

The translations and adaptions of poetry are from the following poems:

"The Pearl" (sung or chanted by Kristinge in Chapter 2)

"Deor" (recited in part in Chapters 3 and 4)

"The Dream of the Rood" (Chapter 8)
"The Seafarer" (Chapter 10)

As noted, the translations and adaptions of these four poems are partly my own—but not without help! I made use of several classic sources, including: John C. Pope's edition of *Seven Old English Poems* including his commentary and glossary; Ralph Quirk and C.L. Wrenn's *An Old English Grammar;* Bruce Mitchell and Fred Robinson's *A Guide to Old English;* and Sweet's *Anglo-Saxon Reader.* I also give my high recommendation to the thoroughly comprehensive volume, *An Introduction to Old English,* written by Prof. Jonathan Evans of the University of Georgia.

The hermit's song of Chapter 23, by contrast, is *not* my translation. It seems to date back at least to ninth century Ireland. When I first saw it many years ago, I copied it word for word thinking it would fit beautifully into the mouth of my seventh-century monk Kristinge, trained as he was by the Irish monk Willimond. Unfortunately, I have lost my source for this poem. However I have since been able to find the same translation in two books: *The Foundations of Christian Art* and *St. Francis of Assisi and Nature.*

The Biblical stories and songs sung by Kristinge are more or less my own versions, but they were largely inspired by another Old English epic poem known as *The Heliand*, or "The Saxon Gospel," which actually comes not from England but from Francia during the Carolingian dynasty (which succeeded the Merovingian). Here I am indebted G.Ronald Murphy's beautiful translation and commentary, *The Heliand: The Saxon Gospel.*

As a final note, some readers may wonder why I used Old English rather than Old Frisian poems as inspiration. The most important reason is simply that, essentially, there is no surviving literature in Old Frisian—nothing from before the twelfth century. There are, however, numerous surviving poems in Old English. And one should keep the following points in mind before worrying too much about the differences, or about putting Old English poems in the mouth of a Frisian bard singing in Francia and Denmark. Not only was Old English (or Anglo-Saxon as it is sometimes called) closely related to both Old Frisian and Old Danish, but as the story notes there were even many Saxon tribes and villages in Friesland. Songs and poems often traveled from one people to another, and similar tales can be found all over northern Europe—thus the presence of an Irish bard such Dyflines in Friesland would not have been altogether unheard of. Willimond came to Friesland from Anglo-Saxon England and would have brought its stories with him. Of course it is also simply the case that I myself, the author of this work, am English speaking and all of this tale has in one way or another been translated into English.

As a lover of this poetry, I am delighted to share it with my readers. In the end, though, my primary goal was to tell a good story and a true story, and to tell it in the best way I know how.

GLOSSARY OF TERMS
AND OF PERSONS,
HISTORICAL AND FICTIONAL

Terms

axwei: From Old English, an "ox way" or "cow path" around the outside of a terpen village.

hearthwerod: From Old English, this term could be rendered literally "hearth companions" but that would miss the depth of meaning of the term; it signified a strong bond of community of a chieftain and his most trusted warriors and advisors who lived together, fought together, slept together, and shared together the fellowship around the hearth fire in a Saxon or Frisian mead hall.

rood: a wooden rod, or tree, and the first Old English word used to signify the cross of Christ.

scop: a Germanic poet or bard, but also (especially in Denmark) one with religious teaching duties as well.

terp: an artificial hill or mound, often created from old cow dung or clay, upon which settlements (such as Ezinge) were built offering both elevation above oft-flooded lowlands as well as a more defensible position against raiders and other enemies.

torc: a band of twisted or wound gold worn around the neck of a chieftain as a sign of wealth and authority.

wic: this term could mean simply a "home" or "settlement" near the sea, but it is often associated with a seaside location for trade. In this novel, following hints of an older meaning, it refers to a "beach" or especially a sandy place where merchants could safely come ashore in longboats to trade. Coastal villages might themselves be called wics, or they might have nearby associated wics. The variant "wic", "wich", and "wick" often appear as a suffixes in English place-names.

weregild: in Old English could be rendered simply as "blood gold" or "blood money", but the underlying concept was deeper and was very important in old Germanic cultures (including Saxon, Frisian and Danish). When a chieftain or warrior was killed—in battle or lesser forms of manslaughter—the weregild was the price owed for that person's death, and it was the obligation of the slain one's kin (or thanes) to exact that price from the slayer. Though it might literally be paid in gold in order to prevent a further feud, often times the weregild was poetic metaphor for a revenge slaying.

Persons (Fictional)

Aelfin, son of Aeltar: a chieftain in the Frisian village of Ezinge, and once a friend and thane of Finnlaf, son of Finn.

Aeltar: a one time loyal thane of Finn, and a chieftain of the Frisian village of Domburg.

Aescholt: a Frisian warrior and cousin of Eomaer; the name means "grove of ash trees."

Aesher: a Danish chieftain, and a cousin of Fjorgest.

Aewin: daughter of Eodan, a Frisian chieftain, and the brother of Eomaer. Was once promised in marriage to the Frisian prince Finnlaf, son of Finn, but Finnlaf was killed before the marriage.

Benetus: a wealthy Gallo-Roman nobleman.

Beow: is the name of both a legendary Danish hero of old and also Frisian warrior who becomes a thane of Folcwalda.

Beowlaf: son of the Frisian warrior Beow and a thane of Finn.

Berigyldan: a peasant in Hwistan during the reign of Finn, and the wife of Lopystre; the name means "golden berry."

Blostma: a peasant in Hwistan during the reign of Finn, and the daughter of Lopystre and Berigyldan, the name means "blossom."

Brogus: a monk at Luxeuil, miraculously healed by Father Petrica.

Brytta: wife of the Danish chieftain Fjorgest, who died in childbirth.

Ceolac: a thane of Aelfin.

Charleson: Oldest son of Charletax.

Charlethax: A Frankish nobleman and landowner.

Chlotair: a (fictional) illegitimate son of the Frankish king Charibert. Becomes a monk a Luxeuil.

Daelga: The poet and bard of the mead hall Finnsburg during the days of Finn and HIldeburh, and a one-time tutor of Kristinge.

Deomaer: A jeweler and coin-maker at Finnsburg during the reigns of Folcwalda and Finn.

Deor: a legendary bard.

Dunnere: a Frisian peasant and goatherd at the village of Ezinge during the time of Aelfin.

Dyflines: an Irish bard in the service of the chieftain Aelfin at Ezinge; the name could mean "one from Dublin."

Ecgwalda: a Frisian chieftain at Domburg during the reign of Folcwalda; the name could mean "sword-ruler" or "sword-might."

Elfhild: daughter of Gundomer and Berta.

Eodan: a Frisian chieftain. The father of Eomaer and Aewin.

Eomaer, son of Eodan: A young Frisian chieftain during the days of Kristinge, and a brother of Aewin.

Eormanic: notoriously cruel Gothic king mentioned in Deor's poem.

Finnlaf: the son of Frisian chieftain Finn, and the older brother of Kristinge. Killed at the first battle of Finnsburg.

Fjorgest: a Danish chieftain of the Hoclinges tribe.

Folcwalda: a famed Frisian chieftain, and father of Finn, who united Friesland and laid claim to being its first king. The name could mean "people's ruler" or "strength of the people."

Friesc: a legendary Frisian chieftain and hero of old, and a forefather of the Frisians.

Froda: a thane of Finn and the brother of Frotha. Died at the second battle of Finnsburg. His father was chieftain at Dorestad, but was overthrown by Radbod son of Réadban.

Frotha: a Frisian chieftain and the brother of Froda. His father was chieftain at Dorestad, but was overthrown by Radbod son of Réadban.

Gundomer: A Frankish nobleman and landowner. Husband of Berta.

Guthlaf: A Jutish warrior who died fighting on the side of the Danes in the battle of Finnsburg. A brother of Hunlaf and Oslaf. These brothers are believed to have started the fight at Finnsburg for personal motives.

Guthman: A thane of Finn and brother of Guthric. Died at the second battle of Finnsburg.

Guthric: A thane of Finn and brother of Guthman. Died at the second battle of Finnsburg.

Healfas: a Jutish chieftain, the brother-in-law of Aesher. Owes allegiance to the Hoclinges, a Danish tribe.

Herthor: a thane of Aldgisl.

Hildeburh, daughter of Hoc: a Danish princess who became the wife of the Frisian king Finn. The mother of Finnlaf and Kristinge, and the brother of Hnaef.

Hildegund: Daughter of Gundomer and Berta.

Hnaef, son of Hoc: a Danish chieftain, and the brother of Hildeburh. Died at the first battle of Finnsburg.

Hoc: a famed Danish chieftain, and the father of Hnaef and Hildeburh.

Hunlaf: a Jutish warrior who died fighting on the side of the Danes in the battle of Finnsburg. A brother of Guthlaf and Oslaf. These brothers are believed to have started the fight at Finnsburg for personal motives

Hyse: a thane of Eomaer and younger brother of Treothrym.

Isernfyst: a Saxon chieftain over the clan at Heorotburg, who pledged loyalty to Kristinge. The name means "iron fist."

Kristinge: the son of Frisian chieftain Finn and his Danish wife Hildeburh, and the younger brother of Finnlaf. As a youth he was raised in Hwitstan by the monk Willimond and tutored by the bard Daelga with no knowledge of who his real parents were. He spent six years being trained as a monk at Luxeuil before learning of his heritage and returning to Friesland.

Lawyrke: a peasant fisherman in Hwistan during the reign of Finn, a friend of Willimond, and the father of Lawyrklaf. He was drowned in a fishing accident. His name means "Lobster." Father of Lawyrklaf.

Lopystre: a peasant fisherman in Hwistan during the reign of Finn, a friend of Willimond, the husband of Berigyldan, and the father of Lindlaf. His name means "Lobster."

Maccus: a thane and cousin of Aelfin in the Frisian village of Ezinge.

Oslaf: A Jutish warrior who died fighting on the side of the Danes at Finnsburg. A brother of Hunlaf and Guthlaf. These brothers are believed to have started the fight at Finnsburg for personal motives

Petrica: a monk of Luxeuil.

Radbod the Young: the son of Réadban. He died childless.

Raeban: in a tale told by Dyflines, Raeban wa a Frisian warrior who unknowing offered hospitality to Odin and was given an enchanted (but cursed) sword. He becomes a great chieftain, but after killing his own kin he is an outcast and becomes one of Odin's berserkers.

Réadban: the Frisian chieftain over both Dorestad and Utrecht, and the father of two sons, Ultar and Radbod, who both died in battle while Réadban is still alive.

Sceaptung: a Danish skald in the service of Fjorgest. He collaborates with the priests of the old gods in opposition to Christianity.

Theofor: a Frisian warrior during the days of Folcwalda, and the father of Theoman.

Theoman: the son of Theofor and a thane of Finn during his days of power at Hwitstan.

Tredswar: a thane of Eomaer and younger brother of Treothrym.

Treothrym: a thane of Eomaer; older brother of Tredswar and Hyse.

Ulestan: a loyal thane of Folcwalda and then Finn during their reigns. Was sent with Willimond to the monastery of Luxeuil to protect Kristinge, the heir to the Frisian torc. Died and was buried at Luxeuil.

Ulfgar: a Frankish wagon-master in the service of Gundomer.

Ultar: the son of Réadban, and the father (in this story) of Rathbod (a future king of Friesland).

Wigmaer, son of Wihtlaeg: the Frisian chieftain at Wieuwerd.

Wihtred, son of Wightlaeg: a Frisian chieftain of Aalsum.

Willimond: a Irish-Saxon monk from Lindisfarne who is sent as a missionary to Friesland becomes priest in Hwitstan during the reign of Finn son of Folcwalda. He becomes first the foster-father and then the step-father of Kristinge.

Wyndlaf: A Frisian trader and owner of a longboat.

Persons (Historical)

Adon: the founder of the monastery of Jouarre and a disciple of Columbanus.

Agilbert: a monk at Jouarre, and the brother of the abbess Telchild. Agilbert will later travel to England and play an important role in the Synod at Whitby, along with his disciple Wilfrid who will become one of the first known missionaries to Friesland.

Aidan: an Irish monk who becomes a missionary to the Saxons of Northumbria and the of the monastery at Lindisfarne. In this story he is also the spiritual father of the fictional character Willimond.

Aldgisl: a Frisian chieftain who has become king of Friesland by the end of the seventh century. He welcomes the Christian missionaries Wilfrid and Willibrord to Friesland.

Balthild: a former Saxon slave girl (possibly of noble birth), taken to wife by the Frankish king Clovis. She is the mother of Chlotar (also called Lothair III), Childeric, and Theoderic III. Balthild is the patron of a new monastery at Chelles (outside Paris). After Clovis's death she abdicates her authority to live out her life in an abbey.

Brunhild: the grandmother of the Frankish king Theoderic, who later becomes an enemy of Columbanus.

Charibert II: Frankish king of Aquitaine, and the uncle of Clovis.

Chlotar: also called Lothair III, the son of king Clovis and queen Balthild, who is named a child king of the Franks in 656, and rules (in name) for five years.

Clovis II: the king of the Franks, the husband of Balthild, and the father of Chlotar, Childeric, and Theoderic III. He dies in 657 (not long after the visit from the fictional characters Willimond and Kristinge in this story.)

Columbanus: an Irish monk who becomes a missionary to the Franks and founds several monasteries including Luxeuil.

Dagobert II: the son of Sigibert. At the death of Sigibert in 656, he is sent away to Ireland by the ambitious Grimoald, Mayor of the Palace. In order to put his own son Childebert into power, Grimoald spreads the rumor that Dagobert II had died. In this story I have Clovis hear (and believe) that rumor. Eighteen years later Dagobert II will return to Austrasia and rule as king for four years.

Ebroin: a Mayor of the Palace, who effectively rules the Franks off and on for many years after the death of Clovis. Ebroin was notoriously ambitious, cruel and treacherous,

Grimoald: a Mayor of the Palace, who (at the death of the puppet king Sigibert) names his son Childebert king. Both Grimoald and Childebert are quickly captured and tortured to death by Clovis.

Osanne: an Irish princess who becomes a sister at the monastery at Jouarre.

Rathbod: a Frisian chieftain who had become king (following Aldgisl) by early in the eight century. He is believed to be a kin of Aldgisl. In this novel I have also made him the infant son of Ultar, and the grandson of Réadban.

Sigibert III: Frankish king of Austrasia, and father of Dagobert II. He dies in 656. After his death and the subsequent capture and death of Grimoald, Chlotar the son of Clovis and Balthild is named king of all the Franks.

Telchild: the abbess at Jouarre, and the brother of Agilbert.

Theoderic I: a son of Clovis I (the first Merovingian king of the Franks) who ruled the divided Frankish kingdom of Metz during the days of Columbanus.

Walbert: a former Frankish nobleman who in 628 become the abbot at the monastery of Luxeuil.

ABOUT THE AUTHOR

Matthew T. Dickerson is an author, a professor at Middlebury College in Vermont, a scholar of the writings of J. R. R. Tolkien and the fantastic fiction of C.S.Lewis, and an environmental journalist and outdoor writer. He books include works of fiction, biography, philosophy, and scholarship (including eco-critical work) on fantasy and mythopoeic literature.

As a fiction writer, Dickerson's interests are in early medieval Europe and fantasy. When not writing or teaching, he is a Americana musician, a fly fisherman, and a caretaker of a hillside plot of Vermont land where he boils maple sugar, cuts firewood, and attempts to protect a beehive or two from marauding bee-thieves known as black bears. He has been married for 25 years and has three sons, all born in Vermont.

Dickerson received his A.B. from Dartmouth College (1985) and a Ph.D. in Computer Science from Cornell University (1989)—where he also did graduate work in Old English language and literature. His computer science research has been primarily in computational geometry, though he has also worked in agent-based simulation and the modeling of killer whale behavior in southeast Alaska.

He is the author of numerous non-technical books, among them *Following Gandalf: Epic Battles and Moral Victory in The Lord of the Rings* (Brazos Press, 2003), recently reissued in a revised and expanded edition as *A Hobbit Journey: Discovering the Enchantment of J.R.R. Tolkien's Middle Earth* (Brazos, 2012), which was shortlisted for the Mythopoeic Society's Mythopoeic Scholarship Awards. He also co-wrote *From Homer to Harry Potter: A Handbook on Myth and Fantasy* (with David L. O'Hara, Brazos Press, 2006). Dickerson has introduced eco-criticism to the world of fantasy in his *Ents, Elves, and Eriador: The Environmental Vision of J.R.R. Tolkien* (with Jonathan Evans, University Press of Kentucky, 2006) and *Narnia and the Fields of Arbol: The Environmental Vision of C. S. Lewis* (with David

L. O'Hara, University Press of Kentucky, 2009). And he has contributed chapters or entries to several other volumes of Tolkien scholarship including *The J.R.R. Tolkien Encyclopedia: Scholarship and Critical Assessment* (2006).

Dickerson's first novel, *The Finnsburg Encounter* (Crossway Books, 1991), was translated into German as *Licht uber Friesland* (Verlag Schulte & Gerth, 1996). His new fantasy novel *The Gifted*, the first book of a trilogy titled *The Daegmon War*, is due out in late 2014.

Since 2002 Dickerson has been the director of the New England Young Writers Conference, an annual four-day conference for high school students in Bread Loaf, Vermont, that is associated with Middlebury College.